Unexpec.

Born and raised in Upstate New York, Jason LaPier lives in Portland, Oregon with his wife and a couple of dachshunds. In past lives he has been a guitar player for a metal band, a drum-n-bass DJ, a record store owner, a game developer, and an IT consultant. These days he divides his time between writing fiction and developing software, and doing Oregonian things like gardening, hiking and drinking microbrew. He can be found online on Twitter @JasonWLaPier and via his website: jasonwlapier.com.

Unexpected Rain

JASON LaPIER

Book One in The Dome Trilogy

HARPER
Voyager

Harper*Voyager*
an imprint of HarperCollins*Publishers* Ltd
1 London Bridge Street
London SE1 9GF

www.harpervoyagerbooks.co.uk

This Paperback Original 2015

First published in Great Britain in ebook format by Harper*Voyager* 2015

Copyright © Jason LaPier 2015

Jason LaPier asserts the moral right to
be identified as the author of this work

A catalogue record for this book
is available from the British Library

ISBN: 978-0-00-812071-9

This novel is entirely a work of fiction.
The names, characters and incidents portrayed in it are
the work of the author's imagination. Any resemblance to
actual persons, living or dead, events or localities is
entirely coincidental.

Set in Sabon by Born Group using Atomik ePublisher from Easypress

All rights reserved. No part of this publication may be
reproduced, stored in a retrieval system, or transmitted,
in any form or by any means, electronic, mechanical,
photocopying, recording or otherwise, without the prior
permission of the publishers.

For my grandfathers.

CHAPTER 1

Kane stepped out of the house, gently closing the door behind him. The operator had dialed up a gorgeous evening in the sub-dome block. Stars were out. The constellations were clear and familiar; Orion, the bears, and all that nonsense. There was a low, ambient light on the street, a bit red in color, but it didn't come from the tiny, flickering flames of the decorative street lamps, nor did it cause enough light pollution to obscure the view of the Milky Way.

Of course, Kane knew the stars were all wrong. It wasn't even night on the planet's surface. When people started leaving Earth and building domes on any rock with the right gravity, orbiting a star within a few sleepy decades of the Sol system, they set them up with twenty-four-hour-day cycles, weather, mild seasons, and all the minor natural comforts and annoyances that Earthlings were used to.

In block 23-D of a sub-dome called Gretel, near the primary dome called Blue Haven, just off the equator of the fourth planet from Barnard's Star, it was the middle of the night. All the residents were fast asleep, happy to comply with the artificial temporal configuration. Domers, in general, didn't question much of anything; they took the life doled

1

out to them by their authorities and passively accepted it – were even grateful for it.

Kane had been a maintenance guy since Monday, and so by walking the streets in the middle of the make-believe night, he didn't set off any alarms for the operator on duty. The job was a joke. The actual cleaning and maintenance of domes and sub-domes was handled by small armies of scrub-bots. The dog-sized, multi-legged, mobile vacuum-slash-scouring brushes did all the work during designated sleeping hours, rotating from one block to the next. Kane was supposed to be keeping the little bastards running – that was the job – but the reality of it was that they didn't need any help. During orientation, it was explained to him that once in a while, one of them might get some bit of debris jammed up inside a leg joint, at which point he'd have to run through a troubleshooting script that ended with a call to a technician. Most of the veteran maintenance staff skipped the first five steps of the script, because nine times out of ten, they'd have to just call a tech anyway.

When it came down to it, Kane's job nearly in its entirety consisted of hitting a single button that started the scrub-bots' cleaning routine. As he walked through the fake night, he thought about the faceless operator sitting in front of a console somewhere, tweaking the temperature and humidity. The job of a block operator was only slightly less menial than his own, and not much more difficult. A few more buttons and a few more routines. This went for most jobs in a dome; most people were just button pushers. In a dome, that was the only way to keep everyone employed. It was more or less an artificial economy. Some people liked to say that with today's technology, the whole human race could be kept alive by a handful of engineers, and that everyone else could just kick back and relax. But people never could shake that sense of accomplishment that earning an actual paycheck gives them, the way that a bank statement justifies their lives and measures their worth. They just couldn't bear to live without capitalism and a so-called free market, that arena where money can teeter-totter endlessly between producers and consumers.

Kane stopped walking. His instincts told him to take in his surroundings, to look, to listen, to smell. The perfect avenue he stood in the middle of was devoid of both life and refuse, and the ambient light lit every empty nook and corner. The only sounds he could hear were the whirring machinations of scrub-bots somewhere in the distance. The entire sub-dome was always clean, and smelled almost like nothing. When he took a deep breath, there was that hidden edge, that sugary, candy-like smell of artificial air. The kind of smell so distant that it caused him to sniff harder in an attempt to pin down its origins, which was, of course, a fruitless endeavor. He thought about the block's operator watching a grid, the blip of some maintenance guy just pulsing in place on the street. He snorted and itched his nose, then started walking toward the garden once more.

Instead of monitoring a robotic cleaning crew, an operator monitored the Life Support system of a block and the residents in it. There were no cameras (no doubt to give domers a false sense of privacy), but the operator got to see a readout of the vital statistics of everyone in their block. At that moment, the readout of one of the resident's vitals should be spiking. Kane quickly strode away from the avenue and headed diagonally across the block, aiming to cut through the central garden toward the exit.

Nightmares on any scale were unusual in domers, but not unheard of. The elevated blood-pressure and rate of respiration of a resident would likely be noted by the operator, but would not be an immediate cause for alarm. Kane wiped the blood from the long, spear-like prod used for unjamming scrub-bot legs with a cleaning rag and stuck the tool through a loop on his belt. He stuffed the rag into a waste receptacle on the street and it was sucked off into a network of tubes that snaked beneath the sub-dome and converged at an incinerator somewhere.

There had been a struggle, of course, but Kane was a professional and his target was over the hill. The actual kill was probably the easiest part of the entire job. It'd taken months for Kane to track the man down, hopping from planet to moon to dome. Digging deep to exhume any trace, any footprint, any contact the target had made and subsequently erased since his disappearance almost a year ago. Not that Kane was annoyed or frustrated by the difficulty of the hunt. If anything, he was invigorated by it. And all the sweeter when he discovered the target had come to the domes. That he had assured himself that all tracks were covered, that he was safe to hide in plain sight, to start a new life. To retire in a sub-dome. Dome life afforded a level of safety so extreme that Kane doubted any domers even knew what fear *was*, not truly.

But his target had known fear. It had registered on his face and in his pleas when Kane broke through the thin shell of dome security and sullied the perfect little domicile with his unwelcome presence. Kane had first silenced the begging and the attempts at negotiation by taking a small appliance from the kitchen and fracturing the jaw. Trapped, cornered, and seeing his fate, the target resisted as best he could, but Kane was faster, stronger, and sharper. His specialty was making weapons out of innocuous objects, and thus the sub-dome home was an armory.

4

He'd left the man beaten and broken in his living room after inflicting a deep wound in his abdomen with the cleaning tool, plunging through several vital organs. The target wouldn't die right away, but he wouldn't live through the night. Eventually his vitals would calm down as the internal bleeding caused him to lose consciousness and the operator on duty would assume the resident's nightmare was over. By the time those vitals dropped to critical levels, he'd be beyond the point that emergency medical care could help him.

Kane reached the edge of the garden and heard an odd sound – that almost animal-like whining howl, the complaint of metal being forced to bend and flex in an unnatural way. A brisk breeze brushed his skin and caused the vegetables and flowers in front of him to lightly sway in their plots. He stopped and looked about, trying to identify the source of the sound. It seemed to be coming from every direction at once.

When it got louder, he realized it was coming from above. The breeze grew alarmingly strong and within seconds, the swaying plants were uprooted and swirling about in the wind. He snapped his head back and looked up toward the sound. A red ball of piercingly bright light tore open the night sky, washing out the nearby stars.

It was the light of Barnard's Star, what the locals would call the Sun if they didn't use artificial sunlight instead. It was the morning light.

There was a crack in the dome.

Kane had been in and out of space enough to know the dangers of explosive decompression, and he looked desperately around for something to grab. He took a few long strides toward a four-meter-tall air purifier node, a thin, metal-painted-white, tree-like structure protruding from the edge of the garden. His jumpsuit flapped against his limbs as if it were trying to strip itself away as he ran, arms outstretched.

He managed to grab a branch of the aluminum tree, but the hole in the sky continued to grow and the suck of the upward wind was too strong. With a rush, he was lifted off his feet and turned upside down, hanging helplessly from the metal branch, his body dancing in the air like a kite in a strong wind. The tree slowly bent its arms upward, allowing him to inch higher into the sky. He could see the seams of the air purifier coming apart in slow motion, and he desperately pulled at the branch that was his lifeline, putting one hand over the other, trying to reach the base of the tree.

He could barely hear the pop of the branch coming away from the trunk with the rush of wind in his ears, and then he was airborne, the thin aluminum stick still clutched in his hands.

Kane closed his eyes and let go of the branch, allowing himself to tumble in the wind while the bright morning sun showed red through his eyelids. It was pretty much like falling, except up instead of down.

CHAPTER 2

"McManus, Horowitz, Halsey, Runstom," the fuzzy 3D image of Captain Inmont barked as its pixels rapidly coalesced into view, eclipsing the bombball game. "Report to Briefing Bay Six immediately!"

The holo-vision shut off automatically. In frustration, Officer Stanford Runstom flicked the large silver switch on the base of the HV back and forth a few times even though he knew that when a call came in the HV would be disabled.

"Sonova bitch," he said aloud. "It's the goddamn Sirius Series!" He made a kicking motion in the direction of the holo-vision, but pulled back before making contact. The meager entertainment station came with the officer's dorm room and if he broke it, they'd dock his pay. With a grumble, he rolled in his cot and came to a sitting position. Other than the cot and the holo-vision, his small home featured a narrow wardrobe and a foot locker. If he looked at either for too long, he'd start to think about how pathetic it was that all of his belongings fit into such a limited space; and left room to spare.

He stared at the blank HV for a moment, as though if he looked pitiful enough the device would give him a break and put the game back on. It wasn't long before his devotion to the Poligart Pioneers waned as the possibility of a new case edged its way into his thoughts. He reached over the side of the cot and pulled his boots on. It was easy to get sucked into a championship light-years away when there was nothing to do for weeks at a time, but a win for his favorite bombball team wasn't worth a damn compared to a chance to work on a crime scene.

He sat alone in Briefing Bay 6 until the other three officers arrived and signed on to the mission computer. They grunted groggy greetings at each other and sat at the table in the center of the room, away from Runstom. The four of them were part of a crew of officers stationed at a remote base in the Barnard system. They were always on call, but rarely had much to do. Runstom looked at each of them briefly, but they seemed to avoid eye contact, instead involving themselves in some minor preoccupation. Susan Horowitz, her dark hair disheveled, sat there flipping through a magazine and was wearing loose, casual clothing meant for a workout, though she looked too relaxed to have come from the gym. Jared McManus was jittery as always, and his wiry, toned muscles twitched as he looked around the room with narrowed eyes, not focusing on anything in particular. George Halsey had at least bothered to put part of his uniform on, but he looked like he'd just gotten out of bed. The lanky, yellow-haired man stared into space, eyes and mouth both half open as if he were frozen at some point in the middle of a yawn.

It was warm in the briefing room and Runstom felt the urge to unbutton his vest, but he resisted it. He was determined not to feel even slightly embarrassed about being the only one of the four so eager to get to work that he put on the full standard-issue uniform. Instead, he took off his hat and set it on the table, letting the stubble on his head get some air.

After a few minutes of silence, Captain Inmont's floating head appeared on the holo-vision unit at the front of the room.

"Officers", crackled the holo-vid speakers. Inmont's head wavered, interference causing her face to flex unnaturally and a little unnervingly. "We have a very serious incident on Barnard-4, in Gretel. That's a sub-dome of the dome-city Blue Haven. Possible mass-homicide."

"Captain," Horowitz interrupted as she pulled her straight, black hair back into a pony tail. "Doesn't Blue Haven have a local police force?"

"Yes, that's correct. The Blue Haven police technically have jurisdiction over the sub-domes there, but they do not have the numbers to spare for an investigation outside the city proper. The ModPol contract with the Barnard-4 Planetary Defense Coalition puts this one in our jurisdiction."

"Right-o," Horowitz said, tipping back in her chair and scratching her belly with one hand.

"You will be assisting detectives Brutus and Porter on this one," continued the virtual head of Captain Inmont. "We'll need a strict—"

"Uh," McManus interrupted, raising a hand. "Did you say 'mass homicide'?"

"Yes, that's right," the head replied patiently. "And that's another reason we're being called in. The local PD never deals with this level of crime. Life Support failure on a complete block. That's thirty-two residences. Four empty, twenty-one singles and seven couples. Five of those with a child. Forty people in total. We don't know the actual body count yet, but since the incident happened at nocturnal block hours, it's a possibility that we're looking at forty victims."

"Life Support failure?" McManus parroted, letting his hand drop, but only halfway. "Sounds like a job for engineers. Why are we looking at homicide?"

The captain sighed. Disdain wasn't easy to transmit over a blurry remote visual, but somehow she managed. "LifSup engineers are already investigating, remotely," she said slowly and deliberately. "They reported to us that the system log says someone executed a series of commands that simultaneously opened up the top-side inner and outer doors, overriding the airlock safety. Vented the atmosphere of the whole block in a matter of seconds." She paused for a moment, as if waiting for another interruption. When none came, she finished. "The commands were executed from an operator console."

The room stayed quiet for a few seconds, then Halsey piped up for the first time, as if the silence had woken him up. "So lemme get this straight," he slurred sleepily. "Someone intentionally suffocated forty people?"

"Not just suffocated." Stanford Runstom spoke before the captain could respond. "There must have been explosive decompression, too."

"That's right, Officer," Inmont said. "Have you ever seen this kind of thing before?"

Despite the long periods of inactivity, Runstom had worked a few interesting cases here and there. Vandalism. Theft. And one time, a few years back, even a murder. But he easily spent more time in the outpost's library poring over old cases than he did working on real, live cases. The library pastime was meant to be study, but it involved a fair bit of daydreaming as well. What would he have done on each case? Would he have caught the offenders? Would he have brought them to justice?

Runstom sat quietly for a moment. Forty potential murder victims. He was definitely going to miss the rest of the Sirius

Series. "No," he admitted in a low voice. "But there's a first time for everything."

They took a short-range cruiser from their precinct, located in the asteroid belt between Barnard-4 and Barnard-5, down to the surface of Barnard-4. The third and fourth planets of Barnard's Star were the only rocks in the system deemed suitable for dome construction; which is to say, they lacked hospitable atmosphere, but they had gravities somewhere in the vicinity of ten meters per second squared, give or take, as well as minimal natural magnetic fields. Since B-4 was the primary client for their precinct, their station was in an orbit that paralleled the planet's orbit pretty closely and they were coming out of subwarp to make their approach within a few hours.

The planet wasn't much to look at. Runstom watched the surface scroll by on one of the tracking monitors as they descended through a landing trajectory. It was gray and lifeless, pock-marked with craters and nothing else, until the first city came into view. The habitable structures weren't the first thing he saw, of course, but rather the massive atmospheric processors that protruded tube-like into the sky. He knew nothing of how they worked, other than by extracting minerals and liquids from deep under the surface, turning them into oxygen, water, and other useful things, and expelling byproducts into the airless vacuum that surrounded the complex. A kind of temporary atmosphere was created in that immediate space, a mix of toxic clouds and precipitation that boiled off in the lack of air pressure as it dissipated across the planet's surface. It was this mess that began to haze into the monitors as the cruiser drew closer to its destination, and Runstom could only just make out the lights of the city below as they approached.

Mass murder. Murder of any kind was rare enough in the domes. Even other violent crimes such as assault, rape, destruction of property, and so on were lower than they'd ever been. He leaned away from the hazy lights of the screen and scratched the back of his neck, glancing around at the other officers as he did. They joked and bullshitted like they were going on an outing, but he could detect the tension behind their banter. None of them were prepared to deal with something like this. Runstom included himself in that thought, but somehow he imagined it may be worse for him because he couldn't help but take it so seriously, more so than any of them. The others spent their lives floating from one day to the next, waiting for the next vacation, waiting for eventual retirement, but Runstom had always wanted more. He'd spent his whole life waiting for a case this big. And now that it was here, all he could think about was how terrible it was that so many lives were snuffed out in one strike. Families. He brought his hand from around the back of his neck and up to his forehead, which was warm to the touch. The idea that such an event could be an intentional, malicious act caused him to sweat.

This was the job. This was why he was in ModPol. They couldn't bring those lives back, but they could find out who did it and give the people of B-4 some justice. He pushed the anxiety down with a thick swallow and began to rehearse crime-scene procedures in his head as a way to occupy his thoughts.

The cruiser docked at the surface spaceport at about 5:30AM local time, a good three hours after the incident. Ground transport wasn't quite so speedy though, since they had to land at the main port in Blue Haven and then lug their equipment from there to the mag-rail that ran out to the sub-dome called Gretel. Blue Haven was a very densely populated mega-dome, and in the mix of vehicular and human traffic, it took them another two hours to reach the mag-rail station.

The mag-rail itself was pretty quick, once they finally got on it. They were inside Gretel after a scant, eighteen-minute trip. The sub-dome was still set for nighttime shading, so most of the residents were asleep and it wasn't nearly as crowded as the main dome. They managed to grab a hover-cab and get over to the checkpoint outside block 23-D in about ten minutes. A few Blue Haven officers were there, as well as some emergency personnel. Also hanging about were a few groggy LifSup operators, griping about being dragged out of bed.

"Welcome to Gretel, officers," said one of the Blue Haven officers as he directed some others to help the ModPol team with their gear. "I'm Officer Nate Jenkins." He nodded to each of them in turn. Runstom could never get used to the pale, almost translucent skin of the B-foureans, which was compounded by their low-gravity height that had the effect of making them always seem to be looming from above. He nodded back, then made a show of looking at the indicator lights on the wall just outside the mainte-nance door that led into the block. "Pressure's back on in 23-D," Jenkins continued. "They just gotta stabilize and then you can go on in. Med techs'll be goin' in with ya. Check for survivors."

"What are the chances of someone surviving?" McManus asked, arching an eyebrow.

"Well, the air here on B-4 is pretty thin," said one of the emergency medical technicians, a middle-aged man with long, but well-groomed, white hair. "The artificial atmo in the dome would have rushed out pretty quick with the top blown like that. So you've got a pretty good chance of immediate asphyxiation for anyone who didn't get a lungful of air when it happened. Then there's the drop in pressure, so we might see some decompression sickness – you know, the bends – and maybe some embolism." He looked at each of the blank faces of the ModPol officers. "You know, pressure drops ... boiling point drops ... body fluids start to bubble," he said, pushing down on an invisible scale with his hands. "The bubbles can block off arteries and keep oxygen from getting to the brain."

"Yeah, not to mention stuff flyin' around like a fuckin' tornado," chimed in one of the Life Support operators, the last word dissolving into a cavernous yawn. Runstom tried to give the cluster of operators an inconspicuous once-over look. They all looked tired and they huddled together in an almost defensive formation, like a pack of wild animals. They whispered to each other and snickered quietly in between yawns and grumblings.

"Yeah, there's that," one of the other med techs said, a skinny woman who looked too young to be attending a crime scene. "We'll probably see a lot of lacerations, blunt force trauma, that kind of thing."

"People inside housing units probably had a better chance," the first med tech said. "Especially if they were in a small, closed room. Anyone who is alive, we gotta get to pretty quick, in case they're suffering from hypoxia."

McManus leaned into Horowitz. "Do I wanna know what that means?" he asked in a low voice. She didn't look at him, just shook her head slowly. "Hey, pal," he said loudly, addressing the pale-skinned Officer Jenkins. "What's the layout of this place?"

"Well, let me show you," Jenkins said with an unnerving smile. He took a step toward one of the monitors on the wall and pointed. The screen was mostly black, save a few thick, green lines forming a tic-tac-toe grid. Inside each of the squares were lighter lines, grids within the grid. "Block 23-D is a typical sub-dome block." He pointed at one of the smaller squares inside the bottom, left-most square of the main grid. "Four small residential units form a square, their backyards coming together, separated by fences." He traced a couple of the light-green lines and said, "Around each side of these squares is a narrow avenue."

Jenkins leaned back from the monitor and made broad motions with his finger, saying, "Nine of these squares themselves form the block, three rows of three. In the middle square, there's a supply store and a little community garden."

"Bing. Block 23-D," said an extremely calm, disembodied female voice. "Pressure stable. Oxygen level stable." A bunch of the indicator lights that Runstom was pretending to look at turned a welcoming green.

"Ah, there we go," Jenkins said. "We've got atmo. The other systems like the vital-scanners are still off-line. But it's safe for you folks to go in."

Runstom was still thinking about the operators. "These guys all just woke up. Where's the LifSupOp on duty for this block?"

McManus glared at him, but Horowitz said, "Hey yeah. That's a good question."

"Ah, uh." Jenkins pointed a finger in no particular direction. "Your uh, detective. Detective Brute?"

"Detective Brutus," McManus said.

"Right, Brutus. He told us to take the Op on duty over to the BHPD station and put him in holding until someone can interrogate him."

"You mean *question*," Horowitz said. She turned to dip her head slightly and look Officer Nate Jenkins in his gray eyes. "You took him in for *questioning*."

"Oh, no." Officer Jenkins smiled broadly. "We arrested him."

"He's a suspect," one of the other Blue Haven officers said with a touch of pride in his voice. He went back to doing an impersonation of a statue.

"That's right," Jenkins confirmed, cheerfully. "Our only suspect." He nodded once, as if the book were closed on this case and looked around at everyone for a moment, then at the wall with all the green lights on it. "Well, as I said – you folks are all set to go into 23-D now. We'll be here if you need anything."

Horowitz smirked at him. "Thanks for your help," she said overly cheerfully, beaming an obnoxious smile and wide eyes at the B-fourean. Jenkins, apparently unaccustomed to sarcasm, or more likely, unwilling to acknowledge it, simply nodded and smiled.

Runstom was about to ask the B-foureans another question when McManus suddenly slapped him on the back and shoved a CamCap into his gut. "Stanley. You get to be Porter."

Runstom clutched the headgear. "It's Stanford," he muttered, and carefully placed the unwieldy helmet with the camera attachment on his head. A jacket accompanied the CamCap, coiled wires connecting the camera to bulky sonic and magnetic sensors, a transmission antenna, and multiple battery packs. Runstom shrugged into the jacket and felt twenty kilos heavier.

It was customary for ModPol detectives to attend an initial crime-scene investigation remotely. Runstom was pretty low in the pecking order in his precinct and seemed to get stuck wearing the Remote Detective Unit more often than anyone else, except for maybe Halsey. He was generally pretty annoyed by it, but this time he couldn't help but to feel even more annoyed that Brutus and Porter weren't present in the flesh. This was a goddamn mass homicide, not vandalism or petty theft.

Once they got inside, it was a real mess. Debris lay strewn everywhere. Little single- and double-seated hover-cars hung about at awkward angles, their frames split or badly bent. Shards of unidentifiable plastic and metal stuck out of the artificial turf of the yards like crooked, multicolored fangs. A tree-like air scrubber lay precariously across two rooftops, the surface of its metallic branches gleaming dully in the low light, its plastic root system splaying out into the sky over the avenue. The ModPol officers congregated in the Southeast corner of the block, near the maintenance access door, med techs in tow.

Horowitz was staring back at the entrance. "Those motherfuckers are useless, you know that?" she said to no one in particular.

"B-4 cops act like their job is public relations," McManus agreed immediately. "Like criminal justice's got nothing to do with it."

"They act more like fucking waiters than cops," Horowitz said.

Runstom kept his mouth shut, but he had to agree. The pale-skinned B-fourean officers were trained to be the face of the dome government. The crime rate was so low, particularly in the sub-domes, that the cops really were there for PR more than anything else. Smile and make people feel welcome and protected, that's what they were good at. Runstom wondered if he was feeling thankful for the local force's incompetence. The truth of it was, if domer cops were any good at doing actual police-work, he'd always be stuck back at the outpost, perpetually orbiting a slow circle around Barnard's Star, watching HV and reading about other people's cases. He kept his somewhat inappropriate glass-half-full optimism to himself.

"Alright, listen up." Detective Brutus's voice came crackling out of the Remote Detective Unit that was wrapped around Halsey, who looked as uncomfortable in his gear as Runstom felt. "Everyone pair up with a med tech and take a quadrant. We'll take this one. McManus, you take the Southwest. Horowitz, you take the Northeast. Runstom. Take a stroll through the garden and see if you can find any – Halsey! Check your CamCap. I can't see anything."

"Uh, okay, boss," Halsey said, looking over his connections with clumsy motions.

McManus turned back toward the maintenance door. "Hey!" he shouted. "Can you guys switch it to daytime?"

The murmur of voices emanated from the other side of the doorway. After a minute or two, one of the operators croaked out of a hidden speaker. "Okay, here comes morning."

The night sky started to lighten, and as it came into view, the dome seemed to flex and ripple like water. After another minute it was a brilliant, light blue-green hue, radiating light and illuminating the avenue and revealing dents and scratches on the residential units on the corner.

"What color clouds do ya want?"

"We don't need any clouds!" McManus shouted. "Just leave it like this, that's fine." He looked at Halsey. "That better, Detective?"

"Huh?" Halsey blinked.

"Yeah, much better," Detective Brutus's voice crackled out of Halsey's jacket. "Runstom!"

"Yes, sir?" Runstom turned to face Halsey.

"Go to the garden and check it out. I doubt you'll find any survivors there, but make note of any bodies. Then go up to the Northwest quadrant."

"Yes, sir," Runstom said. Halsey seemed to be interested in something sticking out of a nearby yard and turned the CamCap away. "Um. Excuse me, sir. Detective."

"What is it, Officer? Halsey, turn back around so I can see Runstom!"

Runstom motioned to the CamCap on his own head. "Detective Porter? He hasn't connected yet."

"What?" the speaker crackled before erupting into a sudden burst of static. "—wah—drant and look for bodies. Remember, warm or cold, make sure the med tech gets a full scan. Let's move, people."

Runstom looked at McManus and then Horowitz, hoping one of them would offer guidance without his asking for it. McManus ignored him, motioning to one of the med techs and then marching off. Horowitz slapped him on the shoulder. "Have a nice walk in the sweat-suit, Runny. You," she said, pointing to a med tech. "Let's go."

Halsey was taking one of the other med techs into the nearby unit on the corner. Runstom looked at the remaining med tech; the one he thought was too young to be at a crime scene. She was a scrawny, pale girl with large beady eyes and thin, fidgeting fingers, and would have been a few inches taller than Runstom if not for her slouch. "Hi," she said, sticking a cold hand into his. "I'm Roxeen."

He shook her hand in one up-and-down motion and then pulled away. "Officer Stanford Runstom." He shifted the weight of the jacket around, but it only seemed to make it worse. She peered at him as if he were a specimen under a microscope. "Alright, let's go, Roxeen."

The garden was a shambles. Ex-garden, really. All the plants had been sucked out of the ground. Half the irrigation system lay in a tangle of pipes in the middle of a nearby avenue. Somewhere in the center of the once-garden-muck was a yellowish blob.

"That's a body," Roxeen said, pointing to what Runstom was already looking at. "Let's go scan it."

He nodded, still looking at the body. They began trudging through the slimy mixture of dirt and vegetable pulp. The broken stalks and vines and mashed fruits gave off an odor that to Runstom just smelled like food, and it started to make him hungry. As they got closer to the body, his appetite vanished. The corpse was bloated and bruised. Purple and yellow flesh was only partially covered by the tatters of what was once clothing, maybe some kind of jumpsuit, uniformly gray in color.

"Looks like they got the worst of the decompression," she said, her scanner already in hand. She stalked toward the corpse with morbid fascination.

Runstom took a step and suddenly found himself with one foot submerged in the muck. "Ah, goddammit," he said, trying to pull his foot free. The weight of his jacket shifted and his other leg dropped, the mud reaching his knee. "Oh, come *on*."

"Oh my," Roxeen said, coming over to help him. She took his hand and pulled weakly, making no headway.

"Help me get this jacket off," he said, struggling with one of the sleeves of his burden. "Porter's not even here and I'm lugging this goddamn thing all over the place."

"What's Porter?" she asked as she helped him pull out of the sleeve.

"Detective Porter. The guy who is supposed to be watching through this goddamn camera on my head. The reason I'm dragging around an extra twenty kilos of weight here."

They succeeded in getting the jacket off him, Roxeen pulling on it by one sleeve and falling backwards, dragging the equipment through the mud. After a few more minutes of fighting to get his feet out of the muck and fighting off her attempts to help, Runstom managed to curse and pull himself free.

A few minutes later, they were standing over the amorphous and splotched corpse. Patches of the yellowed skin were marked by uniform squares of red. Roxeen bent forward to run her scanner up and down the length of the body. "Yep," she said with an unnecessary air of authority. "This one got the worst of it."

She rattled off all the conditions already speculated by the lead med tech, and then some. Runstom looked up while she talked. He saw only blue-green sky. Despite the chaos surrounding them, the block was eerily calm. "The main venting doors are probably right above us somewhere. Why didn't this guy just get sucked out onto the planet's surface?"

"Oh yeah," the med tech said thoughtfully as she stood up. "I think there are some kind of protective grates or something between the inner and outer doors."

"That would explain the checkerboard effect," he mumbled, giving the body one last look and then turning away.

"What's a checkerboard?"

Runstom glared at the med tech. Her white face and large gray eyes were innocent and quizzical. "Forget it," he mumbled. He'd only had his thirty-seventh birthday two

21

months ago, but Roxeen's alarming youth was making him feel old. Though it wasn't entirely youth, he supposed. He tried not to let it get to him and instead looked back at the rest of the garden. "Let's get out of this mud pit. I don't see any more bodies."

After slipping and sliding their way back out of the sludge, he set the jacket down on the avenue and made a meager attempt to clean it off. She wandered up and down the street looking for more residents while he cleaned. She didn't find any, and once he got the jacket back on they set out to go house to house.

"So," Roxeen said as they walked, pausing in that way when someone wants to broach a subject they're not sure they should. "Where are you from, Officer Runstom?"

Runstom sighed wearily. "Do we really have to do the small talk thing right now? I'm not good at small talk."

"Well, I was just …"

"I know you were just." Runstom stopped and turned to face her. "It's the green skin. Right?"

"Well," she started, then frowned, dropping her gaze. "I'm sorry."

"Look, you've got medical training, right? Don't you understand? It's the filters and stuff." Runstom hated trying to explain why he was born with green skin. It was really more of a brownish-olive color, but compared to the stark white of a B-fourean like Roxeen, he was a green man. He didn't really understand the science behind it either, and he was always trying to forget how much different it made him look from most others.

"Yes, the filters," Roxeen said meekly. "The atmosphere combined with the radiation filters where we grow up make our skin favor different pigmentation during development."

"Right, something like that," Runstom mumbled, and he turned away and started walking again. "I'm space-born. You want to know where I'm from?" Roxeen didn't answer. "Nowhere, that's where. Born on a transport shuttle, somewhere between one ModPol outpost and another." He trudged down the avenue and motioned her to follow him as he opened the door to the house on the corner. She stood there for a moment, clearly not content with the condensed version of his life story. She gave him a look he couldn't quite read and then walked past him through the doorway.

He stood alone and scowled at nothing. She was just a kid, asking questions a kid would ask. Not only was she young, she was a B-fourean – a domer – living a sheltered life. He decided he'd better go easy on her and he took a deep breath.

Runstom looked up and down the avenue before following Roxeen into the residence. The whole block was a crime scene. It had to be the biggest crime scene in ModPol history, excepting incidents where entire spaceships had been destroyed, of course. He'd certainly never read about anything this big in the outpost's library.

The first four houses shared similar scenes. Debris trailed out of the windows and doorways. Dishes, books, records, artwork, clothing, smaller pieces of furniture, and lots of unidentifiable bits of previously loved possessions. Each unit had a body, all of them dead. They all had managed to keep themselves from being sucked out of their houses, and didn't have nearly as much of the bloat as the corpse in the garden had. The residents in those four units either died due to injury from flying debris or survived the windstorm long enough to suffocate. Only Roxeen's scanner could tell the difference. She dutifully examined them with a morbid curiosity that made Runstom increasingly uncomfortable.

The fifth house was different. The damage inside the house seemed off somehow, but Runstom couldn't put his finger on why. They didn't find a body, just lots of broken glass, ceramics, and plastic. They dug around for a few minutes, just to be sure they didn't overlook a corpse.

"What was that?" Roxeen said with a start as Runstom flipped over half a lounge chair.

"Huh? I dunno, just a chair, I guess."

"No, shh!" She stood still for a moment, and he turned to give her an annoyed glare. "I heard something," she whispered. Her eyes were wide with alarm.

"What?" he said in a hushed voice. He tried not to move for a moment as he listened.

"In the lavatory, I think."

He looked at the bathroom door and stared in silence, straining to hear. He looked back at her, and shifted his weight around. He suddenly remembered that he was still wearing that damned, bulky jacket and Detective Porter had yet to remote in. He disconnected the CamCap from the port in the jacket and shrugged off the latter. He was about to take the helmet off too, but then had a sudden image of Porter trying to call in right at that moment. The last thing he wanted was a demerit, so he plugged the CamCap cable into the regulation Personal Mobile Device in the inside pocket of his ModPol uniform. The PMD had a weak transmitter on it that didn't work well for a long distance up-link, but if Porter tried calling in, Runstom would at least know it and could just plug the CamCap back into the jacket real quick.

"I think there's someone in there," Roxeen said. She inched closer to the bathroom while Runstom messed around with his equipment.

"Okay," he said quietly. "Don't move." He took a step toward the bathroom door, unclipping his holster and touching the butt of his gun. It suddenly occurred to him that if anyone were alive in there, he had no reason to suspect they were dangerous. He kept one finger on the gun anyway, and crept forward. Something about this house was ringing alarm bells in his head.

He got to the door and punched the release handle, but the door stuck firmly closed. Locked from the inside. Someone was definitely in there; whether they were still alive or not, he wasn't sure. He broke the silence with a knock on the door.

"Anyone in there?" It was quiet for a moment, then he heard a distinct, thin cough from the other side. "Hello?" Runstom said, loudly now. "If you can hear me, can you hit the door lock?"

He heard no other sound. "Shit," he muttered, pulling a multi-tool off his belt. He jammed the tool into the side of the door-handle mechanism, popping the safety latch. The panel fell away revealing the manual handle. He grabbed it and yanked the door sideways.

"Shit," he repeated, unsure of how to react to the scene before his eyes. "I think we've got a live one here."

The bathroom floor was red and wet with blood. Sitting on the floor, against the far wall, was a tall, red-skinned, red-haired man. His eyes lolled back in his head, but his chest moved ever so slightly, in and out, in and out. The slow motion mesmerized Runstom for a fraction of a second, and he pictured each corpse they'd examined, each a *thing*, an object to be scanned, but each of them had been more than that only a few hours ago. Each one had once been alive.

"Oh, my!" Roxeen breathed as she came up to the bathroom door. "He's ... he's covered in blood!"

Runstom took a step forward as her words sunk in. He swallowed a few curses before finding the right response. "You don't get outta the sub-domes much, do ya?" He looked at her, and she turned away from the body on the floor long enough to give Runstom a blank look. "He's an off-worlder. Probably from Poligart, that big moon in the Sirius system. Or maybe Betelgeuse-3. That's red skin," he said, pointing to the man. "That's blood," he added, pointing to the floor.

Roxeen's mouth moved a little, but she didn't say anything. "Well, get over here!" he barked at her. "He's still breathing, but I don't know for how much longer."

She stutter-stepped toward the red man on the floor, fumbling with her scanner. She knelt gingerly in the gooey, half-dry, red-brown plasma that covered the tiled floor, planting herself a few feet away from the resident as she stretched the scanning unit toward him. It began blinking and chirping all kinds of warnings and alarms. Runstom couldn't use a med-scanner to save his life, but the device practically quivered with fear as it chattered on about fading vitals.

Liquid oozed out of the right side of the man's mid-section, and Runstom and Roxeen both stared at the open wound dumbly. Runstom's mind clumsily sifted through all the crime-scene procedures he'd been re-memorizing on the flight to B-4 as though there would be some rule or policy on how to handle the situation, something to tell him what to do. A gurgled cough came from the dying man, causing Runstom to throw aside the mental handbook and focus on the life slipping away from them in that moment. He lunged forward and put his hands on the open wound, applying pressure. He felt the goo of a QuikStik bandage. An open med-kit lay on the floor underneath the nearby counter. This guy had managed to partially close his wound, but not completely. The ragged way he was breathing and the agitation of the med-scanner led Runstom to guess there was probably a lot of damage somewhere on the inside.

"Can you do anything for him?" Runstom said, craning his neck to watch the red man's face while keeping his hands on the wound. When the med tech didn't reply, he looked at her. She stared through him with those big gray eyes. "Roxeen!" he shouted.

"They said they would all be dead," she said softly. "They said there wouldn't be anyone alive."

"Yeah, well they were fucking wrong, Roxeen! This guy is breathing!"

The dying man coughed several times in succession. "Uhhhnnn."

"Hey. Hey!" Runstom tried to look into the eyes rolling around in the red man's head. "Hey, look at me! Help is here, you're going to be okay."

"Uhhhhnnn," the man groaned. "Eh," he coughed a strange sound like he was trying to speak. "Eh. Eh."

"That's it, talk to me." Without taking his eyes off the man, Runstom spoke out of the side of his mouth at Roxeen. "Get another QuikStik, so we can close this wound. And we need some syn-plasma. He's lost a lot of blood. Hey buddy – talk to me. Where are you from?"

"Ehh. Ehhh. Kkkkssss."

"Come on, buddy. Stay with me."

Roxeen dropped the med scanner to the floor, where it continued beeping and flashing more intensely, locked on to the patient's vitals. She broke open her own pack, unrolling it across the still-wet tiles and revealing all manner of emergency medical product.

27

"Ehhh. Kkkksss." With an effort, the man raised his blood-stained hands, bringing them up to his face. He tried to put them together, shakily forming a cross with his index fingers.

Roxeen had gotten another QuikStik out of its package and moved Runstom's hands away so she could apply it. With his hands free, Runstom tried to hold the red man's head straight.

The man looked into Runstom's eyes. He crossed his index fingers again, holding them in front of his face for a few seconds before dropping them weakly and going limp. He exhaled one last time and closed his eyes.

The med scanner blared one last mechanical scream and went silent.

CHAPTER 3

After several hours, the Modern Policing and Peacekeeping officers, their remotely connected detectives (Porter did eventually call in), and their accompanying medical technicians found thirty-seven residents and one maintenance worker. Two people who lived in the block were later found to be in the Blue Haven dome during the incident and were detained for questioning, but quickly released. Of the thirty-eight found in block 23-D, nine were still alive. Two of those were unstable and died before the med techs could get them out of the block. The other seven were taken to Gretel Hospital and were in various medical conditions, and despite the likelihood of permanent physical and mental damage, all were expected to live.

The twenty-nine found dead were all scanned and recorded. Many had died from blunt-force trauma and lacerations or suffocation. Many had suffered from various other disturbing ailments, the medical names of which Runstom did not care to remember, mostly related to decompression and lack of oxygen. The remains were removed and the ModPol officers were given one more day to comb the desolate block. This time they were without the CamCaps and weighty jackets.

They found no other remains and the clean-up crews moved in to go to work the next day.

"Seems like we should be in there for a couple more days," Runstom said, sitting at a table in a break room in the depths of the Blue Haven Police Department Precinct One. "It's a crime scene, and they're already cleaning up all the evidence."

"Evidence?" McManus snorted, pouring himself a cup of coffee. "What the hell are you talking about, Stanley? Only one guy could have done this and he did it from outside the block."

"It's Stanf—"

"Mac is right, Stanley," Horowitz said. "It's a pretty open-and-shut case. The dicks like the operator. The sooner they get a confession out of him, the sooner we can go back to base."

Runstom looked at each of them, frowning. Horowitz wasn't even looking at him. She was idly flipping through a mag-viewer in front of her on the table, most of her long, straight, black hair pulled into a ponytail, leaving a clump of bangs to fall to one side, obscuring her face. McManus stood rigidly near the counter and peered suspiciously into his coffee cup. Halsey was half-dozing in his chair, startling awake with a snort when he began to tip over. There were three pale-faced Blue Haven officers looming on one side of the room, smiling mildly, thin hands clasped together at their mid-sections. Runstom thought that if he were to try to read their faces, he'd be looking at a blank page.

"Hey, Whitey," McManus said. "This fucking coffee is cold."

"Ah, thank you, officer," the middle one said. "We're glad you enjoy it."

McManus looked into his blank, gray eyes and then shrugged as he took a slug from the cup, then grimaced before taking another. Runstom frowned at the other ModPol officer, unnerved by the skin-slang. The residents of Barnard-4 were all extremely pale skinned thanks to low-grade filtration mechanisms and the distance from the center of the solar system. People growing up on B-3 – like the other three ModPol officers in the room – were closer to the star, and by necessity benefited from more expensive filters. They all had skin colors that ranged from pinkish yellow to light brown, closer to the hues of many Earthlings.

"Anyway. I don't know what you're complaining about, Runstom," McManus continued, starting a slow pace around the room. "Are you saying you had a good time combing through a giant trash heap, hoping to find the bloated remains of a B-fourean?"

"They weren't all B-foureans," Runstom said, quick to make his argument. "One guy was—"

Halsey interrupted him with a giggle. "Yeah, Stanley wants to go play dick. He wants to in-vess-ti-gate. Maybe go un-der-cov-er. Just like his dear ol' mum."

"You got a problem, Halsey?" Runstom stood up.

McManus moved in front of him. "Is that it, Runstom?" he said quietly. "You think you're better than us? *Detective* Runstom, is it now?"

Runstom imagined slugging the other man across the jaw, sending him sprawling to the floor, but he was determined not to be baited. "Officer McManus," he said in a low voice, matching it with an even stare. "Are you attempting to instigate me?"

McManus gave a huffy snort. "No, *Officer* Runstom." he said through clenched teeth. "I'm not trying to *instigate* you." He took a sip from his cup, bringing it close to Runstom's nose. "I'm just really, really bitten off about how terrible this fucking coffee is." He slapped the empty mug down on the table and walked out of the room.

Halsey gave half a laugh and then leaned his head back and closed his eyes. Horowitz continued flipping through her mag-viewer. The Blue Haven officers maintained their indifferent smiles. Runstom stood in silence for a moment, focusing on suppressing his anger. After he'd given himself enough time to calm down, he announced that he was going for a walk. No one responded, so he left the room quietly.

The local precinct was set up like a maze of hallways and rooms, but everything was arranged in a way that made it impossible to get lost. Domes were all designed on paper by engineers, and everything turned out to have an unnatural symmetry that Runstom could never get used to. Even if you tried to get lost, you couldn't wander long before somehow ending up where you were supposed to be.

There wasn't much to do in the Blue Haven precinct – they didn't even have a library – so Runstom stopped when he came upon a door that led to an inner courtyard. It wasn't very large, but it had some plant life. Even though the trees and bushes were laid out in perfect position, nature still had chaotic reign over the formation of branches, leaves, and bark.

Runstom sat on a bench and tried to breathe deeply. Despite the presence of naturally generated oxygen in the space, the sweet sting of manufactured air was still detectable. He tried to ignore it and think about the case. He was still reeling from the fact that the investigation on the ground was more or less over already. Thirty-one people had died, seven others were injured in the ordeal. How could the investigation of the crime scene be over so quickly?

The detectives, Brutus and Porter, didn't believe it was an accident. They were charging the block operator on duty with murder. Runstom knew they didn't have much in the way of evidence. But even so, maybe they were right. As a rule, you look for the simplest explanation and you'll find your suspect. The only person who could have opened the venting doors was the operator.

So why was Runstom unable to accept such a simple conclusion? He sighed as he sat in the fabricated grove of trees and shrubs. He'd been spending too much time in the outpost library. Poring over old cases with complexities that were just plain absent here.

They did have one key piece of evidence: the operator's console logs. What they didn't have was motive. Runstom wished he could be a fly on the wall in the interrogation room at that moment, where they were currently questioning the operator. Would they get a confession out of him? Would they discover the man's motive for killing thirty-one mostly unrelated people in one fell swoop?

Runstom rolled his head around, stretching his neck. He caught a glimpse of the curved sky above. Maybe the guy just snapped. Dome sickness. It'd been known to happen, although supposedly not very often. Some people just couldn't take it, living in the confined spaces, never being able to set foot onto the surface of the planet that binds them gravitationally. Runstom had never heard of anyone becoming violent from dome sickness though, at least nothing more than a brief outburst. Malaise, mood swings, depression, even suicide, but never such a calculated act of violence against so many people.

He stood up, but he didn't go anywhere. He just continued to stare at the trees confined to their perfect little steel planters. He knew the reason he couldn't accept the simple explanation. He wanted there to be more to the case than there was; he wanted a chance to do something. He wanted a chance to prove himself. McManus' comment had troubled him more than he was willing to admit. Not the skin-slang – he'd learned to live with that stuff – but the *detective* comment. Runstom had been working with McManus, Horowitz, Halsey, and others at ModPol for several years now. So many that were officers at ModPol were probably always going to be officers; especially the likes of those three unambitious clock-punchers. They all knew Runstom was determined to make detective. He was getting a little old for an officer, and he'd been passed over for promotion more than once. The others rarely missed a chance to remind him that despite his efforts, he was as stuck as the rest of them.

Of course, he knew that by making waves in an open-and-shut case like this one, he wasn't going to win any medals. Brutus and Porter already had a less-than-glowing opinion of Runstom. If he opened his big mouth to the detectives, he might never get called for crime-scene duty again. The biggest case he would ever participate in, and all he had to show for it was the cataloging of a handful of bloated corpses.

CHAPTER 4

"Look, Jackson. We don't need anything from you. We've got a murder weapon with your fingerprints on it. We have evidence that places you at the scene of the crime at the time it was committed. We've even got motive. This is your last chance to make things a little easier on yourself."

Jax was quiet. Detective Brutus of Modern Policing and Peacekeeping sat across from him, jacket off, sleeves rolled up, elbows on the table. Detective Porter, also of ModPol, leaned against the wall, quietly watching him. Their strange skin, a hue somewhere between brown and pink, reminded Jax that he was in the company of off-worlders. He liked to think of himself as open-minded and free from prejudice, but these two brown-pink-skinned men made him extremely nervous.

Jax's lawyer, a man by the name of Frank Foster and a B-fourean like himself, sat by his side. Foster leaned over to whisper something to him, but Jax raised a hand to bat away the advice.

"Maybe you should listen to your counsel, Jackson."

All he could think was that it had to be a set-up. There was no other explanation. He didn't say it out loud. There was no point, and he didn't want to sound – or feel – like a cliché. He folded his arms across his chest and stared pointedly at nothing.

"Murder weapon," Brutus said, pulling a printout from a folder and slapping it onto the table. "The murder weapon in this case is the Life Support system. The trigger on this weapon is an active console. These official logs show that only one active console was connected to block 23-D's LifSup system at 2602.03.23.02.03, the time at which the incident occurred." He pointed at the printout with short fingers that sprouted blond hairs the same color as the stubble on his head. "The consoles use biometric authentication to verify operators. This log says the voice of you, Jack J. Jackson, Barnard-4 resident ID 721841695, and the *fingerprint*, of you, Jack J. Jackson, Barnard-4 resident ID 721841695, were used to activate this console at 2602.03.22.10.06." He turned the printout around so that Jax and his lawyer could read it. "It remained active until the forced reset at 2602.03.23.02.14."

The operator continued to stare into space while his lawyer leaned over to look at the printout. After a minute he leaned back. "Mr. Jackson," he started.

Jax threw up his hands, finally meeting the detectives' eyes, each in turn. "Why would I hurt so many people?" He felt like he was watching a scene in a holo-vid, unable to believe it was really happening, that he was under arrest, suspected of murder.

"That's what we're here to find out," Brutus said evenly. "Why would you kill an entire blockful of people?"

"This is ridiculous," Jax said, more to himself than anyone else. Visions of crime dramas were filling his head. How many times had he been entertained as the actor cops went on about evidence, profiles, and motives, all while the suspect squirmed in their little metal chair. "You guys must have done a psyche profile on me," he tried. "This can't be something that fits my pro—"

"Profile?" Porter laughed from the back of the room. He was tall for his kind, lean, muscular, and had darker skin than Brutus, a color some might describe as bronze. The man looked more like a politician – or a used hover-car salesman – than a detective, and Jax couldn't wait to get away from him. "Look, Jackson. No one cares about your profile when there's this much evidence against you."

"And we have motive," Brutus added. "You knew two of the victims."

The detective paused, as if to let Jax try to read him. He seemed to open his face up, letting Jax know he wasn't lying. The LifSup operator didn't know who lived in block 23-D. He wasn't allowed to know. He had access to minimal vital readouts on all the residents in his block, but no names. Just resident IDs. He wasn't a resident there himself, so he wasn't allowed in. It hadn't occurred to him until now that real people lived in there, or in any other block he worked on. Or rather, *real* in the sense that he might know them personally. The operators rotated around from block to block every week. His only concern while on the clock was the Life Support system, not the list of resident IDs that came with the rest of the block data readout.

Detective Brutus pulled another printout from his folder. "Brandon Milton." Attached to the printout was a file photo. On top of that, he slapped down a more current photo of the expired resident. "His wife, Priscilla Jonnes." Again a printout and file photo. Again a postmortem photo taken by a med tech two nights ago. The bodies in the photos looked inhuman, twisted into unnatural angles, skin splotched, bruised, and cut all over. He couldn't even see their faces, but somehow he knew that the names matched the deceased.

Jax couldn't breathe. Milton. His supervisor. Priscilla. An ex-girlfriend. He didn't know she was married. He hadn't spoken to her in a couple of years. He knew Milton was married, but of course, he didn't know his supervisor was married to one of his ex-girlfriends. He didn't like the guy enough to want to know anything about his personal life.

He was frozen, and probably looked like he was going to be sick. The detectives gave each other a knowing look, as if celebrating a silent victory. They probably thought Jax was ready to toss his lunch over the bloated mess of once-human flesh in the photos, but the source of the bile rising in his throat was the same fear that was causing him to feel the walls closing in around him. If there was any doubt in his mind that this was a set-up before, it was gone now.

"Take those away, please," his attorney said weakly. Jax could feel the man next to him fidgeting and anxious, rattled by the images in the photos.

Brutus ignored him. "You know what?" he said, pointing and wagging two fingers at the operator. "You're right. I did look at your psyche profile. That's standard procedure. You want to know what your profile told me about you?" Jax just stared, slack-jawed, so Brutus kept talking. "Too smart to be an operator." He leaned in closer. "Yeah, that's right. A smart guy. Smart enough to go to an Alliance University as an engineering student, anyway, until you dropped out. It makes no sense for someone with your brains to be working this thankless, dead-end job. You should be designing LifSups, not operating them. So what's the deal with that?"

Jax wanted to just be silent, but the detective stared at him, waiting for an answer. He felt railroaded. Worse, he could hear his father's voice inside his head, as if he were standing over Jax's shoulder. *Tell them, Jax. Tell them why you're not an engineer like me. Tell them why you failed. Tell them why you turned out to be a grunt like your mother was.* He narrowed his eyes. He wasn't ready to share his life story with these strangers. "I guess not everyone has what it takes."

Detective Brutus stared at him for another minute, as if he were trying to figure out if the answer revealed anything significant. He shrugged and continued. "Let's start with the girl, Jackson. We know you had a relationship with Priscilla Jonnes." Another printout came out of the folder. Jax began to wonder what else was in that stack of coffin nails that he first thought was just for show. "This is a record of a genetic compatibility test. You and Jonnes must have been pretty serious. A genetic-comp test – that's pretty much a pre-engagement for you B-foureans, right?"

Detective Porter stepped up to the table, leaning over, palms flat on the surface. He put on a concerned face. "What happened, Jackson? There's no grounds for a break-up in this compatibility report. So what was it? What was the trouble in paradise?"

"We grew apart," Jax managed to say. Trouble in paradise, indeed. Priscilla had been a wonderful companion and a dear friend. If Jax could figure out why she left, he'd know a whole lot more about women. Or people in general, for that matter. "I haven't seen her in years," he said sadly, then creased his forehead in annoyance that these off-worlders were getting into his head.

"Mm-hm." Porter nodded, as if that was the answer he expected. He smiled, his teeth unnaturally white and perfect, and winked, as if he'd just made a sale or won someone's vote. He stepped back to his post holding up the wall.

"Milton is your supervisor," Brutus continued. "*Was* your supervisor. Must have burned you up, your boss marrying the love of your life."

"I didn't know," Jax said quietly, knowing they weren't going to listen to him. He looked briefly at his lawyer for help, but the man's gray eyes were wide and empty. He'd probably never defended any crime worse than vandalism before this day.

"The guy who was constantly on your case. The guy whose signature is on a stack of write-ups that kept you from getting promoted this year." Another printout, this one on different paper. "The guy you have an official personal debt to for ten thousand Alliance Credits."

Jax looked at the paper on the table. It was some kind of third-party record, like an escrow company or bank or something. It was covered with official seals and date-stamps, all from the same day, about six months ago. The lawyer took a timid look at the document, and his silence seemed to verify its authenticity.

"What ..." Jax started, but couldn't form any other words. His mind reeled. He never borrowed money – not from anyone, not even his own father. But for some reason someone had forged a document that said he owed money to his supervisor, Brandon Milton. It made no sense to Jax.

"The guy." Brutus pulled the postmortem photo of Milton back to the top of the pile. "The guy who is dead now. Dead by the commands of a Life Support operator. Commands input at your console."

"This is not real," Jax said. The room began to dip and sway in his vision and he placed his hands flat on the table to steady himself. "This is not true. I never owed Brandon Milton any money. I didn't even know he was married to

Priscilla." He got louder, voice rising in panic. "I didn't run any commands that opened up the roof of that block! I didn't kill these people!"

"Well, a confession would have been nice, could have been a straight-to-sentence, no-trial-necessary deal." Detective Brutus held the door open as Detective Porter came into the break room.

"I know, Mike," Porter said. "But you know what they say. Everyone on the prison planet is innocent, donchaknow?" They shared a laugh. "But hey, don't sweat it – that guy is going away for good."

"Yeah, I reckon so." Brutus turned to face the officers in the room. "Okay, everybody, listen up. No confession from Jackson, so that means he'll be going to trial. Now you know we don't do any ModPol trials on-planet. He'll be tried at the outpost, out on the outer ring of the system. And, you know we can't just send a ship out to the edge for one prisoner. But there are a couple of prisoners lining up for trial in Blue Haven right now, so we'll have a full transport by the end of the week."

"Excuse me, detective?" Runstom said, hearing apprehension in his own voice.

"Yeah, Officer. Question?"

"Uh. Well, I was just wondering – aren't we going back to the crime scene at all?" Brutus stared at him expectantly, so Runstom continued. "You know – to make sure there's nothing we missed. Evidence we might have missed."

"That won't be necessary," Porter responded, walking toward the coffee machine.

"Yeah," Brutus said, and seemed to leave it at that. He looked at the back of his partner, and Runstom detected a hint of uncertainty on his face, but it quickly vanished.

"Okay," he said with renewed authority. "We're going to need to keep two of you here to escort the prisoner up to Barnard Outpost Alpha when they're ready to transfer him."

"You. And you," Porter said, fingering Halsey and Runstom. He tilted the coffee cup in his hand, peering at the inside of it cautiously, as if it might suddenly come to life and bite him.

"Okay, good," Brutus said. "You other two are heading back up to Outpost Gamma. We've got some paperwork assignments for you. Any questions?"

They didn't get much time to respond before Detective Porter banged his cup down onto the counter and said, "Nah, they got it. C'mon Mike, let's go." He slapped Detective Brutus on the shoulder and they left the room.

"Bah, paperwork," McManus grumbled after the dicks left. "Just our luck, eh, Sue?"

"What?" Runstom's eyes went wide with disbelief.

"Yeah, fuck you, Mac!" Halsey said. "Paperwork, big deal. We gotta sit around here in this fuckin' dome for three days and then take a ride out to the outer ring! Four days cooped up in a tiny transport vessel with a bunch of cons and—"

"Better check your orbital positioning," Horowitz said. "Alpha is on the opposite side right now. Tack on an extra day and a half."

"Oh yeah," McManus said. "Don't forget about the trip back too, that's a couple more days." He pointedly dropped a half-full cup of coffee into the sink. "Hey, white boys," he said to the three pale-faced officers still standing quietly at the back of the room. "Been nice knowin' ya. Thanks for the shitty coffee."

"It was our pleasure, officers," the middle one responded cheerfully.

"Have a nice trip, fellas." McManus and Horowitz gave them each a nod and walked out the door.

"This is just great, Stanley," Halsey breathed. "Can you believe this?"

Runstom glared at him. "My ... name ... is ... *Stanford.*"

"Well?" Jax stared at his silent counsel.

Frank Foster looked up. "Well," he responded quietly.

The lawyer was sitting in the only chair in Jax's sparse cell. His hands rested idly on a thinly packed paper folder that sat on a small desk. The folder was closed. Jax paced a full circle around the room, which somehow felt familiar. The walls were painted the same blue-green aqua color that his office was painted, but that couldn't be it. Could it?

Jax shook his head, trying to rattle his brain into focusing. "Well, what are we going to do?" He stopped pacing and stared at the other man. "I mean, it's bad, right? Is it bad?"

Foster closed his eyes for a moment, then opened them. "It's not good," he said. "Definitely not good. I have to inform you, Mr. Jackson ..." His voice trailed off.

"Inform me of what?" Jax snapped. He felt like he should be angry at something, but anxiety eclipsed every other emotion.

The lawyer sighed. "It looks like they're going to take you off planet while the investi—"

"Off-planet?" Jax couldn't get his brain to focus. "What do you mean by that?"

"They're going to take you out to one of the Modern Policing and Peacekeeping outposts."

Jax covered his eyes with the palms of his hands. "I don't understand," he said through clenched teeth. "I thought we paid ModPol for defense. Like against space gangs and whatnot." He uncovered his eyes and looked at Foster again. "Isn't that what we pay them for? Why are they even involved in this?"

"Yes, well. Modern Policing – um, ModPol – has automatic jurisdiction over interplanetary issues." Foster looked away from Jax. He was older, maybe in his mid-fifties. His white hair was long but thin and his face sagged in places as if it had begun melting a few years ago, but then stopped and re-solidified. "They can also be called in to assist with any investigation involving a class-four or class-five crime."

"Class four meaning murder or rape." Jax had holo-vision to thank for knowing that classification. Although, with all the crime drama vids he'd seen involving murder or rape, no one ever mentioned ModPol. "What's class five?"

Foster looked back at Jax. "Mr. Jackson," he said, his voice wavering. "This is a class-five crime. Are you aware of that?"

Jax was dumbfounded. "But I didn't do anything! The system malfunctioned, that's the only explanation. The only *reasonable* explanation," he corrected himself, fears of conspiracy creeping into the back of his mind.

"The crime being investigated is mass murder. There were thirty-one deaths—"

"But that's ridiculous!" Jax could feel fear creeping into his voice, causing it to crack and waver. He heard himself get louder to try to compensate, nearly shouting. "Why would I kill all those people? Why would anyone intentionally kill thirty-one people that have no connection to each other? Other than living in the same block—"

"I'm not accusing you, Jack." It was Foster's turn to interrupt. The older man's voice hardened. "Look – I don't know what this is all about. Thirty-one people are dead, and if there's a crime here, that's a class-five multi-murder.

The local authorities never see this kind of thing, so they called in ModPol. Once ModPol shows up, they ... well." He paused and made a motion with his right hand, as if tossing something away. "They tend to take over the whole thing. Investigation, proceedings, trial. All that."

Jax slumped onto his bed. He took a deep breath and stared at the blue-green wall. "So what are we going to do?" He looked at Foster. "I mean, you're my lawyer, right? You have to believe I'm innocent. What are we going to do?"

The other man cleared his throat. "They're going to take you off-planet, Mr. Jackson." The words seemed to crawl out of his mouth. "And there ... there you will be assigned new legal representation."

"What?" Again Jax had to work to focus and control his panic. "Wait, so you're not my lawyer?"

"Well, I am right now," Foster said. "But only for the next few days." He stood up and walked around the desk, then leaned against it. "Look, Mr. Jackson. Jack. Quite frankly, I'm not the right man for this job. We don't get these kinds of cases here. I haven't even worked a class-four case since my early career, when gang violence was still a presence in some of the more remote domes."

"This is just great," Jax muttered. He felt helpless.

"Jack. Listen to me. You're going to get a new lawyer when you get to the ModPol outpost. You're going to get someone who knows what they're doing." Foster stepped forward and put a hand on Jax's shoulder. "I do believe you're innocent. This was an accident. They're going to get testimony from all kinds of engineers and other experts, and the inevitable conclusion will be that it was a system problem. They're not going to cook you for this. You're just going to have to be strong and wait it out."

Jax sighed wearily. He wanted to believe Foster. Whether it was true or not, he had to believe that he was going to be proven innocent. How else would he get through this? He looked up at the lawyer and nodded. "Thanks, Frank."

Foster turned away and walked back over to the desk. He started sifting through some papers. "I've contacted your parents via d-mail." He looked over at Jax. "They haven't responded yet. But it's only been a day. The message might still be in queue."

Right, thought Jax. How many times had he heard someone blame lack of communication on the d-mail queue? He could only imagine what his father was thinking right now. The interrogation by the ModPol detectives came flooding back to him. It seemed like he was being reminded an awful lot about how he'd disappointed his father lately. He supposed after years of building walls, it was bound to catch up. "What did you tell him?" he asked. "Them, I mean."

"Well, just what I was legally obligated to. That you were arrested. But not convicted. That there was an investigation and there could possibly be a trial." Foster sat back down at the desk and concentrated on getting his papers in order. "I can send another, if you like. Normally we'd be asking your relatives to post bail. But in this case ..." he said, then trailed off.

"Right," Jax said. "No bail for the mass murderer."

"Yes. Well, anyway," Foster said. "If there's anything you want to tell them, I can send another message."

Jax sat silent. Would he give his father the satisfaction of an apology? "No," he said.

Foster stood up, his folder in hand. "I have to go." He pressed the button on the door, summoning the guard.

Jax was still thinking about his father. He imagined the man sitting at their home terminal, the one in the kitchen.

46

Drinking his coffee and reading a long-distance d-mail from B-4, telling him that his son had been arrested. Jax resented his father, and he resented the woman that he married after his mother died. His father and another engineer. They took the settlement from his mother's death and were off to greener pastures on B-3 before a year had passed.

But as much as he wanted to, he could not hate his father.

"Wait," Jax said. "I do want to send another message." He stopped and watched Foster turn his head. He swallowed, feeling a tightness in his throat. "Tell my father that I love him. And that I'm sorry."

"I will." The door opened. "I'll be in to check on you tomorrow."

Foster left and the door closed. Jax was left alone with his thoughts in the empty room.

Once again, he stared at the pale-blue walls. Maybe the room really did remind him of his work office. It was so bland, so devoid of any emotion or meaning. Just like everything else in the sub-domes. His mother's office – his real mother, Irene – her office was actually interesting. He'd only visited it a few times when he was a kid, but the memory of the walls painted bright orange and dotted with comical posters always stayed with him. The furniture that should have been in a living room, plush and soft, but yet there it was in the middle of an office. And the windows. Windows that looked out at the planet's surface. The real surface.

Some people will live their whole lives on this planet and never see its surface, his mother used to say. It's dull, gray, and ugly. But without it, we would just be drifting through space.

The world was a smaller place without Irene Jackson. It was a world as small as the room Jax was locked in. It was a world without a surface.

CHAPTER 5

The next day, Stanford Runstom and George Halsey sat in the Blue Haven Police Department break room watching bombball highlights. Runstom fidgeted with his uniform's snaps and Halsey sat stone-faced, staring at the holo-vid, not napping for once.

"*And Sommerset breaks another trap ...*" announced the HV set in a thin but enthusiastic voice.

"He's at the shot zone," Halsey said in chorus with the announcer, his mocking voice dead and monotone in contrast to the energetic sportscaster. "He jogs left, dodging Caruso. He fires. He scores. Krakens take the lead at the half."

"This is the fifth time they've played the same sports show with the same highlight sequence," Runstom said with a groan. He rubbed his eyes with the palms of his hands. "I can't stand this anymore, George."

"You're the big bombball fan," Halsey said without turning away from the holo-vision.

"No, I mean just sitting here doing nothing."

"What else are we gonna do?" Halsey poked idly at the remote and hopped around a few channels, all of which were playing advertisements.

Runstom didn't have an answer. He wanted to do some police work. They couldn't go back to the scene of the crime; the cleaning staff were already all over block 23-D, scrubbing it down. He knew they might be able to talk their way back into the operator room outside the block, but what evidence they might find there, Runstom had no idea. If the whole crime was committed from the console, he wouldn't even know what to look at. There was only one decent avenue of investigation he could think of at the moment.

"We could go interview the suspect," he said.

Halsey finally turned to look at him, mouth hanging open for a moment before curling into a smile. "Yeah, right. Good one." He turned back to the holo-vision. "Can you imagine, though? The dicks would be pissed," he said, drawing out the last word.

"Yeah," Runstom agreed quickly. He blew out a long sigh as Halsey continued flipping channels. "Well," he said. "I'm going for a walk."

Halsey turned around again and gave him a funny look. "Yeah, okay," he said tentatively. "Well, don't go too far. We might have to leap into action at a moment's notice."

"Right."

Officer Runstom found himself standing in the viewing area just outside an empty interrogation room. The B-fourean officers in charge of the holding cells had offered very little resistance when the ModPol officer had requested to have a prisoner brought out for questioning. Technically, they weren't supposed to bring out any prisoners without permission from the detectives that brought them in. The local officers were either blindly submissive to anyone wearing a

ModPol badge or they just didn't really care that they were being asked to bend the rules – Runstom wasn't sure which.

A few minutes later, Jack Jackson was led into the interrogation room and Runstom went in. A B-fourean guard stood quietly against one of the smooth, blue walls after plunking Jackson down in a small, metal chair in front of a long, empty metal table. Runstom quietly took a seat in the comfortable office chair opposite the prisoner. He'd watched a few interrogations go down in his time, and he'd seen many more go down on holo-vid, but he'd never conducted one himself. He hardly knew where to begin.

"Hi," Runstom said. "I'm Off—" he started, then stopped, wondering if he should call himself Detective for the purposes of the interview. He shook off the thought as ridiculous. "I'm Officer Runstom, Modern Policing and Peacekeeping."

The other man stared back in silence. He was tall, slender, and pale-skinned, like an average B-fourean. He looked afraid. His mouth moved slightly as if to make some kind of greeting, but no noise came out.

Another officer came into the room carrying a cup and set it down in front of Runstom. "Let me know if there's anything else you need, Officer."

After thanking the B-fourean officer and watching him leave the room, Runstom got out his notebook. He had tried to make relevant notes about everything he knew about the case so far, but unfortunately he knew very little. He poked at the coffee cup absently.

Jackson spoke suddenly, breaking the silence with a quiet voice. "You don't have to drink it, you know."

"I beg your pardon?"

"The coffee. Off-worlders tend not to care for it. We coldcook our coffee here. Most off-worlders want it hot."

"I see." Runstom picked up the cup. "It's okay. I don't mind it so much." He set the cup back down without taking a drink. "Did you, uh, did you want some?"

"No, thanks," Jackson said plainly. "I only drink coffee at work. And, as you can see, I won't be going to work for a while."

"There was a lot of evidence, Mr. Jackson," Runstom said. "But you maintain your innocence."

"Don't tell me this is another lame attempt at getting a confession out of me." Runstom knew there was anger in the statement, but the man's voice was shaky and unsure, riding on a current of fear more than any other emotion.

"Actually, Mr. Jackson, I was just—"

"Please," the prisoner said. "Call me Jax. My friends – I mean, most people – call me Jax."

"Okay. Jax." Runstom watched the other man for a moment. Maybe he wasn't as average a B-fourean as he first thought. Jackson's brown hair dangled haphazardly down the sides of his head. He had the same dull, gray eyes the others had but there was something else behind them. Fear, for sure, but something else – a glint of pride, a spark of independence. A fire that the other B-foureans Runstom had met seemed to lack. Runstom put his hands flat on the table and drummed his fingers lightly. He tried to remember transcripts of suspect interviews he'd read in the outpost library. "What do you think happened, Jax?"

Jax looked at him quietly for a moment, as if he didn't understand the question. "I don't know what happened."

"The venting doors in the block were opened," prodded Runstom. "But you claim that you didn't intentionally open them."

"I *didn't* open the doors," Jax said, leaning forward in his chair. "Intention's got nothing to do with it. I did not open them."

"But the console logs say you were logged into the console at the time of the incident."

"I was. But I did *not* open those doors." He made a fist at the word *not*, and began to make a motion as if he might bang it down on the table, but instead held back and just flexed his long fingers. "I couldn't have even if I wanted to."

Runstom studied the operator for a moment. The B-fourean's eyes were steady as he spoke. "Why not? The engineers say that someone issued the commands to open the doors from a console."

Jax sighed. "It doesn't make sense. There's a reason there are two sets of venting doors. You can't open one without the other being closed. The system won't let you. Especially not from an operator console. Operators are human and it could easily happen by mistake if it wasn't for the safety checks in the system."

"I see." Runstom wished he knew whether or not that was true, but it made sense. He made a note in his notebook to double-check that detail later when he had a chance to look it up. "So then, Jax. What's your explanation for what happened? If it's not possible for an operator to open both sets of doors, then how did they get opened?"

"How would I know?" Jax replied with a huff. "I didn't do it."

"But you must have some idea." Runstom flipped a few pages back in his notebook. "You've been a Life Support operator for several years now."

"It had to be a glitch in the system," Jax said quietly. He seemed to be deep in thought. "That is the only explanation."

"You don't sound too convinced of that."

The operator sighed and his head dropped. He looked defeated. He was a younger guy, somewhere in his mid-to-late twenties, but the wavy brown hair on the top of his head was beginning to thin, revealing the stark white skin beneath. "Okay, what the hell," he said into the table. "My only other explanation is that I was set up."

Runstom's heart skipped a beat. What a cliché, for a suspect to claim to be set up. He couldn't possibly believe the man. Yet here it was, the kind of explanation Runstom was looking for – one that promised a deeper and more complex case than just some guy going crazy and killing a bunch of people.

"Did you tell that to Detectives Brutus and Porter?"

Jax raised his head slightly and shook it slowly from side to side. "It sounds stupid. They wouldn't have believed me." He looked at Runstom. "I'm sure you don't believe me either."

Runstom thought quietly for a moment before answering. Brutus and Porter would never consider that there could be conspiracy behind these murders. The biggest crime in domed life in decades. Runstom felt like he had to believe anything was possible in such a situation. "I believe that everyone is innocent until proven guilty. That's the law."

The operator's face brightened ever so slightly and he made a noise, something between a sigh and a laugh. "Thanks," he said, and seemed to be at a loss for anything else.

Runstom arched his back in a stretch. "Let's talk about these safety measures you mentioned," he said. "If someone wanted to open both sets of venting doors, they would have to circumvent the safety measures, right?"

"Yes."

"Okay," Runstom said, hoping for more. "How would someone go about doing that?"

The prisoner looked at Runstom warily. "Should I have my lawyer here?"

The officer could feel his brow furrowing in frustration. Then he realized what he was asking: for the only suspect of a crime to describe how the crime in question could be pulled off. He was supposed to be asking a hypothetical question but he was asking the wrong person. He should be asking another operator, or better yet, an engineer. But he didn't know any. And since he was just an officer, not an investigator, he had no resources to find any that he could question.

"You have the right to have your lawyer present," he said, regretting the words as soon as they came out of his mouth. What kind of interrogator tells the suspect his lawyer should be present?

Jax's mouth scrunched up to one side of his face. "I'll keep it in mind," he said. "So far he hasn't been a whole lot of help. But I hear I'm getting a new lawyer." He paused, then added, "Off-planet."

"Yeah, that makes sense," Runstom said, then cursed himself for revealing that he didn't know that fact already.

"The detectives – they were from B-3, right?" Jax said, keeping the conversation off the subject of safety measures in Life Support systems.

"Yeah, that's right. Most of the people in my precinct are B-threers."

"So, if you don't mind me asking," Jax said. "Where are you from, Officer … Runstom, was it?"

"Yes. Stanford Runstom." The ModPol officer glanced self-consciously at the B-fourean officer standing quietly off to the side of the room, observing the conversation with mild interest. "My mother was a detective," he said. "In ModPol. An undercover detective, actually. She gave birth to me while on assignment, in a transport ship. That's where I spent the first few years growing up."

"I see." Jax looked Runstom up and down briefly. The officer waited for the question that always came next, the one that asked why his skin was green, exactly, but it never came. "Is that why you joined ModPol? Following in your mother's footsteps?"

Runstom caught himself in the middle of a weary sigh and tried to stifle it with a polite cough. "My mother did great things and made many sacrifices in the pursuit of justice," he said. "If I accomplish only a fraction of what she did, I'll be proud."

Jax's gaze drifted off to the side of the room as though he were looking into the distance beyond the wall. "Yeah, me too," he said quietly. Then he blinked and turned back to Runstom. He jabbed the table with a pale finger. "This is an injustice, right here, Officer. If I'm convicted of this crime, an innocent man goes to prison."

"Call me Stanford." Runstom watched the prisoner in silence for a moment before continuing. "So you believe this was either an accident, or that you were set up."

"I was set up," Jax said firmly. "Accidents like this don't happen. Plus there was that fake debt – some paper saying I owed money to Milton."

Runstom flipped through his notebook. "Fake debt?"

The operator eyed him suspiciously and again Runstom cursed himself for showing his ignorance. "The detectives had some piece of paper that said I was in debt to Brandon Milton," Jax said after a moment. "He was my supervisor."

"And one of the victims," Runstom added, finding Milton in the list of names he'd recorded. "Wait a minute," he said, looking up. "You mean Brutus and Porter had documentation of a debt – of you owing this Brandon Milton money – and you did not actually owe him money?"

"Right."

"For how much?"

"Ten thousand Alleys."

"Seems like the kind of thing you would remember. If you owed your supervisor ten grand, that wouldn't have slipped your mind."

"Yeah, exactly," Jax said, nodding.

"But it makes a good motive." Runstom tapped his pencil against his notebook. "Killing someone because you owe them money, I mean." Before Jax could object, he continued, "So if someone made this fake document, and did so to set you up, who did it? Who wanted you to take the fall for murder?"

The operator sighed wearily. "I don't know. I've been thinking about it for three days and I just don't know."

"Okay. Maybe it's someone you know, maybe it's someone you don't know. Let's just say for now that someone out there framed you, and we don't know who it is. So the next question is, how did they do it?"

"That's something else I've been thinking about non-stop for the past three days. The way I see it, there's two parts to it." He raised one finger and then another as he talked. "One, they would have had to figure out a way around the safeties on the doors to open both at the same time. And two, they would have had to make it look like it came from my console, because the commands were in my log file. Which means they either ran the commands directly from my console, while I was sitting at it and logged into it, or they ran the commands somewhere else in the system and managed to write the history to my console logs."

Runstom quickly jotted down some notes, although he wasn't entirely sure what the operator was talking about. "So, overriding the safeties ..." he started to say.

"That's the easier one, honestly," Jax said. "Because it's mostly theoretical. From my perspective? It's impossible. But I can tell you what part of the system they would have to break to make something like that work." He put his elbows on the table and brought his hands together, slowly cracking his long fingers one by one. "The safeties are just checks, right? So when every command is punched into a console, it has to pass a bunch of tests to make sure that it's okay for the system to run that command." Jax looked at Runstom, as if trying to read something; as if trying to make sure the officer was keeping up. Runstom put down his pencil to give the other man his full attention.

"Let me give an unrelated example," Jax continued, his voice picking up speed. "There's a command called 'rain'. Now, residents don't like climate-related surprises, so we have to turn on the rain warning at least twenty minutes before executing the 'rain' command." He grabbed the notebook and pencil from Runstom, who didn't resist. "So first you punch up a 'rain-warning' command. Somewhere in the system, a variable is set. Something like this," he said as he wrote two phrases on the paper, one below the other. "Then, if you were to run the 'rain' command, the system would do a test and see if the current time is at least twenty minutes more than the variable we set with the 'rain-warning' command. If it's not, the 'rain' command fails. Otherwise, it starts some subroutine that makes it rain in the dome."

He finished scribbling and flipped the notebook back over to Runstom. The officer took a look and saw what might have been a series of math formulas. The only words that jumped out were RAIN and WARNING, both written in upper case.

"If I were to punch up RAIN at 10:10AM, it would fail the test," Jax said, tracing his finger along the jumbled words on the page. "And I'd get this error message. If I were to do it after 10:20AM, it would succeed."

"What is this?" Runstom asked. "Some kind of code, right?"

"It's complex."

"Yeah, I can see that. Goddamn complex."

"No, I mean it's COMP-LEX," Jax said, exaggerating the syllables. "It stands for Computational Lexicon. It's a common programming language for operational environments."

"Oh." Runstom looked at the operator's scribbled words and symbols carefully. "Okay. So you're saying that if someone punched in a command that opens the inner doors, then some – variable?" Jax nodded and Runstom continued. "Some variable is set that tells the system the inner doors are open. Then when someone runs a command to open the outer doors, the system would have run some check—"

"Yes, exactly. A check on the state of the inner doors. If they are already open, the command to open the outer doors fails and you get an error message. Same goes for the reverse – if you try to open the outer doors first and then the inner."

"So someone might have reset that variable, the one that tracks the state of the doors *after* opening one set of doors."

"Well, it's not that simple. Those are actually system variables. No one has access to them from the console."

Instead of replying, Runstom took a drink from his cup. He managed not to gag, and had another sip, waiting for Jackson to continue.

"Okay," the operator said. "That's where the theoretical stuff ends. I don't know how they changed a variable only known to the system. I mean, the variable names we used here – I just made those up for the sake of a simple example. Operators like me have no idea what actual variables are used in the system, let alone have access to modify them. We

can't even be 100 percent certain of the conditional tests."
Jax paused momentarily, then finished in a soft voice, "That's
stuff only the system engineers would know."

Runstom nodded slowly, trying to absorb the information he'd
just gotten. "Okay, so let's say somehow someone wrote some
code that broke the safety check. Let's go to the next question:
How did they make it look like it came from your console?"

"How did they make it look like it came from my console?"
Jax repeated quietly. "This part I'm not so sure about. I was
logged into the system at my console. I didn't punch in those
commands, but somehow they were run as if I did punch
them in. Or at least it was logged that way." He trailed off.

Runstom took another drink of the cold coffee. He watched
Jack Jackson and began to wonder if that nagging doubt in
the back of his mind was right. That this was going nowhere.
That this was really just a waste of time. He swallowed and
tried to clear his head of doubt. It wasn't as if he had anything
better to do with his time. But he couldn't help thinking that
if an officer couldn't trust his gut, he couldn't trust anything.
He shot for a simple explanation. "Maybe someone punched
it in while you were away from the console? Did you take
any restroom breaks?"

"No, that's not it," Jax said, shaking his head without
looking up. "There's some kind of body-detector at the
console. Any time you get up and then come back to it,
you have to re-authenticate to the system. Biometrics and
all. Even if you just get up to stretch."

"Sounds like a pain in the ass."

"Yeah, it is."

"Look, maybe we need to move to some—"

"Wait," Jax interrupted. "There was one thing. One
weird thing I remember from that night." His cool gray eyes

suddenly lit up. "That's it! That has to be it! There was one time when I got up for a few minutes. When I sat back down, I re-authenticated, and it didn't take. I had to do it again!"

Jax looked at Runstom expectantly. The officer started, "I don't understand, why would ..."

"Don't you see? An op like me has to authenticate to a console dozens of times during each shift! By voiceprint, fingerprint, and typing in a password." He enumerated the three actions on his long, white fingers. "Voiceprint, finger-print, password. Voiceprint, fingerprint, password."

"So you typed it in wrong?"

"No!" Jax said. "Did you hear what I said? Voiceprint, fingerprint, password. Dozens of times during *every shift*. I can type that password in my sleep. You could gouge out my eyes and sit me in front of that console and I'd still be able to authenticate." He had a desperate look on his face, but Runstom, despite trying to keep an open mind, had trouble believing there was any significance to this story. "Check the logs." Jax looked at the B-fourean guard, then back to Runstom. "Tell them to go get the logs. The console logs!"

The guard's smile drooped slightly at being brought into the conversation by the prisoner. He looked at Jax and then at Runstom.

"There's a file for this prisoner," Runstom said. "A file that has to go to the System Attorney out at the court on Outpost Alpha. Could you please bring me that file?" The guard started to move, but hesitated. Runstom flipped through his notebook, as if looking for something. "I have a copy of it, but I left it back in my quarters," he lied awkwardly. "I know the detectives left a copy that gets transferred with the prisoner. Could you please just have someone bring me that copy?"

The guard gave him a conspicuous look, like he didn't trust Runstom completely, but then apparently decided he didn't much care, because he shrugged and left the room. He came back a few seconds later and said, "Someone will bring it in just a moment, Officer."

"Thank you very much," Runstom said. He turned to Jax. "Okay, Jax. What's the deal? What if you did have to authenticate twice? What will we see on those logs?"

"If I mistyped my password, then you'll see an authentication failure. Followed by a successful auth a few seconds later," Jax said. "But I don't think we'll see any failed auths."

"And what does that mean? If there are no authentication failures?"

"It means that I wasn't authenticated the second time. I just thought I was."

"I don't follow you," Runstom said, desperately trying to focus.

"It was another program. Something that gave me a fake login prompt. Even though I was already logged into the system, I saw the login prompt and thought I was not logged in yet. I give it my voiceprint, fingerprint, and password again, and the prompt goes away. And that program runs whatever it is meant to run."

Runstom rolled around the concept in his brain, thinking out loud. "So you see a login prompt. You think you are authenticating, but really you are telling some program to run. This program runs some commands, and it's running them from your console – because you told the program to do it."

"Yes!" exclaimed Jax.

A B-fourean officer came back into the room and handed a folder to Runstom. He was an officer Runstom hadn't seen before, an astonishingly young rookie. Runstom thanked him and the officer exchanged smiles with the guard in the room and went on his way.

Runstom dove into the folder, digging out the console logs. He came around to the other side of the table and he and Jax pored over the printouts together. "The incident occurred at 2:03AM," Runstom said.

"Here!" Jax excitedly poked the page. "Look. Here's when I authenticated, at 2:01AM. No auth failure. Only one auth success."

Runstom stared at the log in silence. His heart pounded as the realization dawned on him that his hunch was right. This was no open-and-shut case, as much as his detectives wanted it to be. There was a wrinkle, and Stanford Runstom was onto it.

"So now what?" Jax said anxiously.

Runstom stood up and paced slowly around the table. He could feel the thrill of the discovery enticing him, but he had to remind himself that this double-authentication trick only meant something if Jax was telling the truth. Even if he weren't deliberately lying, he was only going on a memory of having to log in twice. There was nothing in the printouts that corroborated the anomaly Jax was describing.

"If we could get back into your LifSup system, could we find this hidden program?"

"Yeah, but I wouldn't get my hopes up," Jax said. "Anyone who was smart enough to design this kind of program probably knew enough to cover their tracks." He paused, and Runstom was forced to cock his head in bemusement to get him to extrapolate. "The invasive program's final command was most likely to delete itself."

"Right," Runstom said, resignation in his voice. "Okay. So how did it get there?"

"Well," Jax replied, lost in thought. "There are no data ports on the consoles themselves. And the controls on the console are only set up for running commands. So you couldn't sit at a console and enter in the program code manually. They could have jacked into the LifSup system itself, but access to the hardware is locked down tighter than a drum." He stopped and thought for another minute or two, folding his hands together and bending his fingers, occasionally finding a knuckle to crack. "Of course, there's always the up-link access. There's a satellite up-link built into each LifSup system so that Central Engineering can push down updates."

"Updates?"

"Yeah, bug-fixes and stuff. Revisions to the program code that are supposed to make it run better."

"Okay." Runstom started thinking out loud again. "So someone could have used this up-link to put the program into your LifSup. Does that mean they would have used a satellite somehow?"

"Yeah. Well. Not necessarily a satellite. But in order to speak to the receiver down here, they'd have to do it from somewhere in orbit around the planet. I don't know much about satellite communication. But it seems like it'd be possible for someone in some other kind of space vessel to carry the same kind of transmitter that a satellite would use, and beam the signal down to our receiver."

Runstom took a moment to digest that. "Wouldn't the data coming down from a satellite be secure?"

"Yes, I'm sure there's an identification process," Jax said. "Plus an encryption layer. So we're talking two possibilities here. Either they somehow mimicked a known satellite, which would be tricky, because they'd have to get information used to generate the identification of the specific piece of hardware out there in space."

"And we are already looking at the possibility of someone who has enough inside information about a LifSup system to be able to circumvent the safety checks," Runstom said. "So we can't rule that out."

Jax nodded slowly. "Yeah, true. The other possibility is that they knew of some other channel, some back-door or something into a LifSup system."

"You mean like some other up-link?"

"Well, not really. I mean the same up-link, but during the handshake – when the signals are being sent from each end to identify itself – there could be some kind of code that you could send to the LifSup side to get direct access to the system."

"Why would there be some secret code?" Runstom asked. "I mean, if they can already send updates through the up-link, why would they need a 'back-door' into the system?"

Jax pulled his arms up and twisted his upper body in his chair, popping a few kinks in his back as he did. "Well, it's just an idea. I've seen technicians when they're working on a system that's not behaving normally. When something subtle is off, they like to use a special port somewhere on the LifSup main unit. They plug directly into it with their personal computer and send it some special code that gives them full-access to the system. I figure it's the kind of thing that's universal across LifSup systems, or at least LifSup systems of the same model. It's just there for troubleshooting purposes."

"So you figure that there's another back-door in the up-link that works the same way a technician uses a physical port to get into a system," Runstom reasoned.

"Now, I don't know that for a fact," the operator said, spreading his hands out in front of him. The more he had to explain technology, the more physically mobile he seemed to get. "Let's just say, I wouldn't be surprised if there were such a back-door."

"Okay, okay." Runstom nodded and looked down at his notes. It was all speculation, and it was all hinging on this prisoner being wrongfully accused. Runstom willed himself to resist judgment one way or the other, but he felt like he had to decide if it was even possible for someone to exploit the system in such a way. Was it even possible for Jax to have been set up? "So we have so far. One, someone who knows the internals of Life Support systems writes some code that would open both sets of venting doors on a block. Two, they disguise this code and set it up to run as a replacement for a login prompt, knowing that it would cause some operator to unwittingly execute it. Three, they beam the code down from a transmitter of some kind to the satellite up-link of the LifSup system at block 23-D."

"Yeah, I guess that's about it," Jax said, looking off into the distance. He seemed to be lost in thought for a moment, his eyebrows furrowing and his mouth opening slightly as if he were about to add something else. Then he simply shook his head, then nodded. "Yeah, that sounds about right."

Runstom studied the other man and they both lapsed into silence for a few minutes. The door to the interrogation room opened and the rookie B-fourean officer came through. He held the door open and George Halsey came in after him.

"Oh, hey, George," Runstom said, feeling his face redden with guilt.

"Officer Runstom," Halsey said, standing over the table. "I see you decided to question the prisoner." He eyeballed Runstom. "Just like we talked about."

Runstom stood up. "Uh, yeah. Like we talked about." He tried to make his voice power through the sheepishness he was feeling in getting caught by his partner.

Halsey used the next awkward pause to grab the top of the chair Runstom had been sitting on and wheel it over to himself, swooping it beneath him, sitting, and lifting his feet up and dropping them crossed onto the table in one continuous motion. His head lolled back in a kind of relaxed apathy. If there was an art to laziness, Halsey had mastered it.

Runstom frowned at Halsey, then glanced back at the one-way window that stretched across the back of the room. "So you watched some of the interview, right? Or do I need to catch you up?" He cast a sideways glance at Jax, who was looking at both of them timidly. Runstom was worried that Halsey's sudden entrance undid all the work he'd done to open the prisoner up.

"Yeah, I caught most of it," Halsey said, following Runstom's eyes to Jax. "Lemme ask you fellas this. Do you think that this *alleged* satellite transmission happened right before the incident at the block? Or did someone *allegedly* beam that code you're talking about down to the LifSup months ago and it laid there dormant?" At the end of the question, he briefly speared Runstom with a warning look, then his face relaxed again as he turned back to await Jax's answer. Reproval was something rare to see in Halsey's eyes and it fueled Runstom's lingering doubt over whether he should have started the interrogation in the first place.

"Well, either is possible I suppose," Jax said. Apparently, Halsey's relaxed manner extinguished any previous anxiety, because the operator again spoke freely. "I guess it doesn't seem likely that they would beam it down and let it just sit there on the system for long. In fact, it probably sat hidden in volatile memory, so it would be wiped clear during a reset and no trace of it would ever be found."

Halsey nodded and ran his fingers through his short, blond hair. "Clever," he said. He looked at Runstom. "I'm thinking traffic logs."

"What traffic logs?" Jax asked.

"ModPol keeps record of all space traffic coming in and out of the system, orbiting the planets, going into the asteroid belts, and so on," Halsey said, turning to Jax again to answer the question. He looked back at Runstom. "We could access the logs, find out who was out there at the time of the transmission – *alleged* transmission – and get their approximate position."

"Right." Runstom knew Halsey was going to give him an earful when they left the interrogation room, and yet the other officer seemed to be happy to play along. Then it clicked as to what Halsey was talking about. "Because you would need a direct line of sight from a ship to the receiver dish at block 23-D in the Gretel dome on this planet."

"Exactly. We plot all the coordinates of ships in the system at that time, and then we can isolate just the ones that would be in position to beam a signal down to his LifSup," Halsey said, waving a finger at Jax. "*Allegedly* beam a signal."

CHAPTER 6

"He goes by Three-Hairs Benson. Bluejack is his game. I know he's been here, so you might as well make it easy on yourself."

The proprietor of the card-house smirked. "Listen, lady. We got a strict policy here at the Grand Star Resort." He raised a yellow finger. "We don't ask for names, and we don't give out names. We protect the identities of our clients." He took the raised finger and bent it down, poking the flat palm of his other hand. "You come to a bluejack table, you lay down cash, you get a color, and that's what we call ya."

"I know how to fucking play fucking bluejack, pal," Dava said. She waved her arm in an arc. "You got four tables in this tiny, little shit-hole. At most eight players to a table, and looks like you ain't exactly packin' a full house." She looked around the filthy hovel. "Let's face it. Most of your customers are pale-skinned domers. If a guy came in here with bright-red skin, you'd notice him."

"Hey, I don't judge," the owner said with a used-hovercar-salesman smile. "Alleys are Alleys. Money is Money. I'd even let you play, if you wanted to."

Dava's eyes narrowed. "Even a brown-skin like me, huh? I'm touched. You're a fucking saint." She put a firm hand on the shorter man's shoulder. "Benson had money to play with. And knowing his luck, he probably started losing. Then he thought he had to play some more to make back his losses. That's how gamblers think."

"Read the sign lady. This ain't gambling. The bluejack tables are for entertainment purposes only." The man was sticking to his routine, but Dava could hear the faint touch of fear seeping into his voice. She could almost smell the perspiration emerging from his skin.

"So he was probably in here more than once," she continued, ignoring his fine-print line and tightening her grip. "This stout, tattoo-covered, red-skinned man with a fat wad of Alliance Credits." She leaned in close and got quieter. "You know, I understand what you're doing. He was a good customer, I'm sure. Lost lots of money on your tables. But you should know: that wasn't his money to lose."

The man swallowed and blinked slowly. Dava could see beads of sweat forming on his forehead. He turned away from her and wiggled out from under her hand. "I told you," he said weakly. "It's our policy."

Dava frowned. "That's unfortunate." She walked over to one of the bluejack tables.

"Orange, what's your bet?" the dealer-bot droned as she approached.

"Uh," said one of the three skinny, white-faced players at the table. "Twelve?" He watched Dava nervously. "I mean, I'm um. I'm out." He turned his cards over.

"Green, wha-zzzzZZZTTT—"

She drove a small blade into the top of the dealer-bot's head and pushed a trigger, generating a series of *shinking* sounds. She removed the blade and a thin lick of smoke followed it out of the now lifeless hunk of metal.

69

"Aww, awww," the owner of the Grand Star Resort whined. "Come on, you know how much those dealer-bots cost? Aww, right in the central processor. Come on!"

She walked over to another table and waggled the knife in her hand as she moved. "Maybe you wanna call the cops?"

"Oh come on, lady!" The man ran up and grabbed one of Dava's arms. "Please!" She looked at him for a moment, saying nothing. "Okay, okay," he said. "I saw the man you're looking for."

"And he's a regular?"

"Yeah," the owner said, defeated. "Comes in every night, right about seven. Before the third shift comes on, so's he can get a good spot at a table."

Dava nodded, inspecting the man's face. He seemed just frightened enough to be sincere. "Thanks for your time." She looked around. "Sorry about the dealer."

As she walked out the door, she heard the owner say, "Goddammit, Suzu, go get an out-of-order sign for that table! And while you're at it, get the bot-tech on the phone and see when he can get over here."

Dava found a dark corner to disappear into, just off the large corridor where the Grand Star Resort and a few other squat gambling shacks clustered like mushrooms. Dark corners were easy to find in the massive maze of underground maintenance tunnels beneath Blue Haven. Skinny white B-foureans flitted about like bits of paper, disappearing into the mobile storage units that had been converted into bars and card-houses. The domed cities above looked so pristine and perfect, but every beautiful rock in the sky has a dark side.

She turned her arm over and looked at the small screen that was embedded into the bracer she wore. It was a RadMess; *Rad* meaning radio wave, and therefore relatively short-ranged. *Mess* meaning message; the device had a voice module, but she and her mates mostly used the small keyboard to send text-based messages back and forth silently.

Space Waste was a gang that oozed brash confidence and chaos on the outside, but internally the organization strove to be efficient and careful. When you flaunt the fact that you're persistently circumventing the planetary laws, you have plenty of reason to be paranoid at every opportunity. Quite often, the gang found itself in possession of military-grade equipment, including communication devices with near-unbreakable encryption.

Dava started punching a message into her RadMess bracer. The reason they didn't bother with that military-grade comm stuff was pretty simple. Any dome like Blue Haven was going to have scanners all over the place monitoring radio waves on any frequency. The local authorities wouldn't be able to decrypt any military comm chatter, but its presence would set off a bunch of red flags and attract immediate attention. So when in domes, they used the cheap-as-shit, consumer-grade RadMess.

Of course, being Space Waste, they were still adequately paranoid about it. Rather than trying to layer on more encryption – the RadMess had a base level of encryption that wouldn't stop any authorities, but kept civilians from eavesdropping on each other – they used a manual code. It was a pretty dead-simple substitution cypher. Every letter of the alphabet was represented by a number. It took a little practice, but most Space Wasters could easily memorize the code. It was just a matter of training your brain to see an "A" whenever it saw a "22", and so on. When they typed their messages, they randomly sprinkled in other numbers that were outside the set just to keep chaos on their side.

Any radio scanners in a dome might be checking for frequencies and contexts of certain keywords. A lot of time and money went into developing artificial intelligence smart enough to interpret the meanings behind the words of humans. A string of raw numbers was just static on the wire to them. Geologists taking readings, students answering quiz questions, box scores from a bombball game – nothing worth bothering with.

She sent a message to Captain 2-Bit and Johnny Eyeball, letting them know she'd found a card-house that Three-Hairs Benson frequented. Less than a minute later, she got a response, mentally spelling out the numbers into letters, into words.

Dava broke the silence of her dark corner, groaning at the news that Captain 2-Bit had lost Eyeball. She started to write a message back to tell him to look for Johnny in the bars, but 2-Bit didn't need to be told that. With all the bars in Blue Haven proper, he would be looking all night anyway. She'd just have to go ahead by herself and meet up with them later. She didn't need their help to handle Benson. Eyeball was supposed to be the muscle – he was big, fast, and as deadly with a blade as he was with a pistol, rifle, or ship-mounted laser turret. He was one of the best; but lately he'd been hitting the bottle a lot. It might have been a mistake for 2-Bit to bring him on this job. Something about the domes – the too-perfect air, the too-perfect architecture, the too-perfect people – triggered self-destructive instincts in an atmo-born like Johnny Eyeball.

Of course, Dava wasn't born in a dome either. Her brown skin was a constant reminder that she was actually born on Earth. For some reason, if two brown people left Earth and had a baby on another planet, in a dome, the baby would turn white-skinned within the first year. Or pink, if they lived in one of the upper-class domes. Dava's skin color marked her as Earthen, even though she left there at four years old and her memories of her home planet were fuzzy at best.

Abducted is what she would tell people. *Rescued* was what the abductors called it. Rescued from the Earth, that dying planet. People still lived there, but those that remained were a special combination of rich and stubborn. Rich enough that they could afford to live in an arcology, those massive, all-in-one structures that were the precursors to domes. Stubborn enough to not want to leave their dying Mother and give one of the other nearby planets a try.

Dava was born into a tribe living in the wasteland. She had to admit that the part about being rescued was true to a certain degree – had she spent many more years there, she would certainly have been stricken with cancer due to exposure to solar radiation. But that's where the *rescued* part ended.

Her arm buzzed once more, pulling her out of the wasteland and back into the underworld of the B-4 domes.

The message was a brief order from 2-Bit that Dava should finish the job while he tracked down Eyeball. At least Johnny had 2-Bit to babysit him. That seemed to be the only thing Captain 2-Bit was good for. She supposed that was the perk of being one of the oldest surviving members of Space Waste: no more heavy lifting, no more dirty work. Most young recruits worshiped 2-Bit like he was a war hero, but she didn't see it. He wasn't particularly smart, or fast, or anything, except apparently lucky. It was good though; the troops needed someone to look up to, and, right or wrong, 2-Bit called the shots and they obeyed. Most of the time.

She turned her eyes back on the card-houses across the way. There was perfection above in neat little packages, but it seemed that no matter how perfect things were, it was impossible for the human race to avoid stepping in shit eventually. She watched the sad souls that sought refuge from the transcendence of dome life looking over their shoulders, skittering from vice to vice.

She felt empathy for all of them and sympathy for none.

Three-Hairs Benson came back out of the Grand Star Resort within less than a minute of entering the converted storage unit. He looked desperately from side to side. No doubt the sight of the lobotomized dealer-bot tipped the gangbanger off to the fact that his boss had sent someone looking for him.

Dava frowned as she watched the man start to head one direction, then turn around and head the other. Benson was good and paranoid, as he should have been, but he was not very bright. He was getting older and drugs, alcohol, and age had permanently dulled his senses as well as his wits. Space Waste was full of murderers and thieves, so no one was going to look down on Benson for his gambling habits. But the gangbanger had collected on a delivery and failed to bring the cash back home. Worse than that: he'd obviously lost some – possibly all – of the money.

If you crossed Moses Down, Space Waste's boss, the usual procedure was for someone to liquidate your accounts and for someone else to liquidate your innards. Benson was most likely cleaned out financially, and so the gang would only be performing the latter ritual. It was unfortunate. Dava was one of a handful of people who knew that when a Space Waster was retired and their personal assets were collected by Down, the proceeds got donated to orphanages. Particularly, orphanages that housed children who'd found themselves separated from their parents at some point in their journey from Earth to one of the domed planets.

Not only did Benson fail while he was alive, his death was going to be just as useless. He seemed to be heading for one of the cargo elevators that went back to the surface. Dava sighed softly to herself. The least Benson could do at this point was face up to what he'd done and take his punishment with dignity. But no, the damned fool had to try to run.

She flitted from shadow to shadow until he approached a small drainage passageway. She appeared behind the older man and poked her blade lightly into his back. He froze for a moment, then his head sagged in defeat. She directed him to take the side passage and he did.

Dava and Three-Hairs Benson both disappeared into the darkness of the drainage passageway. A moment later, Dava emerged alone.

CHAPTER 7

"You are just cruisin' for a bruisin', you know that, Stanley?"

Runstom huffed. "It's Stanford." He knew Halsey picked up the damned nickname from the other officers and only used it when he wanted to get under Runstom's skin.

"Yeah, right. Officer Stanford Runstom," Halsey shot back. "Off ... i ... cer."

Runstom sighed, closing his eyes and rubbing his eyebrows with his forefinger and thumb. "Look, George. I know this is stupid, to go against the dicks like this, but you have to admit – there's something not right with this case. That operator in there didn't murder thirty-one people."

Halsey looked up from the holo-screen. "Thirty-two." Runstom opened his eyes to look at the other man, who continued, "I heard earlier today. One of the other victims died in the hospital. Internal injuries."

They sat in silence for a few minutes in the dimly lit workroom that they brought the traffic logs to because it was the only place in the precinct that had a computer with a 3D spacial modeling application on it.

"Shit," Halsey breathed. He scratched at the tightly cropped yellow curls on his head as he stared at the printed-out logs on the desk in front of him. He pulled over a directional lamp that was meant to aid in reading without interfering with the holo-image, which required mostly darkness for proper viewing. "Dammit, I thought this would at least be something to keep busy with, but it's more of a pain in the ass than I thought. And yes, it is stupid to go against the dicks. Especially on the word of an accused murderer."

"George," Runstom said, leaning in close. "Don't you ever want to be more than an officer?"

Halsey narrowed his eyes. "That's none of your business."

"Can't you just humor me and entertain the possibility that there is something more to this case?"

Halsey sighed as he panned around the image. "Yeah, yeah, more to this case. How about you focus and help me figure out the cone of contact from the sub-dome? We get this done and I can give it all to you and wash my hands of it. You can tell them I helped after you get the whole case solved and they award you some kind of medal of honor."

Runstom frowned into the darkness. As much as Halsey drove him up a wall, he had to admit he was very thankful for the help. "How do you even know how to do this?" he asked as he watched Halsey tap away at the keys.

"What do you mean?" Halsey answered without looking up.

"This core of contact—"

"Cone. Cone of contact."

"Yeah, whatever." Runstom started at the holo-screen as it panned across a minimal representation of the Barnard system: translucent spheres sitting on thin, oval-shaped lines. "Where did you learn this stuff?"

Halsey tapped a few more keys and the view zoomed a little closer to one of the planets. He looked over his shoulder at Runstom. "I took a few terms of astrophysics at Alpha. Part of dispatch training."

"But you're not a dispatcher."

"Not yet, but someday I will be," Halsey said, turning back to the holo-screen. "Just got a couple more months of training."

"No offense, Halsey, but you don't seem like the studying type. I mean, you never seem to want to do anything." Runstom started to feel a little guilty for always assuming the other officers he worked with were completely unambitious.

"Yeah, but if I become a dispatcher, I can do even less," Halsey said with a mischievous smile. "And you should be thankful, because the only reason I'm helping you now is that it's good practice. Hand me that planetary rotation reference sheet." Runstom did, and Halsey took it and added, "Those cats are total slackers. Nothin' to do but watch the stars go by."

They worked together for about thirty more minutes getting the computations right. When they were done, they had a narrow, wire-frame cone sticking out of the side of the planet Barnard-4, projecting outward into space. Any ship that passed through the cone had a possible line of sight to the receiver at Gretel, block 23-D. After that, they imported the space-object positional data from the ModPol traffic logs and after another twenty minutes they had little dots of varying sizes all over their model version of the Barnard System.

"You're in luck," Halsey said. "Looks like only three vessels fit into the cone, given the rotation of the planet and the logged positions just before the time of the incident."

Runstom was scribbling notes furiously, knowing he would need all this information as evidence if he were going to convince his superiors that something fishy was going on with this case. "Okay. What are the three ships?"

Halsey punched up the cross-references of the positions and the ship data. "Let's see. We've got a mail drone. An asteroid mining vessel. And ... a cruise ship."

"Okay, we're looking for someone with a beam-based transmitter," Runstom said, thinking out loud. "It'd have to be mounted to the outside of a ship, unless there were another place it could be stored, where it might have a way to send a transmission out of a port or something."

"Stan, you ever think about what it's like on one of those cruise ships? Now that's some serious slacking."

"George, come on."

"Okay, sheesh." Halsey leaned back to stare at the ceiling and scratch through the curls of his hair. "The mail drone seems a little far-fetched. Those things are too small to mount anything on, and they have zero cargo space. Unless you yank out the mail memory modules."

"Yeah, well – that'd give you about half a meter square," Runstom said. "And even then, there's no passenger room in a mail drone. They just aren't outfitted for people. No life support or anything. So it'd have to be all pre-programmed."

"Or controlled remotely. But then, what would be the point?"

"Not to mention, the delivery companies keep track of those drones pretty closely."

"Yeah, okay. So no room on the mail drone, unless it's tampered with, which is highly unlikely, and then it's questionable if you would even have enough room for a transmitter." Halsey made a mark on the report. "So the mining vessel. According to the data, it's a standard Galacaroid Maximiner. Crew of eight. Four front-mounted mining lasers, one front-mounted explosives launcher, and one small top-mounted defense turret with an EMP gun in it. Plenty of cargo space, of course, but inaccessible to the crew when in space. A handful of pusherbots do all the heavy lifting in the cargo bay during mining operations."

"Hmm. Which one is that in the model?" Runstom asked.

"This one here. Farthest out."

"So it'd need a pretty strong transmitter."

"Yep." Halsey punched up some quick calculations. "About 78 megasparks to send a signal that distance and maintain integrity. Plus, this one was only in the cone for a couple of hours, about five days before the incident."

"So it's possible," Runstom said, pausing thoughtfully. "Someone would have to either mount a large transmitter in the cargo bay or yank out the mining lasers and make room for it on the front. Do we have log data of that ship in the system for any time after that?"

"Of course." Halsey fiddled around for a few minutes, importing some of the traffic log data into the model. "Okay, here we go," he said eventually and slapped a button on his console.

The model began to scroll forward in time. The little dot representing the mining vessel bounced around the asteroid field for a few minutes. Halsey yawned. Suddenly the dot zipped away from the asteroid ring and over to one of the outer planets.

"Where'd it go?" Runstom said.

"Uh. Let's see. It went to one of the moons around Barnard-5. There's some kind of refinery based there."

"So it mined asteroids for a couple of hours and then went to a refinery," Runstom said.

Halsey turned around and faced him. "Seems like a perfectly natural thing for a mining vessel to do, doesn't it?"

"Yeah, I suppose so," was Runstom's answer. He wanted to say that just because someone was acting naturally, that didn't mean they were innocent, but he kept that thought to himself. "Let's move on to the last one."

"Sure. Royal Starways Interplanetary Cruise Delight Superliner #5. Crew of 348. Not just ship operations personnel, of course, but including wait staff, maids, pool cleaners, porters, baggage handlers, masseurs, personal trainers, personal entertainers, day care—"

"Right, right, what else?"

"Mmmmmm. I'll skip the weapons detail. Basically, this thing has a slow route that starts at Barnard-3, moves in close to Barnard-1, where it orbits for a short time. Then it goes to Barnard-2, orbits there for a bit. Then on to B-4, where it docks at the sub-orbital platform for a very short amount of time before continuing on. After that it orbits B-5, then orbits B-7, then comes back to orbit B-6, then spends some time near the asteroid belt, then it makes a slow cruise back down to B-3."

"Those things take a couple years to do their whole route, don't they?"

"Yep." Halsey punched up some other data. "About nine years in total. A slow tour of the whole system, hanging about in orbit around the uninhabitable planets, stopping at a moon here and there. The full planetary experience for folks with too much money and even more free time. Of course, some people only go part way. It's only the richest B-threers that can afford the full cruise."

Runstom huffed. "Anyway – there are only like eight or nine or ten of these superliners, right? Just doing their slow loops of the system?"

"Yeah, something like that. So you can catch one at least once a year. Ours is number five of the pack." Halsey went back to the holo-screen. "She's this big dot here, in between the orbits lines of B-3 and B-4. I'll load up her path data. I'll start a couple weeks back in the log since she's so slow."

The dot jumped back a few inches on screen, which was probably a few million kilometers in real space. Halsey hit a few buttons, and it started to crawl forward. The cruise ship was traveling much slower that the miner had been, so he tweaked the speed of the model to get it moving. Barnard-4 has a long rotational period, taking about two Earth weeks to make a full spin. The model was moving at higher speed now, and the cone of contact sticking out of the planet swept around with the slow rotation. Eventually, the cruise ship got close enough to intersect with the cone as it crawled through space. A couple of days' worth of real time ticked by as they watched the ship stay within the cone. The date of the incident came and went before the vessel's path took it outside the cone's coverage and it abruptly stopped.

"Two days ago – that's the end of the logs I got. After this, she'll be lining up to parallel B-3's orbit and in a couple months' time, she'll match up to B-3 and hold position while shuttles unload and reload from the planet." Halsey turned away from the model and stared blankly into the darkness. "Well shit," he muttered after a moment of thought. "The cruise ship definitely sits in the cone for a few days."

Runstom closed his eyes. "Okay. Assuming that someone hit the LifSup receiver at sub-dome Gretel, block 23-D with a signal from space. What we now know is that the only eligible spacecraft for the job are a mining vessel and a cruise ship."

"Right. But if spaceships could be suspects, both of these have pretty good alibis."

"Yeah, no kidding." Runstom started writing in his notebook. "If it's the mining craft, they've deliberately run a route that would appear normal. Covering their tracks. They would have planted the malicious code five days before it was triggered to take effect."

"So five days it lay dormant in memory somewhere," Halsey said. "Risking detection or possibly being wiped out with a system reset."

Runstom nodded, and went on, keeping his momentum. "They were pretty far out, so they would have to have a large transmitter. Even if it weren't mounted on the front, it would be obvious sitting there in the cargo bay. In fact, they might have to have the pusherbots move it into position. All eight of the crew members on board would have to be in on the whole plan."

"Right. Otherwise, they'd know something was up, because you couldn't just start mining rocks and throwing them into the cargo bay with your big ol' transmitter in there. And someone would notice when they got home and didn't get paid for a full load of ore."

"Now if it's the cruise ship," Runstom said, flipping a page over in his notebook. "Then you don't have to have any ship operators even in on the act. The cruise ship passes through the cone of contact for a couple of days. Including the day of the incident, making it possible to deliver the code and have it execute immediately on arrival."

"And it's closer," Halsey said, pointing back at the model. He tapped at the console. "Close enough that you'd only need ... three and a half megasparks to power the transmission. If you had a clean shot. And those superliners have plenty of wide-open deck space where the only thing between you and space is clear splexiglass."

"Right, and a sat-transmitter will go right through that."

They sat in silence for a few minutes. Halsey flipped off the holo-screen and then stood up to stretch. "Honestly, Stan. I don't know."

"Don't know what?" Runstom didn't look at Halsey, but stared off into nothingness, trying to envision a scene where someone was lugging a large device around the deck of a cruise ship.

"Don't know if it's worth it." Now Runstom turned to look at the other officer. Halsey continued, "I mean, don't get me wrong. Playing around with traffic logs has been a lot more fun than sitting around watching the crap that passes for vid on this shitty planet."

"But you saw the console logs," Runstom said. "You saw what Jackson was talking about."

"Yeah, but Stan, come on." Halsey spread his arms out. "It's a great story, but how can you trust that guy? I mean, he's a suspect."

"I know he's a goddamn suspect," Runstom muttered.

"He could be making the whole thing up."

"He's not." Runstom still wasn't exactly sure of it, but he had a tendency to irrationally take a stand when challenged.

"Oh." Halsey scratched his head, ruffling his short curls of hair. "But how do you know?"

"Okay, maybe I don't know." Runstom stood up to face the other officer. "You're right. He could be making it all up. But you know this whole thing doesn't add up. George, I talked to that guy in there. He's not a murderer."

"And what, you're psychic?"

"No, I'm not psychic. But you watched me talk to him. You talked to him. He's just an operator. He's not crazy. And he's not a criminal."

Halsey sighed heavily. "Look, Stan, I get it. I know what this is about. Okay? I know you, man. We've been working together for a long time. As soon as the dicks wanted to close this thing, you wanted to open it wider."

"What's that supposed to mean?" Runstom began to raise his voice, but something held him back.

"You've been getting the shit end of the stick for years, Stan. You should be a detective by now but they keep finding reasons to hold you back. Reasons to say you're not there yet. To say you're not good enough."

Runstom pursed his lips together and narrowed his eyes at Halsey. "I am good enough."

"Yeah, you are fucking good enough," Halsey said, pointing a finger at Runstom's chest. "That's what I'm saying. You should be a goddamn detective. But you're not. Are you?"

"No."

"So you got something to prove. You're always looking for a chance to prove that you should be a dick."

Runstom frowned. "So what? So what if I have something to prove. The dicks got this one wrong, George. Brutus and Porter aren't even trying. We're officers of Modern Policing and it's our duty to make sure every angle of this thing is looked at."

"Oh spare me," Halsey said, rolling his eyes. "Shit like that comes out of your mouth so much, sometimes I think you actually believe it."

Runstom crossed his arms. "George, you know something's not right with this case. I know you know."

"Stan, seriously." Halsey took a step back. "I hate to be the one to break this to you, but you're not making detective. Okay? It's not your ability or your dedication. You've got plenty of both. It's your skin. It's your—"

"Don't even fucking go there, you sonova—"

"Stan, listen to me." Halsey took another half-step back. "All I'm saying is you know there are people in ModPol that have a problem with your mother. They're gonna hold you back as much as they can. And some of them are just looking for an excuse to bust you down even farther into the shit. If you go trying to play detective on something big like this, and you're wrong, it's over, man."

"People don't know shit about my mother."

"I know, Stan. Believe me, I know. They don't know shit. But they think they do. And those people that think they know something are always watching you. Always looking for a way to make you the fall guy."

Runstom swallowed and looked down at nothing. He clenched his jaw and swallowed a few more times before speaking. "Okay, George. You're right." He spoke so quietly that the other officer had to step forward to hear him. "But there's a limit to how much longer I can do this, you understand? I don't have something like – like becoming a dispatcher to look forward to. If I don't make detective – I mean, there's a limit to the number of times I can be passed over for promotion before I can't ..." He trailed off, unable to find the words.

Halsey put a hand on his shoulder. "I know, man. I know. All I'm asking is that we just think this shit over before you go doing something rash. We should have a couple more days before the transport gets here. We'll talk to Jackson some more and see what else we can come up with. Let's just not go crazy, okay? We gotta play by the rules just enough to try to minimize the amount of trouble we get in." He shook Runstom's shoulder lightly. "Okay, Stan?"

"Yeah." Runstom met the other officer's eyes. "Okay."

CHAPTER 8

The next morning it became apparent to Jax that the prisoner barge had arrived when a new set of guards began filtering into the cells and escorting prisoners out. He counted sixteen pairs of cuffs going out before it was his turn, and then he was secured into a wall restraint in his new cell on board the transport. He couldn't move his head after that. In the cell corridor, the guards loudly read off case numbers as they brought in each defendant, and he counted twenty-one of those.

Thirty-eight defendants in all (including himself) for the week, which to Jax seemed relatively low considering the population size of Blue Haven and its sub-domes. Of course, B-foureans were in general a peaceful people, mostly thanks to a well-established culture of passive good will, which was reinforced by holo-vision public service announcements and audio/visual media broadcast all around the domes. In parks, in mag-trains, in elevators – it was hard to get away from the stuff.

Some off-worlders called it brainwashing, but Jax wouldn't go that far. They still had free will. A person could choose to drown out the barrage of messages. They could choose to read books – particularly, off-world books – instead of watching holo-vision. But most people didn't have the motivation to, and Jax couldn't fault them too much. Life in the domes might have been mundane, but it was easy. That was more than you could say for a lot of other places in the known galaxy.

Those who knew Jax always wanted to know why he wasn't living up to his potential. He had good skills with math and science, and with his father's connections, he could have sailed through engineering school. Forgoing that, he could have at least earned himself a promotion or two in the Life Support operations world. Jax didn't hold some kind of personal grudge against his supervisor – the now deceased Brandon Milton – nor vice versa. Milton didn't like Jax for the same reason most people didn't. Jax just tended to rub some people the wrong way.

Life on B-4 was easy-peasy, and so the crime rate was low. And because of the low crime rate, the governments of the planet did not dedicate a lot of resources to law enforcement. It was easier for them to subscribe to the services of Modern Policing and Peacekeeping, as it was for many of the governments of the inhabited planets and moons of the known galaxy. ModPol was like an organization of security guards and mercenaries, packaged up along with prosecutors, lawyers, judges, and juries. If you wanted to buy ModPol's protection, you bought ModPol's version of the law as well.

The ModPol grunts – including the detectives that first questioned Jax, and the officers who came later – probably didn't know the crime rate was so low on B-4. They'd seen crimes of passion that were unimaginable to the mind of a B-fourean, but commonplace elsewhere. But a crime like this – over thirty people killed by one person – was unimaginable anywhere. It was as if the only way they could deal with facing such a slaughter was to put a face to the criminal as fast as possible. Jax could imagine them telling each other, *Let's get the sick sonova bitch that did this and make him hang.* And Jax happened to be the sonova bitch in the wrong place at the wrong time.

Which is probably why they jumped at a chance for a revenge angle. Angry ex-boyfriend and disgruntled employee. Jax actually never took it personally when his company passed him over for promotion, time and time again. That part the ModPol detectives could not be more wrong about. He really just did not care. He only kept the LifSup job to pay the bills.

They wanted to know why he wasn't an engineer, as if not becoming one was the source of his pain and a catalyst for vengeance. He couldn't care less about that. Not to mention he couldn't stand engineers. His father was an engineer. His father married another engineer when his mother passed away. Jax couldn't explain it, but he just had the feeling that if he became an engineer too, he'd feel like he would somehow lose the memory of his mother. He and his father and step-mother would become one happy family of engineers, forgetting all about the late Irene Jackson.

Jax's mother had worked in pre-construction air processor assembly. When there's little or no atmosphere, it's difficult to make headway building domes and sub-domes, so there's a whole pre-construction phase that has to happen initially. Irene Jackson worked with a crew that put together temporary air processors to provide atmosphere for the workers and equipment under the massive tents that enveloped a construction site. During construction, Irene and her crew worked tirelessly to maintain the proper levels of various gases inside the tents, checking for leaks or contamination. When a job was done, they tore the processors back down and moved on to a new site.

On her final job, Irene Jackson and several of her crew were investigating an anomaly in the gas mixture in an isolated section of a construction grid. The source of the contamination was an unseen fissure in the surface of the planet. Due to the pressure of a methane gas bubble just beneath the surface, the initial ground density survey had cleared the area for construction. When Irene and her crew-mates brought their equipment in on trucks to the section where the oxygen alarms were buzzing, they unwittingly placed an excessive amount of weight over a fragile square of the planet's surface. Before they could react, they were in the middle of a massive sinkhole. They were suited up, but their suits were designed to withstand the harsh atmosphere of Barnard-4, and the jagged, gray, ugly rocks inside the cavern that opened up beneath their feet tore their suits open like the claws of a predator slicing into prey. Trapped in a newly formed canyon, the air processor techs could only lie on their backs and admire the stars while the oxygen slowly bled from their suits.

Jax thought he was lucky the detectives focused on his so-called career failures. He was lucky they didn't ask him why he was even still on B-4. Because that question he could not answer, even when he asked himself. He was a few years away from turning thirty, and he knew he couldn't stay on this planet. But he had nowhere else to go. Moving in with his parents on B-3 was not an option he could accept. He shuddered when he saw the irony of this whole situation. He was finally going to get to go off-planet; and in a way, he was looking forward to it. Even if it was to be put on trial and probably executed, at least he'd be out of the domes for once. It was as if he had to become a prisoner to break free.

So was this whole thing really just happenstance? That was the question burning in the back of his mind for the last couple of days. Was it just wrong place, wrong time? Or was there more to it? Obviously, he'd been set up, but why him? Was he targeted for something he'd done in the past? Did he piss off the wrong person? Or was he just picked because someone had to take the fall, and he just happened to be the mark?

The cops in the off-world crime dramas (the only holo-vision Jax could stomach was foreign) would always ask that question. *Do you know anyone that might want to hurt you?* Yeah, sure. There were people in Jax's life that didn't like him. Maybe even wanted to hurt him. And they probably tried to hurt him, in their own B-fourean way: by denying him constant offers of assistance and shovel-loads of gratitude. But no one Jax ever met could have possibly devised a scheme to set someone up to take the fall for a mass homicide.

He daydreamed about crime drama holo-vids to keep his mind off the alarming and unexpected weight of the thrust of the barge as it lifted off, and the even more alarming shudder and shake that quickly followed as they tore through the sky.

Once they broke away from the planet's gravitational pull and the ship's acceleration dropped, Jax's restraints loosened and he was allowed to move about his tiny room. It was pretty much a standard jail cell; a bunk-bed, a toilet, a sink, and a small table with a chair. The sparse holding cell in the Blue Haven Police Department was plush by comparison. A stack of papers and a handful of pencils on the table reminded him that he was allowed to write by hand, but would not be permitted access to electronic devices of any kind.

After he pulled himself out of the wall-mount, he found himself face-to-face with his cell-mate. The guy had been out cold when they first boarded, and Jax had only heard his case number when it was read off by the security detail. Jax suspected the guards had drugged the large, muscle-bound, yellow-skinned, multi-tattooed man who now stood before him, cracking his neck from side to side and rolling his shoulders. Jax was used to being taller than the handful of off-worlders he'd met, but this man was tall enough to look him in the eyes, and almost twice as wide.

"Hello," Jax said. "I'm Jax."

The man smiled at Jax, showing off an almost-perfect set of teeth. "Hey, roomie. I'm Johnny Eyeball." He winked.

"Oh." Jax was about to ask if that was a nickname, but then realized he himself hadn't exactly given his real name either. "Nice to meet you, Mr. Eyeball."

Johnny Eyeball winked again. It was a mildly angry wink.

"So, uh," Jax started nervously. He began to think about all those off-world crime dramas, and all the psychotic criminals that roamed the galaxy outside the sanctuary of Barnard-4. "What, uh. Whaterya in for?"

This question seemed to put the other man in a good mood. "Ah, now that's a great drinking story. We got a couple days together, so I'll leave that 'til another day." He winked again. "In one part, I get an eighteen-minute laser shoot-out with an unarmed maitre d-bot." He winked a couple of times, rather wildly and gleefully. "Tell me, Mr. Jax. What's a pale-skin like you gotta do to land on a con-barge like this?"

"Mass homicide. Sus—" he started. He was about to qualify the charge with *suspected*, but the look in the unwinking eyes of Johnny Eyeball made him realize it might be a little easier to sleep at night if he left his innocence out of it. *We're all psychos here*, he imagined saying, adding a maniacal grin.

"Fuck you," Eyeball breathed. "Really?"

"Yep," Jax said, trying to sound confident. "Class five."

"No shit."

"Yep." Jax's roommate looked him up and down, so Jax returned the look. "I like your tattoo, by the way. Is that a smart-tat?"

"Oh yeah." The larger man flexed his bicep and his tattoo morphed from a series of abstract lines into three arrows, bent into a circle, each arrowhead pointing at the start of the next arrow. Johnny grunted, twitching his fingers, and the arrowheads bent and twisted vaguely outward. "Get it?" he said, smiling. "Fuckin' chaos, brother. That's what I do. Take the cycle of order and turn it into fuckin' chaos."

Jax nodded. "You know something, Johnny Eyeball? I rather like that idea."

The one major difference between the current accommodations and a jail cell on-planet was the small, round, window in one wall of his room. Through this porthole, Jax could see the inky darkness of space, pinpricked by stars, and occasionally he could see distant planets and even spacecraft traveling the same lanes (keeping a safe distance of several thousand meters, of course).

For the first time in his life, he was drifting through space. Well, first time he was literally drifting through space. Jax felt like he'd been figuratively drifting through space his whole life. Or at least the chapter of his life that began when his mother passed on. The woman was his best friend, the one person he felt like he could connect to. B-foureans – or maybe it was all people, but he only had B-foureans to go on – seemed to be alien to Jax. People Jax interacted with on a day-to-day basis, whether his co-workers, clerks in a shop, or passers-by on the street on the whole seemed to have some ability or inborn trait that allowed them to avoid showing any significant emotion. Even their happiness felt halfhearted. They laughed with an air of bland bliss, and never at an ironic situation or humor born of satire. They beamed with glee about the work that they and their fellow citizens did, but rarely indulged in too much pride or envy. Jax's mother and her co-workers, however, laughed heartily. They poked fun at each other, and they poked fun at life. And they were proud people. They were proud of the work that they did and they were proud of their families and they were proud of their accomplishments. Jax's mother was proud of Jax, and she rarely passed up a chance to wallow in his pride.

She was proud of Jax for who Jax was, not for who he was supposed to be.

A few hours later, Jax was still staring out that window. His roommate was sound asleep in the top bunk. When he heard the clinking sounds of the auto-lock on the cell door, he didn't turn around, but instead watched a small commuter ship cruise past in the distance, heading the same direction as the prison barge.

"Hey, Jax," Officer Runstom said to his back. "Halsey and I wanted to fill you in on what we found out."

Jax stood there for a minute more, watching the little ship fly on. "Never been off planet before," he said, distantly. "Never could afford it. Get framed for a mass homicide, get a free trip all the way to the outer rim." He chuckled to himself. "I'd love to tell my friends about that little loophole." For no real reason, he added, "'Cept I don't have any."

"Nonsense," Halsey said. "You've got Stanford here."

Jax could hear Runstom grumble something at his partner. He turned around and faced the two ModPol officers. "I'd offer you a seat," he said. "But as you can see, I only have the one chair." He sat down on the bed and leaned his back against the wall. "I guess you guys can fight for it."

The bed above Jax's head creaked as his napping roommate rolled over. The big man coughed a few times, then stuck his head over the bed. "Hey," he croaked. "You da cops dat arrested dis guy?"

The ModPol officers both looked at Johnny Eyeball and said nothing.

"Yeah," Eyeball said, as if speaking for them. "Tell me. What's dis guy in for?" Jax couldn't help but to grin at the criminal's thuggish accent, apparently switched on just for the benefit of the cops.

"Mass homicide," Runstom replied.

"Thirty-two people," Halsey said.

Johnny whistled. "Fuckin' psycho," he breathed, then rolled back over. He was snoring within seconds.

Runstom and Halsey both stared at the top bunk warily for a moment, then looked at each other. "It's okay," Jax said. "I think they gave him something. He hasn't been awake for more than a few minutes at a time since he came on board."

Halsey shrugged and sat in the chair, leaving Runstom to stand. Runstom didn't seem to mind. He stood in front of Jax with a notebook in his hands, holding it tightly as if it were a precious artifact. "Jax," he said, quietly and cautiously. "We're not supposed to be in here chatting with you. We're just on escort duty."

Jax nodded slowly. "I understand. Thanks for coming."

Runstom looked at Jax for a moment, then opened up his notebook. "Halsey and I constructed a model," he explained. He went into great detail about the rotation of Barnard-3, a cone of contact, and the paths of all the ships in the traffic logs. It took several minutes and Jax tried to follow, but astrophysics was definitely not his forte. As he strained to stay focused, he felt saddened by the thought that under more fortunate circumstances, he probably would have found the math involved very interesting. As he grew uncomfortable sitting on the thin mattress of his cell, he wished Runstom would just get to the point.

Eventually, he did get to the point, which was this: Runstom and Halsey had narrowed it down to two possible ships that could have sent a mock-satellite signal to the LifSup system at block 23-D. He told Jax all the details around the mining vessel and the superliner.

"Any chance the traffic logs could have been doctored?" Jax asked at the end.

"Doctored?" Runstom appeared taken aback. Jax realized the two officers might have been clued into the possibility that conspiracy was afoot, but hadn't considered that someone within ModPol might be part of it.

"I compiled those logs from multiple tracking modules, all over the system," Halsey said. "Someone would have to hit every one of those to erase a ship – and I mean physically, because they only have one-way transmitters, they don't receive incoming data. The logs weren't doctored. Not unless they were doctored by me."

Runstom gave his partner a suspicious glare, prompting Halsey to spread his arms. "Oh, come on, Captain Paranoia! You know what? You go do a random sampling of my log sources. Verify that they match up with module data." Halsey looked at Jax. "You got this miner and this cruise liner. That's it."

"Unfortunately, both of them make good candidates," Runstom said, apparently sidelining his paranoia.

"So where do we go from here?" Jax asked.

The two ModPol officers exchanged worrisome glances. "Halsey and I have talked it over. We don't know if this is enough evidence to change the minds of Detectives Brutus and Porter. But we have to take it to them first. That's the chain of command."

"You mean, *you're* gonna take it to them," Halsey said, putting his hands up defensively, palms out. "All I know is that Officer Runstom asked me to compile some traffic logs for him. Leave me outta the whole 'accusing our superiors of incompetence' bit."

"Okay, okay, George. I'm leaving you out of it. But I'm not accusing anyone of incompetence. I just want to show Brutus and Porter that there could be more to this."

"And if they don't buy it?" Jax asked warily. He didn't like the idea of those asshole detectives getting the first pitch of this story.

"Then Stan calls up our captain," Halsey said. "And if she won't hear it, then he can go to the major. Or to the commissioner." He paused, looking at Runstom again. "If he hasn't been fired by that point. And he's still looking to push his luck." Runstom didn't reply, but his frown deepened.

"But if we even have to go that far, chances are, they won't listen," Jax said, venturing a guess.

"We wanted you to have the information, so you can take it to your attorney," Runstom said. "Halsey and I don't know courtroom law. We figure your lawyer will know best what to do with it."

Jax sighed, feeling hopeless. "Unless you can convince your detectives to investigate those two ships, I don't think I have much of a chance. And I know how hard that will be. Miners tend to be independent types who don't cooperate with authorities unless forced to." Jax paused, then added sheepishly, "I mean, at least that's how they are in the holovids. I've never met any in person."

"Yeah, they don't much like ModPol," agreed Halsey. "Truth be told, they're generally out of our jurisdiction, unless they come to civilization. And they rarely do that, since traders make regular trips out to the refineries."

"Someone would have had to get a large transmitter out to them," Runstom said. "If we can start an investigation, we could go back to the traffic logs and find out what ships have been out to that miner's refinery. Check their cargo manifests."

"And we don't know how far back to go," Halsey said grimly. "Someone could have dropped off the transmitter a year ago, for all we know."

"What about the cruise ship?" Jax didn't like the mining vessel for this job. It was too inconvenient and expensive. The superliner seemed to scream convenience. Coming into range of signaling the Gretel sub-dome over the course of multiple days. And close enough to use a small transmitter. One that could fit in a large suitcase, if disassembled.

"Well, she's technically in our jurisdiction, being operated by a company based on Barnard-3," Runstom said. "They wouldn't be real happy about a raid on the entire ship, and we wouldn't know where to start. Over 300 crew members and more than four times as many passengers. Some passengers that've spent more Alliance Credits on that ship than any of us could make in our lifetimes. We'd have to be real certain, and I don't think our bosses would risk it."

Jax wanted to scream at them, call them useless for getting nowhere. For allowing their colleagues to arrest and prosecute an innocent man. But he knew they were doing the best that they could. "Thanks for this, at least," he said. "It means a lot to me that you even listened to me. And I know you've gone out on a limb. So, thanks."

Runstom pulled a few pages out of his notebook. "Here," he said, handing them to Jax. "I made copies of everything." Jax got off the bed and took the notes. "Listen," said Runstom. "If it comes down to it, I'll testify. Don't let your lawyer call Officer Halsey. If he really has to, tell him to call me to the stand."

"Okay," Jax said quietly. "Thanks, Stanford." He was at a loss for words. It'd been a long time since anyone stood up for him. He shook hands with Officer Runstom and then with Officer Halsey and they left him alone to stare at the stars through the tiny porthole.

CHAPTER 9

Klaxons bellowed and the bombball game on the holo-vision was suddenly replaced by the blazingly bright, red, flashing image of an alarm-bell icon. Runstom cursed and looked away, the ghost of the image already burned into his retinas.

Halsey yelped awake and fell off his cot. Tangled in a blanket, he tried desperately to stand but was having a difficult time with the action. As low-ranking ModPol officers, their accommodations were barely better than those of the prisoner they were escorting. Their room was a little larger than Jax's cell, and featured two flimsy cots, a table, and a couple of chairs. Runstom slapped off the holo-vision – the one item they had that prisoners didn't – and got up to help Halsey to his feet.

"What the fuck is going on?" Halsey had to shout to be heard over the alarms.

"I don't know," Runstom yelled. He opened the door to their room. The hallway walls flashed red and the klaxons were even louder.

After a minute of confusion, the alarms quieted enough for an announcement to be heard. An unnatural and unperturbed female voice calmly stated, "Alert. The ship is under attack. This is not a drill. The ship is under attack. Gunners, report to battle-stations. Guards and prisoner escorts, report to the prisoner bay. This is not a drill. Repeat. This is not a drill."

"Well, fuck me," Halsey said in a normal voice, just before the alarms started blaring again. "Come on, Stan," he shouted. "Let's go!"

They ran down the maze of corridors that led them from the guest rooms to the prisoner bay. Various uniforms ran with them, others ran the opposite direction. Once they hit the prisoner bay, they ran into real chaos. Most of the prisoners were still in the yard and barge guards were desperately trying to corral them into their proper cells. This did not go over well with most of the prisoners, who – quite correctly – assessed that the cells were the least safe place to be during a fire-fight between the barge and other spacecraft.

Things went from bad to worse when something got past the barge's defenses and the walls shook violently and the floor lurched out from beneath them all. Artificial gravity started to falter, causing everyone to bounce around like they were on pogo-sticks. The guards suddenly became less concerned with getting the prisoners back into their cells and more concerned with finding something to hold on to.

"Stan!" Halsey yelled. "Stanford Runstom! Over here! I found Jackson!"

Runstom got himself turned around and saw Halsey holding Jax from behind, his arms hooked under the operator's armpits. Jax's head lolled around, his eyes barely open. Runstom made his way over to them, trying not to run, lest he send himself flying out of control in the weak gravity.

"Jax, wake up!" Runstom yelled once he got to them and got a hold of Jax's chin.

"I think he hit his head," Halsey shouted. "We need to get the hell outta here!"

Runstom looked around desperately as he racked his brain trying to remember the layout of the barge. He'd been briefed on it at some point in his ModPol officer training, but that was long, long ago. "This way," he shouted, pointing. "To the kitchen. I think if we go through there, we can get to the storage room. We might be able to find shelter in there. Inside packing crates – or something."

Halsey nodded and moved around Jax so they could get on either side of him, each with one of his arms hooked over their shoulders. The extra weight actually made it easier for them to move in the low gravity and they got to the kitchen without injury, dodging bouncing guards and prisoners as they went. They tried to yell to people they passed to tell them to get to the storage bay, but it wasn't apparent whether or not anyone was listening.

The kitchen was a total mess and they had to pick their way carefully through the chaos of cookware and upended food. Once they made it through, they found the short hallway that hooked up with a large corridor.

"This is the main supply corridor," Runstom said. The alarms rang furiously in the distance, but not in this section of the ship. "I think the supply deck might detach. There will be some minimal controls in there. If the barge takes too much damage, we can try to pull off and float away."

"Yeah, and hopefully not draw any attention." Halsey looked back through the kitchen, the way they came. "You think anyone else got the idea?"

"I hope for their sake, someone does," Runstom said. "Come on, let's go."

They moved down the long, wide corridor toward the primary supply deck. Once they reached the end, they punched the door release and the storage bay opened widely before them. Everything inside was strapped down tight and mostly unaffected by the drop in gravity.

The floor lurched violently, one way, then the other, back and forth a few times. The three of them ended up in different parts of the room. Runstom found himself near the doorway and on his back, staring at the supports high above along the ceiling. Suddenly, a high-pitched, eardrum-piercing, nails-on-a-chalkboard sound screeched from the main supply corridor.

Runstom lifted himself off the deck and hooked his arm over the rounded edge of the door frame, getting a good look into the large hallway. Bright, white light sprayed in showers of sparks on either side of the corridor. Runstom froze, unable to comprehend what was happening, unable to react. After a minute or so, the white light was just a red ghost in his eyes. A few metallic clangs, and suddenly a round section of the wall popped out and hit the floor with a clatter. Almost instantly, three more circles of wall were projected out, one on the same side as the first, the other two on the opposite side.

There was a moment of eerie silence, save the distant klaxons, which from here were beginning to sound like an alarm clock, pestering him to wake up already. The silence didn't last. Shouts and cheers emanated from the new holes in the corridor, and were soon followed by human forms. Human forms armed to the teeth with all manner of projectile, chemical, and even bladed weaponry.

"Fuck me!" Halsey breathed, suddenly at Runstom's side. "Fucking gangbangers!"

"Shit," Runstom said in a hush, trying not to draw any attention. "Why are they attacking us? There's nothing of value on this prisoner ba—"

Runstom stopped himself as the gangbangers met in the middle of the corridor. There must have been twenty or so of them. He caught sight of the symbol on the back of one of their jackets. Three arrows in a circle, arranged as if one flowed into the next, but with the arrowheads bending outward.

Halsey must have seen it too. "Space Waste!" he whispered.

No further explanation was needed. The two officers didn't have a need to know much about space gangs in their relatively low-key planetary assignments, but Space Waste was legendary in ModPol circles. One of the largest gangs in the known galaxy, and certainly the most well-organized, Space Waste had a knack for showing up without warning, taking what they wanted and then disappearing. More often than not, they left no living witnesses; only hundreds of InstaStick decals featuring their twisted-arrows logo.

"If Space Waste is hitting a prisoner barge," Runstom started quietly, turning away from the doorway and slouching against the wall so he could face Halsey, "they must be here to break someone out."

"How did they get aboard?" Halsey came around the other side of him to get coverage behind the wall.

"They must have used those tubes." Runstom gestured vaguely. "Reinforced, pressurized boarding tubes that can extend from one ship and form a seal with the hull of another ship." He'd been asking himself the same thing for the last several minutes and finally worked it out. "They're flexible, to account for drift. They were originally designed for rescue operations."

"How do you know this?" said Halsey, cocking an eyebrow.

Runstom shrugged. "I saw it on holo-vision once. It was one of those rescue documentaries."

"But if they cut through the hull, what happens when they disengage the boarding tubes?"

"Well, in a rescue operation, it's a last resort. They only do it when they know LifSup is failing on the endangered ship, and they want to get as many survivors off as quickly as possible."

"So lemme guess," Halsey said grimly. "The Space Wasters won't be so humanitarian."

"No, I would think not," Runstom replied calmly. He wasn't actually calm – far from it – but the situation was beginning to feel like it wasn't real. Like it was just a holo-vid show. "They'll probably get whoever they're after, and then re-board their ships and disengage the tubes without bothering to attempt to re-seal the hull breach."

"Shit," Halsey muttered. "This is too much explosive decompression for one week." Runstom shot Halsey a sour look and the other man put his hands up innocently. "What? It's not like Jackson will get framed for it this time."

Runstom suddenly stood up halfway, his eyes darting as he scanned the storage bay. "Where is Jackson?"

"Sit down!" Halsey said, pulling on Runstom's arm. "We'll get him in a minute. We need to figure out what to do! We don't have much time!"

"Okay, okay." Runstom crouched back down and spoke in a low voice. "They've breached this main supply corridor. So the rest of the ship might be okay, once they detach the boarding tube. But only if someone can hit the emergency air locks, then they can cut the rest of the ship off from this hallway and be safe."

"Safe from decompression, anyway," Halsey said. "If the Wasters have boarded us, they must have taken out our engines. When they get what they came for, they might just sail out to a safe distance and waste us."

"Yeah. Well, we can't do anything about that. The only option we have is to close this hatch on the supply deck and hope they leave the storage bay alone."

"Then we're on the drift until someone comes along and rescues us. As long as they decide to leave us alone." Halsey frowned, then his face brightened suddenly. He arched his head up and peered around the curve of the doorway. "There is one other option ..."

"What?" Runstom tried to follow his partner's gaze. The hallway was clear. The gangbangers had mostly moved on, to somewhere in the main part of the ship. Two of them stood there near the breaches, their backs to the supply deck.

"We get aboard one of those ..." he started, then stopped. Runstom guessed he was trying to imagine what kind of ships were at the other ends of those tubes.

"Did you grab your sidearm?" Runstom asked. "I only have a stun-stick," he said, indicating the thin rod hanging off his belt.

"Shit, I don't have anything," Halsey said, padding around his uniform. He turned to look back into the storage bay. "There has to be something in here. Let's go look around."

"Okay. I'm going to find Jax first and check on him."

"Forget Jackson, Stan! We're going to die out here if we don't move right now!" Halsey was trying to yell in a whisper, and it made the veins in his skinny neck bulge.

"Listen, George," Runstom said, pushing down with his hands and trying to take the other officer down a notch.

"Let's just pretend for a minute that Jack Jackson is innocent. We're about to attempt to commandeer some kind of space-gang vessel. We won't even know what it will be until we're on board. You and I are qualified to pilot one- or two-man patrollers, but anything bigger than that and we'll have our hands full." Halsey frowned at this, but kept his mouth shut. "Now I'm only trying to think a few steps ahead. *If* we manage to get away from this situation alive, and we're out there in the middle of nowhere in god-knows-what kind of ship, I guarantee we'll be glad to have another hand, especially a Life Support op!"

"Goddammit," Halsey grumbled. He sighed. "Okay. Go find that goddamn operator. I'll look for arms. Now let's go, for fuck's sake!"

They gave another look over at the two gangbangers farther up the corridor and then carefully made their way through the storage bay, ducking behind crates and shelving units as they went. The breach-guards seemed to have no inkling that someone might be hiding out on the supply deck. Or maybe they just didn't care; which was worse news, because that would mean they knew it was going to be a quick in-and-out for their cohorts.

Runstom found Jax lying on top of a crate, about three meters up. With the low gravity, he must have been flung up there, and now he lay unconscious, one arm dangling off the side. Runstom crouched and then sprang his legs, thrusting himself up to Jax's level, and then beyond. He had to stick his arms up to keep from banging into the high ceiling, and he angled himself so that he'd land on top of the crate on his float back down. He slung Jax over his shoulder and lightly dropped off the side of the box. They landed with a soft jar, and Jax made a quiet whimpering grunt as they did. "Still alive," Runstom breathed.

Halsey came bounding over to them, carrying a small bundle of thin, black rods. "Fuckin' stun-sticks was all I could find. Oh, and this med kit," he said, unhooking a white plastic case from around his shoulder. "We could keep looking."

"No, let's not waste time. I have an idea." Runstom popped open the med kit and started rummaging through it. Fortunately, it was the consumer model. Everything was clearly labeled and marked with icon-laden instructions. He grabbed a case labeled *Insta-Wake*. He had no idea what this stuff was, but he'd seen it used before more than once while on the job. He popped open the case and pulled out the single-shot needle-gun.

"Hold him down," he said, and Halsey braced Jax as best he could. Runstom put the needle-gun up to the operator's neck (as per the icon on the inside of the *Insta-Wake* box) and pulled the trigger. Jax coughed and his chest heaved, and Runstom quickly covered his mouth. His eyes fluttered open, slightly at first, then suddenly they were wide and intense.

"Shh. Jax. We've got a bit of a situation here, and we need you to be calm." Jax's eyes were still wide, but he nodded. They took their hands off him and he sat up and rubbed his head. "We don't have time to explain everything, so just trust us on this ..."

There were so many things that Dava loved about a low-grav fight. The sheer panic that accompanied the loss of control. The recoil of firearms working against their shooters. The majestic deadliness of someone trained to use acrobatics and blades in such a situation.

She was the first one of the Wasters to come out of the kitchen and into the yard, a massive open cube in the largest part of the barge. The tables around the room were bolted to the floor, but just about everything else wasn't and there was debris everywhere. She scanned up the sides of the cube at the walls lined with cells, stacked up for five levels. Guards and prisoners bounded clumsily about the space, each body with its own trajectory and intention, none of them aligned. She spent a tenth of a second drinking in the pure chaos and then went to work.

The plan to target the artificial gravity pump at the bottom of the barge and then penetrate the rear corridors had worked as well as they could have hoped. Now all that remained was to find Johnny Eyeball and Captain 2-Bit.

A stun-stick came her way, with a bulky uniform in tow. She drew her short, curved scimitar and snapped the stick in half with a quick cutting motion. The guard stumbled backward, half-falling, half-floating. She braced one foot against a nearby table and launched herself at him, her sharp blade slicing clean through the midsection of his cheap armor.

She moved on without bothering to finish him off, making her way toward the starboard-side wall of cells. Another guard flew over her head, arms and legs flailing, before slamming into the back wall with a crunch. She looked toward the source of his trajectory to see Eyeball wrestling with another guard, both of them trying to gain control of a low-end ModPol pistol.

With a few long leaps she got close enough to witness Eyeball bring one of the guards' bare hands close to his face. She caught herself between a grin and a grimace as the man howled in pain while Eyeball sank his teeth into the soft flesh just above the thumb. The gun came free and Eyeball grabbed it with one hand and with the other, shoved the guard into a sprawling tumble across the space.

"Hey Dava," he said with a dripping-wet crimson smile. "They fly pretty good in this gravity, eh?"

"Johnny," she said. "Seven minutes left, then you better be at the rear corridor just beyond the kitchen."

"Right," he said, checking his newly acquired weapon. "Where's 2-Bit?"

"Third level, opposite side."

They'd come for both, but she knew Eyeball could take care of himself. The higher priority was getting 2-Bit out of there. Her boss had made a big stink about how important it was to bring 2-Bit back home, how much the others looked up to him, how critical his experience was to the gang. It was that last bit that made Dava wonder. She always thought 2-Bit was an idiot, but he did have *experience*, which may have been another way of saying he *knew things*, things that Space Waste didn't want to turn over to ModPol. Locations of caches, plans for upcoming operations, informants sprinkled around the galaxy, those sorts of things. Secondary, everyone seemed to think that there was an advantage to having a couple of Wasters get arrested: recruitment. And 2-Bit was just the right man for the job. They knew that if they rescued him, he'd have a cartload of fresh meat to bring home as well.

She headed for the opposite wall. When another guard raised his pistol at her, she kicked to her right and balled up to avoid the shot. The kickback threw his arm up high and her scimitar swept across it, severing the hand soundlessly. The shocked victim was almost as soundless with his gasp and before he could fall to his knees, she planted one boot on his helmeted head and vaulted herself up, grabbing the railing along the edge of the second-level walkway. From there, she got to the top of the railing and leapt high enough to grab the floor of the third-level walkway, pulling herself up quickly and easily in the low gravity.

"2-Bit," she called out. "Captain, where are you?"

A yellow-gray hand appeared through the bars a few cells down. "Down here!"

She approached and saw the old man standing tall and healthy as always. She couldn't tell if he was exceptionally cool-headed given the situation, or if he was just oblivious to the imminent danger. Of course, 2-Bit had only gotten arrested because he was trying to rescue Eyeball from the mess he'd created back on B-4. She had to admire his ability not to lose his shit over the mistakes of his kin.

"Dava, boy is it good to see you," he said with a genuine smile. "The force fields went off when the gravity took a hit. Safety and all that." He tapped on the bars. "But then these came down."

With a laser cutter and enough time, she could get through them – they weren't more than cheap steel, probably designed for keeping things from flying out of the cells more than actually keeping prisoners in for any length of time – but the clock was ticking.

She switched her RadMess to voice mode. "Thompson, I need the cell doors on the third floor opened up."

The reply crackled over the tiny speaker a second later. "Which one on the third floor?"

"Just open all of them."

"Right, you got it, Dava. I'll get someone on it."

"Dava." 2-Bit gestured to a form huddled at the back of the cell. "I got a man in here with me. He's from B-3, but was runnin' some racket on B-4 where he was selling cheap vacation getaways to naïve B-foureans. He would get them aboard his ship, rob them, and drop them in the next dome over."

111

"Sounds like a real charmer," she muttered.

"Point is, he's a pilot," 2-Bit said. "Claims to be a pretty good one. And you know we always need more flyboys."

Her bosses were right, only 2-Bit could turn a jail term into a recruiting opportunity. She half-laughed at the thought. "Alright, bring him along."

A buzzer sounded and 2-Bit flinched and took his hands off the bars as they slid upward. "Come on," he said to the back of the cell.

A soft-pink-skinned B-threer came out of the darkness. "Thank you, thank you so much," he said, then stopped short when he saw Dava. "What's this?"

"What, boy?" 2-Bit said. "Come on, we need to move."

"She's with you?" he said, pointing at Dava. "This shitskin?"

The emergency lighting began to fail and the yard grew darker, which had an effect of shocking the stream of chaotic shouts and clamoring into a sudden silence. Dava went empty in her center. It had been more than a decade since she left the domes of Betelgeuse-3. She'd left at the age of fifteen, after spending nine years of her life in that whitewashed, shopping-mall civilization.

Children had been better than anyone at reminding her that she didn't belong. That she came from that refuse-planet Earth, that she deserved to be incinerated and broken down into molecules like any other trash. She had to bear such barbs almost every day in those domes. She was branded with it, the mark of the unwelcome, the never-clean.

But she had not had to bear it since joining Space Waste. Ten years since she'd even had to hear slang such as that.

2-Bit was at her side, quietly nudging her back to the present. The B-threer seemed frozen, still inside the cell, the hateful eyes burning like those of the nasty dome children. She lifted the tip of her blade slightly and he stepped back.

"Close the cell doors on level three," she said into her armband.

"What? We just opened them, Dava."

"Close them," she said.

Inside some supply hold, leaning against some towering crate, Jax groaned loudly. "Help. Someone. Is anyone there? I'm hurt. I need help! Can anyone hear me?" His voice cracked with fear – most of it real.

"Ello? Ooze over der?" came a rough voice after a minute. "Com'on outta der!"

Jax's mind raced. Whatever it was Runstom gave him to wake him up was giving him the shakes. "I … I can't move. It's my leg. I think it's broken. Who is that? Can you help me?"

Jax heard another voice that he couldn't make out. Then the rough voice again, "Ee says 'is leg's bustid. Huh? Okay, okay. I'm going." The voice got louder as it was directed back at Jax. "Okay, you. I'm comin' over. Don't move. I'm uh … I'm a medic."

Jax rolled his eyes, which caused a spike of pain to shoot through his throbbing head. He tried to keep his hands from shaking and sit still, his back to the large crate they'd found him lying on. He heard a movement, the *tok-tok-tok* of boots on the metal floor off to his right, and he turned his head. A scruffy, scarred, yellow face came around the side. "Ey, boy. You got a gun? You armnnNNNHHHHH—"

The body that came with the face flexed violently, hands dropping some kind of bladed, rifle-like weapon with a clatter and after a couple of seconds, the man spun around and crashed to the floor, his shocked face staring at the ceiling. Bubbling drool oozed out of the side of his mouth and down his cheek.

Halsey came around the corner of the crate, three smoking stun-sticks bundled together in one hand. He stared at the unconscious man with a tight grin on his face.

"Goddamn," Jax whispered. "That was a little extreme, wasn't it?"

The officer gave him an innocent look. "Well, I had to be certain, right? He's a big boy!" He stuck one of the stun-sticks through a loop in his belt and dropped the other two as he bent down and snatched up the loose weapon. It looked like a stubby rifle with a pair of blades extending slightly away from the barrel at two different angles, forming a vague V-shape.

Jax was about to ask Halsey if he knew how to use that thing, but then thought better of it. Whether he did or not, Jax didn't really want to know, and there was no point in calling the officer's ability into question now.

Halsey turned around quickly, rifle secured in both hands, as a shout and a grunt came from the other side of the room. Jax stood up and carefully peered around the other side of the box.

Runstom was about twenty meters away, his right arm wrapped around the neck of another scruffy-looking man. These men were part of a gang, apparently – at least, that's as much as Runstom and Halsey had a chance to tell Jax before they turned him into bait. The officer was at a slight disadvantage, height-wise, and he swayed horizontally from the back of the gangbanger, who was making use of the low gravity to try to shake him loose.

Halsey slung the rifle over his shoulder and snatched up the extra stun-sticks. He ran over to the spinning officer–gangbanger combination and stopped short, trying to figure out how to get a clear shot.

"Put those goddamn things down," Runstom said between huffs. "The current will run through him and hit me!"

"You're gonna have to let go!" Halsey yelled, legs bent at the knees, trying to keep the other two directly in front of him.

The Space Waster spun around and faced Halsey, perhaps perceiving him to be a more immediate threat than the man trying to slowly asphyxiate him. He bent his head forward and, using the weight on his back for leverage, he lumbered at an alarming speed toward the other officer.

"Let go now!" Halsey shouted as the big, yellow man bore down on him. He thrust out his two stun-sticks, one in each hand. From his angle, Jax could see Runstom just barely manage to jump free, but he was pretty sure Halsey had his eyes closed. The sticks connected with the big man's chest and he went down with a jaw-clenched scream through his teeth, sinking to his knees and then keeling over backwards.

Jax ran up to the officers. "Where's his gun?" Halsey jerked his head erratically from side to side.

Runstom looked in one direction, strode a few meters, and snatched up another blade-gun type of weapon. This one appeared to be more of a single-hand weapon; a smaller but terrible and jagged blade attached to a large pistol. Most of its bulk was due to its battery pack. Runstom flipped a switch on the side of the gun and a small, red dot appeared on the crate next to him. He looked up at them. "Okay, let's move. Jax, you wait until we say it's clear. We're going for the closest hole on the right."

Their choice of breaches was, of course, entirely arbitrary. They had no idea what to expect as far as the attached ships went. Jax watched from behind the curve of the storage-bay doorway as Runstom and Halsey quickly moved down the long corridor, guns pointed forward.

Runstom looked back over his shoulder long enough to yell, "Clear! Come on, Jax, move!"

Jax tried to angle his legs so that his strides pushed him forward more than up, but he was completely unprepared for athletics in low gravity. He covered the distance of fifty meters to the first breach in what seemed like several agonizing minutes, but it could have been much less.

When he got within a few meters of the officers, he was jarred by the clapping sound of Halsey's rifle. The officer was shooting a projectile weapon of some kind, an old-fashioned gun that actually fired bullets, and the force of the recoil in the low gravity caused him to stagger backward and lose his footing. "The door on the far right side!" he yelled, trying to get back to his feet. Runstom started firing his laser down the hall, blindly shooting down the right side.

Gunfire echoed down the hallway and Jax was sure he heard something whiz by his head. The oval corridor was a good twenty or thirty meters across, and while Jax and Runstom were taking position near the wall on their right, Halsey was closer to the opposite side. He got to his feet and dove into a nearby breach. The officer then set himself in a position where he could brace his back against the side of the tube and lean out to fire his rifle down the hall without getting pushed backwards.

Jax watched the scene with bemusement, until Runstom turned and shoved him into the boarding tube. He came in after the operator and leaned out the side of the tube, sending laser fire down the corridor. After a few blasts, he turned to Jax and shouted, "Get down the tube to the ship. Make sure we can fly the thing outta here!" Jax started to turn, but Runstom yelled "Wait!" He unhooked the stun-stick from his belt and handed it to the operator.

"What am I supposed to do with this?" he said, fear creeping into his voice.

"There might be a pilot standing by. Just press the button on the handle and poke him with the round ball at the end." Jax stared at the stick in bewilderment. "Go, now, goddammit!" Runstom shouted, and the look of intensity and violence in the officer's eyes made Jax want to go down the tube and face someone less terrorizing. Like maybe a bloodthirsty gangbanger.

Runstom stuck his gun back out the breach-end of the tube and with a battle cry, continued blasting. Jax could hear Halsey join in, and for that brief moment he imagined the ModPol officers were a two-man army, fighting off a wave of invaders. He spun around and headed down the tube.

The tube itself was barely large enough in diameter for a grown person to stand. Being B-fourean, Jax was taller than many other humans and had to crouch as he picked his way through the flexing tube. There were handles dotting the length of it, and he quickly discovered their intended use. Once he was off the barge, the failing artificial gravity was no longer a factor, because there was no gravity at all. The tube was some kind of segmented metal. It was not transparent, and for this, he was thankful. It didn't seem like a good time to be confronted with the vast emptiness of space.

After a minute or two and some distance Jax couldn't judge, he reached the end. He could still hear Runstom shouting and blasting, and he was pretty sure he could make out the clapping of Halsey's rifle even at this distance. The hatchway at this end was open. That seemed like a terribly dangerous thing to do, and Jax had to imagine it violated all kinds of safety regulations. *So, yeah,* he thought as he slowly pulled himself through the hatchway. *Add that to their list of atrocities.*

The ratio of ducking to returning fire for Runstom and Halsey was steadily growing in favor of ducking. There was a palpable increase in pressure coming from the center of the barge as the gangbangers reassembled their forces and returned to their only escape route. It seemed like a good plan, but now Runstom was having his doubts about getting between a legion of Space Wasters and their ships.

"George," he said in between blasts of his laser pistol. "George!"

Halsey stopped shooting and leaned back into the tube he occupied on the opposite side of the corridor. He struggled with an extra ammo clip that was affixed to the side of the heavily modified rifle. "My last clip," he yelled. "We need to get out of here."

The gangbangers didn't waste time taking advantage of the short pause. Runstom and Halsey were both forced to lean back into their tubes as the hallway crackled with machinegun fire. Runstom panted as his heart threatened to climb out of his throat. He and his fellow officers had combat training, but it didn't come close to preparing him for something like this mess. He looked down at the cellpack in the laser pistol. It was down to about a ten-percent charge. He had no idea how many shots that translated into.

The continuous rain of bullets smoothed into a series of rhythmic bursts, and for a brief moment he thought that maybe it meant the gangbangers were running low on ammo as well and were attempting to conserve it. This thought gave him a flicker of hope until he remembered all the blades attached to the guns. Maybe he was better off getting shot before it came to that.

A new sound caught his attention, a strange metal-bouncing-on-metal sound. He and Halsey both looked into the corridor from their opposite-sided shelters. A cylindrical object bounded along and continued all the way to the supply hold they'd come from only minutes before.

"Shit." Runstom wanted to yell to Halsey that it was a grenade, but the explosion beat him to it. The heat of it blew up the hall and into his tube, but there was nothing more than that. He ventured a peek back down toward the hold and saw the burned scarring just inside the open doors.

He realized in that second that whoever had thrown the grenade hadn't accounted for the low gravity. The next one came with an adjusted aim, rolling to a spot directly between them where it stopped and spun idly like a bottle in a party game.

Halsey took two steps into the corridor that was still being peppered by cover fire and swung his rifle like a club, smacking the cylinder with one of the blades at the end of the barrel. The grenade flew back down the hall and Halsey cried out as a spray of red burst from his forearm. The rifle clattered to the floor and he dropped back on his ass and kicked at the floor with his feet, pushing himself back into the tube.

"George!" Runstom reflexively stepped toward his partner, but the spray of bullets drove him back.

The returned grenade blew and the cover fire was momentarily interrupted. Runstom didn't have time to wonder if it actually took anyone out, he just used the space of a breath to dive across the hall and into the other tube. He grabbed Halsey by his good arm and hoisted him to his feet, but the other officer cried out as he stood.

He pulled away the bloody arm to reveal thicker, darker blood coming from his abdomen. "Stan," he gasped, reflexively holding his wound once again. "You gotta go."

"No." Runstom tugged roughly at Halsey's arm. "Come on, George. We're both going."

Halsey groaned but didn't protest further. Runstom tried to think but he had no time. They were outnumbered, outgunned, and it was clear the rest of the barge had fared even worse. Space Waste had won. He looked down the nearby tube. No doubt there was a ship at the other end, but he'd already sent Jax down the tube opposite. More than ever, Runstom thought their only chance at escape was to stick together.

In the several seconds that had passed, the gunfire had not returned. "Come on, George," he said with a tug. "Now or never."

They limped across the width of the spacious hallway. A burst of gunfire sent them diving for the tube. Runstom felt the bite of one shot in his thigh and the ripping sting of another across his midsection before he hit the inside of the tube. He spun around to see Halsey twisting in the corridor, spitting curses and clutching his leg.

"George!"

Another cylinder bounced along the floor, thumping Halsey in the chest. He grabbed at it, bobbling it until he spun it around and found the safety clip. He clutched at it and looked at Runstom. "Go, Stan!"

"George, what are you doing? Throw it back!"

"Go!" He started belly crawling toward the tube. Sporadic bursts lit up the air. "Go before I blow us both up!"

Then it clicked. He was going to blow the tube loose so that no one could follow.

"Damn you," Runstom said and turned away from his only ally.

He flung himself as deep into the tube as he could, then scrambled to yank himself along by the handholds when the gravity disappeared altogether.

Still coping with the weightlessness, Jax pulled himself through the small ship slowly and carefully. He was in what appeared to be a passenger-seating and load-out room. There were twelve or so "seats" on the walls which were angled in a way that, if there were any gravity, one could walk up to them and strap in securely without actually sitting. They were similar to the mount that was in his cell, only made for voluntary use. On the other side of the room was a series of racks that contained a few spare guns and what looked like suits of armor.

On the opposite wall from the hatchway was another door. This one was closed, and apparently locked, according to the lit sign on the front of it. There were a few flimsy-looking spacesuits hanging haphazardly on either side of it. Jax realized that this was probably the cockpit door. It was a small ship indeed; a personnel carrier, probably hijacked from a military outfit at one time. Just enough to get a boarding party from one big ship to another. They'd be lucky if it could even do Warp.

Jax knew the cockpit door wouldn't open unless the outer hatchway was closed. He'd have to cut off the ModPol officers long enough to secure the ship. He put a foot against the wall, hit the door trigger on the hatchway, and sprang his body across the chamber to the opposite side, grabbing onto the latches on the wall and hiding himself behind the spacesuit closest to the cockpit.

He waited. The seconds passed. He tasted bitterness in his own saliva and he forced his breathing to slow, trying desperately not to vomit. Finally he heard the internal mechanisms of the door sliding around, eventually clinking into place. The door slowly opened.

"Hey, fellas," a voice said. "Back already? Hello?"

Suddenly, unexpected to both Jax and the pilot, there was a series of clanging sounds coming from the outer hatchway.

"What the hell?" said the pilot to himself. He was still out of view from Jax. The banging of something solid on the metal hatch came again. "Okay, I'm comin', I'm comin'," he shouted, then said in a quiet aside, "How did those idiots manage get the inner door to open without coming through the outer door?"

Jax could hear the snapping sound of belts being unclipped. He tensed and poked the little ball at the end of his stunstick between the sleeve and the midsection of the spacesuit, pushing the sleeve aside just enough for him to watch his aim. A body began to float by and he hit the button, jabbing the stick forward.

"AAAhhhhhnnnnNHHHHH!" the pilot screamed, his body contorting with almost mock-athleticism in the absence of gravity. After a few seconds it went limp, and he hung there, arms dangling like a scarecrow-bot.

"Shit, guys," Jax breathed. "I hope that's you." He didn't know how to fly a ship, so he figured he was dead either way if it wasn't Stanford Runstom or George Halsey on the other side of that hatch. He punched the close button on the cockpit door and floated over to the hatchway.

He hit the release and Runstom came through. He quickly spun around and slammed on the button to close the hatch. He looked wounded, blood oozing from different parts of his uniform. Jax tried to look into his eyes, but the officer was looking down, eyes squinted in pain.

There was a low boom and the ship seemed to drift slightly, an odd sway that moved around them while they floated weightless in the center of it.

"Stanford," Jax started.

"Halsey," Runstom rasped quietly, looking at the closed hatch.

"Shit." Now Jax read the pain on Runstom's face differently. He wasn't good at dealing with grief, but he suddenly thought of his mother and it felt like something was tearing apart his stomach. "Stanford," he said, putting a hand on the officer's shoulder. "He was a good man."

Runstom swallowed a couple of times. "That asshole was the closest thing I've had to a friend in years. He didn't deserve to go like that." He closed his eyes for a moment and Jax stayed quiet, despite being terrified of the danger they were still in. After a few seconds, Runstom opened his eyes. His lips quivered and pursed and his forehead creased as his eyebrows tensed. Jax could only guess what was going through the other man's mind. Pushing down the pain, burying it for another time. "We don't have much time," the officer said finally. "We have to move."

Runstom grabbed the floating pilot and briefly checked his pulse. He took a restraint band off his belt and pulled the pilot's arms together and bound them. "Strap this guy into one of those," he said to Jax, pointing at the harness-seats. "And then get up to the cabin. I'm going to warm up the engines."

Jax did his best to strap the unconscious pilot in, and then floated into the cockpit. There were four seats, each facing a long, narrow window that looked into the blackness of space. Runstom was already strapped in, and Jax picked a seat at random and followed suit.

"I'm detaching the boarding-tube now," Runstom said, and Jax could hear the crack in his voice. He cleared his throat and then turned with a quick jerk. "Do you have the notes I copied for you?"

"Yeah, of course. They were the only thing I grabbed when the alarms started." Jax had a standard, prison-issue satchel strapped to his body. He pulled the collection of papers out of it and handed them to Runstom.

Runstom took the notes and quickly found the page he was looking for. He set them down on the console. "I'll need to navigate away from the barge a few thousand meters, then we'll be hitting Xarp speed."

"This thing can do Xarp?" Jax asked, trepidation in his voice. Warp was light-speed, and that was terrifying enough, but Xarp was even faster; a speed appropriate for mammoth interstellar vessels, but insanely dangerous in such a small ship. His experience with space travel was about to compound as it went from a day and a half of looking at the stars through a porthole the size of his hand to a faster-than-light escape from a murderous space gang.

"She's an interplanetary, military personnel transport. Designed to be launched in packs, usually about a hundred or so at a time, delivering squads of elite soldiers to a target without warning. Usually sent from deep, deep orbit on the outermost part of a system, where a warship can sit undetected." Runstom looked up from the console for a moment, but not at Jax. Not at anything in particular. "She's not much for luxury. All engine and fuel storage. Designed to bring the fight to your enemy's doorstep."

Jax looked around, wondering if he had missed some kind of informational plaque on the way into the cockpit. "How the hell do you know all that?"

Runstom shrugged. "ModPol training, mostly. Plus my grandfather was in the Sirius Interplanetary Navy. And … I guess I probably watch too many documentary vids." He grabbed the throttle and the ship started to move with a jolt.

"Stanford," Jax said tentatively. "You do know how to pilot this thing, right?"

Runstom was quiet, concentrating on the stick. "Every ModPol grunt has to fly patrol for a couple of years before they get to start doing real police work." The ship shuddered and Runstom quickly reached for the panel in front of him, hitting a button and flipping a switch. "Of course, this thing is just a little different than a one-man patroller."

The view panned to the left as the ship rotated, the side of the barge disappearing to the right. Jax leaned forward to angle his head back and forth and take in the view without unstrapping himself. As the emptiness of space opened up before them, he looked at the rear monitor to see the barge coming into view. There was another small craft next to it on this side, tethered by a boarding tube. Next to that he could see the boarding tube that was once attached to their newly acquired vessel, now just floating idly, a jagged hole in one side of it where it was half-hanging from the barge like a misplaced tentacle. Despite the lack of wind in space, it flapped oddly.

"I think the barge is decompressing," Jax said, watching the monitor.

"Nothing we can do," Runstom said quietly. "I don't know if anyone but Space Waste is left. Our problem is that they probably expected all boarding parties to detach at the same time. So we have to get out of here quick before they figure out something is wrong."

Jax looked away from the monitor and back to the view from the window. There was a ship in the distance, but with no frame of reference he couldn't tell if it was a large ship far away or a small ship close by.

"That's the command ship," Runstom said before Jax could ask. "She's pretty far out, but she's got some fighters close by. That's the contact computer." He pointed at a crude holo-screen positioned front and center of the cockpit. It displayed a large red blob surrounded by a handful of green dots. Another green blob sat farther off from the rest. "The red one is the barge. The little green ones are combat vessels. Small fighters and personnel assault ships like this one."

"And the big green one is the command ship," Jax guessed.

Runstom angled their vessel in a direction that would take them away from the barge and the command ship equally and they edged forward slowly.

"Faster might be a good idea," Jax said, realizing suddenly that he was gripping the arms of his chair so tightly that his fingers hurt.

"To run is to be chased," the officer said quietly. "We're just one of them for another minute or two, then we're nothing but Xarp-wake." He seemed to be lost in thought for a moment. "I'm surprised nothing has come across the comm. They must be keeping radio-silent."

Jax thought about that as they inched ponderously away from the action. He thought about these gangbangers, who seemed to him like fictional space pirates, with their ridiculous weapons and uniforms. The fact that he had not really gotten a good look at any of them only served to fuel his imagination more. The very idea that they were so organized; able to cripple the barge and board it, all while maintaining such a committed level of stealth. Radio silence meant sticking to a plan, it meant discipline and competence. These were qualities one didn't associate with anarchist space pirates.

He hadn't noticed the wide but short flat panel that ran part-way across the center of the top of their viewport until it lit up and blinked red a few times. It stopped blinking and a series of numbers appeared on it.

Jax looked at Stanford and opened his mouth, about to ask him what they were looking at, but the officer had a grave look on his face as he stared at the numerical sequence that lit up the cockpit. "It's message traffic on the comm." He frowned and looked straight forward determinedly, as if he needed both eyes on the road at that moment. "I don't know what it means."

"Oh," Jax said, realizing. "It's code."

Runstom cast him a sideways glance and Jax read interest on his face for a fraction of a second before he re-gripped the throttle and stared back into space. "Code?" he asked idly.

"Like a cypher." Jax tried to get at his satchel, which was wedged between his thigh and the seat restraints. "Want me to write it down? We could try to—"

"Forget it," Runstom said. "And hold on. Xarp in thirty seconds."

"Stanford?" Jax said quietly. "Where are we going?"

"I flipped a coin," the ModPol officer said. "We're going to go find that superliner."

CHAPTER 10

Runstom and Jax stared out of their wide, short viewport, marveling at the magnificent beast only a few hundred kilometers distant: Royal Starways Interplanetary Cruise Delight Superliner #5.

Of course, Runstom hadn't actually flipped a coin. Jax saw him as a cop, through and through, and as such, he knew the officer left as little to chance as possible. Cops in the holo-vids were always saying that they "like" someone for a crime. The operator came to understand that this did not mean they enjoyed the company of the suspect in question, but rather that of all their choices, if they had to pick one person to be guilty, this was the one. That small "like" was a code-word that represented lots of reasoning, possibly some hard evidence, and, more often than not, a fairly large helping of instinct.

The ship was massive, like a floating city or a small moon (if a moon could be oblong in shape), a seemingly perfect oval when viewed from any angle. The clean, white surface was dotted by small half-bubbles of glass; although they only looked small in comparison to the rest of the drifting hulk. Up close, those little bubbles were a few thousand meters in diameter, giant pockets of different flavors of paradise. Endless beaches, tropical islands, quaint villages, majestic mountains, vast canyons, hip and sleepless clubs, rolling green hills. Any paradise you might dream of, you could find fabricated just for you in one of those immaculate domes floating through deep space.

They had started out by Xarping randomly once, then again. The third time, they headed to the last logged position of the superliner based on the notes Runstom had made, since that was the only reference they had. The officer explained that the first two jumps were necessary to throw off any pursuers. The gangbangers could easily plot a trajectory based on their first Xarp away from the barge. Following that trajectory at Xarp speed was extremely difficult, but by stopping, turning, and Xarping elsewhere, Runstom pretty much guaranteed their escape.

Once they came out of Xarp the third time, the wake of their target (in the form of radioactive discharge) left a clear path for them to follow. It didn't take them long to catch up. The gargantuan ship was barely capable of Warp speeds, and most of the time she cruised around at sub-Warp. Her flight crew only used full Warp to shorten up some of the longer stretches between the outer planets.

Currently, she was making a lazy trek somewhere between the orbits of Barnard-4 and Barnard-3. There were numerous docking bays up and down the sides of her hull, used by small shuttles that ferried passengers to and from inhabited planets and moons wherever a sub-orbital docking station was absent.

"How are we going to convince them to let us dock?" Jax said as they took in the sight. "As in, dock our stolen-from-a-space-gang-who-stole-it-from-a-military-outfit personnel transport?" He shot a glance at Runstom. "Do you think they made markings on the outside? We haven't even seen the outside of this ship!"

"Yeah," Runstom said calmly. "I'm assuming they did."

"Oh." Jax tried to match the other man's passiveness. He looked back at the superliner. "So you have a plan?"

"I tell the truth," Runstom said. "Well, part of it anyway. We were in a ModPol vessel. It was attacked by a space gang. We escaped by commandeering one of the attackers' ships and fleeing at Xarp speed. By luck we happened on the superliner's wake, and we followed it. We're almost out of fuel, and we just need to dock and ride it out until the cruise ship gets closer to B-3."

"Huh. Sounds like a reasonable story, I suppose. Although, I just have to point out: it sounds a little ... well ... made up."

"I can beam them my ModPol credentials. They're coded to my genetic profile. Impossible to counterfeit. And if they need further corroboration, they can ask the fly-boy tied up in the back."

The fly-boy in question – the Space Waste pilot they more or less kidnapped (Jax was pretty sure Runstom never read the man his rights) – was named Prosser. That was about the full extent of information they got out of him during the flight. Any attempts to communicate with the gangbanger usually resulted in a spew of vulgar threats against his captors, and given the reputation of Space Waste, they were inclined to believe him. After two attempts to question Prosser, Jax couldn't bear to listen to the guy anymore. His nightmares were bad enough already.

Jax remained unconvinced of Runstom's plan, but it actually worked out pretty well. They got authorization to dock with the cruise ship and had their gangbanger pilot (he refused to talk to anyone on the superliner, too, of course, but evidently his presence alone supported their story) transferred to the small brig on board. Runstom even convinced them to give their newly acquired transport ship a quick paint job. They had never gotten a chance to see the outside of it, not that it mattered to either of them. They got a room reserved for emergency use, down in the servants' quarters, and managed to scare up some spare clothes.

"Well, then," Jax said, after taking a look at their meager accommodations. "Now all we have to do is find a sat-transmitter somewhere on this boat that's the size of a metropolis." He sat down wearily on one of the bunks. "If only we had some kind of equipment that we could use to detect a transmitter. Not that we could detect one unless it was in use anyway."

"Right," Runstom said. "We're going to have to do this the hard way. We canvas the ship. We talk to everybody."

"Ugh," Jax groaned. "Ask a cop how to find a needle in a haystack, and they'll tell you: 'One straw at a time.'"

Runstom grinned. It was the first time in the few days they'd known each other that Jax saw the officer actually look happy.

"Jack, this is Bob. And this is Karr, and this is Jainel."

"Hey, everyone," Jax said, reaching out to shake hands with the woman first, then the two men. The three of them were dressed in standard-issue Royal Starways maintenance jumpsuits, which were all gray with thin lines of reflective silver running along the sides and down the arms and legs. Like a lot of the working class on the superliner, they were obvious B-foureans, pale-skinned and tall. None of them stood up as he shook their hands; they barely looked up from their lunches.

There was a bit of an awkward silence and Runstom broke it by saying, "We work for the government." He paused, as if trying to remember his line, then added, "The Barnard-4 Planetary Government." The three maintenance workers ignored him, and he nudged Jax.

"Yeah, that's right. We work for a division of Planetary Defense," Jax said. This turned some heads, but also inspired some scoffing. Jax cleared his throat. "Nothing military or anything," he said hastily. "We work for the Rogue Celestial Object Detection Center."

"What the heck does that mean?" the worker called Bob asked with a tone of mild interest. He was the youngest of the three, with short, mousy, brown hair and a distinctly smooth chin.

"Means another way to waste money," Jainel said after a grunt. She was a middle-aged woman with blond hair, cropped short above the ears. She didn't look up from her lunch.

"Well, uh." Jax struggled to remember Runstom's instructions to just relax as he pretended to be someone else. He directed his answer at Bob, since he was the only one of the three not presently stuffing his face. "We look for celestial objects – uh, mostly asteroids – that are on a path that might intersect with Barnard-4." Bob arched an eyebrow, so he added, "You know, we try to make sure there aren't any asteroids out there that might hit B-4. Like that one in the holo-vid."

"Oh yeah?" Bob said. "You mean like *Day of the Asteroid*?"

"Yee-ah," Jax said, drawing the word out. That wasn't the flick he was thinking of, but he decided it didn't matter. "That's it."

"That's why we're here," Runstom said. "The government is installing some – um – detectors …"

"Asteroid detectors," Jax said.

"Right, asteroid detectors. On every superliner. Since uh – since they …"

"Since they regularly cover so much of the solar system," Jax finished.

"Cool," Bob said, his lunch now completely forgotten. "So what do you need from us?" he asked. Jainel looked at Karr and they both rolled their eyes.

"Uh," Jax started, but he was at a loss for words.

"Well, the problem is, our man Jack here misplaced one of the detectors," Runstom said, putting a hand on Jax's shoulder. The three maintenance staff looked at Jax with mild disdain.

"I was drunk," Jax admitted, forcefully curling his lip into a half frown, fighting the urge to smile.

"Yeah-ha," Karr and Jainel said together, breaking into laughter. Karr pointed his sandwich at Jax. "Man, I've been there buddy." He waggled the sandwich and for a flash Jax thought the stuff between the bread looked like another laughing mouth. "So drunk you don't even know where you've been or how you got home, right?"

Jax nodded and the man and woman laughed again. Bob joined in with a silent, open-mouthed smile, but it didn't last. "Hey," he said, suddenly concerned. "Does this mean we're not going to be able to detect any asteroids headed toward B-4?"

"Yes," Runstom said.

"Well, maybe," Jax added, seeing fear cross the young man's face.

"Anyway, we'll find the thing," Runstom said. "If you guys could help us out, that would be – well, it would be very helpful."

Jax watched their expressions carefully, wondering if they were buying any part of the story. The older man and the woman both narrowed their eyes and creased their brows. Jax took their expressions to mean they were actually paying attention, and he was glad enough for that.

"Of course," Bob said anxiously. "We'd be happy to help!" He tried to pull his excitement back a little. "I mean, we've all got family back on B-4, and we'd want to make sure they're safe." He looked around the room. "Like, from asteroids, and stuff."

"I thought you joined this crew to get away from your parents," Jainel said with a sly smile. She was done eating and was neatly folding up the plastic wrappings of her lunch.

Bob frowned. "Yeah, I did. They were always trying to tell me what to do," he said, lost in thought for a moment. "But that doesn't mean I want anything bad to happen to them."

"We can keep an eye out for your thing," Karr said, finishing off his sandwich. With a mouthful of bread and something gooey, he said, "Whaff it wook wike?"

"Um, well." Jax suddenly realized he wouldn't be able to describe the portable sat-transmitter because he'd never actually seen one. "You'll know it when you see it. It's small enough to be portable, but not real small." He gestured vaguely, hands going in and out indicating a variety of possible sizes. "And it's heavy. With buttons on the outside."

Karr huffed a half-laugh and crumpled up the wrappings of his lunch. "You got it, pal. And maybe if we find it, you can buy us a drink, eh?"

"Of course," Runstom said.

"Hell yeah," Jax said. "Thanks guys."

Karr stood up and Jainel followed suit. "Come on, Bob," she said as she and the older man walked out of the break room. Bob started to clean up his lunch slowly, still deep in thought.

After a moment, Jax said, "I took this job to get away from my parents too." Bob looked up at him but didn't speak. "They're both engineers. They wanted me to be an engineer. I just wanted to do my own thing, you know?" He shook his head, thinking about his father and step-mother. Did they care what had happened to their son, or had they pretty much given up on him? As far as he knew, the last message they got was from Foster, his lawyer on B-4; a message that said Jax was going to be taken out to a ModPol outpost for trial. He knew Runstom wouldn't want him to try to contact them. At the moment he didn't feel much like checking in with them, even if he could without revealing his location. "I never see them anymore. I talk to them maybe once or twice a year."

"Yeah," Bob said, nodding. "My mom and dad wanted me to be a doctor. I can't deal with it though. The blood and guts – that stuff just creeps me out." He visibly shuddered. "Besides, I wanted to get out of the domes, you know? Get out and see the stars. The real stars." He looked Runstom up and down. Like Jax, the officer was wearing a very nondescript outfit: brown pants and a white, long-sleeved shirt. The shirt made his olive hands and face seem even greener than usual. He looked like a smooth-barked tree sprouting a couple of large green leaves. "How about you? You're not from B-4, are you?"

Runstom started to sigh, but tried to bite it back. "Nope," he said, matter-of-fact. "Born on a space station. A way-point for asteroid miners."

"And your parents?"

"My mother was killed in the line of—" he started. "Um, in her line of work. Which was asteroid mining. She was killed in a mining accident. It was a long time ago." His lips pursed together as Bob looked at him expectantly. Finally he swallowed and said, "I never knew my father."

"So, Bob, let me give you the number for the room we're staying in," Jax said, drawing the maintenance man's attention away from Runstom. "That way you can reach us if you come across anything."

"Okay," Bob said as Jax wrote the number on a scrap of paper. "Hey, there's a bombball-cast tonight. You guys want to come down to the lounge and watch with us? Have a few drinks? I can introduce you to some other people – other maintenance and cleaning staff and whatnot. Other folks that might be able to help you find your asteroid detector."

"Sure, Bob," Jax said, smiling. "That would be great. Stan here loves bombball."

"Sirius Series!" Runstom said, his mood lifting suddenly.

"Hell yeah," Bob said and the two men slapped hands. "Okay, see you tonight," he said cheerfully and jogged out of the break room.

Alone, Jax and Runstom stood in silence for a moment. Then Jax couldn't take it any more. "I have admit, I thought you'd be better at this undercover stuff."

"Better?" Runstom shot him a glare. "What's that suppose to mean?"

"Well, I mean, you just need to act a little more natural, that's all. Didn't they ever teach you how to go undercover?"

He frowned and dropped his shoulders. "No. I mean, I tried. I volunteered for the training. But I'm not qualified."

Jax wasn't sure what he meant by that and decided not to probe. "Well, don't sweat it too hard. I don't think these people care all that much."

"I think they have no reason to be suspicious."

Jax laughed. "Yeah, I guess living on a ship like this, you'd have to be more naïve than domers."

Runstom's mouth opened and closed awkwardly. "Look, Jax, I didn't mean that—"

"No, it's okay," Jax said, putting his hands up. "You don't have to tell me how sheltered life is in a dome. Gotta be even more sheltered on a giant cruise ship."

Runstom nodded slowly as though digesting that statement, perhaps along with the rest of the situation. "Right. It's good that people won't be on guard. We're going to need to talk to a lot of people if we're going to find that transmitter. *If* there's a transmitter to find."

Runstom couldn't get the question of undercover training out of his head. He'd done what he could independently, but when it came to getting more advanced training, he was shut down. It wasn't because of his abilities or anything. Anyone with a relative who'd done undercover work at ModPol was automatically disqualified.

These were the thoughts that were distracting him as they tried out their asteroid-detector story on a few more souls around the cruise liner. They were in one of the common dining rooms that were designated for the least expensive ticket-holders; not that these people were lower or even middle class, of course; they were just at the bottom of the extreme-upper-class population that could afford a cruise of any kind. They didn't seem to mind the presence of a couple of government employees in their dining hall, and Runstom suspected it was out of a built-in humility they felt at being the bottom of the economic barrel for once.

"It's the Rogue Celestial Object Detection Center," Jax was saying to a couple of men who were at the silver-topped bar that ran along one side of the dining hall. They were pink-skinned B-threers and wore matching blue slacks and shirts. They weren't as dressed up as some, which made starting a conversation with them easier.

"Where is that?" one asked.

Jax looked at Runstom, who jumped in. "We're with the Barnard-4 Planetary Government. Of course, our center is jointly funded by the B-3 and B-4 governments." Every time he had to describe their fictitious employment, his skin prickled. The center they were talking about was real – Runstom remembered seeing a news story about it once and looked it up so he could remember the name – and so his biggest fear was that they would run into someone who actually knew something about rogue celestial objects.

"Oh right," the man said. "That would make sense."

"What makes sense about that?" the other said, taking his drink from the bartender. "Rogue Object Whatdjacallit?"

"Celestial objects, Tommy," the first said, giving his partner a nudge. "You know, like meteors and asteroids and shit."

"Oh, oh, like that flick *Meteor Hailstorm*," Tommy said.

"Right, like that," Jax said.

"Ugh, that was terrible," the first man groaned. "So far from reality."

"You know something about asteroid detection?" Runstom asked in what he hoped was a casual manner.

"Kender loves all that space shit," Tommy said with a wave of his hand. "That's why we're on this cruise. They got all kinds of beaches and nightclubs and he keeps dragging me to the observatory."

"It's a beautiful universe," Kender said wistfully before taking a pull of his cocktail. He swallowed and his face perked momentarily. "Hey, can I take a look at you guys' setup?"

Jax and Runstom looked at each other. The drinking story was fine for telling workers on the superliner, but probably wouldn't go off as well with passengers.

"Sure," Jax said.

"We're going to be setting it up on various parts of the deck," Runstom said, trying to think on his feet. "Wherever there is a clear line of sight into space." He handed the one called Kender a card. "If you see it, just pop us a call and we'll come by and let you take a look."

"Great," Tommy said. "Now you'll have him looking on every deck for some kind of space-detector equipment. Fellas, it was a pleasure, but Kender owes me a dance."

They said goodbye and once the men were out of earshot, Jax leaned in to Runstom. "I feel like we need a better story."

"Yeah, I think so too."

"We're getting a little better though."

"We just have to try a few different angles and see what sticks best," Runstom said. Then he smiled and shook his head. "I don't even know how you're managing this."

Jax laughed. "Yeah, me neither. I think I'm just so thankful for not being in prison. Or shot. Or blown up. Or sucked into space."

Runstom joined in with a laugh of his own. "Seeing the glass half-full. That's so B-fourean of you."

"Oh sure," Jax said. "Well, keeping me out of prison and from getting shot and all that stuff is every uh – what do you like to be called?"

Runstom's laugh turned into a sigh. "Space-born, I suppose. My mother was from Sirius-5, if that helps."

Jax peered at him thoughtfully. "You were telling the truth to those workers earlier. About not knowing your father?"

"It helps to sprinkle the truth into these conversations," he said. "While undercover, I mean. Makes it easier to get into the flow if it's not one hundred percent false."

"I see. So, your mother?"

"That part I made up." Runstom looked down for a moment and then back at Jax. "I'm sorry. I know you lost your mother when you were young."

Jax shook his head. "It's okay." After a moment of silence during which they nursed a pair of drinks, Jax changed the subject. "Do you think we'll find it? I mean, is it even here?"

Runstom blew the air out of his cheeks. "There's a chance. And we better take it. We were lucky to make it out of that attack alive."

He stopped suddenly, his voice catching in his throat. They *had* been lucky, and many others had not. Fellow ModPol employees. Convicts who weren't innocent but didn't all deserve to die. And people like his friend George Halsey. He had to take another sip of his drink just to swallow. It was weak and cheap, as they had been at it all night and needed to stay sharp so they could talk to as many people as possible. But in that moment, he wanted the strongest drink they made. It was as though he hadn't even realized that George was his friend. His only friend. And now he had none. He had an association with an alleged murderer. Maybe he believed Jack Jackson was innocent simply because the only other option would be for Runstom to be completely alone.

"I believe it's here," Jax said. "Because if it's not, I'm fucked."

Runstom smiled and slapped the tall, thin man on the shoulder. "Yeah, you are. Probably me too, when my bosses find out I'm helping you. So come on. Let's get deeper into trouble while we still can."

Day after day rolled by. They interviewed hundreds of people. The floor of their room was piled high with notebooks, the walls covered with the profiles of suspects. Runstom had declared that someone had to fit into one of three categories to be worth considering. First: a crew-member, either greedy or desperate for cash. Second: a passenger that looked out of place, like someone else had footed the bill. And third: someone who could afford a cruise, but had a past. Someone who got to where they were by stepping on others. Someone in a position to be extorted.

Jax thought the last category was pretty far-fetched, but the ModPol officer was always reminding him that anything was possible, and they had to consider all potential scenarios, even those that seemed only remotely likely.

As the days rolled by, Jax's life as a LifSup operator began to feel farther and farther away. It was like being on a vacation that he knew would never end – or at least, it wouldn't end with a Monday back at the office. Day and night they talked to people, made notes, compiled them, and debated. Their lives became nothing but eating, sleeping, and trying to find anyone who might own or who might have seen a transmitter.

Somewhere around the fifth day, they got word of their own deaths. ModPol had managed to keep the attack on the prisoner barge quiet for a couple of days, but eventually the press had their way. Space Waste wasn't named specifically, but they learned that the barge had been decimated by space-to-space torpedoes. Life on the cruise ship seemed to be a world of its own, and Jax and Runstom might have even been alone in watching the news report, for all they knew. Certainly none of the other passengers or crew talked about it. The only two survivors of the attack refrained from the subject as well.

It was that closed-world feel of the cruise that allowed the two to so easily talk to as many people as possible. Everyone there was overly comfortable with everyone else – as long as they dressed the part, they fit right in. The stack of Alliance Credits they found stashed in the Space Waste-stolen personnel transport helped out. They acquired a few fancy outfits at some of the many shopping malls on the superliner. They bartered with wait staff, ship operators, cleaners, and other workers about the ship for various uniforms.

For weeks, they pretended to be other people. Once Runstom loosened up, his old dreams of going undercover seemed to take over. He was able to role-play more naturally, hamming it up with everyone they met. It was amusing to see him in action, this rigid, awkward man fitting in so easily – as long as he was pretending to be someone else. After a while, the undercover stuff started to rub off on Jax, and he came to terms with the fact that at the present he should be either locked up and awaiting a fixed trial for charges of mass homicide or alternatively slaughtered at the hands of a bloodthirsty space-gang. Instead, he had to play-act to hundreds upon hundreds of people for the next few weeks, and if that stoic, hard-nosed ModPol officer could enjoy it, then Jax might as well enjoy it too.

The working class on the ship were generally pretty friendly, and the two men, while undercover, felt like they could come right out and ask most people if they'd seen anything strange – like a large electronic device with an antenna or dish sticking out of it – and they'd get an honest answer. Most people didn't even want an explanation, and those that did earned an earful of Jax's half-nonsense technobabble. One day they might be looking for some device used to measure background radiation in space, and the next, like they told Bob the maintenance guy, it was a rogue asteroid-detector. Whenever anyone did ask too many questions, Runstom would manage to deflect suspicion – more often than not with bombball talk. The galactic pastime was a big hit with people who had spent years of their lives working on a floating island of isolation.

The paying passengers – most of whom were B-threers – were all too eager to socialize, being heavy subscribers to the it's-not-who-you-are-but-who-you-know philosophy. Names dropped out of their mouths like water from a faucet, and they carried around pictures of off-ship material possessions, presenting them like badges of honor. Runstom and Jax decided it was better to lose the work talk and to pretend to be rich and on vacation when talking to passengers. They didn't have any photographic evidence to back up their fabricated existences, but that didn't inhibit anyone from believing them. If anything, it seemed to make folk more enamored, reveling in the mystery of the two newcomers, closing their eyes tightly and letting their imaginations run wild as the two men described their worldly riches in great detail. Runstom's exotic skin color helped with the fiction, and after a while Jax learned to take advantage of his own skin color, inventing stories that took him from B-4 rags to B-3 riches.

The cruise patrons weren't bad people; Jax had to keep telling himself that. Some of them were just unfortunate enough to be born into more money than anyone could spend in a lifetime, and victims of the shallowness that comes so naturally to that lifestyle. One thing they loved more than anything was gossip, and Runstom and Jax learned to trade rumors and hearsay on the superliner like cigarettes in prison. They had established a system for determining the value of each tidbit of information they came home with; how likely it was to be true or false. Jax had them calculating numbers based on corroboration between a number of people and whether each person had more falsehoods or more truths in their gossip-wallet. Boiling things down to logic and numbers was the only way the operator could get his head around the mountainous task of getting to know the motivations and secrets of as many passengers as possible. Besides, it felt so odd to be away from a console for so long that he felt like he had to do something with formulas and variables or he'd forget his own name. To these mathematical determinations, Runstom added his natural cop gut-feeling intuition, which Jax had to admit, was generally pretty accurate.

Roughly three weeks after the day they boarded the super-liner, they decided to take a more focused approach.

"We've only got a few more weeks before we get in shuttle range of Barnard-3," Runstom said while doing push-ups on the floor of their tiny room. "And then we'll lose some passengers and take on new ones. We need to start playing the odds. How many of the employees have we talked to now?"

Jax sat on his bed and flipped through a notebook that contained the most recent summary information. "We've covered about 95 percent of the employees."

"And their guilt-probability scores?"

"All relatively low." There was gossip among the workers, just as there was among the passengers, but the workers didn't talk much about shady pasts; their gossip mainly had to do with who was sleeping with whom. The *working-class stiff out to collect a big paycheck* suspect classification had nearly been eliminated by this point.

"Good," Runstom said. "I think we need to target the highest-scoring passengers."

"What do you mean, 'target'?" Jax asked, looking up from the notes. "We've already talked some of them blue in the face."

"Exactly. It's time to start looking for hard evidence." Runstom stood and walked over to the profile wall, where they hung details of some of the higher-scoring passengers. "We've become close enough to some of the workers. I think we can get some of them to go into rooms for us. Cleaning crews, maintenance crews – those types can come and go as they please without arousing suspicion." He turned and looked at Jax. "We'd have to compensate them somehow. We've still got a few thousand Alleys—"

"Eh," Jax grunted, cutting the other man off. "These people, they don't want money. They can't spend it. They get room and board as part of their employment here. They don't have any bills. They get a big fat paycheck when they get done with their multi-year tour of duty. We need something that can entice them here and now."

"Then what?" Runstom said. "We can try to buy something of value from some passengers, but I don't think they'll be interested in selling. They've got more money than they can spend as it is."

Jax looked down. He had hoped to keep this little secret to himself, but he felt like it was time to come clean. "Remember when we came out of Xarp, and I didn't talk for the next five hours or so?" he asked, head still down.

"Yeah. Worst case of Xarp sickness I've ever seen. Like a junky, stoned out of—" Runstom stopped in mid-sentence as Jax looked up at him. "You sonova bitch," he whispered. "Drugs? On my ship?"

"I'm sorry, Stan. I was a little freaked out. The near-death experience and all."

Runstom looked back at the profile wall. "Where did you get them?" he asked, his voice like ice. "And what are they?"

The officer's suddenly cold and indifferent tone made Jax's hairs stand on end. "They were stashed in one of the equipment lockers, behind some guns. Delirium-G. Pill form." He left out the part where Prosser made a deal with him to reveal the hiding place of the pills in exchange for feeding him a dose. The foul-mouthed Space Waste pilot was pretty heavily restrained in the cargo bay and Jax had felt a little sorry for him, so he agreed.

The officer was quiet for a while, and Jax just let him be. There were worse things in the world than D-G, and Jax knew that Runstom knew it. Let him throw his little cop-minded mini-tantrum. Finally, he said, "I should make you jettison them." Then he turned around, his demeanor lighter. "But ModPol law on drugs varies to a large degree from one contract to another. And since I'm only well-versed on the Barnard-4 contract, I have no idea what the law is regarding Delirium-G on a Royal Starways Superliner."

"Oh," Jax said, a little thrown off by that statement. Having never left his planet before this month, he had not considered the fact that the law wasn't the same everywhere. He'd always thought that part of the point of having an organization like ModPol around was to have a consistent set of laws across multiple populations.

"Additionally, we're currently conducting an improvised undercover operation, so I cannot make any attempts to call this in to ModPol HQ. Furthermore, it is acceptable to commit minor criminal or questionable acts while undercover in order to establish connections or discover evidence."

"It is?" Jax said, wishing he hadn't questioned that last part as soon as it came out of his mouth.

"Well, yeah. I mean, they do it all the time in the holo-vids."

"Oh, yeah, that's true." Jax was lost in thought for a moment, and Runstom was too, apparently, because a silence grew between them. After a few minutes, he decided it was time to lay out the obvious, for the sake of progress. "So, uh. Here's an idea: how about we offer some Delirium-G to some employees in exchange for getting them to do a little digging into the rooms of a few passengers?"

"Let the record show that I do not condone the use of these drugs," Runstom said in some bizarre, half-wooden voice. "But I agree that this may be our best course of action at the current juncture, and time is of the essence."

What record? was the response that Jax managed to keep to himself. "So noted," he said, in a mock-official tone. "Let us proceed, Officer Runstom."

Jax didn't have a whole lot of experience with Delirium-G, but he'd encountered it a few times. Maybe more than the average person; especially the average B-fourean. After his mother passed, he went through a phase during which he spent a lot of time in the underground corridors of Blue Haven. He mostly drowned his grief in a glass, but he did some occasional gambling, and that had led him to his first introduction to the stuff. In one of the more shady gambling dens, during a card game, a woman had tossed a pill onto the table in place of money. A final, desperate attempt to win back some of her losses. It had not been long since Irene Jackson was in the accident when Jax first learned that his father was going to move to B-3 with his soon-to-be second wife. That night, Jax was on a mission to hit rock bottom, trying to gamble away the small amount of savings he had left. Fate conspired against him and doled out a stingingly ironic streak of good luck. Jax had taken many hands over the course of a few hours, including the one with the Delirium-G pill as a bet.

He was feeling low enough to abuse a substance he'd never encountered before, figuring that if he couldn't lose his money, he could at least lose his mind. Again his intention to bottom out was thwarted. The drug did not have the detrimental effect that public-service announcements often described. He couldn't remember most of the experience anymore, but he could remember finding a small amount of peace with the loss of his mother for the first time that night.

Despite the benefits the drug had brought him, Jax knew better than to fall into a trap of relying on it. It had gotten him over a hump (or perhaps more accurately, out of a trough), but he knew the danger in becoming dependent on a chemical. After that first encounter, he'd sought it out again about a week later, while still frequenting the underground. The second time was already noticeably weaker than the first, so he decided to avoid it after that. A few years later, he'd gotten a couple of pills because his girlfriend Priscilla wanted to try it. Since then, he hadn't even seen it again until that day on the stolen transport, when Prosser told him where some was stashed in a compartment on the vessel.

Since they had gotten the stuff out again to use as currency with the employees, he pocketed one. He wasn't sure if he even wanted it, and maybe he would just get rid of it. But it was hard to pass up the last chance to hold on to just one.

For a few days, it burned a hole in his pocket. He wouldn't be able to hold on to the pill for long; he knew he'd be in real trouble if Runstom found out he'd kept one. He thought he'd better just flush it, but then one day Runstom was gone for a while, off bargaining with some cleaning staff. Jax was left alone for a few hours.

As much as he generally disliked life in the domes on Barnard-4, it was his home, and being away from it for so long was having an effect on his nerves. It didn't help that he was working with a cop who was a lot more used to both the travel and the work. The whole being falsely accused of mass-homicide and facing life imprisonment thing just might have been another factor in the fraying of his edges, but who was he to say, really? He popped the pill and headed for one of the mini-domes that speckled the superliner.

He found himself sitting in a deckchair, watching the stars go by impossibly, yet not imperceptibly, slowly. He felt the weight of gravity – not heavier, just pulling more significantly. Tugging, more accurately. A sporadic tugging at his limbs, never all at once, just one here, then there, as if he could detect the microscopic machinations of the artificial gravity pumps deep in the center of the ship. His vision wasn't affected much, as long as his head was still. If a sound caught his attention and he turned to look, the scene seemed to pan slowly, as if some unseen holo-vid director was attempting to create a sense of bigness and tension. His thoughts ultimately unfocused on the final destination of his gaze, instead lost in the journey it took to get there.

He watched the buzzing of the humans around the ship, the little clockwork bees with jerking movements of the limbs zipping to and fro, stopping to get pollen from the bar and storing it somewhere internally, as if there were a plan to return it to a hive where it could become sweet, sticky honey over time. They sometimes visited him to make conversation, which he would review in his head, as if he were a book-reader at that moment rather than a participant in the dialogue.

At some point he found some headphones. They might have been delivered by a deckhand, or they might have been in his pocket. They were on his head now, and the clockwork bee-people danced across the deck, their legs slaves to the rhythm of the bass-a-tron, their arms and heads swaying with the wavtar. Music was almost non-existent on B-4. It was there, but it was always in the background, always light and airy. There were never percussive rhythms or the warping and layering of instruments he was hearing now.

Eventually, he would have to use the restroom. The internal reminder system was polite and patient, but he knew it would be too humble and it would let him ignore it indefinitely, which would ultimately lead to some other discomfort. If he tried to psych himself up for the journey across the deck to the facilities, the anxiety would overwhelm him. The best course of action was to pretend it wasn't going to happen, then simply surprise himself by standing up and walking. A few steps in, once the surprise had faded, he had to regulate his speed. The temptation to run was strong, but he knew to run would mean to fall.

"Do you know what it's like to run? Do you know what it's like to live in fear?" The attendant-bot didn't answer his question, but instead offered him a towel. He took it, and cleared his throat. "I accept this gift on behalf of all humans in the galaxy. This is a momentous step forward for robo-human relations." He hugged the thing, but it was not exactly receptive.

There was a well-known D-G rule about being in the bathroom: never look in the mirror. If you happened to look in the mirror, for fuck's sake, do not make eye contact with yourself. There's a very good chance that you won't recognize the person staring back at you.

Jax looked in the mirror.

"Murderer," he said, maybe out loud, maybe in his head. "Fugitive. That's not me. That's the body I have to occupy because I didn't play their game. I didn't fulfill my *potential*. I didn't grow up to be anyone *important*, so I got to be a pawn in someone *else's* game." He looked at the attendant-bot. "I was like you, you know? Instead of handing out towels in a small bathroom, I handed out oxygen in a small residential block. People lived there, you know. Thirty or forty real, live people. They were just restroom patrons to me."

He grabbed the bot by the towel-arm. "What happens when you don't give someone a towel?" He shook the arm, to little effect. "What happens, huh? Do they die? Do they fucking die? Because that's what happens when you don't hand out oxygen. People fucking die."

Jax looked back at the mirror. "You killed thirty-two fucking people, you sonova bitch. You worthless sonova bitch. You held the gun while someone else pulled the trigger. You pawn. Run, pawn, run. Run one square at a time, like the pathetic pawn you are."

He found himself at the bar. The D-G was starting to fade away, bit by bit. He sent a drink into his system to try to throw it off. "Here, work on this. Keep the D-G around for another hour." Then he had another drink because this was a superliner and the drinks were goddamn fantastic.

"Maybe you're better off this way," he said, back in the bathroom, looking in the mirror. It was either the same visit or a return visit, he wasn't sure. Maybe he was just remembering it. His reflection stared at him expectantly. He felt older. His baby-face had finally begun to age properly, and staring at himself now, his features reminded him of his father. "You disappoint me, Jax," he said through his father's mouth. "This never would have happened to you if you'd gone back to engineering school; if you'd come to live with us on B-3 and got out of the sub-domes. If you'd done something with your life, besides *waste* it." The word "waste" was a tearing sound, like the jagged whoosh of someone ripping paper.

It was the nose and mouth that were his father's, so he began to look elsewhere, searching for his mother. Did he have his mother's eyes? He looked at his own eyes, into the pale-gray irises that he shared with almost all other B-foureans, searching for his mother there among those listless clouds. He felt lost and sad, and the clouds grew darker, thicker. His eyes watered and he blinked briefly, and then suddenly she was there. She did share his eyes, and he could see her seeing him. She had no mouth and no voice, but she could see him. She couldn't tell him what to do. She could only watch.

He wanted her to tell him what to do. He wanted to hear her voice come out of his mouth. But she could not. And he knew that she would not have if she could. She never told him what to do. Even when she knew he was doing something wrong – she just watched.

He blinked again and she was gone. He looked at his mouth, but his father was gone too. He felt very alone. No father to tell him what to do, always disappointed. No mother to watch over him, always proud, abstaining from offering guidance. Was this what he wanted, to be on his own, to make his own decisions, to guide his own fate?

He looked away from the mirror. Whether or not he wanted it, his parents weren't there. No more wallowing in pity or self-doubt. If he had any chance of getting out of the mess he was in, he was going to have to grow the fuck up.

Runstom found him later in a rain room, sitting soberly in a plain, white, plastic chair at a small, white, plastic table underneath a canopy, rain drizzling down on three sides.

"I never understood this," muttered the officer, taking in the scene. "There are beautiful views of the stars from all over this ship. Now the sun rooms, I can understand. The little fake beaches and the little green parks with the blue-sky domes. Sure, stars are beautiful, but feeling like it's night every hour of the day – yeah, I can see why people would want sun rooms. But a rain room?"

"Back in Gretel," Jax started, staring outward. A small, thin cluster of trees surrounded the canopied area, rain pattering against their leaves. "In Gretel, we make rain in our blocks. Remember, the RAIN command? And its stupid warning requirement? Hard to get spontaneous rain in dome cities. Air scrubbers regulate the amount of water in the controlled atmosphere. We can't have people getting wet in their perfect little bubbles. Sometimes I wonder what it's like on a planet with a real atmosphere."

Runstom sat down next to the operator. "I've been to a few. Only moons, though." Jax turned and looked at him, a tiny hint of expectation on his face. "It rains more often than you'd think, in some places. And you have to get all kinds of rain-gear, to keep from getting soaked, and to keep your equipment safe. Sometimes it's damn cold, and instead of rain you get snow or hail. You have to wrap up, or get into a heated suit." He looked out into the rain, thoughtfully. "Sure does break up the monotony, though. Real weather is good at keeping you on your toes."

"I come here sometimes," Jax said. "I'd like to say, I come here to think, but everywhere I go on this ship, I go to think. But sometimes I come here, and I try not to plan it. I try to get up in the morning and tell myself I'm in for something unexpected today. And then I find myself in a rain room, and I go stand in the rain for a minute and pretend that the weather changed without warning, and I'm caught in it." He laughed suddenly. "They don't like it when you do that, you know. They don't want you to go out there," he said, gesturing toward the trees. "The walls start beeping at you and if you stay too long, some security guys will show up and tell you to 'get the hell outta the scenery'."

"Mm," Runstom murmured, letting a bit of quiet time pass before continuing. "One time I lived in a jungle for a couple weeks, on a moon in the Sirius system. Rained all the time, without warning, then it would be sun again. Rain, sun, rain, sun, nothing in between. It was hot there, though, so hot that the rain felt like a warm shower. People didn't run around hysterically when it came, like they do in other places. They just kept on living. If you had any equipment that wasn't waterproof, you knew you better protect it before taking it outside. Other than that, people didn't even use umbrellas. The rain would come, and we'd just walk around in it. Just another fact of life, like the need to breathe oxygen or the laws of gravity."

"When this is over," Jax said, "however it turns out, whether we catch the people that did this or not, I'm not going back to B-4. I can't."

The officer stood up and put a hand on the other man's shoulder. "Someone out there is responsible for the deaths of thirty-two people. I've seen plenty of death in my job – mostly accidental, but sometimes by murder. But I've never seen anyone do something this foul." He squeezed his grip. "I am going to find out who did this. And you're going to help me. And when we're done, you can go wherever you goddamn well please, Jax. As will I."

Jax looked up at him, but was at a loss for words. Runstom said, "Come on. We've got work to do."

CHAPTER 11

Not everyone was interested in the Delirium-G offer, but the number of people that were surprised Runstom. Before long, they had a miniature army of investigators at their beck and call. They searched, they scoured, they dug deep into the room of every suspect. These workers knew all the hiding places; the corners of drawers and cupboards, the inconspicuous maintenance panels, the insides of furniture cushions. No stone was left unturned.

It was a few days later when there was a single knock at the door of their room. When Runstom opened it, he saw no one in the hallway. There was an envelope taped to the outside of the door. It contained a slip of paper with a number on it and a MagiKey card.

They cross-referenced the room number with their list of suspects. They didn't know everyone's room, but they had this one. It was Linda Parson, from the city-dome Yorkenshire on Barnard-3. She was a politician; head coordinator of a sub-dome of Yorkenshire called Jersey. Runstom looked over the other notes they had on her. She was only riding the superliner from a research colony in the asteroid field just outside B-4, back in to B-3. She'd made a visit to the colony to support efforts to find a cure for gravity-lag, a debilitating condition that many planet-hoppers experienced. She had coincidentally timed the end of the visit to align with the passing of Superliner #5, and had hopped aboard to rub elbows with some large pocketbooks that also happened to suffer the effects of gravity-lag every few years or so. It was rumored that she planned to run for mayor of Yorkenshire in the next cycle. However, this was a pretty unsurprising revelation since mayorship was the next rung up on the political ladder, making it a common goal for sub-dome coordinators.

Runstom's favorite detail about Linda Parson was that she'd won the election for Jersey head coordinator against her closely matched opponent, Timothy Eagelson, when it was unexpectedly revealed that Eagelson's wife had undergone controversial magnetic-flux therapy to treat her depression. Despite the Eagelsons' denial of the whole ordeal, the press managed to get a hold of some damning documentation of the procedure, and many pundits questioned whether the Eagelsons might be part of a particularly small and unpopular cult whose beliefs centered around the power of magnets over the body and mind. Parson won the election in a landslide. A suspicious political victory; Runstom allowed himself to feel a lightness, a small amount of hope, because this put her high on his list.

Runstom and Jax put on their cleaning-crew uniforms and found the room. It was on the fourteenth deck, room number 1468. They knocked politely and waited a few minutes. After a silent exchange of anxious looks, Runstom stuck the MagiKey card in the door and they went in.

The place was a mess. Clothing was strewn about the room recklessly. There was a definite smell of something sour, something past its prime. There was even a hint of smoke, like something had burned at some point. Something plastic.

"Okay," Runstom said. "Let's hit the cupboards and the closets first. Then we'll check the hatches and—"

"Uh," Jax said, interrupting him. He was standing next to the desk in the room. He cautiously lifted a soiled towel (soiled with what, they chose not to investigate), and revealed a large, silver box.

Runstom came over and they inspected the box. It was about thirty centimeters tall, and thirty centimeters wide, but not a perfect cube; maybe forty or so centimeters long the other way. There was a small panel on the top that featured a handful of buttons and indicator lights. There were large red arrows painted down each of the long sides of the box. A black cable stuck out of the back of it, and coiled about two meters in length along the floor.

"What do these buttons do?" Runstom asked. "And the lights – what do they do?"

"Only one way to find out." Jax grinned, giving Runstom a look the officer wasn't sure how to read. "Plug it in. We either do it here, or take it back to our room and do it."

"That's the operator in you talking," Runstom said, fingering some screws in the sides of the box. He looked Jax in the eyes. "An *engineer* would say, let's pop it open."

Jax's mouth twisted in multiple directions, then he let it curl into a smile. "A playful jab from Officer Runstom. Someone's in a good mood." He looked around the room. "We could find something to stick under the towel. I wonder if she would even notice that it was gone."

"Probably not." Runstom nudged a thin, cardboard box on the floor with his toe. The box was lying on its side and documents were half-spilling out of it. "She doesn't appear to be very organized."

"I guess it's a matter of whether she plans to use it again. We've already considered it might have been a one-shot thing."

"Yes, but then she would have gotten rid of it," was Runstom's logical conclusion.

"That would make sense," Jax said, rubbing his nose. "But then again, she hasn't bothered to get rid of whatever is producing that nauseating odor."

"Good point. So, to reiterate – *if* this is the device we're looking for, we don't know if it was used for a one-shot attack or if the owner is planning to use it again, say, when we get closer to Barnard-3."

"So we'll just borrow it for a night and then bring it back tomorrow," Jax said. "Whether it was going to be used again or not, the owner won't miss it for a while. We won't be within range of B-3 for another week at least."

"Alright. Let's get moving." Runstom made a move to pick the box up off the desk, but it was stuck there. He put a little more effort into the action, and it popped off after a moment of tugging. Something sticky was revealed on the desktop, and the pair looked at it disdainfully.

"Here's a question," Jax said. "If they have all these cleaning crews on this ship, why has this room not been cleaned in a month?"

"Because I told you motherfuckers to stay the fuck out of my room," slurred a voice that followed the opening of the door. "Hey," the woman said halfheartedly. "You should put that thing down. Actually, take it with you. Just get rid of it, it's garbage." She eyed the box, then looked up at Runstom, then over to Jax, then back to Runstom. "Yeah. Jettison it, okay? Or incinerate it. Whatever you guys do."

The two men stood motionless and dumbfounded. Linda Parson, a middle-aged woman, wearing a platinum, formal-wear jumpsuit, stumbled about the room with purpose. From a cupboard she produced a small foil package. She tore the package open. "You boys hungry?" She leaned in toward Runstom, and he could smell the sweet tang of alcohol from several paces away.

He felt his face harden. The officer had seen this level of degradation before. Linda Parson was a successful woman. She was on a goddamn cruise. She wasn't stressed about her life or her work. No – she was drinking herself stupid to escape something. The mark of a guilty conscience. Runstom shoved the box into Jax's hands and walked over to the door, slapping the trigger to force it closed.

"Linda Parson," he said.

She turned to look at him, then looked back at Jax and the box. She took a step back to try to get them both in view, but there just wasn't that much room, and she fell backward, landing on the bed. "Hey!" she said, agitated. "Who the fuck are you guys?" She looked long and hard at Runstom. "Why are you painted green? Are you cleaners or what?"

"No, Linda Parson," Runstom said. "We're not cleaners." He looked at Jax.

"I'm a LifSup operator," Jax said. "From block 23-D, Gretel, sub-dome of Blue Haven, Barnard-4."

"What?" Linda Parson said, bewildered. Then a look of recognition crossed her face. "Oh, shit," she breathed. "Oh, shit. Oh shit oh shit oh shit—"

"My name is Detective Runstom, of Modern Policing and Peacekeeping. Here are my credentials."

"Oh fuck." The woman didn't bother to look at Runstom's creds. "How did you find me?"

The men exchanged looks, and Runstom wondered if Jax noticed that he threw the word *Detective* in front of his name. With a hard stare he willed the operator to play along.

Jax set the box on the floor in front of Linda Parson. "Show us how it works. Please."

She looked at the box, then to Jax, then to Runstom. The officer said, "You'd better do as he says, ma'am." She stared at him blankly. His voice rose ever so slightly. "Show us. Now."

Goosebumps formed on the woman's arms. She sank off the bed and knelt in front of the box. "Are you going to arrest me? I didn't know what it was for!"

Jax looked at Runstom briefly, then knelt down beside her. "Linda. You've been set up to take the fall for something. Something terrible. If you help us, we can help you. Tell us about this box."

"No, I didn't know," she started. "Wait, yes – set up – that's what it was. It's not my box."

"And someone showed you how to work it, right?" Runstom strained to be consoling rather than hostile. "Just show us how to turn it on."

She nodded slowly, looking from Runstom to Jax. "Okay," she said finally. She ran her fingers over the panel and hit one of the switches. Nothing happened. "Um," she said, her face twisting in confusion.

Jax picked up the long black cable and handed the end of it to Runstom. "Off – err – Detective. Could you find an outlet for this please?"

Runstom took the cable and plugged it in. Linda Parson tried the switch again and the box whirred to life. The side that the red arrows were pointing to slid open and a small transponder-dish emerged from the inside of the device. "It's a transmitter of some kind," she said weakly. "But I didn't know what it transmitted. You gotta believe me!"

"Okay," Runstom said, putting his hands out. "Relax, Linda. Take a deep breath. Tell us what happened."

She tried to breathe deeply, but it came in shudders. "I got the transmitter when I was on Glomulus Serpentus. It's a research facility, near the asteroid ring. They use them to beam data back and forth between different-sized asteroids. For gravity-lag research." Runstom nodded, waiting patiently for her to get to the point. She continued, "Anyway, one of the workers on the base gave it to me. He told me I'd need it for my cruise back to B-3. It was all boxed up. I didn't even know what it was when they gave it to me."

"So when did you discover it was a transmitter?" Jax asked.

She flipped open a panel on the box, revealing a small slot. She poked at it, and a thin, little black square came out, about two centimeters long. "I had to put this in it. And then just take it to the outer deck, and set it down under my table. Turn it on and sit there for about twelve hours." She gave the black square to Runstom, who looked at it for a few seconds, then passed it to Jax. "It's some kind of chip. It arrived in a package, a few days after I got on board."

"What kind of package was it, Linda?" Runstom said, calmly.

"Um." She began fumbling over her words. "It was a box of cookies. It was a brown-wrapped package, like from one of the interplanetary delivery companies. Inside, it was a box of cookies. And this chip was hidden in that. He told me I'd be getting the chip in a package. He said to use the chip in the transmitter exactly four days after the package arrived."

"He?" Runstom stepped closer to her. "Who is he? Who told you to bring a transmitter on board?"

She swallowed hard. "He ... I don't know his real name. He's X."

"X?" Jax asked, and Runstom waved at him before he could ridicule the nickname.

"What delivery company was it that brought the cookies?" Runstom asked. "Do you remember? Do you still have the package material?"

"No," she said, quietly. "I threw it away."

Jax made a choking sound. "That'd be the only thing she threw away," he muttered under his breath, earning a sharp glance from Runstom. He frowned, then held up the chip. "The stealth program that infected my LifSup system – I'd bet everything I own that it's on this chip." He paused for a second. "I mean, pretend I actually own stuff – stuff that's really valuable. We need to get to a computer terminal or something with a port on it that can read this."

"What about the box?" Runstom said.

"It's just a transmitter. I doubt there's anything else of value in it. Of course, that would be assuming we believe Coordinator Parson's story." Linda Parson hung her head while the other two talked.

"Right." Runstom knelt beside the woman. "Linda. Tell us about X."

She lifted her head and stared forward at nothing. "I don't know who he is."

"But he knows you. He has something on you," the officer prodded. "You're in debt to him."

"Yeah." She nodded slowly. "It was the Jersey head coordinator elections. It was such a close election. I knew if I missed that chance, I'd never get a shot at a mayorship in the future. Losing an election can destroy your career. No one understands the risk you take when you run!"

"So you set out to make your opponent look bad," Jax said.

"Well, yeah. But it wasn't my idea. It was one of my aides, during the campaign. She said she knew a way to give me an edge. She said I wouldn't have to know how, that someone else could take care of it." She sniffled a little bit, and cleared her throat. "I said okay, just as long as no one got hurt. My aide said that X would take care of it. I just kept campaigning. After a couple more weeks, I even kind of forgot about the conversation. When Eagelson's wife made the news, I was as blown away as everyone else."

"When did you learn it was X?" Runstom asked.

Parson sighed. "Two days after the election results were in. I got a bouquet of flowers. I mean, I got lots of gifts from friends and supporters. But one bouquet had a note that just said, 'Congratulations on your victory.' It was signed 'X'. Normally I wouldn't have given it much thought. But something in the back of my mind warned me."

"Did you ask the aide about it?" Jax asked.

"She was gone. She collected her last paycheck and didn't show up to work after the election."

"Okay," Runstom said. "So when did you hear from X again?"

"It wasn't until I got the cookies. There was a card. Wait, I think I still have it!" She got up off the bed suddenly, wavered for a second or two, then went into a set of drawers and dug around. She pulled out a small, white, folded-over slip of paper and handed it to Runstom.

He opened it and read it. Jax tried to lean over and get a look, but the officer just folded it back up and stuck it in his pocket. "Okay, Linda. We're going to take the transmitter and the chip. You're not going anywhere for a while, so we're choosing to trust you. We'll be back to check on you ever other day or so. If you know anything else, it'd be wise to let us know."

"I just can't believe this," she said, her voice cracking. "I heard what happened to that block on B-4. I didn't believe it was me who did it. But now I know. I killed those people. I killed those innocent people!"

"No, Linda," Jax said, stepping in front of her. "You loaded the gun. I pointed the gun. But someone else pulled the trigger. This is not your fault, just like it's not my fault. Do you understand?"

She stared at Jax, or maybe through him. Runstom thought about his words, words he knew the operator was telling himself as much as he was telling Linda Parson.

Runstom said, "We're going to find this X. Just don't talk to anyone else about this whole thing. Nothing links you to any of this. Just ride out this cruise and then go home. We'll keep in touch."

"Okay," she said, with a swallow. "Thank you."

They walked most of the way back to their room in silence. When they reached their hallway, Jax finally spoke.

"So what are we going to do now?"

Runstom sighed. "I should be arresting her, or at least detaining her. Bring her in for questioning." He stopped.

"But you won't do that. Why not?"

"I'm not sure," Runstom said in a distant voice. "It feels – it just feels like there's a lot more to this."

Jax didn't ask for any more clarification. He thought back to Runstom identifying himself as *Detective* while talking to Linda Parson. As soon as Detective Runstom reconnected with ModPol, he'd go back to being Officer Runstom. And then it would be out of his hands. How far was this guy willing to go? How badly did he want to know the truth? How badly did he want to prove himself? Would he see it through to the end? Jax wasn't sure if it wouldn't be smarter to just turn himself in with the evidence they had up to this point, or if they needed more. Knowing in his heart that he'd been set up, he didn't want to put his faith in the ModPol judicial system just yet.

"And what did the note say?" he asked.

Runstom thrust the box into Jax's arms and got his MagiKey out to open the door. Then he took the box and set it down on the desk in their room. He pulled out the note and handed it to Jax. "First, you need to pull this box apart and check it for any other memory modules that might be able to store the code that was beamed down to your LifSup system's receiver. Second, we need to find out where the trash goes on this ship. We need to get a hold of that package that those cookies came in."

Jax read the note.

My back itches. Place the metal cookie in the box exactly four days from this very moment. Take the box up to a sitting deck on the port side, plug it in, and flip the green switch. Stay with it for twelve hours. —X

"What the hell does this mean? My back itches?"

"I scratch your back, you scratch mine," Runstom said. "As a politician, Linda Parson knew exactly what that means. She got help from our mysterious X, and she owed him a favor. She could either comply, or he could expose her. He probably has all kinds of evidence that ties her to the Eagelson controversy – which was probably fabricated."

"So if she didn't perform this seemingly simple task, she knew she'd be committing political suicide," Jax said. "She'd probably even go to prison."

"Exactly," the officer said, sifting through some of their notes.

Jax stared at the note thoughtfully. Then something struck him. "Did you just suggest we're going to go digging through the trash?"

"That's right. We need that package. It's our only lead."

Jax's first instinct was to get all incredulous about the notion that an empty package was a lead. He caught himself, and tried to think like his partner for a moment. "Um. Because it was delivered. By a delivery company. And we could figure out where it came from and maybe even who sent it?"

"Hey, not bad," Runstom said, still looking at some notes. "You could almost pass for a cop."

CHAPTER 12

A few of their last Delirium-G's and they had earned themselves a pair of Trash Operator uniforms and a full shift of work. Working in the trashitorium wasn't as dirty as it could be; Gar-bots did most of the heavy lifting. The TrashOps supervised the bots, inspected the containers, regulated the amount of trash that went into the incinerator; that kind of thing. Despite being on a superliner, the trashitorium wasn't much different than what the domes had back on B-4. Jax was surprised to find out it wasn't even much smaller.

The incinerator didn't actually have fire in it. It was a high pressure, high temperature structure that a trash container was emptied into and then bombarded with a particular kind of amplified cosmic radiation. All the material was broken down into individual molecules, which could then be sorted by various methods. First, the smallest microscopic holes would open in the structure and vacuums would suck out the smallest molecules – gases and the like. Then a series of increasingly larger holes opened in the sides of the structure while it spun around, creating artificially high gravity and pulling out molecules in groups of one element at a time.

Jax would have found the whole process interesting if he hadn't already seen it. He'd worked in a trashitorium back in Gretel, before he managed to crawl his way up the ladder to the glorious position of LifSupOp. It was a good thing too, because though they traded for the uniforms, they still needed to pretend to know the job, and Runstom had no clue.

With little in the way of hands-on work to be done, Jax and Runstom managed to get themselves a shift all alone, and Jax was showing Runstom the ropes, in particular the intake and outtake schedule.

"This is obscene," Runstom said as they checked out the data on a console. "It's completely backed up."

"Trashitoriums are always behind schedule," Jax said. "Even with such a refined process, it still takes time. And the people on this ship are outputting garbage non-stop."

Runstom nodded and hummed. "That's good then. That gives us better odds that the package is still around, right?"

"Yep," Jax said and tapped at some keys. "The oldest stuff in the containment queue is a little more than two weeks old. Now we just track Linda Parson's refuse."

Another feature of the average trashitorium that gave them an advantage was the almost malicious attention to detail. The bureaucracy enjoyed by TrashOps made them feel extremely important in an otherwise extremely banal job, but it also meant that any particular refuse container spent a significant amount of time in processing.

"Every container is meticulously labeled and verified," Jax explained as they dug through the database. "You want to know which containers have trash that came from room 1468 between this date and that date? It's like going to the library. We don't even really need this database. Someone who knows the system could just walk through the containers on the staging deck and find anything they wanted to."

"Then why are we looking in the database?"

Jax shook his head. "Come on, man, you can't expect me to remember everything from a job I had like eight years ago."

Before the end of their shift, they were down in that maze of refuse containers, following the hints that Jax managed to dig out of the console. After the better part of an hour, they found the container that had the garbage from room 1468 on the given week they calculated, based on Parson's story. The massive container was further broken into smaller cubes, perfectly packed and wrapped in plastic, each labeled with a unique identifier. Jax had to keep hitting the remote to divert the confused Gar-bots that periodically came around to attempt to clean up the mess they made as they dug through the stacks.

Finally they found the bag with the label they were looking for.

"Here goes," Runstom said and tore it open with a pocketknife.

They spread the contents out onto the floor. They'd been compressed and vacuum-sealed, so there was little decay among the organic matter – not that it made it any less repulsive – and the various plastic-based materials were flattened at odd angles.

"That," Jax said, pointing at a brown wrapper. "It says TerroPac, doesn't it?"

"TerroPac Express," Runstom said, flattening it out. "From Terroneous."

"The moon?"

Runstom ran his hand across the empty packaging, either to flatten it out more or to verify it was real and not a figment of his imagination; Jax wasn't sure which. Then the officer lifted his head. "This is it, Jax. This is a real lead."

It hit Jax then how significant the find was. They'd gone from chasing an impossibility to grasping something so tangible it refused denial.

They stood up and moved aside while the Gar-bots undid the mess they'd made.

"Well, shit," Jax said. "Now what do we do?" He wondered if it was time to contact the rest of ModPol, but he hesitated in suggesting it. As solid as the lead felt, he couldn't imagine a scenario in which they would let him off the hook on just a lead.

"I don't know," Runstom said. "We have options. Come on."

"Officer Stanford Runstom. This is Captain Inmont. A ModPol patroller scanned Royal Starways Interplanetary Cruise Delight Superliner #5 last week and according to their docking logs, your credentials were used as identification there a few weeks ago."

"We understand you came aboard the superliner with an unidentified passenger. We're sending a wagon out to pick you up. Along with whomever you've got with you, if it's another ModPol employee or a prisoner. Of course, that's assuming the person listening to this message is Officer Stanford Runstom. If you're not Runstom, and you've illegally used his credentials, you will be arrested immediately."

The audio clip crackled and then died out. Runstom stared at the speaker in silence. Jax stood behind him and turned the empty package they retrieved from the trashitorium over and over, as if he hadn't already examined every centimeter of it.

Finally, Jax said, "Well, I guess you can't stay dead forever."

Runstom didn't look up. "Get everything together. We're leaving very soon."

"How long do you think it will take them to get here?" Jax said weakly.

Runstom ignored him, punching a button on the com.

"ComOp," the speaker said, after a few pops.

"This is Runstom, one of the guests staying in the spare servants' quarters. Room C-28."

"Yes, sir, I've got your room number on the display here. What can I help you with?"

"I just listened to a message. Can you tell me when it was received?"

"Yes, sir." Some tapping came through over the speaker. "The only message you got today came in about two and a half hours ago. It was listened to by you about three minutes ago."

"Please reset its status to 'unlistened'." Runstom's voice took on the tone it adopted when he wanted to be clear that he was issuing a non-negotiable command.

"Um, okay," the ComOp said. "I guess I can do that."

"Then do it."

"Um." Tapping sounds. "Okay, Mister Runstom. You have one message received approximately two and a half hours ago. It has not been listened to. Is there any—"

Runstom stabbed the disconnect button on the com. Jax looked at him curiously. "What was that all about?"

"We don't have a lot of time before they get here." Runstom began rummaging around the room, pulling out a bag and throwing it on his bed. He began pulling notebooks off the desk and tossing them at the bag. "We need to get our shit together and get out of here."

172

"Wait, what? You're not going to wait for your captain?"

Runstom stopped packing and looked at Jax. "We're too close now. We have the data chip and the package it was delivered in."

"And Linda Parson is still on board. With the chip and the package, don't you think that's enough evidence to—"

"No, dammit!" Runstom's olive skin was flush, turning it a strange color. "Listen to me, Jax. If they catch us here, they're going to shut down this investigation. They're going to toss this evidence into a locker and forget about it."

Jax put his hands over his face and began rubbing his eyes. "Look, Stanford. If you leave now, you're going to be in real deep shit."

"What do you know—"

"Don't give me that shit, Stan." Jax pulled his hands away from his face and glared at the officer. "I'm not an idiot. You could just sit and wait for ModPol to get here and tell a harrowing tale of how you managed to escape the attack on that prison ship. They won't be happy that you didn't report in right away, but you'll get off without much more than a warning." He stepped forward, pointing a long finger at Runstom. "This is your last chance, though. If you take off now, they're going to say you're aiding a fugitive. And then you're not going to be a cop anymore. You're going to be a criminal. You can't risk your career – and your freedom – for someone like me."

Runstom was quiet for a minute. He stared at Jax long and hard. The only sound in the room was a low hum coming from the air vent and time seemed to stand still. "Jackson, it's not just for you," the officer finally said in measured tones. "You're innocent. I know that now, beyond the shadow of a doubt. And if you're innocent and they convict you, then they've locked up the wrong man." His voice began to slowly get louder. "When the wrong person is convicted of a crime, that in itself is a travesty. But it's not just injustice for the wrongly convicted. It's injustice for the victims." Now it was Runstom's turn to point, and Jax reflexively took a step back. "And right now if they haul your ass to prison, it means there's a murderer out there roaming free and they are just pretending he doesn't exist. The real murderer is responsible for the deaths of thirty-two people and I'm not going to let him get away with it. Proving your innocence means bringing someone else to justice."

Runstom turned away and started furiously grabbing clothes out of the closet. "Now get your shit together because we need to get off this goddamn superliner ASAP."

Less than half an hour later, they were back in the stolen personnel vessel. It was repainted and stocked up on food and fuel. Over the weeks they'd cleaned it out a little, but there wasn't much in it that had needed disposing of. They'd kept all the weapons, the armor, and the spacesuits. They brought a few changes of clothing with them, a couple crates of wine, and the opened package that Linda Parson's cookies came in.

By the label they could see that it was delivered by TerroPac Express, a delivery company located on Terroneous, one of the moons that orbited Barnard-5. There were some other data on the label, but Jax and Runstom couldn't make heads or tails of it, other than the number of the office on the moon that the package was shipped from. No matter what, getting to Terroneous was the first step; from there, they'd have to find the next.

Jax wasn't really sure about how much trouble Runstom had gotten himself into by this point. He was not convinced that the officer would get off with simply a strict talking-to from his captain, and he was still feeling the pangs of guilt about it as they prepped the ship for takeoff. He knew this was the last chance that Runstom had to turn back and forget the whole thing and live his life just like he did before he met the operator.

Whenever Jax tried to broach the subject, in those last few moments docked in the superliner, he would look at Runstom and see the determination on his face. The officer was capable of making his own decisions. It would be an insult to question his courage or his dedication. Runstom was a detective stuck in a dead-end officer position, much like Jax was stuck in his dead-end life. Except Runstom actually had the will to move up. Jax had the talent, and had always allowed himself to wallow in mediocrity. Just because he'd always been content to be stagnant, he didn't have the right to discourage Runstom from taking control of a situation. Even if it did mean cutting off the easy route.

"Fuck the easy route," Jax said, not exactly to himself as they sat in the cockpit of the vessel, about to undock from the superliner.

Runstom gave him a look, but it wasn't a look like he wondered what the hell Jax was muttering about. It was more of a look that said, *It's about damn time.*

CHAPTER 13

It was probably a day, or a couple of days, maybe, before they reached Barnard-5. Xarp time was hard to gauge. They didn't have the benefit of cryo-sleep, like an inter-stellar ship would, and they couldn't do a whole lot of moving around. Jax wanted to bring up the point that this was why the gangbangers had Delirium-G on board, but it wouldn't do him any good anyway; they bartered the whole supply away on the superliner. Eventually, count-less hours into the trip, he started to mention it out loud anyway. Whether it would do any good or not, he needed something to gripe about to keep from losing his mind. Runstom mostly ignored him.

"What did you say?" Jax asked after they'd come out of Xarp speed and set a course for the moon orbiting the nearby planet.

"Huh? I didn't say anything," Runstom said groggily. "I thought you were talking."

"Oh. I thought you said 'approximate a yurt'."

"What's a yurt?" Runstom said, raising an eyebrow.

"How the hell should I know?"

"Approximate a yurt."

"What?" Jax looked at Runstom, trying to focus on the other man's face with intense concentration. It blurred in and out of focus elusively.

The whole cockpit turned red. "Warning," said someone other than Runstom. Jax watched the other man's lips not move. "Proximity alert."

A rushing, screaming sound came out of nowhere with an alarming crescendo and the whole vessel shook. After a second or two the sound died out and a streak of white crossed the black of space visible through their front viewport.

"Warning," mentioned an electronic voice. The red light of the cabin pulsed with each syllable. "Proximity alert."

"What the fuck was that?" Jax tried to shake himself awake. "Was that another ship? What the hell were they doing?"

"Goddamn. Yeah, it was. I don't know what they're doing. Where's that contact map, goddammit?" Runstom asked himself as he poked and prodded at some controls. The small holo-vision screen in the middle of a panel just below the viewport in front of them lit up with a series of concentric ovals on two axes. A pair of green arrows floated about on the screen.

"Looks like there's two of them," Jax said. The green arrows were on opposite ends of the holo-view. "Are they trying to circle us? Can the computer tell us who they are?"

"They're friendly," Runstom said, allowing himself to relax a little, which only made Jax more anxious, afraid that his partner was letting his guard down. "Don't worry about it. If they were hostile, they'd be red."

"Oh. Um. How does the – uh – contact map – know when another ship is hostile or not? I presume from your over-whelmingly calm demeanor that it knows sometime before they start shooting at you ..."

"Yeah, you know." Runstom talked through a yawn. "Drive signatures and stuff. The contact computer has a little database of the stuff that makes ships unique. Green means it's a vessel your contact computer knows to be a friendly. Red is a known hostile. Yellow is a vessel it can't identify."

"Okay." Jax tried to keep his breathing steady, but then he stopped breathing altogether. "Tell me you had this contact database reset back when we were docked with the superliner."

"Huh? Why would—" Runstom bolted upright suddenly, straining against the seat restraints. "Oh, shit. We're in a Space Waste ship! Green means friendly to Space Waste!"

Runstom grabbed for the throttle. Suddenly, a series of high pitched waves of sound could be heard all around them, and the cockpit shook violently.

"What the hell do we do?" Jax screamed over the ship's steady stream of sudden warning messages.

"I gotta get us out of here," Runstom yelled, yanking on the throttle. "They're firing on us. They must recognize this ship as the one that was stolen during the prisoner-barge episode."

"Can we Xarp away?"

"We're too close to Barnard-5," Runstom said, still trying to wrestle with the throttle. "You need as close to exactly zero Gs as possible to hit Xarp or you'll rip yourself apart."

"Primary thrusters are off-line," stated the ship's disembodied voice. The viewport showed the planet in the distance slowly moving from side to side.

"All I got left is stabilizers." Exasperated, Runstom slapped the control stick away.

"Doesn't this thing have any guns?" Jax said desperately.

"There's an auto-turret." Runstom flipped a switch. Nothing happened.

"Auto-turret inactive," the computer said. "No hostile targets available."

"Motherfucker, are you kidding me? The contact computer is still showing them as friendly!" He looked at Jax. "Activate the terminal in front of you! You have to tell that thing that those bastards are hostile!"

Jax fumbled with the controls at his station. A panel rolled over exposing a keyboard and one of the larger monitors lit up. It read "SYSTEM READY."

"What do I do?"

Runstom was poking at other controls at his own station. "I'm patching you in to the central computer. You gotta talk to it. I don't know how to reprogram it."

"What the hell makes you think I do?"

"You're a goddamn operator!" Runstom yelled. "They're coming back around – do something, and do it fast!"

Jax looked at his screen in disbelief. He closed his eyes for a second, took a breath, and imagined himself caught in an unexpected rainstorm. He opened his eyes.

```
SYSTEM READY.
CONTACT COMPUTER MAINTENANCE MODE
ACTIVATED. PLEASE ENTER COMMAND.
> HELP
AVAILABLE FUNCTIONS: LIST-CONTACTS,
INSPECT-CONTACT, CONFIG-CONTACT, CONFIG-
AUTO-TURRET, CONFIG-ZOOM
> LIST-CONTACTS
CURRENT CONTACTS:
1 -> COMBAT-CLASS VESSEL NEXUS MK 4
2 -> COMBAT-CLASS VESSEL NEXUS MK 4
> INSPECT-CONTACT(1)
```

```
COMBAT-CLASS VESSEL NEXUS MK 4
BEARING: 195, -15
CONTACT-TYPE: FRIENDLY
CONDITION: NO DAMAGE
APPROXIMATE SIZE: 18 TONS
CREW: 4
WEAPONS: 4 FRONT-MOUNTED HEAVY LASERS,
2 SIDE-MOUNTED SPACE TORPEDO LAUNCHERS
DRIVE: SHORT-RANGE, WARP-CAPABLE
> CONFIG-CONTACT(1)
CHOOSE FROM MUTABLE PROPERTIES:
 1 -> CONTACT-TYPE
> 1
ENTER NEW VALUE FOR PROPERTY "CONTACT-
TYPE" [FRIENDLY]:
> HOSTILE
VERIFY ON CONTACT "COMBAT-CLASS VESSEL
NEXUS MK 4" CHANGE PROPERTY "CONTACT-
TYPE" FROM "FRIENDLY" TO "HOSTILE" [Y/N]:
> Y
```

Jax looked up from the screen and at the contact map. One of the arrows turned from green to red.

Runstom laughed heartily. "Yes! Do the other one!"

Jax tapped away at the keys, and a few seconds later both arrows were red.

"Arming the auto-turret," Runstom said. He paused, looking at the contact map.

"What's wrong?"

"One of them is coming back in close. The other one is hanging back, just slowly circling us. I think the one coming in close means to board us."

"Really?" Jax's brain seemed to experience some sort of traffic jam as it tried to imagine the possibilities of what might happen if gangbangers boarded the transport.

"Yeah," Runstom said. He seemed to be thinking out loud. "The Space Wasters probably want to find out who it was that stole one of their stolen ships. Plus, it's pretty valuable property to them – they probably want it back in one piece. That's why the first shots were a very carefully placed barrage intended to take out the thrusters, so we couldn't get away."

Jax thought about this for a moment while they both watched the arrows on the contact map. "And they probably knew the contact computer wouldn't fight back, since it's one of their own ships."

"Yeah, probably," Runstom said. "Time to play a little rope-a-dope," he added, quietly.

"What-a-what?"

"Rope-a-dope. We lie here helpless and let them get close. We gotta make sure we hit 'em hard. If they slow down to get close to us, the auto-turret will have a much easier time blasting those bastards to bits."

Jax nodded, not so sure of the plan, but not willing to question the officer right at the moment. They both sat in silence, holding their breath for the next several seconds. One of the red arrows slowly ticked toward the center of the contact map.

"Okay," Runstom said to himself. "Right ... about ... NOW!" He slapped a button on his panel. Nothing happened, as far as Jax could tell. Runstom slapped it again. "What the fuck!" He slapped it again. The red arrow ticked closer, but no weapons fire was incoming.

On Jax's terminal, a message appeared repeatedly, in sync with Runstom's frantic button-slapping.

```
UNABLE TO ACTIVATE AUTO-TURRET. AUTO-
TURRET PROPERTY "POWER LEVEL" CURRENT
VALUE: 0. REQUIRED VALUE FOR ACTIVATION
[1..9].
UNABLE TO ACTIVATE AUTO-TURRET. AUTO-
TURRET PROPERTY "POWER LEVEL" CURRENT
VALUE: 0. REQUIRED VALUE FOR ACTIVATION
[1..9].
UNABLE TO ACTIVATE AUTO-TURRET. AUTO-
TURRET PROPERTY "POWER LEVEL" CURRENT
VALUE: 0. REQUIRED VALUE FOR ACTIVATION
[1..9].
> CONFIG-AUTO-TURRET
CHOOSE FROM MUTABLE PROPERTIES:
 1 -> POWER LEVEL
2 -> TARGET PREFERENCE
> 1
ENTER NEW VALUE FOR PROPERTY "POWER
LEVEL" [0/0..9]:
> 9
VERIFY ON AUTO-TURRET CHANGE PROPERTY
"POWER LEVEL" FROM "0" TO "9" [Y/N]:
> Y
```

"Try—" Jax started to say, but the ship's sharp, electronic voice interrupted him.

"Auto-turret activated at power level nine."

Runstom slapped the button again.

"Target acquired."

High-pitched screaming erupted from somewhere above the cockpit and the viewport lit up with blinding white light. A series of thundering explosions quickly followed and their personnel vessel shuddered and began to spin in a sickening manner, sending the stars spiraling in no particularly identifiable pattern. Jax was still strapped in, but he grabbed onto his station and held on for dear life.

"That was too close!" Runstom said, finally getting the ship to stabilize by wrenching on the throttle. He leaned over to look at the contact map. Only one arrow remained, still fairly distant from the center. "What the – I think we vaporized him!"

"Warning," the electronic voice said soothingly. "Battery level is now critical. Auto-turret deactivated."

"Oops," Jax said.

"What? What do you mean, 'oops'?"

"Well," Jax said timidly. "I may have jacked up the power on the auto-turret a little too high." He looked down at his screen.

UNABLE TO ACTIVATE AUTO-TURRET. AUTO-TURRET PROPERTY "POWER LEVEL" CURRENT VALUE: 9. REQUIRED VALUE FOR ACTIVATION [0..2].

He reconfigured the turret for power level two, the most it could handle at the moment. "We'll be—"

"Auto-turret activated at power level two."

"I don't like the sounds of that," Runstom said. He turned their ship around until the arrow was in the forward section of the contact map. They could see the Space Waste fighter ship in the distance through their viewport. Jax wasn't really sure if it was getting closer, but he had to assume it was. "I wish this stupid auto-turret could target a specific part of that fighter," the officer continued. "Like his thrusters. Then we'd be on a little more even ground."

"I saw a target preference setting somewhere," Jax said, tapping at the keyboard. "Okay, it's set to target 'engines/thrusters'."

"Target acquired. Error. Unable to identify adequate line of sight to targeting preference. Resuming default firing mode."

The high-pitched screech emitted from above them again, but this time it sounded small and distant. A streak of white light appeared, originating from the top of the viewport and fading into the distance ahead of them. A few seconds later, streaks of light came from the other direction, sporadically, all around their view. Popping sounds could be heard here and there and the cockpit shuddered and jiggled.

"So much for taking out their thrusters," Runstom muttered.

"What are our chances?"

"Well." Runstom's mouth twisted around as if he were chewing on his thoughts. "This personnel ship has a lot of armor, especially front-side. It can take a beating head-on. Once this guy gets close though, he'll probably bullet right past us, make a quick maneuver and hit us before we can get turned around to face him. Probably dive under us and hit us from down there where the auto-turret can't get to him."

"Communications are off-line," the ship said as pulses of laser fire pounded away at it.

"So," Jax said. "Not so good."

"Nope." Runstom waggled the throttle in frustration. "If we could just get close enough to Terro's gravity, we could land." The view bobbed and slid side to side, slowly. "These damn stabilizers are only giving us rotational movement. I need thrust!"

"Warning. Proximity alert."

They looked at the contact map. Two more red arrows came in from the right side. Jax leaned over to look out the viewport off to the starboard. "There's two more ships coming in. Looks like they're going to meet up with this guy. Maybe come at us with full force? Triple team?"

Runstom was quiet. Jax saw a look of hopelessness cross the other man's face.

The small barrage that had been peppering the personnel vessel stopped. They could see the fighter now it was so close. It turned off to face the other two ships, and they could see streaks of light flying between them from left to right and back.

"What the hell?" they both said in unison.

After a few dozen seconds, the fighter peeled off and began to head in their general direction again, its movement erratic.

"I think he's trying to out-maneuver torpedoes," Runstom said as they watched. "Wait a sec – the red arrows – they're hostile to this ship, because this is a Space Waste ship! Those must be ModPol patrol ships! The ones that were trying to catch up with us back at the superliner!"

A moment later, explosions appeared across the fighter and the two men cheered.

"Target disabled."

"Shit," Runstom said. "Looks like they're going to bring us in after all." He looked over at the operator, frowning. "Sorry, Jax."

"I suppose I should be happy we're still alive," he said grimly, but he couldn't convince himself of that argument.

"Target acquired," the computer said.

"What?" Runstom's eyes widened. "Those are friendlies! Tell that goddamn thing those are friendlies!"

Jax hammered away at the keyboard. He tried to ignore the screeching of their auto-turret and the sudden alarming sound of incoming laser fire. Rather than trying to configure the contact settings, he managed to set the auto-turret back to power level zero.

"Auto-turret disabled."

"This is unbelievable," Runstom said. "I can't get the fucking com on-line. We're sitting ducks and we have no way of hailing them." He looked up. "At least we stopped shooting at them. Once they realize we're disabled, they should just try to—"

"Warning. Proximity alert."

"It's a torpedo!" Jax yelled, looking at the contact-map holo.

Runstom grabbed the stick and started turning the ship. "Our thrusters are already blown. If we can get the torpedo to hit back there, it will do the least amount of damage. We might be able to keep Life Support."

"Warning," the computer said. "Collision imminent. Impact in twenty seconds."

A few minutes later, they were streaking through the atmosphere of Terroneous. It was all the time Runstom had put in with the flight simulator back at the precinct that gave him some tricks to try with the stabilizer thrusters. By combining that with a whole bag of blind luck, they were actually headed in the right direction. The torpedo blast at the rear of the vessel had sent them hurling through space at an angle, like a colored billiard ball getting whacked by the cue ball. Runstom managed to steer them enough toward the moon to catch its gravity. Had they missed it, they would have gone straight on to being caught in Barnard-5's gravity, where they would have been crushed under their own weight as they approached the unstable surface of the gas giant.

Instead they had to contend with a very stable surface rising up to meet them much faster than was necessary. Thankfully, Jax was completely silent for the time being. No screaming about how they were sure to die, no yelling at Runstom to do something. He just sat there and let the officer do his job. He either had complete faith in Runstom or just realized there was nothing he could do to help the situation except shut up and stay out of the way.

Runstom didn't exactly have a lot of faith in his own piloting abilities. He actually rarely flew spaceships these days. He'd spent a lot of time with the one- and two-man patrol ships, of course, but his experience with anything larger than that was mostly via simulation. Docking with other ships in space was pretty easy, no matter what the ship – the computer could handle most of the maneuvering in that case. Landing on the surface of a planet was generally not recommended. Your typical planet had all kinds of waystations and orbiting docks and the like that spaceships could come to. Transportation to and from the surface of the planet was handled by sub-orbital shuttles and strato-elevators and whatnot. It was much more efficient to build Warp/Xarp-capable vessels without landing gear, tons of retro thrusters, huge take-off thrusters, or even wings (in the traditional sense, made for lifting and supporting a craft in an atmosphere).

They had only one advantage: the personnel transport was designed to be flexible enough to have the ability to make a surface-based attack. It didn't have any of the taking-off components, of course; the idea being that a cluster of these ships could land hard and fast, blitzkrieg-style. If the soldiers on board were able to dominate their objective, then another shuttle could come down and retrieve them later. If they failed in their mission, there was no going back.

187

Runstom fussed with the controls, trying to find the switch that would extend the shock-system at the bottom of the ship. Finally he found what he was looking for.

"Surface-landing sequence initiated." The computer's voice was barely audible over the sudden rush of wind. Some lights came on, turning the whole cockpit yellow. A steadily increasing beeping sound began to pierce through all the white noise. Runstom guessed that was an indicator for the distance to the ground.

They felt the vessel shudder as it attempted to right itself, keeping level so the shocks on the bottom would hit the surface squarely. Runstom let go of the controls. There wasn't much he could do from here, except let the ship do its thing. He looked at Jax, who just nodded and checked his seat restraints for the umpteenth time. The beeping got faster and faster. It was the only warning they had before they hit.

It took them a few minutes to recover from the impact. They'd both probably experienced multiple mini-heart attacks during the descent and had to work hard to control their breathing. Jax dry-heaved a couple of times; since they hadn't eaten much of anything during the Xarp trip, there was little matter to vomit.

Finally Runstom unstrapped himself. "Take your time, catch your breath," he said to Jax, his own voice coming out haggard and weak. "I'm going to look around."

He opened the cockpit door and stepped into the main bay of the vessel, closing the cockpit behind him. Guns, armor, ammo, packages of food and water, everything was all over the place, like it'd been hit by a tornado. The whole ship sat at a funny angle, not exactly level. He carefully stepped through the mess and approached the outer hatchway. He reached for the switch, then instinctively bent down and picked up a nearby rifle instead. He checked to see that it was loaded, turned off the safety, and opened the hatch.

They were in the middle of a field of blue-green ground vegetation. It was mostly quiet, the only sound being the crackle of something underneath the ship, the hiss of air as the retro-thrusters vented something, and the flap of something that sounded like plastic above him. There was a distinct smell of burning plant matter mixed with the unnatural smell of melted metal and plastic. There was no sign of life in the immediate area, so he stepped out. Holding his rifle, he stalked all around the landing area and scanned the horizons. Other than some taller, tree-like vegetation in one direction and hills in another, he didn't see much of anything. A few small, avian-type creatures flew about the blue-gray sky in the distance.

He turned back inward, toward the ship. The grass-like stuff on the ground was all scorched and blackened in a rough circle around the vessel. The shock system was exposed and he could see the pneumatic columns, asymmetric in their lengths, accounting for the lopsidedness of the transport. A couple of white parachutes hung from small hatches somewhere out of the top of the ship and flapped about in the light breeze.

Runstom slung the rifle over his shoulder and came around to the back of ship just as Jax was coming out of the rear hatchway.

"Hey," Jax said, his voice rough. He had a couple of boxes in his hands. "You hungry? I'm starving."

"Yeah," Runstom said, smiling. "We're alive. This is going to be the best-tasting meal you've ever eaten."

A few hours later they were trekking through the wilderness. Most of the electronic equipment on board was damaged in the rough landing, but there were a few packs of low-tech survival gear. Compasses, maps, ocular-zoom-scopes, flares, fireboxes, hatchets, blankets, and even a couple of tents.

Jax knew everything there was to know about Terroneous because Runstom knew it and recited it as they prepared to set out. As part of his ModPol training, he was required to learn the minimal stats of every inhabitable rock in the Barnard system. Jax wasn't sure why he was getting the whole spiel, but he thought the officer might have intended to make him feel safe in the emptiness and relative silence of the wilderness.

So Jax learned that Terroneous was pretty hospitable to life as far as celestial bodies go. That it had an atmosphere made up of a lot of nitrogen and a fair amount of oxygen. Not as much O2 as you get in most domes, which tend to overdo it a little, but enough to sustain humans, especially if they stick around long enough to get used to it. Gravity around 8.2 meters per second squared. Most importantly, a magnetic field and magnetic poles at either end of its rotational axis. It was large for a moon, but quite a bit smaller than the average non-gaseous planet.

According to Runstom, the roughest part about life on Terroneous was the lack of sunlight. He explained that while the moon rotates on a nice steady basis, resulting in the same effect of night and day that you'd get on a regular planet, it also revolves in its orbit around the gas giant Barnard-5, causing it to get blocked from the sun altogether for several days at a time. Fortunately, Barnard-5 radiated enough heat to keep Terroneous from becoming inhospitably cold, despite the extended lack of sun exposure. But even with the comfort of heat, the prolonged darkness could be taxing for some people.

They had a map of Terroneous. They'd pulled it out of an aging military-issue paper atlas, so it wasn't exactly up-to-the-minute accurate, but it showed them the handful of locations with any civilization. They managed to get a vague geo-location out of the ship-board computer before the power died completely. The solar panels were damaged beyond repair, along with just about every other feature of the personnel transport. It was just as well, because the sun was disappearing behind the edge of B-5 and they had no idea when it would be back. They took survival supplies and a rifle for each of them. Runstom said it'd be wise to have some weapons in case they had to hunt for food or fight off indigenous predators. Also there was some mumble about Terroneous being a fairly lawless planet. Jax hadn't quite caught the words exactly, and wasn't sure he wanted to.

Most of their wine was smashed, being that Jax had insisted on getting the classic, glass-bottle variety. He'd never tasted anything like it until the superliner, and he grieved more over that loss than anything else on the ship. He stuffed the two remaining bottles down in his pack before they headed out.

Then they walked. For several hours they walked, the thinness of the air making them slow and tired. They saw a great variety of plant life on their journey, as well as a number of bird-like creatures. They saw a pack of what looked to be predators of some kind, but the multi-limbed, large-fanged, thickly-furred creatures seemed uninterested in them, sparing the two men only a sidelong glance before moving off through the tall blue-green grasses.

At first, the whole place made Jax very uneasy. He was on the surface of a planet not protected by a dome for the first time in his life. The longer they walked, the more it felt natural to be in those surroundings. It was like being in a dream. The smells in the air had an effect on him. He kept breathing deeper, trying to take in the strange, fresh, raw odor of the local flora. It would change ever so slightly as they moved from the plains to a grove of trees to patches of brush, and each time he would make himself dizzy trying to smell as hard as he could, desiring so badly to recognize those subtleties that he had never smelled before.

When they finally reached Fornwood, the closest town they could find on the map, they were exhausted. The town was a lot of wood structures, the likes of which Jax had never seen before. It wasn't an overly large town, but there were a number of residences, a market area, a railway station, and a small shipyard. A real shipyard, as in a place where wooden boats were built: rafts, canoes, sailboats, stern-wheelers, those kinds of things.

The people of Fornwood were a bit bizarre to Jax. Their skin was generally light pink but with a bluish hue. They wore a lot of clothing that looked like it was pieced together with animal pelts, and they had such odd accents that Jax would often have to stop and think about what someone said before he could understand them. There were, of course, other off-worlders about, but not many. The Fornwoodians were very friendly to strangers, inviting everyone to stay awhile, perhaps do some shopping and visit a few restaurants while they were in town. The town was safe, they assured the visitors. Not like other places on Terroneous.

They still had some money, and after asking around, found themselves in a room at an inn. They got the same overly-hospitable treatment there that they encountered everywhere else in the town. They were too exhausted for much banter, so they ordered meals right there at the inn and had them delivered to their room. What arrived was some kind of stew, with hunks of animal meat floating around with big cuts of roots and vegetables. On the side there were pieces of a bluish, bread-like food that was kind of tough to chew, unless they dunked it in the stew first. Despite being so tired that he could barely keep his eyes open, Jax was aware that it was the most amazing and flavorful meal he had ever eaten. Runstom said it was because they grew plants right in the ground, in farms just outside of towns. The same went for livestock – they had enough space to raise large meat-bearing creatures naturally, by allowing them to roam large pastures. No hydroponics and factory meat. The officer said it was food made nine-tenths of the way by the planet, then assembled and cooked by people.

Jax slept well that night. Better than he could remember sleeping in a long time; even back in Gretel, on Barnard-4. His home-world was only the next planet inward in the system, but it was millions of kilometers away, and to him that life felt millions of years in the past. In his dreams that night, he was a large, furry animal, stalking unsuspecting prey through tall blades of blue-green grass with his pack-mates.

When he awoke, he felt renewed and ready to move ahead on their only lead. Runstom was in a similar mood. Being on Terroneous lit a spark in the officer that Jax was glad to see. ModPol had no jurisdiction anywhere on the moons of Barnard-5, and so Runstom wore the plainest set of clothes they had managed to salvage from the personnel transport. Jax dressed similarly, but in the back of his head he had half a mind to go into the market and pick up an animal-hide coat.

There was a small postal house in town. They asked if the clerk could look up the TerroPac Express office by the number they had on their package, and she was happy to oblige. The office they were looking for was in a town called

Sunderville several hundred kilometers away, but they could reach it very easily by mag-rail.

They picked up some proper luggage at the market, and Jax got himself a lovely animal-hide coat. The saleswoman told him it was *leather*, which was what they called animal-hide once it's been cured for durability. She assured Jax that if he took care of it, the coat would outlast his own life. Jax decided not to mention that he was probably living on borrowed time anyway, so that wouldn't be much of a feat. They stayed one more night at the inn, had another magnificent meal, and then caught the mag-rail to Sunderville first thing in the morning.

CHAPTER 14

"I'm sorry, sir," the clerk said. He was a tall, old, frail-looking man with yellowing, wrinkled skin, but despite his appearance, he held his ground steadily and adamantly. "I cannot give you a customer's information if they have chosen to send a package anonymously. That," he said with a glower framed by bushy gray eyebrows, "is our policy."

"So let me get this straight," Runstom said, ratcheting up the indignity. "If someone was to send me a box of *poisoned* cookies, and they did so using your anonymity feature, I would have no way of finding out who had just tried to *kill* me?"

"Well, sir," the old man said. "They've a saying, you know. Tis not the poison cookie what kills a man, nay, tis the baker."

"What?" Jax said. "Is that really a—"

"And furthermore," the clerk continued. "If ya be on the receivin' end of a pointed stick, look not to the man at the other end for guilt, but look to ya-self. Chances are, ya've earned that poke in the ribs."

"We don't have such sayings on the law-patrolled planets," Runstom growled. "And thieves and murderers can't hide behind a mask of anonymity."

"Aye, tis true, we're a bit lax on lawfulness in these parts," the old man said, raising a crooked finger. "But we make up fer it in *respect*, young man. Laws are only necessary for people who don't *trust* no one else. And when you can't trust someone, you can't rest unless you *control* 'em."

Runstom was fuming, but Jax put a hand on his arm. "Okay, Stanford. They have a policy. The clerk is just doing his job. Let's go."

A few minutes later they were walking briskly down the street away from the TerroPac Express office. Runstom was practically sprinting in anger, and Jax had a hard time keeping up with him.

"Stanford," he said. "Hey. Stan!" He grabbed the officer by the arm and spun him around, earning a burning glare from the dark eyes on the olive-green face. "Slow the hell down. I have an idea."

This statement seemed to soften the other man's face ever so slightly. "What?"

"Well, when we were in that office, I got a look around. I noticed that another one of the extras they offer on delivery is a return service, so if you send something to someone and they send it back, TerroPac will ring you up and you can come pick up the package. They even have a deal where you can get that as a combo with the anonymity thing. People probably reject a lot of anonymous packages, so in some cases you might want to make sure, if they rejected it, that you would get it back."

"Okay," Runstom said, his eyebrows furrowing. "What are you thinking?"

"We have the original package, or at least the outer wrapping." Jax pulled the folded brown paper out of his satchel. "Look, here. There's a code on here that says RTSOF. Return to sender … something."

"On failure."

"Right! Return to sender on failure. Which means whoever sent the chip to Linda Parson requested the return service feature."

Runstom's face finally lit up. "So we make a new package, wrap it up with this wrapper that has the sticker with the sender's ID on it, seal it up, and *return* it to TerroPac."

"Yes!" Jax said. "And they'll give the sender a call and we can stake out the office and see who walks out with the package."

They talked the plan out as they walked to a store to buy a box of cookies. Runstom rubbed his hands together with an almost frightening enjoyment for subverting the TerroPac Express anonymity feature. Jax felt a little guilty about it, being that he actually thought they had a pretty strong point. He'd never really thought about it much before, laws and control and all that.

They booked a hotel room so they could get their package together and give themselves another day before they "returned" it. Sunderville was quite a bit larger than Fornwood. There were plenty of residences, including some apartment complexes, and there were stores and restaurants offering a wide variety of products. There was even at least one school that Jax had noticed. The smaller buildings were mostly brick or wood or a combination of both and the larger buildings were made of steel and featured a lot of glass windows.

People mostly got around town on foot and on cycle. In fact, it was a bit of a contrast to Fornwood. Where the smaller town was almost all foot-traffic, this town had lots of dedicated, paved roads for cycle and small motor vehicle traffic. Some other massive, truck-like vehicles were restricted to use on the outskirts of the city or near delivery docks and transportation hubs. All the cycles and motor vehicles Jax saw were the ancient wheeled variety – no hover-bikes or hover-cars in this town.

Their hotel room was pretty high up, fourteen floors, and the view out of the large glass window was breath-taking. Jax had never seen anything like it. They saw rolling hills in the distance, covered in the blue-green fuzz of vegetation, those tree-like plants dotting the landscape. The planet, Barnard-5, was beginning to sink into the horizon and he could see its long curving surface, as if it were just a mostly-hidden circle positioned right behind the nearby hills.

Standing in front of that window, Jax felt like his insides were turning to jelly. It felt like he'd always had this life goal to see the surface of another planet, ever since his mother showed him the dead, gray surface of Barnard-4. And here he was, on a giant moon that was teeming with life. He'd walked across this moon's surface. He'd reached out and touched the plants that grew from its living soil. He'd watched the animals who lived on it naturally move about freely; freer than any human who lived in a dome. He wished Irene Jackson could be there to experience it with him. But even if she couldn't be there, he knew his mother didn't have to be alive to be proud that her son walked on the surface of any celestial body other than Barnard-4.

Jax was really beginning to like it on Terroneous. He kept that information to himself, though. In fact, he tried to keep it *from* himself. It was dangerous to the mission. If he started to think too hard about it, he might decide it was not worth tracking down the next lead. He might start thinking about making this moon his home; a new home, beautiful, quiet and remote, where ModPol and any part of his old life would never bother him.

"That's it. That's the package. I can see the red X we marked on it."

"Give me that ocular," Runstom said, grabbing the scope from Jax. He took a look for himself and saw the small red X on the side of the package. It was being carried out of the TerroPac Express office by a tall man with broad shoulders and a massive midsection. The clothes he wore hung about his frame haphazardly, covering most of his pale-pink skin.

The target frowned heavily and walked with a bit of scorn in his step. He was clearly frustrated about having to pick up the package. Runstom wondered if he'd yet realized it wasn't the exact size of the package he had sent out. He didn't seem paranoid or suspicious of anything – just grumpy – as he strode head-down toward the trike he had ridden up to the TerroPac Express office.

The hotel had provided Runstom and Jax with a pair of bicycles as part of their room package. The cycles bore the flashy logo of the hotel on them, which made them look like a couple of tourists. Jax had been agitated about the notion of being identified as a tourist, and Runstom was detecting some sudden urge to fit in coming from the other man. The officer reminded him that if they looked like tourists, no one would suspect they were staking out the TerroPac office.

The charade continued to be useful as they trailed the big man on his tricycle through the streets of Sunderville. He showed no signs of being aware that he was being followed, and certainly made no attempts to shake the two tourists who coincidentally turned the same way he did, time and time again. It was fortunate, because Jax had never been on a human-powered bike before, and as a result, he bumbled around like a drunk. This vehicular disability was undoing all the *fitting-in* that his new leather jacket had bestowed upon him. The jacket was, however, helpful in keeping his clothes from being torn to shreds as he proceeded to fall off the bike every few minutes.

Finally, the heavy-set man stopped at an apartment complex. Jax and Runstom rode past him and stopped at a store across the street. They watched as the big man put his three-wheeled bike in a shed in front of the complex and then headed inside. Runstom quickly stuck his bike in the auto-locking corral in front of the store and grabbed the key-card that popped out when he engaged the locking mechanism. Jax followed suit and they sprinted across the street and into the apartment building.

No one was in the lobby. There were two elevator doors and Runstom noticed that the digital floor number readout next to one was quickly ticking up: 8 … 9 … 10. It slowed down and stopped at 12. He looked at Jax.

"I guess we can hypothesize that the big man didn't take the stairs," the operator said.

Runstom nodded and hit the elevator call button and they took the other car up to the twelfth floor. When they arrived, they stood in the hallway and looked left to right. There were about ten rooms on either side of the elevator, doors on either side.

"Well, now what?" Jax whispered. "We can't just knock on every door."

Runstom gave his partner a half-smile, and Jax rolled his eyes. "Come on," the officer said. "Let's start at this end."

The big man was behind the fourth door, not counting the ones where no one answered. He looked at them mildly confused, just like the other three people who answered their doors did. "Can I help you?"

"Your package got returned," Jax said before Runstom had a chance to speak. He glared at the operator.

"How did you know—" the man started, looking quickly to Jax, then to Runstom, then back. "Who are you? What do you want?"

"We work for X," Jax said. "And we need to talk."

Fear darkened the man's face like blinds closing over a window. "I – I tried to send the package. I don't know why it came back," he stammered. "X said that I should send it anonymous!"

"Let's step inside," Runstom said, before Jax could pull anything else. He made a mental note to deck the operator at his earliest convenience for taking the lead. Sure, they didn't exactly have a plan, but Jax's ruse was just reckless. The big man was frozen in the doorway. "Now," Runstom said, putting his hand on his hip and revealing the laser pistol he'd kept since the shootout with the Space Wasters.

"Okay," the man said, putting his hands up and slowly backing into the apartment. "Okay. Okay."

"Sit down." Runstom motioned toward a chair at a small table. The apartment was a fair size for just one person, but it was clear the man lived alone. It was open, the kitchen looking directly into the living area. An easy chair sat in front of a holo-vision on one side and a single bed on the other. A large picture window displayed a spectacular view of the city and the hills beyond.

The big man sat down. Jax stood in front of him, apparently trying to be intimidating. Runstom paced about the kitchen, making observations. The package was sitting on the counter, unopened. There was some other mail there as well. Half-opened bills, mostly, all addressed to one Markus Stallworth.

"I did what he said," the man said to Jax. "I did exactly what he said to do."

Runstom turned away from the counter and faced the man sitting at the table. "Markus Stallworth," he said. The man looked up at him. "When X called you—"

"X didn't call me," the man interrupted. "He d-mailed me."

"Of course he d-mailed you," Jax said venomously. "X doesn't have time for backwoods parts of the galaxy like this shit-stained moon."

"When he d-mailed you," Runstom continued, stepping closer, "he didn't tell you what the purpose of the program was, did he?"

"No!" Markus Stallworth spread his hands out. "No, of course not! All I did was encrypt it and put it on a memory chip! I got the d-mail with the program and the d-mail with the voiceprint and fingerprint and password. He said to encrypt this program in a package that will make it unreadable to anyone who didn't have voiceprint, fingerprint, password." Stallworth counted off on his fingers as he said the last three phrases.

"But you must have had a look at the code before you encrypted it," Jax said. Runstom could see the operator trying to keep a lid on some very real anger. The phrase *voiceprint, fingerprint, password* took him back to that very first interview back at the Blue Haven Police Department on B-4, the operator detailing the console login procedure.

Jax continued his grilling. "You must have gotten an idea about what it was for!"

"No!" Stallworth looked away from Jax and to Runstom. "I swear. I mean, I saw the code, sure. It was so obfuscated though – I couldn't tell what it was. I don't do very much COMP-LEX programming." He wiped beads of sweat from his brow with his dingy sleeve.

202

Runstom watched Jax's expression. He had no idea what Stallworth was talking about, but his partner seemed to believe the man. He could see it on his face: defeat. This was yet another pawn in some unknown player's game. Jax turned away from both of them.

"Please," Stallworth said, looking at Runstom. "I did what he said. Tell me he's not going to cut off my lines. I have all these customers lined up. Big-time customers, with big-time orders. If I don't get the materials for my factory, I'll be ruined." He started to stand up, knees bent and hands out. "Please. Tell him I'll double his take. Just don't cut me off."

Runstom turned away from the man, disgusted by his begging. Some people are taken advantage of, others put themselves in the path of extortion through their own greed. He guessed Markus Stallworth was the latter. He picked up the package.

"We're taking this. And we're going to make sure it gets delivered." Runstom turned back to Stallworth. "We'll deliver your offer to X. You better hope he's in a good mood. You are just one little card in his hand."

"Yes, yes, I know." Stallworth was on the verge of tears. "I've always been faithful," he tried, almost blubbering. Jax looked over his shoulder and shared a look with Runstom. The site of such a large man acting like a baby was stomach-churning.

"Markus," Jax said sternly. "Where's your terminal? We need to d-mail X and give him an update."

"Right over here," Stallworth said, heading into the living area, pointing at a small desk with a green monitor and keyboard on it.

Runstom nodded to Jax, and the operator walked up to the terminal.

"Unlock it," Jax said. The large man did as commanded and then backed away. Jax sat down and began tapping at the keys.

"Markus," Runstom said from the kitchen. "Do you have anything to drink in this shithole? I'm dying for a beer."

"Of course." Stallworth hurried back out to the kitchen. He dug around the cupboards and produced a bottle. "Does he—" he started, pointing toward the living area.

"No, he doesn't drink." Runstom took the bottle and positioned himself in front of the large man, blocking him into the kitchen for a few moments. He slowly drank the beer and watched Stallworth, who stood frozen, beads of sweat trickling down one side of his pink face. The quality of the beer took him aback momentarily. "This is goddamn fine beer. Where'd you get this?"

"Uh," Stallworth said nervously. "They uh. They brew it here. Just outside of town, I mean. There's a brewery."

"Hmm," Runstom said, drinking slowly and thoughtfully. "Like nothing I've ever had before. Must be you can only get it here on Terroneous. That right?"

"Yeah, I suppose so." Stallworth didn't seem to really know, or perhaps care, about the beer at the moment.

"Okay, let's get the hell out of this place," Jax said, coming out of the living area. He stormed out the door.

Runstom took a final swig and set down the empty bottle. "See ya around, Markus Stallworth." He headed for the door, then turned and shrugged. "Although I suppose for your sake, let's hope not."

He closed the door and left the big man standing in his kitchen, whimpering softly to himself.

CHAPTER 15

"Next time you plan on pulling that intimidation shit, you better let me know in advance, goddammit," Runstom was saying. "Jackson, I'm talking to you! What the hell are you doing?"

They were back in the hotel room and Jax was getting some of his stuff together, pulling clothes out of the closet. He stopped to pick up the notebook and hand it to Runstom. "We gotta go back to Barnard-4. Look at the address that one of those d-mails came from."

Runstom looked at the notes that Jax had scribbled down while digging through Markus Stallworth's terminal. The d-mail that the program was attached to didn't have a sender ID. The other d-mail – the one that had Jax's voiceprint, fingerprint, and password – came from Brandon Milton, Block 23-D, Gretel, Blue Haven, Barnard-4.

"This is your supervisor, right?" Runstom said. "Brandon Milton?"

"Yup," Jax said, stuffing clothes wildly into a suitcase.

Runstom grabbed Jax by the arm. The operator tried to twist away, but Runstom was stronger. "Brandon Milton is dead, Jax."

"He set me up," Jax said, eyes blazing. "He sent my biometrics to Stallworth. He set me up to take the fall."

"But he's dead, Jax. He's—"

"No!" Jax shouted. "He's X! Don't you fucking get it, you goddamn cop? He's X and he set me up!"

Runstom bit back the urge to slap some sense into the other man. He let go of the arm. "Tell me something, Jackson. How did you know Markus Stallworth wasn't X?"

"What?" Jax said, voice shaky and eyes bleary.

"The first thing you said to Stallworth was that we worked for X. How did you know it wasn't going to be X answering the door of that apartment?"

"I didn't," Jax said with a laugh. "I mean, I figured it was a safe question. His reaction would tell us right away if he was X or if he knew who X was."

"I don't buy that." Runstom stared at Jax. "You knew."

The operator chewed his lip. He spoke quietly. "I don't know what you mean."

"You knew. You knew Stallworth wasn't X. You knew he was another one of X's pawns."

"How'd I know?" Jax yelled suddenly, eyes watering now. "Another pawn can recognize another pawn when they see one. That's how I fucking knew. I just had to take one look at the guy." He began to pace, throwing his arms into the air. "Stallworth is just trudging through his life. He's got nothing. He's no mastermind. He's a loser. He's a fucking tool."

"And you knew this."

"I mean, do you think X is the type of person who would let someone trail him from a goddamn parcel delivery office?" Jax continued. "To a tiny, shitty, studio apartment in a place like Sunderville? Of course he wasn't X."

"Then you know goddamn well that Brandon Milton isn't X, don't you?" Runstom fired, his voice strong and stern. "Brandon Milton was another pawn and now he's dead."

"No," Jax said weakly. "He didn't deserve it."

"No, probably not. But an old man told me recently that if someone jabs you with a pointed stick, you probably earned it."

"But what did Milton do? How did he earn his death? He was a good man. He wasn't some loser on some backwater moon. He was married," Jax started to say, but the words choked off.

"We don't know," Runstom replied. "Look, Jax. You have to trust me – you don't know everything about everyone. You can work with someone on a daily basis, but you don't know their secrets. Maybe he was into bad drugs. Maybe he was a gambler and he owed the wrong people money. He crossed paths with the wrong people. I'm not saying he got what he deserved. But I am saying that there's a very good chance that Milton didn't have a clean past."

"But then what about me? What did I do?" Jax said, tears streaming down his cheeks. "Why am I a pawn in this bastard's game? What did I do to earn this?"

"Listen to me, Jackson." Runstom put a hand on the other man's shoulder. "You're not a pawn. All of these people, they did something willfully. They can act like their hand was forced, that they had no choice, but it's not true. They all had a choice and they chose to turn a blind eye to what was happening and allow themselves to be a link in the chain of events that led to the deaths of thirty-two people.

"You didn't allow yourself to be used," the officer continued, trying to look into Jax's wet, gray eyes. "You didn't do anything of your own free will. You were in the wrong place at the wrong time. You're as much of a victim as those thirty-two people. There's only one difference between you and them. You're not dead. You're still alive and that means you can set this straight."

Jax coughed and pulled away, trying to wipe his face. "Do you understand me?" Runstom said. "You are not this man's pawn. You are the unexpected wild card in an otherwise stacked deck. And you're going to be the one to bring down the house of cards."

"Okay." The operator was making strange noises, half-crying and half-laughing. "I get it, Stanford. You can stop with the ridiculous mixed metaphors."

"Okay, so d-mail. Drone-mail," Jax lectured after Runstom asked him why they were on a small, low-altitude, passenger air-vessel, bouncing through turbulence on their way up to Terroneous' north pole. "Electronic mail works great when you're on the same planet, but in order to send e-mail to another planet, it has to be transported physically by these Zarp-drive drones."

"Gotcha, Xarp-drive drones." Runstom looked uncharacteristically queasy as the craft bobbed erratically.

"Not Xarp," Jax corrected. "Zarp."

"Huh?" Runstom's face bunched together, creating ripples of light-green and dark-olive lines.

"Zarp. With a 'Z'. Not Xarp with an 'X'."

"What's the difference?"

"Well, Warp is light-speed, right?" Runstom seemed to nod, but with all the bouncing, it was hard to tell. Jax continued anyway. "Xarp is FTL – that's faster than light. Zarp is an order of magnitude faster than Xarp."

"I never heard of Zzzarp—"

"Well, of course not," Jax said. "People can't use it to travel. Zarp moves too fast for animal or even plant life to survive the trip. The time-space alterations cause any organic matter to reverse-compose. So only automated drones can actually do Zarp."

"Oh," Runstom said. Jax gave him a few seconds in case he had any other questions, but he didn't say anything else. Jax was a little thankful, because honestly, that was about the limit of what he knew about Zarp speed.

"Old-school networking principles apply here," Jax continued, back on the topic of d-mail. "A drone will be echoed back when it has been received successfully, and multiple drones with the same data on them are launched together for redundancy. The drones are actually pretty small and are launched from orbiting satellites so they don't need any rocket fuel. They're just a shell with a bunch of memory cells for holding the mail data and those little Zarp engines. And of course a computer to drive them, with minimal artificial intelligence."

"Okay, I get all that. But I still don't understand what we're going to do up there." He motioned vaguely into the distance. "Up at the mail dock, or whatever you call it. The d-mail that the program was attached to didn't have any sender inform—"

"I know, I'll get to that," Jax interrupted. Runstom rolled his eyes and let him continue. "Okay, first what happens is that a drone lands at a d-mail dock. Then its contents are downloaded and those messages and electronic packages are sent on to their intended recipients, using the regular local communication technology – satellite, fiber optics, whatever. Once a drone's memory has been downloaded, it goes into this queue – for re-use. So there's this whole queue of drones

209

that are sitting there waiting to be filled up with new mail so they can be sent back out into space." He paused to see if that was sinking in. "See what I'm getting at? If the drone with that d-mail that had the program in it is still in the queue, we can find it."

"You mean they don't wipe the memory in the drones after they download all the d-mail?"

"Nah, not right away," Jax said. "They'll get wiped once they get to the front of the queue. And there's always a ton of drones in queue. If our drone came in a couple weeks ago, it'll still be stuck somewhere in the middle." He got his satchel from under the seat in front of him and pulled out their notebook. "And yes, the sender ID was not in the d-mail. But every d-mail has its drone ID added onto it when it's uploaded to that drone. It's stored in the header of the d-mail. Kind of like a stamp on a passport. Mostly there for troubleshooting," he added, as he pointed out the drone ID he had noted on paper. "But also for billing purposes. You can mask the sender ID on a message, but for every block of memory used on a drone, someone somewhere has to pay a d-mail company. And it's not cheap either. Which is good for us, because the high cost of Zarp engines means you'll never see more than a couple hundred drones at any d-mail docks."

"Okay. But even if we find that particular drone, what good will that do us?" By this point, Runstom's normal green luster had paled half-way to an ashen gray.

"Well, each drone comes from a single planet, moon, or space station," the operator replied. "It will have the last d-mail facility it delivered mail from imprinted on it. Right on the outside of the drone, visible to all. Again – they do that for troubleshooting purposes. You know, like if a drone never made it to its destination and it was just out there floating around in space."

"How the hell do you know all this?"

"Don't ask." Jax wasn't in the mood to relive another potential career path he failed to follow. He looked out the window. They were just above the cloud layer, but it was broken and he could see the land below. Blue-green patchwork lying atop soft hills, interrupted here and there by pools of clear liquid. The round shape of Barnard-5 was occupying more of the sky throughout the day, shrouding the land in shadow, and he could see part of the gas giant through the mist. An ever-present guardian, keeping watch over its moon-child.

"Goddamn turbulence," Runstom muttered as they jiggled up and down.

Since his partner didn't seem much up to conversation, Jax found himself lost in thought. The sting of being betrayed by Brandon Milton was very strong, and not likely to fade anytime soon. He knew that. He thought about the last couple weeks of work as a LifSup operator. He thought Milton was just giving him a hard time like everyone else did who wanted to somehow bully Jax into reaching his full potential. Milton taking Jax under his wing. The micromanaging was driving Jax crazy. Now he could picture it all happening in his head. Micromanagement was an excuse to look over Jax's shoulder – a number of times. Learning Jax's password. Helping Jax clean up around his station. Had he stuffed a beverage can into his pocket? One with perfect copies of Jax's fingerprints? And the voiceprint – how hard would that be to get? A pocket recorder. Milton had used one to "talk" notes, rather than using a notepad and pencil. He had gotten Jax's biometrics, no problem whatsoever. Easy peasy.

It felt good to think that over, to "remember" how it all happened. It helped Jax to feel like he should not have been suspicious, should not have seen it coming. But the question of why was still on his mind. This guy X, what was Milton's connection to him? Was it about drugs or gambling, like Runstom guessed? Did Milton get into trouble – get into debt – and ended up owing X a favor? Did X say, just get me any operator's credentials, I leave it up to you to pick your victim? It was possible. Jax supposed he'd better heed what Runstom said and not pretend to know Milton – really know him – just because they worked together.

It was the only thing that made sense for Milton's story. It had to be something bad. Linda Parson, she had political ambitions. Markus Stallworth was running a business and from the sounds of his blubbering about X getting a cut, he'd probably become indebted when the mystery man alleviated some competition or drummed up some not-so-legal lines of inexpensive supplies. But Milton didn't have a lust for power or money. He was just a LifSup supervisor. Just another toiling B-fourean, another ant in the anthill.

And there was the other thing the detectives had slapped onto the table: a debt. A personal debt, as if Jax owed Milton something. The cops had all kinds of official paperwork that said Jax owed Milton a significant amount of money. They even had Jax's signature, and he knew he never signed any such thing, nor had any reason to. Not for the first time, the operator wondered if any of those cops were on X's payroll. They seemed awfully eager to convict an innocent man. Were they part of the conspiracy? Or just being mildly incompetent cops? The debt, though, was something. Maybe it was payment. If Jax had been convicted of murder and there was an outstanding debt with a citizen, then according to law, Jax's savings would have been used to pay off the debt.

Maybe Milton was in some kind of money trouble and along came a solution. Someone says, set someone up to take a fall and we'll make sure you get a payday. Milton probably didn't even know his payday was supposed to come in the form of an IOU from a convicted murderer – that by framing someone and getting them sent to prison, he'd be getting a payment out of the personal savings of that same person when they were convicted.

Of course, Milton probably didn't know a lot of things. He didn't know that when he stole Jax's credentials, they would be used to murder a whole block. Otherwise he wouldn't have set up the Life Support operator on duty for the same block he happened to reside in. But then again, how could he have known that was going to happen? Jax himself had to be convinced that it was even possible for someone to write a program that could circumvent those block safety protocols. Milton must have had no idea why X wanted an operator's credentials, or what he would use them for. If Milton really knew anything, he wouldn't be dead.

This guy X, whoever he was, was starting to take the shape of a mob boss in Jax's mind. How many people did he have in his pocket? How many people owed him, and how many people worked for him?

Talking their way into the processing facility at the d-mail docks was not as difficult as they anticipated. The people working in the extremely remote location (on the already remote moon) were more than happy to give in-depth tours to anyone who bothered to make the trip. Jax talked about being interested in going off-world to school to learn more about drone engineering. He spoke some of the same language that the d-mail techs spoke, and within twenty minutes of their arrival, the staff on hand were treating Jax as one of their own.

Jax again began to feel the pull. The allure of just letting go of the incident at block 23-D and staying right there on Terroneous. The large moon was not in ModPol jurisdiction and they might never bother to look for him if he just laid low. He imagined getting a job at the d-mail facility – the site was remote, but to make up for it the people there worked in shifts of one month on, one month off, still collecting a paycheck. The place was like a hotel for most of them who had their own homes in different cities and towns only a few hours away by plane.

Whenever he looked at Runstom, Jax knew he had to keep going. He could see the officer carrying around the deaths of those innocent people, the hunger for justice. The deeper they got into this case, the more hungry the man looked. Every lead was an appetizer for the next course. It was infectious, that hunger. That desire to find this bastard "X" and put him away for good.

They spent a few hours there at the d-mail facility, and Jax had plenty of time to scope out the drone he was interested in. It was an interstellar drone from the Sirius system. After Jax had a little more time to enjoy the company of fellow tech-heads, they said their goodbyes and took a mag-rail to the nearest city with an interstellar port.

Two days later they were in cryo-sleep in a long-range passenger vessel, headed for Sirius-5.

CHAPTER 16

"Alright," Moses Down said, his voice resonating deep. "Slow the hell down, 2-Bit. Tell me what happened. From the beginning."

"Right, right," Captain 2-Bit said. The aging gangbanger took a deep breath. Even over the low-res vid-screen he was visibly antsy. "We're out in my cruiser, right? Just took off from Terro with a load of that dark Terro beer that the boys all love, right? I mean, we cleaned 'em out – got a couple dozen barrels of—"

"Get to the point, Captain."

"Right. So we left Terro and we check our contacts before Xarping, just as normal, right? And what do we see, but hello, that personnel transport that went missing during the raid on the prison barge. You know, when y'all sprung me and Johnny Eyeball, right?"

"Yeah, you told me that already," Down said, motioning with his large brown hands. "So what happened? You went after her? Did you get 'er back in one piece?"

"Well, see, I sent two fighters out after her, right? I told those boys, take out her thrusters so she can't split, right? Then we can hop aboard, grab anyone we find, and take back our ship, right?"

Down nodded. "Good thinking, 2-Bit. So they took out her thrusters?"

"Yeah, they did," 2-Bit said, getting a little excited. "She didn't even know it was comin', right? They get on one side of her, one boy does a flyby, real quick-like, and they got her surrounded." He tried to model the scene with his hands. "She doesn't even react to the flyby, right? So the boy, he comes back around and BAM! Takes her thrusters out, perfect cluster." He poked at one hand with the fingers of his other.

"Nice," Down said, grinning wide, stretching the short, curly beard that framed his jaw. "You've trained your boys well, Captain."

"Right," the captain replied, then followed with a sigh. "See, my boy, he's thinkin', the ship can't go nowhere now, and they don't know how to work the weapons on it or somethin', because they didn't put up no fight. He comes up on her real slow-like, right? So's he can board 'er. But he's bein' careful to make sure she's not gonna fire back."

Down's mouth turned downward. "But not careful, enough," he said. 2-Bit didn't reply right away, so he prompted him. "Is that right?"

"Well, he got right up on her. And outta nowhere, the auto-turret – you know, those personnel transporters we lifted from that Sirius Navy outpost – they got this beautiful auto-turret, right? Dumb as a rock, but that sucker packs a punch, right?"

"The auto-turret dusted your fighter," Down guessed.

At this, Captain 2-Bit took his hat off and held it over his heart. "Aye, boss. Complete disintegration."

"Okay," Down said after a grimace and a moment of silence. "So then what happened? You tell the other fighter to take him out?"

"Well, sure, I thought about it. See, the transport had no thrusters, and my boy could fly circles around her. Plus she shot most of her power away with that first shot." 2-Bit looked grim. "But some ModPollies came out of Xarp right then. Patrol vessels – same trajectory – I think they was followin' the personnel ship."

Down growled, a deep and guttural sound. "Goddamn ModPol motherfuckers. They got no right comin' anywhere near Terro."

"So I tells my boy, come on back," Captain 2-Bit continued. "But these boys are like dogs, right? He could smell blood, and he wanted to finish off that transport. But the transport, we armored the hell out of that sucker, right? He blasts it, but it's strong, and after a minute or two those cops are getting closer. So he tries to peel off, but the ModPollies was on him with torpedoes."

"Goddammit," Down muttered. "Those ModPol wanna-be cops, they can't even fight you in a straight-up dogfight. Fucking torpedoes."

"Yeah." 2-Bit looked down at his hat again for a few seconds, then looked up with a smile. "But get this, boss. After they waste the fighter, the ModPollies get too close to the transport and the auto-turret goes and starts poppin' at them!"

"What? No shit!" Down's face brightened ever so slightly. "What'd they do?"

"Well, they's cops, right? They get shot at, they shoot right back. Torpedoed the sonova bitch. Smacks it right in the behind, the transport goes flyin'. We tracked it down to the surface of Terro. Cops got no jurisdiction there, so I guess they either figured the crew for dead or not worth goin' after, cuz they Xarp out after that."

"Goddamn ModPol motherfuckers," Down muttered again.

"Yeah, so we went down there after a while. Checked out the wreckage, right? The transport, well, she's taken a beating, and now she's on the surface and no way to get her back up into orbit without a lift-ship. Not much worth salvaging, 'fraid."

"Did you find any bodies?"

"Nope," Captain 2-Bit said. "No bodies. The ship had its shocks stuck out the bottom, so they must've survived the landing. A bunch of stuff was looted out the ship. We took the guns and armor they left behind."

"If they walked away from the wreck, they must have left a trail," Dan said, speaking up for the first time in the conversation. He was standing next to Moses' chair. "Did you track them?"

2-Bit was quiet. Down prodded him. "Did you track them, Captain?"

"No, boss."

Down frowned. "You're still in orbit around Terroneous, right, Captain?"

"Aye, boss."

"Okay. Wait there. I'm sending Bashful Dan, Johnny Eyeball, and Dava to meet you. Now listen." Down leaned in toward the vid-screen. "Dan is the best tracker we got, so you pay attention to his advice. And Johnny spent some time on that prison barge and got a good look at all the ModPollies that were on it. We know it was one of them that took the transport, so he might be able to recognize them if he sees 'em. But you gotta keep him sober, 2-Bit." He paused. "You understand me? Keep Eyeball outta the bars and outta the bottle."

"Right, boss." The captain hesitated. "Do we really need Dava?"

218

"I want to make sure this gets done right," Down said. "You got it, Captain?"

"Aye, boss."

"Good." Down closed the connection and turned to Bashful Dan. "Can you still track them?"

"No problem," Dan said. "People don't respect a trail these days. Space covers all tracks, they think. Those guys who crashed the transport, whoever they are, landed on Terroneous. No doubt they had to walk through tall grass, probably dropping ration wrappers the whole way. Probably went to the closest town, got themselves a hotel. Stuck out like sore thumbs, like tourists."

"Dan," Down interrupted. "If they slow you down – 2-Bit and Johnny E, I mean – you just ditch 'em. Don't let the trail go cold."

"Aye, boss. I'll find 'em." Dan was quiet, then asked, "Why are we taking Dava?"

"Because whoever these guys are, they've already killed a couple Wasters stealing that transport," Dava said from behind him. He nearly jumped out of his waxy orange skin.

"Fuck me," Dan coughed. "Do you have to do that?"

"And killed another Waster outside Terro," she continued, ignoring the tracker's question and pacing around the shorter man like he was soon-to-be dinner. "And not only that, you've got ModPol all over your asses on this one. Someone has to protect the li'l boys."

"That's right. Just remember," Down said, waggling a finger at Dava. "I'd like at least one of them alive. I want to find out how they did it. You know how I get," he said with a toothy smile. "We learn from our mistakes. We practiced that prison barge break-out scenario over and over, and didn't anticipate that someone might get one of our ships

219

out from under our noses. So if you can get one alive, do it. But if you can't, then just waste 'em."

"Mmm. Aye, boss," the assassin said, with a long, lightly-curling smile.

"Go get prepped, Dan."

"Yes, boss." Dan nodded at Down and gave Dava a hesitant look, then tripped his way out of the comm room.

"He might be a good tracker, but he has zero situational awareness."

"Dava," Down said. "You should be nicer to them."

"Sorry, Moses," she said. He had a way of making her feel like an admonished schoolgirl at times.

"It's okay. I just want you to get along."

She frowned and turned away from him. "I know. But I work better alone."

"No, you don't," he said firmly, placing a hand on her shoulder and turning her to face him. "When I found you, you were alone."

"Moses," she murmured. She didn't want to be reminded of those days.

He let go and laughed then, his inexplicable amusement jarring her. "Dava, Dava," he said. "You're like that ExpandoKnife you love so much. Constantly puffing up and then shrinking back away again."

"You gave me the damn knife," she said.

"I know. I'm starting to question whether it was all that good of an idea."

She frowned at him. "You taught me to be an assassin. Can't I just do that? Why do you have to bitch at me for not playing nice with the others?"

He sighed and gently shook his head. "You're more than an assassin, Dava."

"Right," she mumbled. She wanted to make for the door, but she could feel his presence rooting her to the spot.

He reached up and stretched his arms, which practically touched the ceiling, then brought them back down. "Why did we go after the prison barge."

It was a question, but it came out like a statement. She felt like a schoolgirl again, now being quizzed. "To rescue Johnny and 2-Bit," she said, guessing he was testing her camaraderie.

"Why else."

She thought about it. There wasn't anything of value on the barge. They didn't leave with anyone but some prisoners. "Fresh meat?"

He grinned at her widely. "Yes, that's true too. 2-Bit did well, finding six quality cadets. Future Wasters."

"Yeah, he did okay." There would have been seven recruits, but she chose to leave one behind. She wanted to vent to Down about the racist asshole – because he would understand – but she didn't want to revisit it. There was nothing to gain from it.

"Why else."

She narrowed her eyes at him, not getting the game. "I don't know. Sure as fuck wasn't anything worth stealing." She bit her lip in thought, then added, "I guess we got to fuck with ModPol a little."

He nodded, his grin fading. He seemed to be inspecting her, searching her face for something deeper. Something that wasn't there, because she didn't know what he was looking for.

"ModPol," he said. "They're only half the problem. A massive industry based on security. Based on what should be a human right. Exploiting people that just want to live in peace. People who want peace so badly, they won't invest in police or military. ModPol exploits them for having a dream."

221

She huffed. "Kind of hypocritical coming from a crime lord," she said with a smile.

He grinned back, but only mildly. "Yes. They're naïve to have that dream, but I admire them for it anyway."

"What's the other half of the problem?"

The grin melted again, this time into a full facial scowl. He turned and paced as he talked. "Some of these dreamers, these utopia-seekers. They see the path to the perfect end – to peace – they think it can only be accomplished through a kind of cleansing. See, the exploitation goes both ways. They use ModPol as a way to *export* their criminal element. These peace-thinkers, they looked over the history of civilization and they seen a pattern. They seen the prison-system cycle. Small-time crime, do the time, but when you get out, you're worse off than you were before. And you got no means but to do more crime. The cycle."

She watched his deliberate and slow strides around the comm room. "So they outsource the prison system."

"That's right," he said, turning to face her. "Out with the system, out with the cycle."

"Why did we attack the prisoner barge?" She knew the answer, but she asked anyway. She wanted to hear him tell it. She wanted to know there were people like Moses Down in the world.

He stared at her silently for a moment before launching in. "These people want to systematically eliminate scum like us from their happy little supermall lives. But they underestimate us as much as they loathe us. We are resourceful. We are organized. And we will break their fucking toys. We are the stones that clog their perfect machines. We are the grime that refuses to be washed out of the universe."

222

CHAPTER 17

"Well, now what do we do?" Runstom said as they tried to stretch themselves awake after disembarking from the long-range space-bus.

"Blarg." Jax rubbed his eyes. "I need coffee."

"First time in cryo, eh?"

"Merf." Jax flexed his fingers. "My hands feel like oatmeal."

"Come on, let's get out of this terminal." Runstom grabbed Jax's suitcase and passed it to him. He picked up his own suitcase and nodded toward the exit. "There's always a few good cafes right outside these places."

A few minutes later, they were pouring coffee down their throats as fast as they could without scorching themselves in a little cafe that was packed to maximum capacity.

"So anyway," Runstom said. "What's the next step?"

"I feel heavy." Jax lifted his arms experimentally. "Is this the effect of the cryo? Is it going to wear off?"

"That's gravity-lag. You didn't complain about feeling lighter on the superliner or on Terroneous." Jax gave him a furrowed look. Runstom continued, "Anyway, gravity is heavier here than it is on Barnard-4. It will take some getting used to. Probably a couple of weeks."

"Fuh, I hope we're not here that long," Jax grumbled.

"Which brings me to my original question. What's the—"

"I heard your goddamn question," Jax snapped. It felt like his brain was running on rusty gears that were caked in mud. He frowned and looked at the officer. "Sorry, Stanford. I guess I need more coffee." He took another gulp and sighed. "This damn coffee is hot. Why is it so hot?"

Runstom grabbed his arm. "Come on Jax, snap out of it. We have to figure out our next move."

Jax pulled away hard, almost knocking over his coffee, catching it at the last minute and pulling it close like it was a precious loved one. "Well," he said, closing his eyes tightly for a second then reopening them. "The person who wrote that program is somewhere here on Sirius-5."

He looked out of the window of the cafe and into the streets of Grovenham. It was a domed city, the largest on Sirius-5. Buildings rose into the artificial skies all around them. The streets were packed with people. Most of them were white-skinned, like Jax, being born and raised in a large dome where the cost of living was "economical" and therefore featured low-end solar filters, though their white skin was different than his. Sirius is a white star, or technically a pair of white stars, whereas Barnard's Star is a red dwarf, so no doubt that difference accounted for the slightly more beige color of the local skin, making Jax's look pale gray by comparison. The people were, on average, stouter than B-foureans, who were often tall and skinny. Probably a side-effect of the higher gravity.

"Shit," Runstom said, his voice rising, pulling Jax's attention away from the streets. He sounded surprised about something. "That's all you've got, isn't it? You dragged us from one star to another and our only lead is *somewhere on this planet!*" he said, waving his arms around as if to encompass all of Sirius-5.

"Well, you're the cop! You tell me what we should do—"

"Oh, *I'm* the cop now?" Runstom said, standing up and pointing to his chest. "I get to be in charge? Are you sure you don't want to just walk out onto the street and start bullying people? Like the little stunt you pulled with Markus Stallworth?"

"Yeah, well, if it wasn't for me we wouldn't have even found him. I—"

"Oh yes, I see." Runstom nodded his head vigorously. "The unappreciated genius that is Jack J. Jackson. Thank you, Professor Doctor Jackson for narrowing our next lead down to a single planet. Just let ol' Officer Stanford take it from here, no fucking problem!"

"Yeah, Officer Stanford. Officer." Jax felt like he was listening to himself, his voice acting on reflex, but he didn't stop it. "That's what I'm dealing with here. Of course you don't know what to do next. Why would an officer know what to do?"

Runstom glowered. "I may be just an officer, but I saved—"

"Sure, sure," Jax said. "Saved my ass, I don't even know how many times now. But the whole reason I'm in this mess is because of your fucking incompetent organization. Mod-fucking-Pol. Great police work, ModPol."

"Oh, big loss. Big loss, Jax. What an important life you were living in some cookie-cutter dome on Barnard-4. Pushing buttons all day and then going home to your family and friends."

"I didn't have any friends," Jax said before his slow brain processed the sarcasm. "Goddammit," he muttered.

"I wonder why," Runstom said. "You're such a charmer. A real pleasure to be around."

"Oh, excuse me for not being happy-go-lucky about being wrongfully accused of mass murder." Jax threw up his hands. "An *injustice* that you're supposed to trying to fix, Mr. ModPol."

"I'm trying to fix it." Runstom stabbed the table with a finger. "I'm trying Jax. But I can't do everything. I thought you had a plan for once. Isn't that why we came to this planet?"

"Dammit, yes," Jax said. He rubbed his blurring eyes. He tried to fight through it. Was it the cryo? Was it gravity-lag? Or was he finally cracking? If he wasn't so tired and heavy, he might be reaching the breaking point anyway. They'd come so far, but for what? To prove his innocence, something he shouldn't have to do in the first place. So far. Too far to just give up, but he couldn't think. "The original code came from here," he said, forcing the words to come. "We just have to find it."

"Just search the planet?" Runstom grabbed him by the arm and started speaking with a hushed intensity. "Jax, listen to me. We are back in ModPol jurisdiction. How long do you think we have to do this? We're on the clock. Get ... your ... shit ... together," he said, shaking Jax's arm with each word.

"Okay, you know what?" Jax stood up and yanked his arm away. The weight of his own body made him instantly tired and he closed his eyes for a moment, rubbing them with the palms of his hands. "I can't think with you yelling at me. And I can't take any more this fucking hot coffee. You want my help?" He opened his eyes and pointed out the window to a bar across the street. "I'll be having a real drink. Otherwise, you can fuck off."

Jax took one more reluctant gulp of the coffee (for the sake of the caffeine) and slammed the cup down on the counter. He turned and shoved his way past the crowd in the coffee shop and out into the street. He didn't bother to look back to see if Runstom was anywhere behind him. He headed for the bar – a narrow structure stuffed in between office buildings – and pushed through the swinging doors and into the darkness inside.

Stanford Runstom fumed for a good hour or so, walking the streets of Grovenham. The gravity-lag was starting to get to him a little, despite his adamant attempts to ignore it. They kept the gravity on ModPol outposts relatively high so everyone would be in their best shape no matter where they went, but in the last couple weeks he'd spent time on Barnard-4, a prisoner barge, a cruise ship, a large moon, and had done a whole lot of space flight in between. As much as he hated to admit it, Jackson was right about one thing: it was time for a drink.

He went into the next bar he passed as he was walking down some-number-or-letter street. The place smelled sweet and spicy, of candles burning. The lighting was low, and there were plenty of unoccupied tables. There were maybe twenty people in the large room where a few hundred could comfortably congregate.

Runstom took a seat at the bar and asked for the darkest beer they had on tap. The tend-o-bot complied, bringing him a glass and registering a tab for his seat with a series of clicks and whirs. About two and a half minutes later, he ordered another.

"Hey, Greensleeves," said a woman's voice. "Got troubles?"

The hairs on the back of Runstom's neck stood on end. He was looking into his glass, and found himself clenching it tightly. McManus had used that slur once, and Runstom had cold-cocked him so hard the other officer spent three days in the infirmary. Of course, Runstom earned a month on asteroid watch as well as several demerits for "starting" the fight.

He turned slowly toward the woman. "What?" he said through gritted teeth.

When he got a look at her, he blinked. Runstom's skin was a deep olive, but this woman's skin was greener, almost a forest green. Dark-brown hair fell around her face in waves, and she half-smiled at him, one corner of her mouth curling up fiendishly. Her light-brown, almond-shaped eyes glittered in the low light.

"I asked if you've got troubles," she said. "But I suppose that's a bit of a rhetorical question, because I can see that you do." She turned to the tend-o-bot. "Gimme what he's having."

They sat in silence as the bartender brought the woman her drink. "I'm Jenna," she said, offering her hand.

He took it lightly. "I'm, uh, Stanford."

"Pleasure to meet you, Stanford. We don't see a lot of space-borns in Grovenham."

Stanford nodded. "No, I suppose not. I've been to a few domes in my day, and I don't see many—" He was cautious with the word. "Space-borns. In domes. In general." It was probably more politically correct to refer to green-skinned people as space-born, but the distinction felt just as segregating to him.

"Ah, so you get around a bit, do you?" she said, with a playful smile. She tasted the beer and her eyes widened. "Mmm. Dark and sweet. Not usually my style, but I could get used to this." She took another sip, keeping her eyes fixed on his while she tipped the glass to her mouth. "Tell me, Stanford. What is it that you do?"

"Uh," he started, unsure of what to say. He felt a sudden shame about telling someone his profession. He wasn't sure where it came from. Was he ashamed of Modern Policing and Peacekeeping in general? Or just ashamed of his own failures?

"Wait," she said, putting up a small hand. "Don't tell me. I like the mystery. It's more fun." Her index finger traced around the top of her glass. "I'm an engineer. Don't tell anyone though, it's dreadfully boring. I've been in Grovenham for a couple years now." Her voice seemed to pitch up and down lightly, as if it were bouncing along her words. "My parents were both cops though, that's how I got the green skin. I was born in a ModPol outpost and grew up living there for my first couple of years." She looked at him, as if trying to read his reaction.

"Oh," Runstom said. "My mother was a cop. She was a ModPol lieutenant. My father," he started, but then paused. "I mean, she wasn't always a lieu. Lieutenant," he said, trying to cover the cop-lingo slip. "She had me when she was an un— … um, an investigator. I spent my first couple of years between or on ModPol outposts." His childhood story came to an abrupt and unsatisfying end. "So that's, um. That's why I've got the green. Skin. Too."

"Well, I suppose there really are only a few kinds of greensleeves in this galaxy," she said, taking a sip of her beer. "Navy-brats and ModPol-brats. Unless of course, you want to count space gangs."

"I'd prefer not to," Runstom said in a low voice.

"Yeah," she said and smiled. "Me neither, I suppose."

They sat in silence for a few minutes, until Runstom finished his beer and she ordered him another.

"So what brings you to Grovenham, Stanford?" Jenna asked. "Business? Or pleasure?"

Runstom stared at his glass. He watched his reflection come and go as brown clusters of foam floated just on top of the beer, as if his head was a moon in a cloudy, brown sky over a world that smelled wet and malty, with hints of coffee and chocolate. "Business. I guess."

"Hmm, that's no fun," she demurred. "How long are you in town? Or should I be asking, on-world?"

Runstom thought for a moment. "Until my client gets what he wants," he said finally.

"Oh," she started to say, but he interrupted her.

"You see, I've taken on a – client – who has a – case." He picked his words carefully, like picking the best footing while climbing a rocky slope. "And sometimes, you take a case that takes much longer than you thought it was going to. But you have to keep remembering why you took it."

"Because it pays well, I hope," she said with a short laugh.

He huffed a half-laugh. "Yeah. I suppose that it does pay well, if you broaden the definition of pay beyond monetary reward."

"Ooh," she said, her lips curling into a tight circle. "Perhaps Stanford's *client* is a *lady*."

"No, he's not," Runstom said reflexively, then wished he hadn't. He wished he hadn't said anything at all for the last few minutes, in fact.

"I see," she said. She slid off the barstool and he turned to face her. She looked him up and down, her head cocked to one side. "I have to use the little girl's room. Order me another beer, would you please?"

"Sure," he said, although it wasn't necessary. The tend-o-bot heard her request and filled her order without Runstom's help. He watched her walk away. She wore some kind of white jumpsuit with lots of small pockets all over it. Something an engineer would wear.

230

He sat there quietly for a minute, wondering if he should pay his tab and extricate himself from any further conversation with this space-born stranger. The beers were stacking up and the alcohol, along with the gravity-lag, conspired to dull his wits. He almost jumped when he heard her voice again.

"Justice," she said. He turned to face her. "That's it." She pointed at him, poking him lightly in the chest. "If it's not money, and it's not a girl. Then it's justice, you're after. That's you, Green Man. It's in your blood, your dad was a cop."

"My mom was a cop," he corrected her in a dark voice.

"Oh yeah," she said. "Mom was a cop."

He turned away from her. "You got justice in your blood too? From your cop parents?"

She didn't respond. He turned again to look at her after a few seconds of silence. She had her head tipped back, draining her beer. With her eyes closed, she set the glass down lightly and smiled. "Mmm. I don't usually drink the dark stuff. But I can see why you like it."

Jenna produced a card from her purse and cleared her tab with a swipe. The she leaned over, close enough for Runstom to smell her. A mix of light perfume and the sweet scent of alcohol. She cleared his tab with a swipe, then put the bank card back in her purse and drew forth another card, clear and small.

"Now you owe me a drink," she said, handing him the translucent square of plastic. "See you around, Stanford. The Green Man out for Justice." With a blur of long brown hair, she twirled around and walked out the door.

The White Angle Saloon was about as close to dank as you could get in a dome bar. Which is to say, it was dark, mostly devoid of patrons, and had a lot of watered-down beer on tap. Jax was learning that last part the hard way. He was on his sixth glass and still on edge.

What made things worse was the bartender seemed to be avoiding him. Although, Jax had to admit, he was probably being just a tad too talkative. So he had a few things to get off his chest. What do they pay these bartenders for, anyway? This guy was lucky not to be replaced by a tend-bot.

Jax looked around the bar. No women, all men. He was the only one at the bar; everyone else was seated at tables. Three greasy-looking guys sat together, talking in hushed voices, occasionally bursting into raucous laughter. Two other men sipped cocktails out of straws in tall glasses and pushed papers back and forth across their table. A man sitting alone kept nodding his head, as if he were about to fall asleep in his half-full glass of flat beer. Another man had a small bottle of liquor on his table and a shot glass. He poured himself a shot and winked angrily at Jax. And one other loner was slowly drinking a beer and involved in some kind of card game with himself.

"Wait a sec—" Jax said, facing a full beer. The bartender had managed to pour him a new glass and scoot away before Jax could talk to him. So he talked to himself. "Did that one guy just wink at me?" He looked at his glass as if addressing his beer. "Wink angrily?"

He turned back around and saw a vaguely familiar face. "I think I know that guy," he said. "Maybe I should go talk to him." He hopped off the barstool and took a few seconds to regain his balance. The alcohol in the last several beers had finally gathered enough strength to have an effect. It joined forces with the high gravity and threatened to pull Jax to the floor. He put a hand on the bar and took a deep breath, then picked up his beer and sauntered over to the winking man's table.

"What the fuck do you want?" the man said as Jax loomed in front of the table, looking him over.

"Don't I know you from somewhere?"

"Beats the shit outta me." The yellow-skinned man poured himself a shot, dropped it into his mouth, then slapped the shot glass back on the table hard, causing the glass and the table to voice a small protest. The man stared at Jax, then winked.

Jax shrugged and sat down, a passive act that was more about succumbing to gravity than intentional motion. He looked at the man, thinking about his yellow skin. He looked around the room again briefly, and it occurred to him that he was the only white-skinned person in the bar. Outside, this being a domed city, there were plenty of pales. Jax wondered why they called this place the White Angle Saloon when white-skins seemed to avoid it. Maybe it was for the irony. Maybe it was a coincidence. Maybe it was just a terrible name for a bar. It sounded like someone couldn't decide between Wide Angle and White Angel and just took something in between.

"I like your tattoos," Jax said. The yellow man was covered in tattoos, but one on his arm in particular struck Jax as interesting. "Hey," he said. "Is that a smart-tat?" He was struck with a strong feeling of deja-vu.

"I hate these domes," the other man said. "Fuckin' domes. Fuckin' shit-ass fake air. That's why I gotta drink, you know. They always yell at me." The man put on a mocking, sour face. "Johnny, why you gotta drink so much? Don't drink so much, Johnny! Stop shooting people, Johnny!" He poured himself another shot. "It's the fuckin' domes, man. They don't fuckin' get it!" He tossed back the shot and set the glass down slowly and deliberately and winked at Jax.

"You were born in a real atmosphere," Jax decided. "I can see why the domes upset you. I lived my whole life in a dome. Only recently did I get a chance to experience real atmosphere." He stared into the distance, remembering the blue-green grass of Terroneous. "I was only there a couple days, but still, I miss it." He took a slow pull of his beer.

"Fuckin' domes," the other man muttered.

"Did you say your name was Johnny?" Jax sat up straight suddenly. "Johnny Eyeball?"

The man gave him a fiery, glaring wink.

"Yeah!" Jax slapped the muscled man on the shoulder. "We were cell-mates, man! A couple weeks ago. You remember?"

Johnny Eyeball stared at him long and hard, frowning with thought. His mouth slowly churned and curled upward. "Yeeaaaah," he said. "You're the fuckin' mass-murderer!" he shouted, overjoyed in that way that only a drunk who has remembered something from more than a fortnight ago can be.

"That's right! Jax, the mass-murderer!" Jax whooped as Eyeball slapped him on the shoulder, nearly knocking him out of his chair.

Eyeball poured himself a shot and raised the glass. Jax met the little shot glass with his beer glass and they both drained their respective drinks. The White Angle Saloon was eerily quiet.

"Hey," Eyeball said after Jax called over to the bartender to bring him another beer. "Hey. Hey. Wait a sec. Wasn't you my cell-mate on the prisoner barge?"

"Huh?" Jax said, turning away from the bar and back to Eyeball.

234

"I mean, how'd you get here? We took some recruits from the barge – and you ain't one of them. Rest of the cons, we dropped at the asteroid colony."

Jax's brain tried to kick into high gear, but it was back to rusty gears churning through mud again. The alcohol had undone all the work that the caffeine had accomplished. "Uh," he tried. "What, uh. What barge?"

"You know, the prisoner barge. The one we – DOOSH", Eyeball said, making an explosion sound. "The one we blew up."

"Oooh," Jax said. "That was you? Yeah, no. We were cell-mates on Barnard-4. In Blue Haven. We were in the little jail they have there."

"Oh," the yellow man said. He thought quietly as the bartender brought Jax his drink.

Jax's dulled brain didn't want to give the other man a chance to remember that they actually were on the barge together. "Hey," he said. "Why did you drop prisoners at the asteroid colony?"

Eyeball grunted. "They always need workers in the mines. It's a shit job, but better than rottin' in a cell. Plus we get a finder's fee."

Jax stared at the other man for a moment, not really processing his words, but trying to keep him talking. "So, uh … why do they call you Johnny Eyeball, anyway?"

Eyeball glared at him. "You probably didn't notice," he said in a low voice. "But one of my eyes doesn't close."

"Oh." Jax thought about that for a second. "You mean, not ever?"

"Not in a very long time. War wound."

"Oh," Jax said again. He was about to ask *What war?*, but was suddenly sidetracked by another slow-moving thought process. "Hey wait a sec. Did you say 'we blew up the barge'? That was you? Who is 'we'?"

"Yeah," Johnny Eyeball said, grinning widely. "Space Waste!" he shouted suddenly, flexing his arm. The smart tattoo morphed from a vague cluster of lines into the triangle of out-turned arrows.

"Wait a sec," Jax said to himself, but out loud, the gears churning through more mud, this time actually making progress. "That symbol is for Space Waste? Fuck me, I didn't know that."

"Space Waste!" Eyeball shouted again. "You wanna know how we did it, Psycho Jack?"

"Uh." Jax lost his tongue for a moment. He really hoped that nickname wasn't going to stick. "Yeah," he said tentatively. Then he realized he really did want to know how they pulled that raid off. "Yeah. How did you guys do that?"

Eyeball rubbed his hands together with delight. "We went to a ModPol auction, see? We're all in disguise and shit. Like, not me, but some other dudes. ModPol makes tons of Alleys, so they're always buying new ships and shit. They decommission the old ships and put 'em up for auction."

"Uh-huh," Jax said, trying to follow Eyeball's excited gestures.

"So we bought us an old prisoner barge," Eyeball continued with a series of quick winks. "Because Space Wasters are always gettin' arrested, see? So we get an old prisoner barge, take 'er out to deep space, and then start raiding 'er!"

"You bought a barge and then attacked it? Attacked your own barge?" Jax gave him a sideways look.

"Doncha get it, Psycho Jack?" Eyeball leaned closer, as if he were about to speak in a low voice, but continued at the same volume. "We *practiced* on the old barge!" He sat back, grabbed his bottle of liquor and laid it on the table sideways. Fortunately, the cap was screwed on and the contents remained inside. "A couple of guys gotta sit in the thing and play defense. The rest of us track the ship." He surrounded the bottle with his shot glass, Jax's beer glass, and a salt shaker. "Then we come up on it and start hittin' it with boarding tubes!"

Johnny Eyeball picked up the bottle again, popped the top, and refilled his shot glass. He pushed Jax's beer back over to him and held up his own glass, as if making a toast. He grinned and winked. Jax picked up his beer cautiously and clinked it against the Space Waster's shot glass. They both took a large gulp.

"Took us a couple tries, to get the timing down good." A sad look crossed Eyeball's face. "And the first time we do it for real, I gotta be on the inside and miss half the fun." He sighed. "Ah, but anyway – even from the inside, I knew my own part in making the whole thing go smoothly. Practice makes perfect."

"But I thought you were all about chaos," Jax said acidly. He probably should have kept the challenging comment to himself.

Eyeball put his index fingers and thumbs together, forming a vague circle. "Order," he said, then spread his fingers wide. "Into chaos. Crime takes discipline, you know." He pointed at Jax. "I mean, *you* know. Right? You didn't kill a couple dozen people without some planning, didja Psycho Jack? You must've had a practice run, didenja?"

The operator's brain seemed to lock up and it tried to go in two directions at once. One of them was his real self, the one that wanted to stand up and declare his innocence, over and over again. The other was the criminal that he was pretending to be when he talked to Johnny Eyeball. The one who did this, the real psycho.

I know I'm innocent, he told himself. *Now let's just take a trip down this other road and see where it goes.* He was afraid that if he went that way, he'd somehow relinquish that innocence, like confessing to a crime he didn't commit. It was a risk he would have to take. It was time to be the murderer for a few minutes. If he was going to track down a murderer, maybe he should give a go at thinking like a murderer.

The criminal sitting across from Jax had a point. If he wanted to wipe out a whole block of people, he would have to do some planning. And clearly, X did some planning. He did some exploiting. But when it came down to it, whoever wrote the program, that's the killer. That's the hit-man. Maybe it was X himself, maybe it was someone who worked for X. Markus Stallworth and Linda Parsons were just pawns. Brandon Milton was a pawn. They didn't know what they were passing along, what they were contributing to, and they didn't want to know. But the programmer, whoever he was, he knew what he was doing. He might not have delivered the bomb, but he created the bomb. And when you make a bomb, you know it's only used for one purpose.

The programmer who was somewhere on this planet, Sirius-5. Whoever he was, he knew he was making a murder weapon when he wrote the program that would open up a hole in the roof of a block.

"Yeah," Jax said in a low voice. "I had to practice. You see, I killed those people by messing with their Life Support system. Inside a dome, the residences are all divided into blocks." His hands chopped invisible squares into the table. "In each block, you have somewhere between twenty and fifty people. Each one has a Life Support system that functions mostly independently. That way if anything … bad … were to happen, you could isolate the incident to a single block."

Jax took a pull of his beer, mainly to give himself a second to think, then continued. "So I needed a LifSup system to practice on. Just like you guys had to practice on a barge. My LifSup system couldn't be one that was hooked up to a block, because then real people would get hurt and they'd be on to me before I got a chance to go after my real target. And if I went right after my target without practice, I'd never be able to be sure it would work right."

"What do you mean by 'it'?" Eyeball asked quietly. His eyes were unwinking and transfixed on Jax. "'It' would work right?"

"It," Jax said. "Is a program. It's a program that tricks the LifSup system into opening the outer and inner ventilation doors in a block at the same time. Many of the people – my victims – many died from being thrown about, along with all their worldly possessions, due to explosive decompression. Others who managed to keep from being impaled or crushed eventually asphyxiated."

"Suffocated." Eyeball held his breath as if trying just a taste of a horrible death by lack of oxygen.

Jax nodded, allowing his criminal-self, the role he was playacting, to revel in the untimely deaths of his victims. After a moment, he went on. "So in order to write the program, I had to get myself a LifSup system to test on. Decommissioned systems would be too unreliable, and most of them are recycled for parts anyway. They don't auction those things like ModPol does with their ships that are only a few years old." He was hypothesizing about this part, but the logic seemed firm. "So my best bet was to get one straight out of manufacturing."

He paused and thought about the next step carefully. "I could have made friends with someone in LifSup manufacturing, got myself some contacts and acquired a unit that way." Now he was more or less thinking out loud. "But I wanted to leave as small a trail as possible. I know all about these LifSup systems, so I went and got myself a job at a plant. I knew exactly what they'd be looking for to hire someone that would work in the final stages of production. Like – an inspector, for example." Actually, he wasn't sure if the programmer posed as an inspector or something else, like a floor engineer or shift supervisor, or whatever. In any case, the idea that he got himself a job at a plant was sounding pretty good.

"So I go to work in this plant," Jax continued. "And I manage to get myself a LifSup system. Part of one anyway – the part that's programmable. I take it home, and I write my malicious little program, and I make sure it works against my LifSup system." He paused for a few seconds, then added. "I even wrote myself a little test routine, so I could run it again and again – just like you Space Wasters practiced your raid a couple times until you got it just right."

"Hmm," Eyeball said, looking through Jax, into nothingness. "Psycho Jack, kills people with a program," he said to no one in particular. "So how did they catch ya?" he asked, but before Jax could answer, he sat up with a start. "Hey, if you weren't on the barge, how the fuck did you even get out of jail?"

"Oh, I don't fucking believe this!"

Jax and his table-mate were both startled by the loud and haggard voice that cut through the bar like an old, heavy ax. A couple of men came across the room, swift and blurry in

Jax's dark and foggy vision. They were large, tattooed, and apparently fairly well armed.

"Johnny!" said the older of the two men, slamming a fist down on the table. "What the hell are you doing? You're not supposed to be drinking, goddammit!"

"Sorry, Cap'n," Eyeball said, hanging his head. "You know how I hate these fuckin' domes."

Johnny's captain sighed wearily. "Yeah, Johnny. I know." He bent down on one knee and put a hand on Eyeball's shoulder. "We all hate 'em. But we got a job to do, ma boy, right? We brought you here for a reason. Dan is trying to track down that ModPol motherfucker that stole that transport ship from us, right? And we need your help, Johnny, because you seen most of the cops on that barge with your own eyes."

The captain stood back up, which took a little effort. His skin wasn't quite yellow like Eyeball's, but more of an orangish color. He was older, maybe by a decade or so. "Now come on, Johnny. Hell, drinkin' in domes is what landed ya in jail in the first place. The sooner we can find these cops, the sooner we can get the hell outta here."

Johnny Eyeball sighed heavily, leaving his lips pouted outward. He hefted himself out of the chair, making a bit of a production of it. He slid the bottle closer to Jax. "You better take this, Psycho Jack."

"Thanks, Johnny," Jax said. "Good luck with the hunt," he added.

"Yeah, thanks," the gangbanger mumbled. He turned to the other man that came in with the captain, the one who hadn't spoken yet. "Tell me you got a trail, Dan."

"We had one," came the quiet but sour reply. "Until we had to come back for you."

"Ooh, whee," Eyeball said mockingly. He swayed slightly; either trying to taunt the other man or simply the result of intoxication. "Bashful Dan ain't so bashful today, issy?"

Bashful Dan ignored him and instead looked at Jax. "Who is this you're drinking with, Johnny?"

"Huh?" Eyeball waved a dismissive hand in the direction of the operator. "Oh, that's just Psycho Jack. We met on Barnard-4. In jail. He killed like, thirty people." He held out his hands in front of him, looking at each of his companions to make sure he had their attention, before profoundly uttering, "*With a program.*"

"Right," the captain said, taking hold of Eyeball's massive arm. "Well, you can tell us all about that when we're Xarping the hell outta here, Johnny. *After* we track down this piece-of-shit ship-thief."

He practically dragged Johnny Eyeball out the door, as the drunk man winked angrily at no one in particular.

Jax realized the man called Bashful Dan was still staring at him. It wasn't an attempt to intimidate or dominate or anything chest-pounding like that. It was with a genuine *interest*; one that made Jax very nervous. He looked at Jax like he was checking off notes in his head. Finally the man turned and followed the other two out the door.

Jax suddenly wished he knew where Runstom was.

Five minutes later, Runstom walked into the White Angle Saloon.

"Hey, Stan!" Jax said, waving an arm. "Over here."

Stanford walked up to the table. Jax was clearly inebriated. "Jax. I just saw some Space Wasters. We gotta be careful. They might be after us."

"Oh-ho." Jax nodded heavily. "They're after us, alright. After you, 'specially." He aimed a weighty index finger at the officer.

Runstom sighed. "Yeah, me especially." He looked around the dark bar. "You had your fill of this place yet?"

The operator gave him a funny look, as if he were wary.

"Look, Jax. I'm sorry I yelled at you. I got a little frustrated. Grav-lag, and cryo-hangover, and all that."

Jax looked down for a moment, then looked back up at Runstom. "Okay," he said. "I'm sorry too. For the whole Markus Stallworth thing. I shouldn't have done that without telling you what I was gonna do."

"Thanks," Runstom said.

"And I'm sorry about all that stuff I said. About you being just an officer. And about ModPol being worthless and all that shit," Jax continued.

"Right, okay," Runstom sighed. "Thanks."

"And I'm sorry for the other stuff too. You know, when I said you're all just a bunch of repressed assholes and ModPol is just a company that makes money off the suffering of others and stuff."

Runstom's face contorted. His eyebrows dipped and creased and his jaw slid back and forth. His nostrils flexed and flared.

"You said that to me, pal," the bartender said from behind Runstom. "Hey, buddy. You wanna drink or what?"

"Oh," Jax said. "Oh. Ohhh. Well then I apologize to you, Mister Bartender." He looked at Runstom. "Err, and you, too, of course. For all that stuff I said just now. Totally wrong."

Runstom turned around. "No, I don't want a drink. I'm leaving."

"Wait," Jax said. Runstom could hear the chair squeak as he struggled to his feet. The operator came around the front of him and blocked his way out. "Really, Stanford. I'm really sorry. But I have good news!"

"What?" Runstom said with a sigh.

"I know what we need to do next!" he said, grinning widely. "I know how we can get a lead on the programmer."

Runstom mulled over a few dozen ways he could end the operator's life right then and there. It afforded him a small amount of satisfaction and it allowed him to move on. "Okay, Jackson. What do we do next?"

"We need a hotel with a terminal. Not just a cheapo public terminal. An advanced terminal with privacy."

CHAPTER 18

They got a room at Hotel Destino. It was a little upscale, but it was the cheapest place they could find where they could get an advanced private terminal in their room. Since they only had cash, they had to put it all up front, and now their stack of Alliance Credits was dwindling down to nearly nothing.

Jax had insisted on the terminal access. He said they couldn't be certain what was in the unencrypted version of the program he had made a copy of when they were at Markus Stallworth's apartment. He didn't trust a public terminal. And he needed to be able to step through the program with debugging tools, which, he explained laboriously, meant that your run-of-the-mill standard terminal wouldn't do.

The operator was alternately hammering away at the terminal, scribbling in a notebook, and taking slugs from a large bottle of Drunk-B-Gone they'd picked up at a corner store. The stuff was chock full of vitamins, electrolytes, caffeine, proteins, bacteria, enzymes, and god knows what else. It was designed to make the body process alcohol through its system faster. It was highly recommended that one drank excessive amounts of water alongside

Drunk-B-Gone, and it was even more highly recommended that one had free access to a lavatory when consuming Drunk-B-Gone.

Jax hopped up and ran to the bathroom. Runstom strolled over to the terminal. The screen read:

```
230 IF X3 = 100 THEN GOTO 410
240 LET FG8 = X3
245 INPUT R9
```

… and so forth. Runstom's eyes watered at the sight. He picked up the notebook. Jax had drawn a table, and in one column, there were things like A, B, C, FG6, FG8, R1, R9, X1, X2, and X3. Most of the column next to these strange codes was empty, although there was an occasional number or word.

"Scuse me," Jax said, edging his way past Runstom and sitting back down at the terminal. He took the notebook from the officer's hands. "See, this code is all obfuscated."

"Right," Runstom said. "What, uh. What exactly do you mean by that?"

"Well, for example: usually when a programmer writes code, they use meaningful variable names." Jax flipped the notebook to an empty page. "Like if I wanted a variable to represent my block name, I might use *block name*," he said, writing the phrase out to look like *BLOCK_NAME*. "But if I wanted to obfuscate the code – if I wanted to make it harder to read – I would name this variable something unrelated. Something random." He crossed out *BLOCK_NAME* and wrote *X2*.

"So you're trying to figure out what all those random things are?"

"Right. The fun part is, some of them don't even mean anything." Jax turned to look at Runstom.

Runstom must have given the operator a confused look, because Jax laughed. Or maybe he was just giddy from the side effects of Drunk-B-Gone. The operator's hair was frazzled, matted in some places and spiking out in others. His eyes seemed to burn with intensity and when he blinked it was almost like he was blinking *hard* – squeezing his eyes shut tight for a second then springing them open again. No further explanation came, so Runstom was forced to say, "I don't follow."

"Okay, first let me show you a real simple operation." He wrote on the notebook:

LET BLOCK_NAME = "23D"

"All I did there was set one variable, BLOCK_NAME, to have a value of '23D'."

"Let block name equal 23D," Runstom read aloud. "I guess that makes sense."

"Exactly, it makes sense like that, but watch what happens when we do some obfuscation." Jax scribbled several lines of nonsensical math-like code into the notebook that caused Runstom to feel seasick.

```
10 LET X1 = "3"
22 LET X2 = "2"
30 LET X3 = "7"
34 LET X4 = "9"
40 LET X5 = "A"
51 LET X6 = "D"
60 IF 1 > 0 THEN GOTO 80
```

```
70 LET Z1 = X1 + X2 + X3
80 LET Z1 = X2 + X1 + X6
```

"There, you see?" Jax said. "This is a bit of a contrived example, but anyway. This Z1 variable, that's the same as our BLOCK_NAME above. But instead of a simple variable assignment operation, we have all this extra junk in here. First of all, we have these line numbers that don't exactly fit a logical pattern. That right there is going to send a well-disciplined programmer running screaming for the hills."

"Running for the hills sounds nice right about now," Runstom muttered.

Jax ignored him and continued. "Anyway, if you were scanning this code, visually, you might see this line 70 here and think that the Z1 variable was assigned to X1 + X2 + X3. Well, then you'd look back at those X's," he said, pointing to the first couple of lines and then writing *"3"* + *"2"* + *"7"* just above the *X1 + X2 + X3*, "and think that Z1 was given a value of '327'."

Runstom added the three numbers in his head. "I would think it'd be 12."

"Oh yeah, well that's another confusing thing. These are numbers, but when you put quotes around them, that makes them strings. A string can be any number of characters, and when you use a plus operation on two strings, you concatenate them." He held out his palms facing upward and slid them together, so that his pinky fingers touched. "The two strings become one long string."

"Right, of course," Runstom said and took a step back, pulling his eyes away from the maddening notebook.

"Anyway," Jax continued before Runstom could come up with a reason to escape. "This line 70 never even gets executed. Because if you look at line 60, it says, 'if one is greater than zero, then go to line 80'. Well, one is always greater than zero!" he exclaimed, throwing up his hands. "So this code right here is *always* going to skip line 70 and go straight to line 80."

Runstom was filtering out most of what Jax was saying, but a thought crossed his mind. "So it's like a smokescreen."

"Yeah, pretty much." Jax seemed to chew on that for a second or two. "Or more like a big wad of tangled-up wires, that all need to be unraveled so you can figure out which ones are connected to anything and which ones aren't."

Runstom was quiet for a moment. "Well," he said, shrugging. "I don't suppose there's anything I can do to help."

"Nope." Jax's fingers tapped away violently. "Probably not." With that, he hopped up and sprinted to the bathroom.

The ModPol officer went out for a couple of hours. He knew he probably shouldn't be out wandering around, being that Space Waste was on the hunt for him, but he figured that since he knew they were looking for him, he had the advantage. He watched his back for tails and crisscrossed through the crowded streets of Grovenham, sailing his way through the sea of stout, white-faced people.

He came upon a park block and thought that maybe the artificial groves of trees would help clear his mind. He went inside and was surprised to find it much less crowded than the street. A few people strolled down the faux dirt pathways, many of them in their later years. Runstom trekked through the park and after a few minutes, found himself caught in a light, artificial rain.

It wasn't particularly cold, and it wasn't heavy, but the general wetness was mildly uncomfortable, so Runstom headed for a gazebo he spotted farther down the path, sitting in a clearing of trees. As he walked up and found himself a seat on a bench, he started thinking about the rain talk he once had with Jax. He realized that the rain he was caught in was probably a scheduled event, and that would account for the low occupancy of the park.

An older couple approached the gazebo and sat down on a bench across from him. Apparently Runstom wasn't the only one to appreciate a light rain and a vacated park. They spoke in soft tones to each other from time to time, but mostly they sat quietly, hand in hand, staring out at the rain. He tried to share their sentiment in spirit, tried to enjoy the rain, but it was too much like water from a faucet, smelling clean and lightly metallic and chemical-like. Not like the wet, musty smell of genuine planetary precipitation.

Runstom felt a little awkward now that someone else was there, and he felt a compulsion to find something to be occupied with. He dug out his notebook. He had lost his original notebook back on the prisoner barge, but had made copies of all his notes for Jax, who, thankfully, managed to hold on to them. During the few weeks they spent on the superliner, Runstom realized the benefit of having a backup copy of the notes and began to re-copy the important bits into a new notebook. Ever since then, he and Jax would periodically lend each other their notebooks, so they could make their own copies up to date. Of course, their copies differed. Runstom's notes contained details about people that in all likelihood were extremely trivial, but could possibly be identifying elements. Jax had no such interest in tracking such an intricate level of detail on individuals they'd encountered, but he did track technical details that Runstom couldn't even understand, let alone see their importance. In the interest of being thorough, he asked Jax to mark the most relevant and valuable information so that he could copy it without losing his mind trying to duplicate everything.

He turned to the pages where he'd last written, as that's where his bookmark was, but then realized he didn't really want to review recent events. He felt like he'd had enough going around in circles with the few solid facts they knew right now. He flipped back to the beginning of the book. The notes he took from the initial investigation. The event seemed to have happened a whole lifetime ago.

Thinking about the investigation at block 23-D made him wonder what McManus and Horowitz were up to. He wondered if they missed Runstom, or if they were just glad to be rid of their awkward, green-skinned co-worker. He thought of George Halsey, and allowed himself to be sad that the galaxy lost a few good people on that prisoner barge. Halsey was always an asshole, but on the inside a good cop was buried under defense mechanisms and stifled emotions originating from years of always getting the short end of the stick, despite all the dedication and loyalty you could ask for. He hoped that back on some Modern Policing and Peacekeeping outpost, they recognized Officer Halsey for his better qualities posthumously. A hole appeared deep beneath his sternum as he realized that their friendship may have been born from some kind of bond between rejects, but it had become a lot more than that. He cursed himself for not realizing it while the man was alive.

He returned his thoughts to his notebook. His original notes had listed the full name and age of every single victim of block-23D, along with their occupation and cause of death. When he made the first copy for Jax, he had made sure to include those names, and once he began re-copying the notes, he made sure to save the names again. So much of this case seemed to be unrelated to the victims. That was a giant, gaping hole in their investigation. The victims almost always have something to do with the crime. Nobody goes through this many hoops, pulls this many strings, to kill off a block of people at random. Sure, there are some psychopaths out there, but this attack was so deliberate, so focused. So precisely planned.

Runstom ran over the list of names three times. None of them were ringing any bells, no matter how badly he wanted them to.

For some reason, he thought of the word *obfuscation*. The smokescreen – or as Jackson said, the tangle of wires – that the operator was trying to unravel, trying to see order among the chaos. The list of victims was like that. One victim was relevant; one victim was the real target. The rest served only to obfuscate the details of the crime. Runstom should have realized this fact from the beginning; but then again, he was just an officer trying to play detective.

In a murder investigation, when you have no leads on a suspect, you start looking at the people closest to the victim. The ModPol detectives, Porter and Brutus, seemed to look at the block of over thirty people collectively. To look at them as individual victims was too daunting a task. But then again, there was no standard procedure for dealing with that kind of homicide. No precedents had been set by previous mass-murder cases. Especially not in domes, in the civilized world. In deep space, gang-related crime was the only thing that came close, and gangbangers didn't bother covering their tracks. In fact, most of the time, they let it be well known who was responsible for the mayhem left in their wake.

Runstom stared at the list of names one more time. A proper investigation would involve multiple detectives delving into the lives of each of these victims. He didn't have multiple detectives at his disposal, or even access to the details of any of these victims' lives, other than what was written in his notebook. He only had Jax, the LifSupOp and alleged murderer. They were coming at this case from the wrong side, and he feared that eventually they really were going to hit a dead end. They had been caught up in the moment, following each new clue as they found it, never looking back. It wasn't a real investigation. And it was just a matter of time before they'd get brought in by ModPol and would have to face the music.

When Runstom got back to the room, he found Jax passed out on one of the beds, notebook clutched tightly in his arms. He pulled on the notebook, managing to wriggle it free from the operator's grip. Jax rolled over in his sleep.

The notebook was folded over, and Runstom looked at the last page. A dark, multi-lined circle highlighted: *ZZZ-356201-RG*

He flipped back through a few pages, but the chicken-scratch was difficult to make out, and what he could read he didn't understand anyway. He looked at Jax and thought about waking him up. The operator was sleeping hard, and Runstom wasn't even sure if he could wake him if he wanted to.

He tossed the notebook on the desk and decided to take advantage of the fact that they had rented a room for the night. The way things had been going lately, he didn't know when the next time that he would have the opportunity to sleep soundly in a good bed might be.

"It's the manufacturer's fake block code," Jax said. "See, blocks are labeled with an alpha dash number dash alpha. Dome, sub-dome, block. So block 23-D is actually C-23-D, but we usually just refer to it as 23-D, because everyone knows we're talking about dome C, which we know as Blue Haven."

"Okay," Runstom said. "So the ZZZ part refers to some dome ZZZ?"

"Right. Well, yes and no. The ZZZ is the dome designation, but there are no domes called ZZZ on any planets. See, when a manufacturer rolls out a new Life Support system, they don't know what dome, sub-dome, and block it's going to be sent to. And they have to run a bunch of tests on it before they can ship it off somewhere. So they give it a dome number of ZZZ. As soon as you see that, you know it's a fake. A test code."

"Gotcha." Runstom hoped that this was going somewhere useful. "So what about the rest of it?"

"That's the good news," Jax said, grinning. "That seemingly random sub-dome identifier." He looked down at the page and read off the number. "3, 5, 6, 2, 0, 1. Every plant has a unique identification number. It's a standard, agreed upon and accepted by the different companies that do systems fabrication."

"So the number is a reference to a specific factory?"

"Yup," Jax said, smiling. The optimism on his face and in his voice was infectious, but Runstom had been through too much to get his hopes up just yet. "And if we get to a library, we can find a directory that indexes all those identifiers," the operator continued. He pointed at the terminal. "The programmer who wrote this code obtained his test system from a specific plant, and now we can find out which plant that was."

Runstom nodded. It was better than having a whole planet to scour, but still seemed to leave things a little too wide open. "So you're thinking the programmer is, or was, an employee at this plant?"

254

"Well, it's how I would do it," Jax said, shrugging. "That's the easiest way to get access to a system like that."

"Okay." Runstom figured it was best to play along since this was all they had, and it was better than nothing. What other choice did they have? He pretended to be satisfied with their only option and did some thinking out loud. "If we can get in and get talking to the right people, we might be able to find out if there were any employees that worked for a suspiciously short amount of time there. Would they have tested the program on a system inside the plant?"

"Possibly," Jax said. "But I think they might have tried taking it off-site to work on it. And then brought it back when they were done."

"So in that case, there'd have to be some kind of record of it. Checking out equipment, checking it back in."

"Yeah, most likely."

Runstom was making notes. "Okay, good." He looked back over his notepad. "What about RG?"

"Arr-gee?" Jax said absently as he gathered some things together.

"At the end of the ID. ZZZ-356201-RG. What does the RG mean?"

"Well, normally that's the specific block within a sub-dome." Jax stood quiet for a few seconds, thinking. "I'm not sure what it means on a test system. Maybe when we get to the library we can find that out."

"Ah, the fab-combination," Jax said, pulling his head out of a book. "This is very good!"

The Grovenham Central Library wasn't anything like the library Runstom frequented back at ModPol Outpost

Gamma. The precinct library had been very compact and largely digital, though there were a few shelves of physical books and periodicals. He'd spent most of his time there at work desks and terminals, cross-referencing events and notes related to specific crimes that caught his interest – both solved and unsolved – and studying the reports and the video and audio evidence. This dome library by contrast was almost entirely populated by physical books, despite the fact that all literature was generally consumed by domers electronically.

The library was also fairly well occupied by readers. In some spaces, small groups of people gathered, having hushed but spirited discussions over the subject matter surrounding them. It only just occurred to Runstom that a common place like the library might be a natural socialization point for domers. He'd always been alone when he visited the library back at the precinct, and had associated it with escape and solitude, not a place for people to commingle.

Once Runstom and Jax had found the relevant materials, the library's patrons melted into the background as they furiously searched for the information they desperately needed to make their next move. Jax's voice had broken a long silence.

"What combination?" Runstom was flipping through a manufacturer directory, trying to find the 356201 ID in the index. Rather obnoxiously, the listing was sorted alphabetically by company name, rather than numerically by ID, so he'd been flipping and scanning for almost twenty minutes. The pages were not paper, which he'd encountered very rarely on visits to environments with enough atmosphere to support actual plant-matter – such as Terroneous. Instead these pages were the standard, everyday, all-purpose plastic that everything in a dome was composed of, from candy wrappers to clothing to buildings.

"Well, apparently, during the fabrication process, the Life Support systems take a certain path," Jax said, paraphrasing his book. "They come down an assembly line, then they get imprinted with their core code set, then they get a physical inspection, and finally a system-level inspection. But it's not always the same from one to the next. They mix it up so that problem areas are easier to find. So that different inspectors are inspecting different fabrication and imprinting lines. The last two letters of that ID string represent a combination code."

"Okay," Runstom said, only half paying attention, still scanning the index. Another reason they had to come to a building full of physical books was that the information they needed wasn't actually available in any electronic form. The corporations that were located on colonized planets such as Sirius-5 were required to make all of their manufacturing process details public – along with their organizational structure and finances – but most of them weren't happy about it. So rather than provide the required data through one of the digital networks, they complied with the transparency regulations by obtusely printing physical books and distributing a handful of copies to the public library.

"Don't you see?" Jax grabbed Runstom's arm, but not his attention. "The system that was used to test the program had a fab-combo designated 'RG'. That means, there was a specific assembly line that it came down, it was imprinted by a specific system-imprint operator, it was physically inspected by one specific inspection team and one specific inspector ran system-level tests."

"Ah ha!" Runstom said. "I got it!"

"Oh," Jax said. "Good." He sounded disappointed. "I guess I don't have to explain in detail for once," he muttered.

257

Runstom ignored the comment and read out of the book. "Vitality Systems, Incorporated. Plant number 11."

"Oh, that. You found the plant ID? Does it give a location?"

"There's another reference here." Runstom flipped through some pages. "Okay, here we go. It's in Industrial Sub-Dome A, Grovenham."

Jax lit up. "That's only a short mag-rail trip from here!"

"Let's roll," Runstom said. "You can explain that whole fab-combo thing to me again on the train."

The mag-rail had deposited them in the center of aptly-named Industrial Sub-Dome A. From there they'd taken the walkways to the main office of Vitality Systems, Incorporated. The VSI plant occupied roughly a quarter of the entire sub-dome, so the main office wasn't far away from the mag-rail stop.

Runstom had been anxious to flash his credentials upon arrival, but Jax had managed to talk him out of pulling them out first thing. The operator wanted to have a chance to try a less hostile approach.

"So that's the story," Jax said to one of the Sirius-5 plant managers that had come out to greet them. "I'd signed up for the exchange program as part of the Continuing Education Training requirement we have in the LifSup department in Blue Haven. But somewhere between there and here, I lost track of the paperwork." He shrugged sheepishly and murmured, "It's my first interstellar trip."

The office itself was small and Jax felt the ceiling looming just above his head, though it seemed to afford the squat Sirius-Fivers ample room. The plant manager was a woman in her mid-fifties, with shoulder-length black hair and the same beige-white skin that everyone on the planet had. Her face registered a mix of emotions as Jax talked: annoyance, suspicion, exasperation, and then finally turned positive at the mention of education.

"I think the training programs are very important," she said. "But it's just that the office staff couldn't find any record of you in our system. We'll have to d-mail Blue Haven and have them send us a verification."

"D-mail all the way to Barnard-4 is going to take days," Runstom muttered.

"Ah, that's true," Jax said. The manager gave Runstom a sideways look and Jax gave a short laugh to regain her attention. "You'll have to excuse my *sponsor*, he's just looking out for my best interests."

Runstom pursed his lips together and managed a smile. "Is there any way we can at least have a look around?"

"A tour?" Jax added. "A little preview, something to give me a taste of what the program will include?"

The manager looked from Runstom to Jax quietly, then finally said, "How long have you been a Life Support Operator, Mr. Johnson?"

Jax cringed at the uninspired alias they'd come up with just before entering the office, then tried to shake off the discomfort. "Four years now. For the first couple of years I mostly worked with the BreatheTime 6000 series and the Cloud-i-Dome DXr and DXs, but more recently with the VSI 12K line."

"Yes, that's good to hear." The plant manager brightened significantly. "The 12K stuff is some of the best. Very efficient for the price. Efficient and economical."

"Ah," Jax said with a smile. "I don't know much about the cost, but I know how much easier it is to operate than the other systems I've worked with."

"I suppose a tour of the plant wouldn't harm anything," the manager said. "After all, you came all the way from Barnard-4."

She led them into and through the mazelike plant. Jax tried to keep up the façade of interest while trying to keep a lookout for anything that would give them clues about how the inspections worked, and especially for anything marked with inspector identifiers, *R* and *G*. It wasn't that he wasn't interested – in fact, under normal circumstances, he wouldn't have minded at all to get a better understanding of what went into the systems that he'd been on the operating end of for the past few years. But the truth of it was, the familiarity of it all was yanking him back into a life that didn't exist any more, and it was seriously fucking with his head. Was this a life he even *wanted* to return to? The safety of the domes? Wasn't it?

"We'd like to meet some of the inspectors," Runstom said as they neared the end of the line. Jax flinched at his bluntness. Clearly the officer was running out of patience.

"Our inspectors?" the manager said. "Well, there are some inspection engineers in another section of the plant. But I'm afraid that part is not open to the public. For protective reasons."

"You mean, it's dangerous?" Runstom asked.

"Well, no." She seemed to consider the question for a moment, her eyes drifting upward. "I mean, if anyone saw what we do to test the systems – well, it's just not for public eyes."

The three of them stared at each other in silence for a moment, then Jax said, "She's just obeying the rules."

Runstom frowned and shifted his body anxiously, tugging at his shirt to straighten it. Finally he said, "We need to know what inspectors are under the combined ID of 'RG'."

Jax wanted to say more, but he knew Runstom was right. They had no more time to mess around. The manager cocked her head, then took a reflexive step backward. "What is this? Who are you?"

He got out his credentials. "Stanford Runstom, Modern Policing and Peacekeeping. We're investigating a criminal case and we need to know the names of those inspectors."

An hour later, they were on another mag-rail, back out from Grovenham, this time to a residential sub-dome called Tamillan. They had come back from Industrial Sub-Dome A only to pass straight through Grovenham and out the other side. On toward what could possibly be their final destination on Sirius. They rode in silence for the first half of the trip out. Runstom knew Jax wasn't happy that he'd pulled the ModPol card, but they'd gotten the results they were looking for.

"What are we going to do when we get there?" Jax said, finally broaching the subject.

Runstom had his notebook out, but he wasn't really reading it, just kind of staring at it. "I don't know exactly."

The officer fidgeted. This was it. They had the name of their suspected programmer. Their last viable lead. They were just about out of cash. They were probably long overdue for getting caught by ModPol. In any case, ModPol would be on them very soon now. Runstom's credentials only held weight when they could be verified, which meant someone at the plant office had to run them through the system. Normally, cred-validation would get logged for some ModPol drone to review the details as they worked through a backlog. But Runstom knew that there would be a flag somewhere just for him that would set off alarms.

Only one of the VSI employees that were part of the "RG" team had checked out a LifSup system for an off-site inspection in the last couple of months: a core-programming inspector by the name of Jenna Zarconi. She had identified a particular quirky flaw in one of the systems coming off the line and logged her reasons for needing to take it home over the weekend for analysis. The check-out log also mentioned that the problem could be systematic, and that there was a potential that other systems coming off the line could suffer from the same issue. She had needed to investigate further, and couldn't wait until the following week.

The core of the LifSup system was basically just a specialized computer. It was small enough without the peripheral components that she would have easily transported it home, probably just taking it with her on the rail. The check-in log a few days later showed a mea culpa, with an explanation having something to do with a false-positive on a poorly designed test. Jax postulated that the management was probably so relieved to find out that there was not a serious issue on their line, they overlooked the fact that the flawed test was actually written by Jenna Zarconi herself. The phrase *who examines the doctors?* came to Runstom's mind when Jax explained this detail, though he couldn't remember where he'd heard it. It had the ring of something his mother would say. In any case, it seemed the inspector had written a test that she knew would fail so that she would have an excuse to take the component home. That little detail made her a prime suspect in Runstom's book.

"What worries me," Jax said, one hand inside the other, cracking the individual joints in his fingers one at a time. "Is that she's probably not X. That she's another pawn. But she knew what she was creating. She was a pawn who knew she was creating something that would hurt people." He was almost arguing with himself.

"Maybe she's not a pawn," Runstom said in a low voice. "Maybe she's a partner." He gave himself a minute to digest his own insight. Maybe she was X's partner. She was close enough to the worst part of the crime that it was possible. "In any case, you're right. She knows what she did, and that makes her dangerous."

"Great," Jax mumbled.

"We have to get it out of her first," Runstom continued. "We have to make sure she was the programmer. She's capable, based on her employee profile."

"If it was her, and she's being exploited, then X has to be behind it."

Runstom frowned and looked out the window of the train. The desolate landscape of Sirius-5 blurred on by. "We can start with that angle. Tell her right up front that we're after X, and we know she was involved."

"But that we believe she did it against her will," Jax said, nodding in agreement. "At the very least, we'll probably get some reaction out of mentioning X at all."

"Yep." Runstom knew they'd get a reaction, alright. The officer was not so eager to find another pawn. Another in the long line of victims of exploitation. He was ready to find someone who was guilty. He was ready to find justice.

The scenery went black as the train entered the station tunnel inside the sub-dome Tamillan. He turned and faced the operator. "Now or never."

CHAPTER 19

"Oh. Hello, Stanford. I thought you were going to call."

Jax looked from the woman in the doorway to Runstom and back. The woman who answered the door had green skin, similar to the officer's, although slightly … greener. She was also a lot prettier.

"Hi," she said to Jax. "I didn't expect Stanford to bring a friend. Well, to tell the truth – I thought he was going to call me, not just show up." She stuck out her hand and as he looked at it, he thought about how the color of her half-sleeve, button-up shirt was the kind of white that most domers couldn't get away with wearing without it clashing against their skin. "I'm Jenna."

"Hi. I'm, uh." It occurred to Jax that he should use an alias, but then again, this woman had used her real first name. And Runstom's. "I'm Jack." He took her hand and shook it.

They both turned and looked at Runstom, whose mouth was stuck somewhere halfway between open and closed. "Hi," he said, finally. "Hey. Jenna. Hi."

She smiled warmly at him. "It's good to see you again, Stanford."

"Um. You too," Runstom said with a cautious hand motion in her direction, like he was waving to someone he didn't want to see his friends waving to.

She nodded, still smiling. "So," she said after an awkward pause. "You fellas want to come in? I was just about to open a bottle of wine."

"Sure," Jax said. "That sounds great." He looked at Runstom, who just blinked meaninglessly at him. The officer's skin had paled into a kind of ashen, gray-green color.

They followed Jenna inside. Jax went in first, as Stanford lagged behind for a moment, sticking his hands into every pocket and digging around frantically. The woman had a nice place. They walked straight into the living room, which was a fairly large space and featured four very comfortable-looking sitting chairs.

"Have a seat," she said. "I'll go get some glasses."

She went off into another room. Jax gave Runstom a look, trying to mouth the words, "What's going on?" Runstom just shook his head and sat down. He stared ahead at nothing and put his fingertips to his temples and held them there, as if trying to keep something from escaping out of his skull.

Jenna Zarconi came back into the room with three wine glasses in one hand and a bottle in the other. The men stood up and she gave each a glass and poured them some wine, then portioned some out for herself. They all sat down and tasted the wine. Jax got the sense that he wasn't the only one thankful to have something to occupy his mouth momentarily.

"So, Jack," Jenna said, after a minute or two of uncomfortable silence. "Did Stanford tell you he met me in a bar yesterday? Over in the main dome."

"Oh," Jax said, looking briefly at Runstom. "Yeah, actually, he mentioned that."

"Are you two – partners – of some kind?" she asked. "Stanford didn't exactly tell me what he does."

"He's a consultant," Runstom said before Jax could say anything. "A technical expert, if you will. I hired him to assist me with this case that I'm working on."

"I see," she said, smiling. This bit of information seemed to put her slightly more at ease. She folded her hands together around her glass.

Jax returned the smile. He felt like he was in the middle of a slow-moving spaceship collision. Like two vessels, neither with any thrusters, drifting toward each other at a crawl. Nothing to do but wait and watch the events unfold; and pray that you're on a vessel whose Life Support stays intact.

A concerned look suddenly crossed her face. "Stanford?" she said softly, not looking directly at the man. "That card I gave you didn't have my home address on it." It was clearly a statement, but she quickly turned it into a question. "Did it?"

Runstom didn't say anything. Jax thought he looked as guilty as if he held a smoking gun. So much for those undercover instincts.

The silence spoke volumes. "How did you find my house, Stanford?" she asked, quietly but firmly. "My address – it's not listed publicly."

Runstom sighed wearily. "Jenna. Jenna Zarconi. Do you work at Vitality Systems, in plant number 11?" The question came out wooden and clipped. "Are you an inspector? An inspector of Life Support systems?"

Jenna Zarconi's eyes widened. "Yeah, I am. How did you know that?" she asked under hushed breath. "I didn't tell you any of that last night."

"I know, Jenna." Runstom leaned forward, cradling his wine glass in his hands. "It's the case." He looked at her and then looked at Jax.

"What are you talking about, Stanford?" Zarconi said. She looked at Jax, then back at Runstom. She arched her back as if to stand, but remained sitting. "Who are you guys?"

Runstom was still looking at Jax, as if giving him permission to take a whack at directing the conversation. "Jenna," Jax said. "Do you know anyone who," he started, faltering. Out of context, it seemed like a pretty ridiculous question. "Do you know anyone who goes by the nickname 'X'?"

The green-skinned woman dropped her glass. It landed on the soft carpet without breaking, and all three of them jumped out of their chairs. She bent down and fussed about with a napkin, trying to sop up the few drops of wine that had been left in the glass.

She stood up slowly, keeping her head low, and spoke into her chest. "Yes, I know X."

"How do you know him, Jenna?" Runstom asked. Jax could hear the struggle between being a consoling friend and being an interrogating cop fighting it out in his voice.

"We're not here to hurt you," Jax said. "We're just looking for answers."

She lifted her head. A tear was running down one cheek, giving it a bright, green stripe. "I ... do work for him. Sometimes."

"What kind of work?" Runstom prodded.

"Well," she said, hesitant. "Usually programming. Nothing outright malicious. But writing programs that ..." she paused and swallowed.

"That are subversive in some way?" Jax asked. He could have asked her to finish her thought, and maybe she'd be

267

more specific, but he was getting more and more nervous and wanted to move the conversation along.

Zarconi didn't answer the question, but she nodded briefly. Runstom turned around and walked to the window. He was quiet for the next few moments, and Jax and the woman stared at his back.

"Jenna," Jax said cautiously. "Our investigation has led us to believe that someone wrote a program." He took a step toward her, trying to draw her attention away from Runstom. She turned to face him after a few seconds, and he continued. "A specific program, written to work on a Life Support system."

She looked at Jax and nodded so softly it was almost imperceptible. She didn't say anything out loud.

Jax went on. "Our investigation has led us to cross paths with a few people who contributed in some way to a crime. Each of these people seemed to know only their own part. Their own job. They were apparently not aware of the overarching crime. They were all manipulated in some way by someone. Someone they each referred to as X."

She sniffed. "Do you know who X is?" she asked, her voice quiet and croaky.

"No," Jax said, frowning. "No. We don't." He paused, meeting her eyes again. "Do you know the real identity of X?"

Jax watched the woman. Her head didn't shake or nod in any direction. Her lips trembled, and more tears formed in the corners of her squinting eyes. He thought she looked afraid. Very afraid.

"It doesn't matter." Jax felt ashamed for being unable to push her. She obviously knew X, and they needed to get it out of her. He didn't know what else to say to her. He felt like he needed to open her up more. "Did X force you to write the program?"

"Yes," she said, creakily.

"Did he force you to follow me?" Runstom said loudly. Jax and Zarconi turned to look at the officer, who was still staring out the window.

"What?" she said.

Runstom turned around. "Listen, Jenna," he said sharply. "We can help you. But you have to be honest with us." He took a step forward and she stared at him, frozen. "It was no coincidence we met at the bar yesterday. Grovenham is not that small."

"Okay," she said, blinking back tears and clearing her throat. "I know X. I've known him for a few years." She paused, her face twisting. "We used to be lovers." She swallowed, then added, "And partners."

"You mean, like business partners?" Jax asked.

She looked at him and frowned. "You could say that." She turned back to Runstom. "But I left. I wanted to get out of that. I wanted to go straight, live a real life."

"But he never left you alone," Runstom said.

"Yes," she said. "He did. For a while. But then he started calling. Asking me to do things for him. He never asked me to leave my home or my job or anything. He just asked me to write code once in a while." She blinked and wiped half-dried tears from her face. "He always pays me. And he doesn't take no for an answer. He has—" She paused and swallowed, as if the next word were stuck in her throat. "Evidence."

"Of your participation in past crimes," Jax guessed. After the words came out of his mouth, he realized that was supposed to go unsaid.

"Yes," Jenna Zarconi said. "But it's worse than that." She looked at each of them, and Jax could see fear on her face. "He's a cop. He's ModPol."

Runstom's face contorted. "X? X is goddamn ModPol? No way." He folded his arms across his chest. "No goddamn way."

"Stan," Jax said excitedly. "That makes perfect sense! The exploited people, the cover-ups. The way those detectives were so ready to close the homicide case." The look on Runstom's face – like he'd just been hit across the jaw with a bombball plank – made Jax wish he'd held back his excitement about the revelation.

"Shit." Runstom shook his head. "Goddamn Porter." The officer seemed to be talking to himself more than the others. "Didn't even show up to the crime scene. So quick to be done with the case." He shook his head again, closing his eyes. "But still. I can't believe it." He opened his eyes and glared at Jenna Zarconi. "No."

"It's true," she said, almost whispering. "I know you don't want to hear it, but it's true."

"Did you know the target?" Runstom said, suddenly changing the subject.

"What do you mean?" she started to ask.

"You know what I mean," Runstom said sharply, cutting her off. "The program was designed to hurt someone. Someone specific. You knew this. Out of the thirty-two victims, only one was the real target." He tried to steady his voice. "Did you know who that target was?"

She seemed to think the question over. "Yes," she said, finally. "Yeorg."

"I'm sorry," Jax said. "Did you say 'Yeorg'? Who – or what – is Yeorg?"

"He was the other partner." She sat back down in her chair. Jax sensed a rather long story was coming, so he sat too. Runstom remained standing. "When we started out, we were small time. X, Y, Z," she said. "X, Yeorg, and Zarconi."

Runstom walked around the edge of the room, coming to a stop somewhere behind Jenna Zarconi's chair. Jax watched him pull out his notebook and quietly flip it open. He didn't get out a pen, he just read.

"So you think this Yeorg was the one X was going after with this LifSup attack?" Jax asked. "Do you know why?"

"He was in longer than me," she said, hanging her head. "He wanted out. He was older, and he'd had enough. He just wanted to retire to a quiet dome somewhere." She shook her head. "I don't know what happened, exactly. X probably called on him, like he calls on me. But Yeorg said no."

"But didn't X have evidence on Yeorg too?" Jax asked. He watched Runstom's eyebrows wrinkle as he flipped a page over and then back. "Why didn't he use that to push him? Why kill him?"

She shrugged. "Maybe Yeorg threatened him right back. He probably had something on X."

"Yeorg Phonson," Runstom said, interrupting the conversation from the other side of the room.

Jenna Zarconi twisted around in her seat. "Yes, that's right. How did you know?"

"That's J, O, R, G," Runstom said. "Jorg Phonson."

"Yes, that's him," she said.

"Wait a sec," Jax said. "That's Jorg with a J? How do you get XYZ out of that?"

"Well, it sounds like it starts with a Y," she said defensively, folding her arms. "I don't know. That's just how it was."

Runstom was tapping at something on the page his notebook was open to. "Jenna," he said. "Do you have a video player that can take a PMD memory card?"

"Yeah," she said. She stood up. "Yeah, Stanford. Why?"

"Take us to it," he said.

271

"Okay," she said. "It's in my office." She got up and paused for a second, looking at Runstom, then walked out of the room. Runstom followed her, handing the notebook to Jax on the way out.

Jax stood up and looked around the room for a moment. He looked down at the page the notebook was still open to. He saw a list of the residents of block 23-D, along with their occupations and cause of death. He scanned down the page and found Jorg Phonson. Retired. Impaling, blood loss. There was a letter V with a circle around it next to the name.

Jenna Zarconi came back into the main room with Runstom in tow. He was carrying a small screen and platform set. He set it on the floor in the middle of the room. She took a cable out of the back of the set and plugged it into the wall.

"Jenna, you don't have to watch this if you don't want to," Runstom said. "This is a video taken shortly after the incident with the Life Support system. It's a man we identified as Jorg Phonson. He was still alive when I got to him, but only barely so. We tried to give him medical treatment, but he didn't make it."

"Just play it," she said. Her voice was suddenly firm and strong, like she was ready for what was coming.

Runstom poked a button on the machine and pulled a small memory card out of his pocket. He stuck the card in the player, and it winked to life.

It was a 2D recording, shaky and low quality. They saw a woman – some kind of medical technician – in a small house.

"I think there's someone in there," the woman said.

Runstom picked up the remote and hit a button, tracking through at high speed. They saw the view move into the bathroom, where a man lay in a pool of blood on the floor. He started normal playback.

"He's an off-worlder," the recording said. Jax could recognize Runstom's voice, despite the poor quality. "Probably from Poligart, that big moon in the Sirius system. Or maybe Betelgeuse-3. That's red skin."

Suddenly there was a loud knock at the door. It was followed by a distinct clunk, and then a series of clicks.

"Get down!" Runstom yelled, throwing himself at Jenna.

Jax was able to drop to his knees and shield his face just as the front door to Jenna Zarconi's house blew off its hinges.

CHAPTER 20

Dava walked down the street on some look-a-like block in some look-a-like residential sub-dome. The ticky-tacky cut-outs of houses were revolting. They reminded her of her youth, when she was forced to live in the domes. *Blessed* to live in the domes.

The "Start Fresh Initiative". That's what the alliance of corporations involved in various aspects of dome construction called it.

Her RadMess vibrated and she looked down at the face of it, strapped to the inside of her left forearm. She grinned. "ModPol," she said to herself. "Oh, Dan. Don't sound so worried. This is only going to make things more fun." She tapped out a brief message back.

The "Start Fresh" corporations wanted everyone to think dome life was just the cat's pajamas, but they weren't exactly confident of that. They always needed more guinea pigs. And if they could wrap it up in the spirit of giving the doomed peoples of Earth a second chance, well then, all the better. They called it "Start Fresh", but everyone Dava knew called it "Doomed to Domed".

By the time she was a teenager, she was sick of those damn domes. Betelgeuse-3 was her personal prison planet. Back on

Earth, her real parents had already gotten the cancer and couldn't afford treatment. "Start Fresh" was supposed to be their cure. She'd said good night to them when they bedded down into cryo-chambers on the massive transport in orbit around Earth. When she woke up, they were gone. Jettisoned in mid-flight. They were sick, the flight attendants had explained. They should have reported that they were sick. Sick people can't always survive cryo-sleep. Dava had been stuck with a foster family who couldn't deal with her anymore once her age hit double digits. She spent the middle of her teen years in a home for "troubled youth".

She was in that home when she met the man who changed her life. He came as a counselor, an example of how an orphan could become successful. Apparently the orphanage was desperate enough for that sort of speaker that they didn't look too deep into his story. His name was Moses Down; thinking back on it, she always got a kick out of the fact that he didn't bother using an alias. Moses Down was rescued from Earth about a decade and a half before Dava was. He was dark-skinned and tall, like she was. He spoke about taking control of your life. He spoke about overcoming the hand you've been dealt. He said if you've got a bad hand, you have to learn to stack the deck.

Dava approached Moses Down after his speech. There weren't a lot of other dark-skins in domes, and he was the first adult one she'd ever seen. And one of the few she would ever see. Oh sure, she'd see one occasionally here and there, especially in Space Waste. But as generations moved forward, there were less and less dark-skinned Earth-borns. Instead there were white-skins – and not like the white people she remembered back on Earth with the light, pinkish-beige skin. White-skins were white, sometimes a grayish-white, like the color of newspaper. White skin meant they spent their first developmental years in a dome. Then there were the shades of pink, red and yellow skins. Some were born into domes as well; early domes where the skies filtered out certain things or didn't filter out something else, in systems with different types of stars and differences in sunlight. Yellow-to-red skin was for people like Johnny Eyeball; born in real atmospheres. Outside of Earth, the only places a person could survive the real atmospheres were certain large moons. Like most people, Dava never really understood the science behind the permutations of pigmentations, only that colored skin made people different in an immediately visual way.

So she knew Moses was special. She knew he would understand her pain. He asked her how old she was. She lied and said she was eighteen. She'd been getting away with that for a while. Domed people didn't know what to make of the tall, dark-skinned girl and always assumed she was older than she was. Moses probably wasn't fooled quite so easily, but if that were the case, he never let on. The next day she and a couple other kids sneaked off the grounds of the home with their bags and hopped aboard Moses Down's shuttle.

Her arm buzzed again. Dan reporting that the cops were moving in.

They were serious about this place. These guys that stole the Space Waste ship must be into something deep. She started double-timing, breaking into a jog. If they killed anyone before she got there, she was going to be pissed.

A minute later, she saw Bashful Dan crouching in the bushes across the street from their target house. She could see through the front doorway of the house. They'd probably blown the door off its hinges.

"How many?" she asked Dan.

He jumped, not hearing her approach. "Shit, Dava," he panted. "The green man and the white skinny guy went up and knocked. A green-sleeved lady answered the door and they went in. Then—"

"Dan, I swear to fucking god, if you say 'green-sleeve' one more time I'm going to cut a hole in your gut and make a noose out of your intestines."

"Oh, shit," Dan whispered. "I'm sorry, Dava. It just slipped out." He held his breath as she glared at him. She nodded for him to continue. "And then four cops showed up. They popped the door and walked in."

"How long ago was that?"

"Right when I messaged you," he said. "Like maybe five minutes ago."

"You got confirmation on these guys?" She looked around for a moment. "Hey, where's 2-Bit and Johnny?"

"Well, to answer the first question, yes," Dan said. "After we saw that B-fourean guy in the bar," he started, then paused. "You know, Johnny, he was trashed in the bar. But he remembered that guy, just the same. From the prisoner barge. He was Johnny's fuckin' cell-mate! I mean, the guy tried to tell Johnny that they were cell-mates back on B-4. So Johnny just plays along. He sits there and has a conversation with the guy!"

"Damn, I love Eyeball," Dava said. "You never know when that guy is too smashed to remember his own name or when he's on the clock."

"Yeah, right," Dan said. "One of the best. Anyway, we drag Johnny out of there to get him sobered up; but I leave the captain to babysit Eyeball so I can get to work. I stake out the bar, and sure enough, along comes the green guy. He goes in, and a few minutes later they come out together. I trailed them to a hotel. An hour or so later, the green guy comes back out, goes for a little walk." Dan laughed softly. "The guy went all over town. I think he's paranoid, because he snaked all over the place just trying to get to the park."

"Ain't paranoia if people are really after ya."

Dan thought about that for a moment. "Yeah, shit. Well, he's still pretty green. I mean, I know he's green colored, but I mean he didn't shake me. And he never saw me. Anyway, I call up Johnny and Captain 2-Bit and have them meet me outside the park. Only one entrance, so we knew he'd be coming back out of it."

"So Johnny got a look at him?"

"Sure did. Said that was one of the ModPol officers he saw on the barge, a prisoner escort. We said, you sure Johnny? Moses wants us to be sure. He says, yep. Get this, Dava. He says he had a goddamn conversation with the guy. Because he came to their cell to talk to that B-fourean."

"You guys get names yet?" she asked, mostly out of curiosity, but partly because she was getting sick of the labels.

"Well, not the green dude," Dan said. "But Johnny calls the other guy Psycho Jack. Says he was in for mass homicide."

"No shit. Does he believe that?"

"Not really sure. Eyeball is hard to read, you know? Sometimes he's winking at you like a normal person, to mean he's just kidding or something. Other times," Dan paused. "Well, you know."

"Yeah," she said. "He's just trying to blink." She was quiet for a few seconds. "What the hell is the deal with these guys? A cop running around with a guy who should be on trial for mass homicide?"

Dan shook his head. "Yeah, don't make sense. But seeing how that same cop had come to this Psycho Jack's cell while Johnny was there, must be something going on."

"Yeah, I guess. So where are they?" she asked. "2-Bit and Johnny, I mean."

"Well, to be honest," he said. "I had to trail these two guys all day, waiting for a good time to call you. They went out to some industrial sub-dome, then back to Grovenham, and finally out here to the 'burbs. Johnny got sick of waiting around and started drinking again, so I asked the captain to keep an eye on him. I figured you and I could handle one cop and a skinny, random B-4 dude." He paused, looking at the house. "Maybe I should call them. I mean, those other cops showed up. I don't know if," he started, then stopped himself.

She just looked at him. "We're not waiting for them to get all the way out here. I have a feeling some bad shit is going down in that house right now." She started checking her weapons. "We're going in before something happens to our target. Nobody is killing the assholes who stole a Space Waste boat before we get a chance to torture them." She grinned widely and she could see goosebumps form on Bashful Dan's skin.

"Okay," he said quietly. He looked at the house again.

"Get a smoker and wait here. I'm going to go get in position near a window. When I buzz you the signal, throw the smoker right through that open doorway."

Dan had a small satchel on his waist. He opened it up and pulled out a flat, gray canister. He checked it over and then fished out a small mask, handing it to Dava. She took the mask, gave him a silent nod, and was off.

CHAPTER 21

"Jack J. Jackson. You are under arrest for resisting arrest, class five murder, property damage in the first degree, and impersonating a law enforcement officer of Modern Policing and Peacekeeping. Jenna Zarconi, you are under arrest for conspiracy to commit murder and aiding and abetting a known fugitive."

Four ModPol officers came through the empty doorway, following the announcement on the bullhorn. Three of them had guns drawn, but held them rather haphazardly at their sides.

The fourth man turned to one of the others. "Thanks, Jerry. Let the record show that we entered the domicile of one Jenna Zarconi and encountered one Jack J. Jackson and one Jenna Zarconi. There was no one else on the premises." He cast a sidelong glance at Runstom, who was picking himself back up off the floor. He mentally scanned his body, but felt nothing more than the shock from the fall.

The fully-armored ModPol cop took off his helmet, revealing bright-red skin and a bald head. "Now that that's out of the way," he said, setting his helmet down on a small table near the front door, "we can go off the record."

"Mark," Jenna said, breathlessness making her speech airy and faint. "What … what are you doing here?"

"I want the three of you on your knees with your hands behind your heads," the cop said, ignoring her question. "Now!" he shouted.

The other officers came around the big chairs swiftly and aimed their guns at the occupants. Jax and Jenna quickly knelt down and put their hands up.

Runstom glared at the un-helmeted cop as another tapped his temple with the tip of his firearm. "Get down on the ground, now!"

He knelt down and let the cop cuff his hands as he held them behind his head, not taking his eyes off the red face of the other cop. "You're X, I presume?" he said after the cuffs clicked on.

"That's right," the man said with a snarl. "I'm X. And you're a ghost. The late Officer Stanford Runstom. An unfortunate event on a prison barge, where Mr. Jackson managed to steal your credentials before he escaped."

"ModPol credentials are genetically verified. He wouldn't be able to use them."

X laughed. "Yeah, keep putting all your faith in technology. No one ever exploits technology." He pointedly looked at Jenna and Jax. "Isn't that right, you two?" He laughed again and looked at Runstom again, pulling a small, empty vial from inside his flak jacket. "Anyway, we don't know exactly how he did it. But we did manage to find a sample of your DNA on him." He put the vial back inside his jacket. "But we'll get to that in a minute. After we deal with these two."

"What's your real name?" Runstom said. X frowned at him. The bunching lines of his forehead were made more prominent by his bright-red, bald head. "Come on, X. You're going to kill me anyway. You've got me cuffed and under a gun. You gonna hide under some stupid pseudonym your whole life?"

"It's Mark Xavier," Jenna Zarconi said.

The room got quiet as everyone seemed to look at X for a reaction. He was staring past those kneeling on the floor, looking at the vid-screen.

"Get another QuikStik, so we can close this wound," came Runstom's voice thinly through the tiny speaker. He was kneeling in a pool of maroon, cradling the head of a bloody, red-skinned man. "And we need some syn-plasma. He's lost a lot of blood. Hey buddy – talk to me. Where are you from?"

"X," was Jorg Phonson's response. It was drawn out and haggard. "X." At the time, Runstom thought the man was just making dying noises. Now he could hear the letter X clearly.

"Come on, buddy," the on-screen Runstom said, lightly brushing the face of Jorg Phonson. "Stay with me."

"Phonson," X said loudly, bringing everyone's attention back out of the vid. He looked at Jenna Zarconi. "It's Mark Xavier Phonson, you dumb bitch. Brother to Jorg Phonson." He approached the woman, bending down to glare at her. "The man you murdered. You murdered my brother, you goddamn psycho."

The green-skinned woman looked genuinely stunned. "W-what?"

"Yeah, I know." X stood up straight again and walked past them, approaching the vid-screen. He stared at the device with a frown. "How do I turn this thing off?"

"Oh," Jax said loudly, cutting off Jenna Zarconi before she could say anything. "Just hit that red button there on the front. Yes, that's it – the round one."

X crouched down and hit the button. The screen blinked, then reflected the scene in the room, causing him to stand up and take a step back to get a look at it.

"Now just hit that large, flat, gray button on the very top of the screen," Jax said in a calming tech-support voice.

"You didn't know he was my brother, Jenna. But you did this," X continued, not willing to lose his momentum. "You killed him." He pressed the gray button on the top of the device. The screen flickered and went black, and he turned back around to face her. "Didn't you?"

Jenna Zarconi's face turned into a scowl. "Yeah, well. We did it together, Mark. I couldn't have done it without you," she said at him, over her shoulder. Then she turned her head around forward and stared at nothing. "Even if you didn't know you were helping."

"Jenna, what the hell are you talking about?" Runstom demanded.

"You and your stupid operator," she snarled, turning to face him. "Yes, I tracked you down. After I got a d-mail from that fat idiot Stallworth. He was supposed to be a buffer. All the connections ended with him. But I should have known anyone dumb enough to be in Mark's pocket willingly was going to crack like an egg under pressure. He begged me – he thought I was Mark, of course – begged me to let him off the hook after getting a visit from a couple of thugs. One tall, white-skinned guy and one green-sleeves."

"How did you find us?" Runstom's voice sounded small and weak, even to himself.

"Oh, give me a break, Stanford," Zarconi spat, her brow creasing. "There's only one interstellar port here on Sirius-5, and it's in Grovenham. And flights from Terroneous don't come every day." Still on her knees, she leaned closer to him.

"You're a fucking green-sleeves, just like me. I'm reminded every day of how much I stick out."

"So you waited for me at the spaceport. Watched for a B-fourean and a space-born. Followed me for a bit until I went into that bar alone." Runstom was trying to remain calm, but he felt the rage building inside him. He closed his eyes. He knew there was something off about that woman when she sidled up next to him and started buying drinks, but at the time he was too upset with Jax to think straight. His anger had clouded his judgment then, and he tried not to let it happen now. He swallowed and opened his eyes. "When we went into the other room to get the vid-player, we passed your bedroom. I saw suitcases on the bed. You were going to take off, weren't you? When you found out we were on your trail, you were going to—"

"Shut up!" she screamed suddenly, louder than Runstom had ever heard her. "Did you get a nice taste of *justice* yet, Officer Runstom?" Her green face glowed an almost yellow color, and her brown eyes were blazing and wet. "Because it's going to be the last thing you ever taste!"

"Oh, come now, dear Jenna," X said, still standing behind them. "Officer Runstom here was just trying to do his job." He leaned forward, sticking his head between Runstom and the woman. "Weren't you, *Officer*? Or should I say, ex-officer. Hey, how about that – you'll be an X just like me!" He laughed at himself and straightened back up.

"Wait a second," Jax said, who'd been quiet up to this point. "Um, Mr. X. Sorry to interrupt. I just want to see if I got this right." He looked around at everyone to see if they were going to let him continue. They all looked back at him. "So you're saying, Jenna here killed this guy Jorg? Who also happens to be your brother? And engineered the Life Support

284

failure to cover up the murder? But why did everyone think that you did it, and not her?" His tone wasn't accusing, but sounded like genuine curiosity. Runstom thought to himself that he would be lucky if X didn't decide to gag him then and there.

"Excellent question, Mr. Jackson," X said. "I figured you must be a smart one. Being that you're still alive and not in jail and all that." He looked at Zarconi and spread his hands out, palms up. "Lady Z – you want to take this one or shall I?"

Jenna Zarconi dipped her head for a moment, then raised it again, revealing a teary streak down one cheek. "They wouldn't let me out. The bastards. They were always calling me for favors. Always threatening me. And they never gave me a fair cut. They never let me in on their take. It was XYZ! I was the Z!"

"XYZ," Mark Xavier Phonson scoffed. "Gimme a break with that shit. It was never XYZ. You were just the dumb broad who wanted to turn a partnership into a love triangle." He came around the front of the three kneeling captives. "If anything, it was XY. The *men* doing the real work. You, the woman, just wanted to screw things up."

"That is extremely sexist!" Jax remarked, sounding more fascinated than offended. A few sharp glances pointed his way and he swallowed. "Um, I mean. From a dome upbringing. I mean, you know – I don't know the whole story or anything, so I don't want to jump to conclusions." He swallowed again and looked away, narrowing his eyes, as if his attention were suddenly grabbed by that remarkable painting on that wall over there.

"Yeah, yeah," Jenna Zarconi said. "The *men*. Guess I showed the fucking men something. I showed them what a

woman can do. You and your men – you're all so stupid."
She sneered at him, creases forming on her green face. "Do
you know how easy it was to send a d-mail to one of your
hitmen? To pretend to be you, telling him Jorg was threatening
to go to the cops? Telling him that Jorg was threatening to
bring you down and he had to be taken out?" She laughed,
an unamused, unnerving sound. "The jerk was so excited to
make with the violence, he didn't bother to verify the target."

X looked down, and a real expression of sadness seemed
to cross his face. "Ah, but your hitman made sure to let you
know it was done," she said, reading him. "Didn't he? After
it was too late? Dropped you a note to say, 'Jorg is dead,
just like you wanted'?"

"Yeah, Jenna," X said somberly. "You know what? You're
right," he added, a tad more lightheartedly. "You showed me
something. I underestimated you. That's my sin. I underestimated you and now I lost two good people. Maybe it should
have been XYZ. But now, it's just X."

He looked over at the blank vid-screen and was quiet for
a moment. "Of course, I'm stuck with your set up. I'll have
to use it – to keep my rep. And yes, when I got the call from
Kane, I had to throw some weight around to keep ModPol
from digging too deep. Now I'm working on spreading a
rumor that the Life Support accident on Barnard-4 was a
cover-up. That I, the man known to most only as X, had
Jorg Phonson killed because he tried to cross me. So much
work, cleaning up after your mess." He sighed wearily, then
attempted a dismissive shrug, which Runstom thought looked
a little forced. "I lost two good people – but on the bright
side, I get a nastier rep."

X looked thoughtfully at Jenna Zarconi. "If I had time,
I'd come up with something for you too. A rumor that lets

everyone know you tried to cross me too, and paid for it." He shrugged again, this time raising his hands slightly. "Ah, but never over-complicate, I always say. No, I'm afraid you'll be fatally injured while resisting arrest." He glanced at Jax, and waved a hand at him idly. "You too. Sorry, Mr. Jackson. You don't deserve it, but sometimes life gives you the short end of the stick. And someone has to take the fall for this mess."

Jax laughed. Quietly at first, just a giggle, then breaking into full-on, raucous merriment.

"What's so funny?" Runstom said, before anyone else could. By now, the officer was used to Jax's tendency to exhibit inappropriate behavior and as such he was the only person in the room who wasn't stunned to silence.

"Hey," Jax said. "Yeah, sorry. You know, Stanford. We were having that conversation the other day, about how this bad guy X has all these pawns that do his bidding. Remember? About how some of them knew they were being used, but I didn't."

"Yeah," Runstom said quietly. He didn't like where this was going, but they were all done for anyway, so he let Jax go ahead and dig their graves deeper.

"Well, it just occurred to me that this whole time, the big bad X is the pawn!" Jax said, laughing. "This Zarconi psycho-lady here was pulling all the strings." He cocked his head in thought. "Yeah, that's it. Just imagine there's this puppet master, right? And he has all these strings that lead down to these puppets. Well, when he's not looking, she comes up and tugs on the strings, moving the puppets and making it look like he's doing it!" Keeping his hands on his head, he made an awkward motion toward X. "Get it? *You're* the pawn, in *her* game!"

Mark Xavier Phonson's face grew hard and he pulled his baton off his belt. Jax's giggle faded and he tried to cover his head, but the club came down hard. As Runstom watched Jax's body go limp, the room grew smoky, and he felt his own body grow heavy and disconnected, as though he were the one that got clubbed in the head.

Dava crouched outside one of the windows on the back side of the house. She could hear voices inside, but couldn't make out the words. She carefully lifted her head just enough to get a look through the window. She was looking at some kind of little kitchen. It was unoccupied.

She pulled out her thermal cutter and fired it up. The blade grew instantly red from the heat, and she quietly sliced through the locking mechanism on the window, then silently slid it open. She crept over the ledge and onto a tiled floor.

From behind a cabinet, she leaned out just enough to see down the hallway and into the main living room of the house. There were a couple of ModPol officers decked out in full armor standing around with their pistols drawn. It looked like there were a couple of people kneeling on the floor with their hands on their heads. The one closest to her was a green-skinned man.

Her instincts were right. If this was an arrest, there'd be a van here by now. They'd have these guys face down in the lawn, not kneeling in the privacy of the living room. Some bad shit was going down here. They were probably squeezing these guys for information, and once they were done, they'd fade 'em.

She could hear their voices now. She could hear someone laughing, and she tried to get a look. One of the people on the floor, it was a tall, skinny, white-skinned guy. That must be the B-fourean. He was laughing rather raucously and saying something about puppets and pawns.

"Sounds like Psycho Jack is trying to get himself killed," she said to herself. It was go time. She punched a few numbers on her RadMess and stood up, drawing her small ExpandoKnife from a sheath inside her jacket.

She gave the scene one more good look. There were four large, cushy chairs in a circle in the middle of the room, a cart with a vid-screen of some kind on it, and two small, low drink tables that sat between the chairs. Infrared wouldn't pick up much of the furniture, so it was important to know where it all was. Bashful Dan had said four ModPol cops had entered the house, and indeed, she counted four purple-armored men, on their feet. One had his helmet off, exposing the bright-red skin of his bald head. He had a baton in hand and was hovering over the B-fourean. He didn't have a gun drawn, but the other three did. She'd have to take them first.

The little gray canister bounced its way into the room just as the red-headed cop struck the B-fourean across the temple, hard. Psycho Jack went down like a sack of rocks, and the room started to fill with thick black smoke.

She slid the mask from around her neck up to her mouth and the infrared-enhanced goggles from off the top of her head down to her eyes. She took one breath to make sure the mask was working, then sprinted into the main room.

The powered-up shot-poppers that were ModPol standard-issue lit up like little orange toys, floating around the smoke, barely attached to the red snowman-like blobs that flailed around the room. One gun spun around in an arc toward her as she approached and she batted it aside, sliding her knife into the center of the owner's chest. The purple armor that the ModPollies favored was woven out of a material designed to reflect and filter light-based attacks as well as repel attacks of high-kinetic energy, making them extremely resistant to both hand-held lasers and hand-held projectile weapons, but ineffective against knives, clubs, and so on. The officers' combat training was supposed to save them from hand-to-hand attacks.

The small blade of the ExpandoKnife penetrated quickly, and she hit the button on the hilt. The cop made some gurgling noises, a mix of sounds coming out of his mouth and from inside his chest, as the knife rapidly doubled in surface area, retracted, and repeated the process six times in a second or two. His knees buckled a little to one side and his top end fell away and down, the small knife in Dava's hand coming away from his body with little resistance. The infrared showed the bright heat of the inside of the man's chest as he slid to the floor.

She scooped up the downed cop's gun with her left hand and crouched low, backing away from the middle of the room slightly. Dava could see three forms on the ground now, red hand shapes covering red head shapes close to red body shapes. The three men standing up waving their guns were shouting at each other, trying to get a sense of their locations in the blindness that the dark smoke created. None of them dared fire a single round without knowing who might be in the line of fire.

One of the men was off to her left and the other two were off to her right. She reached up with her arm and aimed the gun she had just picked up at the one to the left. She popped off several shots quickly, then yanked her hand back down. She could see the man's gun light up instantly as he returned fire in a vague sweep, causing the other two men to go diving for cover.

"Ow, goddammit!" one of them yelled. "Who the fuck shot me?"

She pointed the gun to the right and fired off a few more rounds.

"What the fuck?" one of them screamed. "Stop fucking shooting!"

One of the forms to the right ducked down, crouching and covering his head with both hands. The other stumbled off in the other direction. He must have caught a glimpse of sunlight through the smoke, because he made a break for the doorway. He stepped through and there was a definitive FFZZAP, and his form flew out of view to the right side of the front yard. That armor might be laser-proof and bullet-proof, but a close-up blast of electricity from Bashful Dan's shock-gun was going to hurt, no matter what.

With the front door wide open, a cross-breeze was already clearing the smoke. Dava cursed herself for leaving the kitchen window open. Fortunately, the can was still streaming, and would be for a few more minutes. With the cop to the right ducking defensively, she looked to the one to the left. He had managed to back himself up against the wall and was carefully scanning the room, gun tracking in a slow sweep. The smoke was probably thinner farther away from the canister, so she watched the patterned movement of the orange shape of his gun and came at him when it was off to the far side.

She moved with her left hand forward, aiming the popper at his outstretched arm. She fired off a cluster of shots and he cried out in pain, his gun clattering to the floor. Even their sleeves were bullet-resistant, but the armor was semi-soft, favoring freedom of movement over protection. The shots might not penetrate, but their impact at close range had to be terribly painful. He looked around desperately, cradling his arm and cursing frantically.

Stepping forward, she kicked the cop's gun aside and then took a wide swipe with her blade across the halfway point between the red blob of his head and the red blob of his chest. The thinner smoke was allowing more light through this side of the room, clouding her infrared view, but Dava could have executed the move against the helpless man with her eyes closed. His curses sucked off into a gasping gurgle and his hands reflexively went up to his neck. She kicked him in the stomach for good measure and he keeled over, crumpling to the ground and half-coughing through the chasm in his throat.

She turned back to the center of the room and saw someone standing, making a movement with his arm, as if throwing something. The smoke in the room swirled, and she realized someone had gotten enough sense together to toss the canister out. She made a circle, sticking to the walls, and came up behind the last cop. He was crouching and trying to look about, his gun still drawn but lowered. The air started to clear as she glided up to him and put her blade against his cheek. She stuffed the gun in her hand into the back of her pants and used her free hand to pull off her infrared goggles and pull down her gas mask.

The cop wasn't wearing a helmet, and she could feel his vulnerability through the tip of her blade, as if she were drawing across his flesh with her own fingernail. He started to lift his gun, and she felt herself smile reflexively. "You wanna try me, pollie?" she said icily.

He dropped the gun and raised his hands. "Not smart," Dava chided. "Now you're really defenseless. Oh, I'm sorry," she said, cocking her head to one side, trying to get a look at the face of the bald, red-skinned man. "Did I give you the impression I would be letting you live?"

"Who are you?" he said, his throat raw from smoke inhalation.

"Space Waste," said a man's voice. She looked back to the center of the room. The B-fourean was still on the floor, on his knees and rubbing his head. The green-skinned woman was coughing and trying to crawl around on her hands and knees, meandering as if she didn't know where to go.

The green man was standing tall, a bulky-looking pistol trained on her. She recognized the handgun instantly; it was a Zap-n-Zap, Mk-3 military-grade laser pistol. Several Space Wasters carried that exact same model, ever since a crate of them fell off the back of a transport vessel sometime last year.

"You are under arrest," the green-skinned man said, steadily. "Both of you." He took one step forward and motioned with his gun, and the remaining smoke seemed to part around his outstretched arm and then his chest and head. "Get down on the ground, now!" he yelled with sudden intensity.

CHAPTER 22

Officer Stanford Runstom trained his gun back and forth between Mark Xavier Phonson and the unannounced Space Waste assassin as they both slowly knelt down to the ground, their hands in the air. He tried to survey the room with his peripheral vision, not daring to take his eyes off the loose-cannon cop or the deadly warrior-woman.

The place was a mess. The chairs were bullet ridden, the small drink tables were smashed, and the vid-screen was shot right through the center. Jenna Zarconi was face down on the ground but still moving, inching toward the front door, and Jax was feebly trying to pull himself to his feet, using a chair for leverage. Two of X's escorts lay motionless in different parts of the room, both surrounded by pools of red.

Without taking his eyes off X and the gangbanger, Runstom bent down near one of the downed cops and cautiously unhooked the circular restrainers from his belt with his free hand. He stood back up and tried to get a look at how Jax was doing.

"Jax," he said, when he saw the operator able to stand on his own. "Take these," he started, then changed his mind. "No, take this gun. Keep it pointed at these two. If they do anything funny, just waste 'em." He didn't want to risk sending Jax anywhere near that assassin. She'd already proven she could be fast and ruthless.

"No problem," Jax said in a raspy voice. "Give the gun to Psycho Jack," he added with a wide grin. Runstom gave him the pistol and he happily pointed it at the ModPol cop and the Space Waster. "Don't make a move," he said mockingly.

Runstom slipped a restraint over the wrists of the gang-banger first, fixing her hands behind her back. She regarded him with mild interest that bordered on boredom. Her calm made him nervous. He proceeded to cuff X, who looked frazzled and desperate. The corrupt cop tried to lean away from the woman as far as he could, periodically looking at the other motionless bodies, then quickly looking away. After he had them both cuffed, Runstom scooped up the strange blade the woman had dropped.

"Be careful with that, officer," the brown-skinned woman cooed.

"Mm-hmm. Dangerous, I'm sure," Runstom muttered, sticking the knife into his belt.

"I said, be careful with it," she repeated, a little more sternly. "It has sentimental value."

Runstom gave the woman a sideways look, not really sure if she meant what she said or if she was just being coy. He tried to ignore her.

"You," he said, walking back over to Jax. "Give me that gun, and take these," he said, handing Jax the two small detachments that came from each of the restrainer rings. "Just squeeze the button on these to send a signal to the cuffs and it will shock the hell outta 'em. That ought to keep them from trying anything funny." He looked back over at the arrestees. X still looked like he wanted to get out of the room as quickly as possible. The woman just gave him a look that seemed to express resignation, if temporary.

He looked back at Jax to see if he had the situation under control. The operator held the switches, one in each hand, and grinned. Runstom went out the front doorway.

The canister was in the middle of the yard, spouting dark smoke into the air. Without four walls and a ceiling to contain it, it was no smokier than a campfire, and it was beginning to sputter out. The crumpled form of the other ModPol cop lay off to the side of the doorway. Runstom bent down and felt his pulse. The man was still alive, but unconscious. Whoever blasted him was apparently long gone. He unhooked the restrainers from the cop's belt and flipped him over onto his belly. Then he used one of the rings to cuff the unconscious man, just in case he woke up. He didn't waste time binding his legs – hopefully, the guy was in bad enough shape that if he did wake up, getting to his feet and making a run for it was a little out of the question. He did, however, take a second to grab the cop's squawkbox.

Jenna Zarconi must have gotten the worst of the smoke when the canister first hit the room. She was a little ways down the street, on her feet, but bent over and still coughing heavily. She picked her head up and tried to move at a slow jog, not bothering to look behind her.

In ModPol boot camp, they made new recruits learn how to deal with smokers and other gas bombs the hard way: by sticking them in a closed room and tossing the stuff in. Runstom and some of the other cops knew enough to get low and cover up as soon as the smoker hit the floor. Of course, in the boot camp test, no one was shooting or running around stabbing people.

He began walking down the street after her. He switched the squawkbox over to the central line and pushed the call button.

"Dispatch," the box crackled after a few seconds. "What can I do for you, Officer Pontiac?"

"Officer Pontiac is down. This is ModPol Officer Stanford Runstom, Barnard System, Gamma Precinct."

A few more seconds of silence. Runstom quickened his pace to close the gap between himself and Zarconi.

"Um, okay," the box said. "What the hell are you doing on Sirius-5?"

"Look, I'll explain that to your team when you send them in," Runstom said, impatiently. "We've got one officer down, badly wounded, and two others that are dead. I've apprehended three suspects. Now send someone the hell down here!"

After a second, the box replied. "Okay, Officer Runstom. We've got a ModPol team on the way and we're contacting the locals for Emergency Med support." It paused for a second, then added, "Have your credentials ready, Officer."

"Right." Runstom slid the squawkbox into his pocket and reached out to grab Jenna Zarconi. She offered little resistance and he proceeded to restrain her.

"Can't you just let me go?" she said between huffs. "X is the real bad guy here. You see that, don't you Stanford? He pushed me!"

"I do see that, Jenna," he said. "And I'm sorry. But it's not up to me now. It's up to a court of law."

Tears began to form in the corners of her eyes. "They'll never believe my side of it," she said softly, shaking her head. She turned and looked him straight in the face. "Please, Stanford. You have to let me go. I only wanted what you want. I only wanted *justice*."

297

He looked into those light-brown eyes and that forest-green face. A small part of him wanted to believe her, to help her even. He quickly smothered it. "Your quest for justice resulted in the deaths of a lot of innocent people, Jenna." He pulled her by the arm. "Come on. It's time to go."

"So this is the famous Psycho Jack," the brown-skinned woman said. "Johnny Eyeball told us all about you."

Jax lost half of his grin. "By 'us' I presume you mean Space Waste?"

"Said you were in the lock-up for mass murder. That true, Jack? You kill thirty-some people?"

"Yeah, he did," X chimed in. "But he didn't even know he did it. Like a blind pilot in the cockpit of a passenger ship, flying her right into the sun."

"Hmm, that's disappointing," she said, looking Jax up and down. She shrugged – more naturally that she should have, considering the fact that her hands were bound behind her back.

"Credit where credit is due, I suppose." Jax raised his hands in mock defeat. "I was set up. Mr. Phonson here had much more culpability in the deaths of those thirty-two people than me." He grinned again. "I mean, that's what you're under arrest for. You know that, right, Phonson?"

X laughed shortly. "Yeah, well. Good luck making it stick, operator."

Jax regarded him silently for a moment. "Now that we have some time to chat," he said. "There's something I've been struggling with. Brandon Milton."

"What about him?"

"Did you know him?"

Phonson laughed that short laugh again. "Yeah, sure. I knew him."

"Which means what? He was under your thumb?"

"What's it to you?"

"Well, I'll just be honest, because I don't know where the line is drawn in this course of events – when it stops being you and becomes Jenna Zarconi pretending to be you," Jax said. "Brandon Milton was my supervisor. As far as I can tell, he was the one who stole my voiceprint, fingerprint, and login credentials and sent them to Markus Stallworth, so they could be used to encrypt the package."

X considered this for a moment. "Interesting," he said, finally. "If I remember right, Milton – in Blue Haven, right? Yeah – he was a John."

"What?" Jax said, unable to make sense of the statement.

"We hit the Blue Haven underground one night a couple months back. Busted a whole lotta hookers. I worked that case for a long time, made sure we got as many as we could when we made our move. Any one of their customers who had a reputation to protect got to go free."

"Free, as in they owed you a favor," Jax said. X said nothing. "I never would have figured Milton for the type to do that."

"You'd be surprised, pal," Phonson said, looking away as if bored with the conversation.

"But he was married." To Priscilla Jonnes. Sure, Jax and Priscilla had a falling out, but he still felt a small amount of indignity on her behalf for her husband's infidelity.

"All the more reason to make sure he never got caught." He looked back at Jax. "Milton is just another name on my list. A soul in my pocket. If Milton stole your creds, then he did it for Jenna, thinking he was paying back the favor he owed to me."

"Was," Jax said. "Was a name on your list."

"Ooh," purred the woman. "Did you kill 'im Psycho Jack? For what he done to you?"

"No." Jax was spending a significant amount of effort trying to forget that Milton married a woman that Jax was never good enough for, trying not to think about how while with such a woman, Milton paid for companionship on the side. "Well, yeah. Actually. I did kill him, but not on purpose. He was one of the people in block 23-D." He looked back at X and pointed. "So again – you killed him. And now you're going down for it. No one is going to owe you any more favors."

"I don't know what you're not getting about this, op," Phonson said. "You got nothing on me, and I've got way more friends in ModPol than you or that idiot Runstom."

"Mmm?" Jax walked over to the vid-screen and pushed a button on the front. "I'm sorry, were you saying something?" He turned and looked at the cop. "Did I tell you to hit the round red button to stop this vid unit earlier? Damn, I get so confused about those buttons. That was the record button." He ejected the memory card and held it up. "Pity someone put a hole through the screen. We could watch you bury yourself while we're waiting for Officer Runstom to come back."

The woman started laughing. "Goddamn, I don't know exactly what's going on here, but sounds like you're cooked, pollie." She nudged him, and X flinched with a spasm. "So anyway, Jack. I don't mean to be rude, but you'll have time to chat with this asshole later, I'm sure. I just want to ask you a few questions. While I have the chance."

"Um, okay," Jax said warily.

"How did you manage to make off with a Space Waste transport?"

"Well." He thought of Johnny Eyeball and his story about the trial raids they did on their test barge. "You guys knew what you were doing, right? You had it all planned out. Practiced it."

"Yeah," she said nodding. "We tried a few different attack points. Played out what the defense would look like."

Jax thought for a quiet second. "I suppose that's what it comes down to. All your strategies, they're all attack and defend."

"And?"

He shrugged. "Not everyone had defense in mind, I guess."

She cocked her head. "You mean, you didn't."

"I mean, it was clear the ship was dead in the black. Officer Runstom and his partner weren't thinking about defense, they were thinking about survival. They made for the supply bay because it was the only part of the ship that they could get to that could be closed off if whole barge came apart." He made a motion with his hands to demonstrate pieces of the craft coming off. "Other than the bridge, the supply bay was the safest bet. I'm just lucky they dragged me along."

"Hmm. Well, that's something to chew on, Jack," she said. "I appreciate your candor. Space Waste as an organization takes pride in learning from mistakes."

"Yeah, no problem," Jax said. "You can call me Jax, by the way. I don't generally go by Jack."

"Of course," she said, extending her hand. "You can call me Dava." Jax took her hand and shook it. Then he froze.

"I'm supposed to bring you in for questioning," Dava noted, handing the restraining ring to Jax. "Or kill you, if I can't. But since I already got your story, I suppose I don't need to bring you in." She looked over at X and then back at Jax. "I guess I could kill you now, but I'd hate for this whole thing you've got going on here to go unfinished," she said, making a circular motion with her hand. "You know, the only people I hate more than cops are corrupt cops."

"Um," Jax said. "It was a pleasure to meet you. And thanks for not killing me." That was all he could manage.

"My partner has set charges by now," she continued, ignoring him. "He won't trigger them until I give the word." She looked from Jax to Phonson and then back to Jax. "I'll give you five minutes."

"So what are you, like, an assassin with a heart of gold?" Jax said, then wished he'd picked another time to try to be witty.

"Three minutes," Dava replied with a momentary scowl. "You'll probably see me again sometime," she said idly and the frown curled upward. "And tell your buddy that my knife really does have sentimental value. I'll be back for it, some day."

Dava flitted out of the room and into the kitchen. Jax tried to watch her, but she was gone before he could get a look. So instead, he looked at X.

Jax sighed. "Well, at least I know you're not that good," he muttered.

Phonson's face showed that he took offense at the comment and he started wriggling around, as if trying to work the cuffs free. Jax shook his head and hit the button on the restrainer switch. The cop shuddered and spasmed from the electrical shock he suddenly received and then keeled over, face planted against the floor, panting and drooling.

Runstom was walking up to the house with a restrained Jenna Zarconi in tow as Jax was dragging Phonson out by his feet. "They're going to blow it up!" Jax yelled, huffing and backpedaling as fast as he could. "They're going to blow the house! We only have a few minutes!"

The officer seemed to understand immediately, and he ran up to the unconscious ModPol cop still lying just outside the front door. Runstom hooked his elbows under the man's armpits and half-hoisted him up. He began backpedaling as well, quickly out-pacing Jax. "Over here," he shouted. "Follow me."

Dava watched Bashful Dan as he shifted his gaze from the house to his RadMess and back. He chewed his lip and narrowed his eyes from his position behind a vacant hover-car. He checked his RadMess again and began to tap his fingers nervously on the side of the car.

She was still a few yards behind him, hidden from view by a column of metal painted with an obnoxious fake bark texture. She checked the time on her own RadMess. One more minute, then she would appear and scare the living daylights out of Dan, yet again.

Sometimes she thought they hated her. The other Space Wasters. Sure, she was a cold-blooded assassin, but they were all killers. She just had a different method. They preferred to be loud and theatrical. She did her work quickly and quietly. But that wasn't the problem. They didn't trust her.

And why should they? After all, when it came time to pay the piper, she was often the one who came collecting. A few weeks ago it was Three-Hairs Benson. They all knew he'd crossed Moses and he got what was coming to him. But they were also reminded of what they'd get if they ever slipped up. Benson was another reminder that once you became a Waster, you were a Waster 'til death, and there was no hiding from the hand of Moses when it came to strike you down. And Dava was that hand.

But they knew Benson deserved it. He'd stolen not just from Moses, but from all of Space Waste. Their distrust of

Dava – there was more to it than that. It was because she was Earth-born. She was different. Her brown skin. Her past. It made her different than most of the others. Except for Moses. Moses was a leader, and they embraced his different skin color, his Earth past. Then Dava came along and Moses instantly favored her. They resented that, and they never trusted her.

Everyone had a past. No one joined Space Waste if life had been good to them. And these gangbangers wanted to talk about their pasts. They needed to air out. Get things off their chests. But Dava wasn't like that. So because she never opened up, they all made up stories about her. Like rumors going around a sewing circle. A gangbanger sewing circle.

Sure, they were cordial to her. Everyone got along. It was the whispering, the muttering she heard when they thought she was out of earshot. And Moses was chiding her for being distant. She could never complain to him about the others not trusting her. But what was the truth? Did they mistrust her any more than she mistrusted them? Than she mistrusted anyone who wasn't Moses?

Dava frowned and looked at the back of Bashful Dan's head. Her muscles tensed as she prepared to creep up on him, but then she relaxed. How many years had she taken off this poor tracker's life by scaring his wits out? She coughed lightly and hissed in his direction. "Dan," she whispered.

Dan's head jerked up and almost spun all the way around on his neck as he looked around for a few seconds before spotting her, half-behind the metal tree. She waved at him and bounced lightly up to the hover-car.

"Hey," he said. He seemed a little confused. Probably because she hadn't followed form by trying to give him a heart attack. "Dava. What happened?"

"You set the charges, right?" she asked. They both looked out at the house, a good hundred meters or so in the distance.

"Yeah, they're the directional ones that 2-Bit brought. Should be a nice and controlled demo of the house, leave nothing but a little mess on the rest of the street." He turned to face Dava. "Are they all dead?"

"Mostly." She kept her eyes on the house. They were facing the back of the structure, where she had cut her way through the kitchen window. She couldn't see if Psycho Jack and the others got clear from the front. She didn't know why she cared. She didn't want to know why she cared. "Okay, Dan," she said quietly. "Hit it, and let's go home."

There was a series of snapping sounds so loud that Jax could feel them in his chest. His muscles tightened up instantly and he grabbed his ears to keep them from popping off his head. Just as soon as it started, it was over.

He opened his eyes and saw a light haze of dust and smoke come around the edges of the small utility shed they were crouched behind. Runstom was taking the helmet off the ModPol officer he'd been dragging. He put the helmet on and lowered the clear, plastic eye-shield and peered up over the shed.

Jax looked over at Jenna Zarconi and almost said, *sorry about your house*, but then swallowed his words. The woman sat a few feet away from the shed and stared at nothing as the haze dissipated into the air above them. He wondered if she felt regret. Or remorse.

Runstom turned back around and quickly checked on Phonson and the other ModPol officer. They were both conscious now, but both in a bit of a daze and had nothing to say. They each moaned slightly as Runstom grabbed them by the head and peered into their eyes.

"So." He let go of X and turned to Jax. "They gave you a little trouble?" There was just a hint of amusement in his voice.

"Well, Dava," Jax said. "The Space Waster, I mean. She got out of her cuffs. I don't really know how. One minute she was cuffed, and the next ..." He trailed off.

"Okay," Runstom said. He seemed to be in a good mood. "Don't worry about it. She would just complicate things anyway, right now."

"Yeah. Well, when Phonson here saw that she got loose, he tried wriggling out of his own ring." Jax grinned. "So I zapped him."

"Jax," Runstom said, cutting the other man off. "More ModPol cops are on the way. Now most of this stuff is going to be my word against his," he said, nodding at X. "I don't think you should stick around."

"Ah. Before I forget, I better give you this." He handed the officer the PMD card. "There ought to be enough on there to send X up the river for good."

"I don't ..." Runstom started, looking at Jax quizzically.

"The vid unit recorded most of the conversation. I mean, starting with the point at which X hit the record button."

Runstom grinned. "Ah, no shit. You are a goddamn bastard, you know that?" He took the memory card and stuffed it in his inside pocket, then looked at Jax. "Still, though. I think you should split, all the same. Even with this evidence, it will be a long process for them to exonerate you. No sense in you spending the next couple of months in lock-up on account of red tape."

Jax sighed. "No, I suppose not." He was quiet for a moment. "Stanford," he said. "I can't believe this is finally over."

"Yeah, me neither," Runstom said, his eyes drifting for a moment. Then they snapped back to Jax. "Listen. You have to get out of here. Get back to Grovenham. Give me a few hours. Where can we meet?"

Jax thought about how thirsty he was. "The White Angle Saloon."

Jax had the lonely mag-rail trip back to Grovenham to think about his options. There weren't many of them. By the time he'd arrived, he knew.

He sat in the White Angle for a few hours, pacing himself on the beer. He was thirsty and wanted to drink the whole bar up, but he also wanted to keep enough of his wits to get his ass off-planet.

He flinched every time the door opened and the crack of sunlight would blaze into the dark bar. He'd be stuck staring at the silhouette until it stepped through and resolved into a patron, repeatedly not Runstom, but thankfully not another ModPol officer.

Going back to Barnard-4 was definitely not an option. But what if it were? This was the question he kept asking himself. What was there for him? Was it time to do something different?

But he was afraid. Of course he was afraid. The universe outside the domes was a dangerous place. People who lived without domes, they lived rough lives. He'd grown up so sheltered. Could he handle a life outside the domes?

He'd ordered his fifth beer before the next silhouette to grace the doorway resolved into Stanford Runstom.

"Glad to see you," he managed as the officer took a seat next to him at the bar. His voice wavered, and he wasn't sure if he was fighting tears or alcohol or grav-lag or all three.

"Yeah, you too," Runstom said. "I don't have long. Got some very terse orders to report to the ModPol headquarters here on Sirius-5 and wait for further instructions."

"That can't be good."

Runstom's beer arrived and he took a long pull of it. "I'm pretty sure they're downright pissed at me."

"But the – the others?"

"Oh, all arrested." He reached over and grasped Jax's shoulder. "We got them, Jax. We did good."

"Good," Jax said with a sigh of relief. He pondered the word, which seemed to sound funny in his mouth, like it had a different meaning than it used to. "Good. Good." After a moment of silence, he remembered something. "Stan, before I forget, I need to ask you for a favor."

"Anything."

"Can you get a message to my father – and my stepmother – on B-3? Just to – just to let them know I'm alive."

"Of course." The officer seemed lost in thought, bobbing his head up and down. "I suppose I'm overdue for a letter to my mother too."

Jax looked at him. "Oh yeah? I thought your mother was – I mean, I thought you said—"

Runstom smiled faintly and cut him off with a short wave of the hand. "No, no. She's around. Somewhere."

"I see." Jax figured if Runstom wanted to be more forthcoming, he would. He got the sense that he didn't know where his mother was, not exactly. Jax decided not to push it.

They sat quietly working through their beers for a moment. "Where are you going to go?" Runstom said finally. "I know you've thought about it."

Jax exhaled. "Yeah. I've thought about it. I suppose I'll go to Terroneous. At least for a little while."

Runstom nodded. "That's good. You'll be safe there. ModPol won't bother coming around that moon. Not that I approve of Terroneous abstaining from ModPol services, but I guess in this case it's a good place to go if you need to lay low. They might put out some bulletins, but that'll be it. Find a mid-sized town where it's easy to blend in."

Jax's thoughts were distracted for a moment by that division: the ModPol subscribers and those that go it alone. He'd never considered it, having lived his whole life in a dome where the outsourcing of police and defense services was a given. But on Terroneous people seemed to get along just fine without ModPol. It was something he was curious to explore further, once he started his new life on the independent moon.

"Stanford," Jax said, his mind coming back to the present moment. "What are *you* going to do?"

The officer smiled faintly, perhaps even a little sadly. "Well, I'll stay on until this case runs its course, and I'm sure they've cleared your name. Then," he started, but just stopped. He shook his head. "Hell, I dunno. Maybe they'll finally make me detective. Or maybe they'll bust me down to shipping-lane patrol duty. Who knows?" He paused, then added quietly, "I might even take a little break from ModPol."

They finished their beers. Jax closed his bar tab and they left the White Angle and made their way through the crowds to the spaceport. The same interstellar ship that had made the trip from Terroneous a few days before was heading back later that evening, and boarding was about to begin. They went inside the terminal and Jax bought a ticket with the last of the money they had.

"Listen, Stan," Jax said as they walked away from the kiosk and approached the security scanners. He stopped and turned to face the space-born ModPol officer. "I don't know how to do this, how to thank someone like you. I mean, you stuck your neck out for me over and over again. Risked your life, your career. I am forever in—"

"Stop," Runstom said. "I know. I know. But I need you to understand something, Jax. I know how much it all meant to you, but I have to tell you: I did it for me as much as I did it for you. There was an opportunity to do something I've never done before. To set something right that I knew was wrong. If I had walked away from it all at any point, I – well, I don't know—"

"You wouldn't be you," Jax said.

"I suppose," Runstom said. "And anyway, I have to thank you. I couldn't have solved this without you, there's no way around it. All of it landed on you without you asking for it. I'm glad you never gave up, that you never rolled over."

Jax smiled, and even though it wasn't something either man was accustomed to, he hugged Runstom.

"I'll see you around," Runstom said when they released their embrace. "Someday. Somewhere."

"Yeah," Jax said. "See you around."

And he boarded the ship and flew off to start a new life.

Acknowledgments

First off, let me give a huge thank you to the folks over at Harper*Voyager* for their mission to bring sci-fi and fantasy literature to the world. It has been a real pleasure working with you all.

I'd like to thank all the people who have supported my writing in one way or another over the years. National Novel Writing Month (NaNoWriMo) helped me take a big leap forward, and I thank the NaNoWriMo organizers and community. We have so many great writer communities and organizations in Oregon and I want to thank all of them for their writing workshops, lectures, panels, networking functions, and other opportunities, especially the Northwest Independent Writers Association (NIWA), Willamette Writers, the Wordstock Festival, Literary Arts of Oregon, and OryCon (which is a sci-fi convention but I include it for its obvious dedication and support of the written word and authors).

I also want to thank the dedicated folks at Indigo Editing, not only for the editing support they have provided me, but also for the wide variety of workshops they offer and the always fun Sledgehammer Writing Contest they hold annually.

I participated in many critique groups over the years and I'd like to thank all the participants, including the LitReactor community, Writers Determined to Finish, the People's Ink, and last but never least, Writers with No Name: Wes and Brian, thank you so much for the support, the teachings, and the beatings over the years. You guys are the best.

Cynthia: thank you for always keeping my doors and my mind open, throughout my whole life. You believed I could do anything as I jumped from one creative endeavour to the next. Thank you for everything, mom - including valuable feedback on this very book!

Jennifer: I know that I found the best possible life partner, because your support never comes as an obligation, it always comes as pure enthusiasm. I can't believe all the ways you have kept me going: pull-no-punches critiques, design and marketing work, planning and management, and all the trillions of moments of nothing but love, like the time you built me a trophy for completing NaNoWriMo for the first time. Our partnership has enabled me to pursue my dreams without hindrance, and the best part is that I know I don't need to thank you, because we dream together. But I thank you anyway, because this book is as much yours as it is mine. I am so lucky.

31901060486554

CPSIA information can be obtained
at www.ICGtesting.com
Printed in the USA
LVOW12s0517270517
536012LV00001B/36/P

9 780008 120719